Praise for

The Dark Kings series

"Loaded with subtle emotions, sizzling chemistry, and some provocative thoughts on the real choices [Grant's] characters are forced to make as they choose their loves for eternity." —*RT Book Reviews* (4 stars)

"Vivid images, intense details, and enchanting characters grab the reader's attention and [don't] let go."
—*Night Owl Reviews* (Top Pick)

The Dark Warriors series

"The world of the Immortal Warriors is a thoroughly engaging one, blending powerful ancient gods, fiery desire, and touchingly human love, which readers will surely want to revisit." —*RT Book Reviews*

"[Grant] blends ancient gods, love, desire, and evil-doers into a world you will want to revisit over and over again." —*Night Owl Reviews*

"Sizzling love scenes and engaging characters."
—*Publishers Weekly*

"Ms. Grant mixes adventure, magic, and sweet love to create the perfect romance[s]." —*Single Title Reviews*

The Dark Sword series

"Grant creates a vivid picture of Britain centuries after the Celts and Druids tried to expel the Romans, deftly merging magic and history. The result is a wonderfully dark, delightfully well-written [series]. Readers will eagerly await the next Dark Sword book."

—*RT Book Reviews*

"Another fantastic series that melds the paranormal with the historical life of the Scottish highlander in this arousing and exciting adventure." —*Bitten by Books*

"These are some of the hottest brothers around in paranormal fiction." —*Nocturne Romance Reads*

"Will keep readers spellbound."

—*Romance Reviews Today*

DRAGONFIRE

DONNA GRANT

St. Martin's Paperbacks

DRAGONFIRE

Copyright © 2018 by Donna Grant.

For information address St. Martin's Press, 175 Fifth Avenue, New York, NY 10010.

ISBN: 978-1-250-18287-6

Our books may be purchased in bulk for promotional, educational, or business use. Please contact your local bookseller or the Macmillan Corporate and Premium Sales Department at 1-800-221-7945, ext. 5442, or by e-mail at MacmillanSpecialMarkets@macmillan.com.

Printed in the United States of America

St. Martin's Paperbacks edition / November 2018

St. Martin's Paperbacks are published by St. Martin's Press, 175 Fifth Avenue, New York, NY 10010.

10   9   8   7   6   5   4   3   2   1

PROLOGUE

Carpathian Mountains, Romania
Some years ago . . .

Sabina huddled beneath the pile of old, worn blankets as she listened to the adults outside her caravan. There was laughter and the pop of the fire interwoven with their conversations. She burrowed deeper as her uncle slid his bow across his violin, stringing together several tunes to warm up. Soon, a soft, lilting melody filled the camp.

She was almost asleep when the door opened. Sabina blinked drowsily as she rose up on her elbows and spotted her grandmother. "Gran?"

The old woman was bent with age and walked with the help of a cane gripped tightly by her gnarled fingers. Her dark eyes landed on Sabina. "It's not time for sleep yet, my sweet."

Sabina yawned and scooted over on the narrow bed for her grandmother to sit. "You look upset."

Her gran sighed as she placed both hands on top of her cane and glanced out the window to the fire where the others were gathered. Sabina hated being closed in, so she always left the curtains open. Plus, she liked to watch the adults while trying to figure out what they whispered about late into the night.

"Sabina, I'm not supposed to have a favorite grandchild, but I do." Her gran's head of thick, white hair pulled back in a tight bun swiveled to her. "There are changes coming for you, child."

Now Sabina was confused. "What changes?"

"Your father's murder by the villagers was the last straw for your mother. She wants you to grow up having a normal life instead of traveling with us and being persecuted for our ways."

Sabina couldn't believe what she was hearing. She was outraged, fear turning her blood to ice. She didn't want to leave her family and everything she knew. She sat up, feeling helpless and small and angry at her mother. "I don't want that."

Gran put her wrinkled hand on Sabina's leg, and it calmed her instantly. "Shh, my sweet. It's going to be fine. Matter of fact, where you're going is exactly where you need to be. Though I will never get over the pain of you leaving."

Sabina was well aware that her grandmother had the *Sight*. People came from all over to have Gran read their palms or even the cards. Sometimes, she even told them things without inspecting their palms.

Gran had known of her before Sabina's mother even knew she was pregnant. So when Gran said Sabina needed to go somewhere, she was going to do it. Even though she knew in her heart that it meant she might never see her family again.

"All right," Sabina finally mumbled.

"Good girl." Her grandmother patted her hand while giving her a warm smile. "I'm going to tell you a story. I need you to listen carefully because it's important."

Curious, Sabina shifted to lean against the side of the caravan. "What's the story about?"

"Magic. And our history. Every generation, the story gets passed down. Your mother should be the one telling you, but she doesn't believe."

"Why?"

Gran shrugged. "When you love as deeply as your mother did your da, you'll understand. Your mom is drowning in grief, but with you leaving soon, I have no choice but to take matters into my own hands."

Sabina got the impression that she would be leaving very soon. That made her incredibly sad, but she kept that to herself so she could listen to her gran.

"Do you know why we move from town to town?" her grandmother asked.

"Because people don't like us. They think we steal and cheat."

"Some of our kind do," her grandmother said. "Then there are those who don't like the fact that we're different. We don't try to own the land, my sweet. The land is not there to be fought over but to offer us what we need to survive. Regular folk can't grasp that. We believe in freedom, in following wherever our souls lead. Of course, you know the history of our family."

Sabina grinned. "We're one of the most powerful Romani families. Everyone wants to join our tribe or marry one of us because of that fact."

"Our history goes back even further, my sweet. And that's what I'm going to tell you about now. It's a secret, Sabina. You can only share it with your children."

"Why?"

Gran lowered her gaze, sadness tingeing her features. "This should wait until you're older and can understand. If only I had the time."

Sabina frowned at her grandmother's mumbled words. "I'm old enough."

"I hope so, child, because everything rests on you," she said, pinning Sabina with her dark eyes. "This cannot be written down. It is only passed verbally. You cannot forget anything. Do you understand?"

"I do. I won't forget any of it," Sabina promised.

Her grandmother pulled in a deep breath. "Long, long ago, we weren't the only beings on this planet. There were others full of magic and power so great that we mortals couldn't comprehend it."

Sabina's stomach dropped in fear as well as excitement. "Are you saying these people were immortal?"

"Yes, my sweet, I am. And they weren't people. At least, not really."

"Then what were they?"

"Dragons."

She leaned close to her grandmother to see if there was any hint of a smile or anything to let Sabina know that this was all a jest.

"This is serious," her grandmother stated testily. "I don't joke about any of this. People will tell you dragons don't exist, but they do. The most powerful of them are the Dragon Kings."

"Dragon Kings," Sabina whispered, a shiver running through her as if somehow connecting her to the beings.

Her grandmother wrapped her bent fingers around Sabina's hand. "Our family wasn't always wanderers. We had land and a large home in an area ruled by a Dragon King. He kept to himself high up on a mountain. Occasionally, he came down to the village."

"As a dragon?" Sabina asked in shock.

"As a man. You see, Dragon Kings have the ability to change from dragon to human form at will."

She scooted closer to her grandmother. "What did he look like? What was his name? Where is he now? Why didn't you tell me this sooner? Can I see a Dragon King?"

Her grandmother chuckled softly. "I was just as excited when I first heard all this, too." Her smile slipped as she returned to her story. "No one knows what he looks like as a dragon."

"Why?" Sabina demanded.

"He had the power to make sure no one could see him. When he did change, it looked like thousands of bats flying around him in a swarm."

Sabina shuddered at the thought. "Bats?"

"Whenever he was in his human form, he carried a sword. It was a beautiful work of art. My Sight comes from a long line of those with such abilities. It was one of those ancient ancestors who had a vision of the Dragon King slaughtering our village, and that same vision showed her the way to stop such carnage."

"How?" Sabina asked.

"By stealing his sword."

Sabina frowned as she cocked her head to the side. "I thought you said the Dragon King was powerful."

"He was, which is why it was so dangerous for our ancestors to attempt to steal his weapon. But they wanted to save lives. So, they put together a plan and climbed the mountain. They waited for days for the Dragon King to leave the cave. When he did, they snuck in and found the sword. There were six of them. They each went in a different direction, but only one had the sword."

"And the dragon couldn't find them? I thought he had magic?"

"He was enraged when he returned and found his sword gone. He went to the village and questioned everyone. That's how he learned of the missing six. He then set out to find them."

Sabina waited impatiently for the story to continue. "What happened? Did the Dragon King find his sword? I bet he killed the men, didn't he? Did he eat them? If I was a dragon, I'd eat someone who stole my things."

Her grandmother stared at her solemnly. "He didn't find them. The sword was hidden so that our ancestor's vision would never come to pass. Fearing the Dragon King's reprisal, the family packed up and left the village. For thousands of years, we've wandered the mountains."

Sabina swallowed and stared at her grandmother. "Is that all?"

"The Dragon Kings are still here."

"And the dragons?"

"Gone," she said, briefly looking away. "But that is another story for another time."

Sabina frowned, her young mind not grasping the answers. "Why did the Kings stay?"

"I don't know. But that King will be back for his sword. It was foretold by my great-great-great-great-great-great-grandmother. He will never stop looking for what was taken from him."

"Is that why you're telling me this story?"

Her grandmother leaned close to her face. "I tell you, Sabina, because we've stayed hidden from him all this time. The repercussions of what our ancestors did will be swift and deadly. He can *never* find us."

"What if we talk to him and explain that we didn't do it?"

"If only it were that easy."

"But what if we did?" Sabina insisted.

Her grandmother straightened and hesitated. "He might try to get you to help him find it. And he probably won't be alone."

"That won't do any good since we don't know where the sword is."

"Right."

There was something in her grandmother's tone that didn't ring true. Sabina was about to ask her about it when her grandmother continued.

"If we forget this story, then we might disregard what our ancestor saw. We're saving lives by keeping the sword from the Dragon King. It has cost us our homes, but it's worth it."

"How will I know if I come across a Dragon King?" Sabina asked, her mind racing with possibilities.

Her grandmother smiled. "At one time, there was a drawing of him, but it was lost through the years. That's the reason the story must be told and not written. Things get forgotten once they're on paper. If you have to retell something, you'll remember it. Do you understand?"

Sabina nodded slowly. "There has to be some way to know if we're talking to a Dragon King."

"None that I know of."

Sabina huffed and turned her head away. "I wish I could see a Dragon King."

"It's better that you don't."

"Why?" she asked, returning her gaze to her grandmother. "He ruled the land, but you didn't say that he hurt anyone. Did he?"

"Well . . . no," Gran finally admitted.

"Then why make him out to be a villain? Even with his sword gone, he didn't kill our family."

"Ancestors," Gran corrected. Her lips flattened. "You have a point, I admit, but—"

Sabina raised her brows. "You said he had magic and was powerful and immortal. He could have wiped out all of you, but he didn't. He's not a bad person. He just wants his sword."

Her grandmother smiled softly. "I never thought of it that way. When my father told me the story, I took his word about everything, never questioning it."

"Never?" Sabina asked in confusion. "I question everything."

"I know," her grandmother said with a loud sigh.

"What mountain did the Dragon King choose? Maybe we can go and see if he's there."

"He isn't," her grandmother insisted.

"How do you know?"

"Everyone would know if he returned."

Sabina twisted her lips as she thought of her questions until she found one that hadn't been answered. "What was his name? You never told me."

"Vlad, my sweet. His name was Vlad."

CHAPTER ONE

Dreagan
March

The sun blazed fiercely as it crested the mountains and poured its light into the valley and straight into Roman's workshop.

He paused and closed his eyes as he soaked up the rays. In his mind, he was flying high in the sky, his wings slicing through clouds as the warmth of the sun wrapped around his body.

Roman allowed himself just a few more minutes of the memory before he opened his eyes and took a deep breath. Then his gaze returned to the two-foot-tall metal dragon he'd made. He ran his hands over the silver scales. It was to be a gift for Ulrik.

Now that the King of Silvers had returned to Dreagan where he belonged, it was time the Dragon Kings got down to business. First up was V. His friend had suffered long enough.

Roman placed the sculpture in a box filled with tissue paper and closed the lid before taking it and striding toward the manor. On his way to the great house, Roman saw V standing outside, his gaze directed eastward.

Roman placed the gift outside of Ulrik and Eilish's room before he made his way to V. They stood side by side for several quiet moments, each lost in thought.

While every Dragon King had suffered in some way, the betrayal V bore hit Roman hard. None knew why someone had taken V's sword and hidden it. Sadly, they hadn't had much time to search for it after the theft because they were at war with the humans and then they sent the dragons away.

After that, each of the Kings found their mountains and slept away centuries. They woke in turns, but Roman knew Constantine, the King of Dragon Kings, had always kept a lookout for any weapon that even came close to matching the description of V's sword. Many of those were in the armory because Con sent the Dragon Kings to retrieve the weapons—either by buying, bargaining, or stealing—to see if any were V's.

All the while, V remained asleep in his mountain on Dreagan. The few times V woke, his need to search for his weapon overruled everything else. And the outcome was always disastrous for mortals. Which was why Con made sure that V remained asleep.

Until there was no choice but to wake all the Kings to fight a foe bent on revealing them to the humans.

"You doona have to do this," V stated without looking at him.

Roman shook his head. "Same old V."

Piercing blue eyes swung to him. V's gaze narrowed. "What's that supposed to mean?"

"It means that you still doona understand. All these thousands of eons, and you still believe that you have to do this on your own."

"It's my sword."

Roman glanced at the ground and tried again. "Aye, old

friend. It was your weapon that was taken, but how many times have you gone searching alone?"

A muscle ticked in V's jaw.

"How many of those times resulted in catastrophic events?"

"I didna set the fire in Rome," V argued.

Roman held up his hands. "No one said you did."

"Nor did I cause the Black Plague. Or—"

"None of it happened until after you woke and went looking for your sword," Roman interrupted. "I'm no' blaming you. I'm simply stating facts."

V stared at him for a long moment. "*I* lost my sword. *I* should be the one to find it."

"I agree, but there's no harm in having help."

"You control metal, Roman. It's Kellan who can find it. If any King can help, it would be Kellan."

Roman cocked a brow. "I'll try no' to be offended."

V ran a hand down his face. "That wasna my intention."

"You've spent most of our countless centuries asleep. You've no' interacted with the humans. Or anyone, for that matter."

"So you doona trust me alone?"

"We all want you to find your sword. It's time. And I'm going to make sure that happens."

V looked off into the distance once more. "I can no' remember where I lost it."

"That doesna matter. It's probably long gone from there anyway."

His head jerked to Roman. "You know where I lost it."

Roman held his gaze for a long moment, hesitating just a heartbeat before nodding. "Aye."

"Do the others?"

Fuck. This was so not how Roman wanted this conversation to go. V was unpredictable without his sword, and each time he had gone searching for it, horrible things happened to everyone around him.

"Roman," V growled dangerously.

"After the last time you woke from the dragon sleep, I went looking."

V's eyes blazed with fury as he faced him. "You've known."

"I told Con the next time you woke, that I was going to help you. We would've left sooner if no' for the whole Mikkel issue. I know you're angry, and I'm sorry for that. But let me help."

"I can no' remember anything of that day. I had my sword, then I woke and I didna. Only because I refuse to go any longer without it will I accept your help."

"Good. No' that you could've stopped me from going," Roman said with a grin. "I'll let Lily know so she can get the helicopter ready."

V let out a loud snort. "Nay. We're going ourselves."

Roman opened his mouth to argue the danger, but no words came out.

One side of V's mouth lifted in a smile. "I didna think you'd mind. I've already asked Arian for some help."

Roman looked up at the clear, blue sky but dark clouds were fast approaching Dreagan from off in the distance. "Con's no' going to be happy."

"No human will see us," V stated. "Arian will make sure of that."

After a brief period where no dragon was allowed to fly around the sixty thousand acres of Dreagan, Con had finally lifted the ban. The magic barrier around Dreagan kept most mortals away, and anytime someone crossed it, the Kings were immediately alerted.

Years of being private had been shattered in one night when the Dark Fae released a video showing the Dragon

Kings in battle, shifting in and out of dragon form while battling the Dark. Now, everyone wanted to know if real dragons existed on Dreagan.

A part of Roman wanted the humans to know the truth. Though there was little doubt that history would repeat itself and there would be another war between humans and dragons. Except this time, the Kings wouldn't turn the other cheek. If there were another war, the outcome wouldn't be the Dragon Kings hiding in their mountains for centuries.

A whistle above them had Roman and V turning toward the manor to see Arian leaning out the window of his chamber with his mate, Grace, by his side.

"Well?" Arian asked.

V gave a nod. But Roman watched as Arian's champagne-colored gaze shifted to him. After a brief hesitation, Roman also gave a nod.

"Where are you two headed?" Arian asked.

V swiveled his head to Roman and waited.

Roman looked at the sky, already itching to shift and spread his wings to fly. "Romania."

His advanced hearing caught the sound of Grace's gasp, but he paid no attention. Arian would fill her in on all the details.

"We own homes in every major city around the world," Roman told V. "There's one in Bucharest, but we also have another in Timisoara, which is nearer the mountains."

"Of course you do," V said with a shake of his head while wearing a smile. "And I suppose there is a closet full of clothes for each of us."

Roman grinned. "Con doesna do anything halfway."

"He has always looked out for us, thinking of details few of us ever would."

The clouds were nearly upon them, rolling into each

other and growing darker by the second. Excitement rushed through Roman. He wanted to fly, yes, but it was more than that. Almost as if he awaited something.

Or something awaited *him*.

With every second the clouds took to reach them, Roman's skin grew tighter. He yearned to be in his true form, to inhale and feel the fire rumbling in his chest.

To soar into the sky until the ground below was nothing more than a speck.

"And I thought I was the one with secrets."

V's words caused Roman to look his way. But he didn't deny anything. What good would it do?

With a sad smile, V nodded and took off his black boots. Roman waited for him to remove the rest of his clothes, but V casually set the boots aside away from him.

Roman raised a brow. "Just the boots?"

"I like them. Shara bought them for me," V explained.

Roman hid his smile. Shara was not only a Light Fae, but also mated to Kiril. She'd been one of the first mates to approach V, and she did it with the designer boots.

"What about you?" V asked.

Roman looked down at his clothes. He shrugged and quickly removed them. Unlike V, he tossed his boots toward the manor before wadding up his jeans and shirt and lobbing them near his shoes.

V rolled his eyes with an irritated shake of his head. "You couldna fold them?"

"Why?" Roman asked as a crack of thunder pierced the air.

Roman shot V a smile before he shifted and immediately launched himself into the air. The moment his wings spread and he caught a current, he drew in an easy breath. This was where he was meant to be, not stuck on the ground in a form not his own.

Shifting had made it easy to talk to the humans when they arrived, but he would always prefer being in dragon form. Everything felt . . . right.

The air smelled sweeter. He could feel the electricity from the lightning crackling in the atmosphere. And the rain . . . ah, the scent was divine. He loved how the drops hit his scales and rolled down his body toward his tail.

He glanced down as V came alongside him and spotted Con standing at the backside of Dreagan Mountain.

"Well," V said via the mental link all dragons shared. *"He's no' yelling at us."*

Roman studied Constantine for a long minute. *"He's different now that Ulrik is back."*

"Ulrik is where he was always meant to be," V said. *"Everyone knew that. Even Con."*

Roman flew higher into the clouds and shifted his direction southeast toward Romania. He glanced over and caught the sight of copper scales meandering through the clouds.

They might be on an important mission, but V was enjoying himself. It was such a change from the other instances when V had woken from sleep and left his mountain. Perhaps this time would end differently than the others, as well.

Maybe this time when V returned to Dreagan, he would have his sword with him.

Roman glided upon the air currents and, for just a moment, he allowed himself to believe that the mortals had never come to the realm to settle. That at any moment, his pale blue dragons would join him.

It was a dream he only allowed himself once every few days. And, frankly, it was getting harder and harder to remember what his old life had been like.

"Perhaps you should've slept more," V said.

Roman glanced to his right to find his friend. *"Meaning?"*

"I see the far-off look in your gaze, but more than that, I see the misery."

"I feel like memories of our other life are fading. I can no' hold onto something I can no' remember."

"Maybe it's better if you doona," V said.

Roman's head snapped to him. *"You doona think the dragons will ever return."*

"Nay."

Roman searched his mind and realized that he didn't either. *"We will be hiding for eternity."*

"Give the humans long enough, and they'll destroy themselves. Look what they're doing to this planet. I give them another two hundred years."

"Before they die out?"

V chuckled. *"Before they leave. They're looking for another planet. I'm ready to point them in the right direction to hasten their departure."*

"No' all will leave."

V's lips peeled back to show his long teeth. *"Then we help them."*

Roman had to admit, he liked the idea. If only the Dragon Kings hadn't sworn to protect the mortals. On a realm filled with magic, the humans didn't fit in.

The Kings had felt sorry for them and gave them a place to live. After a couple of generations, a select few mortals were born with magic. They weren't nearly as powerful as the dragons or even the Fae, but they could still do magic.

There was a time when some humans revered the Druids, but those without magic, who wanted a taste of that kind of power, grew jealous and soured the others until the Druids finally gathered in a safe place.

Roman hadn't been to the Isle of Skye in ages, but the Druids survived there even now. Their numbers were dwindling, but they clung to the old ways and their magic. Just as the Dragon Kings did.

CHAPTER TWO

Romania

Something kept pulling her gaze out the window, an unknown, inescapable force. Sabina slowly set aside the jewelry she was making and rose from the chair. A strange, puzzling feeling churned in her stomach as she made her way outside.

Standing in the sunlight, her gaze moved upward. She frowned at the dark clouds in the distance. There was something at work here, of that she was sure. She didn't know how she knew it, only that she did.

Your Sight.

She inwardly snorted to herself. She hadn't tried to use her gift for years, nor had she felt anything that would give her any impression that it was the Sight.

So why now?

More importantly, why did she get the feeling that the storm she watched was heralding something?

A shiver raced through her. She rubbed her hands up and down her arms to warm herself, but it didn't dispel the tumultuous thoughts rushing through her head as fast as river currents.

"Bina?"

She turned at her brother's voice and gave him a reas-
suring smile as he stood in the doorway of the back door.
She didn't want him to know that anything was wrong.
"Everything's fine."

"No," Camlo said, frowning. Wind ruffled his too-long,
dark hair into his eyes. He wiped the strands away, his dark
brown gaze never leaving her. "I saw your face."

She walked to her brother and tilted her head back to
look up at him. He was a big man, tall and muscular, but
he had the mind of a child. Yet, no kinder, sweeter individual lived on Earth than Camlo.

Sabina put her hands on his arms and pulled him down
to kiss his cheek. "I was just looking at the weather."

"It turned. It wasn't supposed to." His eyes lifted to the
storm.

"The weather is fickle. You know that." She raised her
brows until he looked at her and reluctantly nodded. "How
are the animals?"

If there was one thing she could always count on, it was
Camlo's love of animals. He cared for them like a mother
would her own children.

His face split into a smile as he named off each cow,
sheep, chicken, duck, goose, pig, and rabbit they had, telling
her if they'd slept well and how they were eating.

She didn't really want such an in-depth update, but
because it mattered to him, she stood and listened to it all,
nodding and asking questions. Her world revolved around
Camlo. It had ever since their parents died.

While there might be some who would resent their
brother for keeping them tied to the farm, that wasn't her.
She didn't particularly like people, and people didn't like
being around Camlo. It was a situation that suited her perfectly.

No one was there to bother her while she made the

jewelry that supported them. Thank goodness so many people bought things online now. She had orders from all over the world. Since every piece was handmade, she charged extra, and customers still bought it. It kept her busy. In fact, she had nearly ten orders waiting to be filled.

The only downside was when she had to go into town to mail the packages.

Camlo, still talking, turned and wandered back to the barn. Sabina watched him for a few minutes. From the moment he came into the world, she had wanted to protect him. Camlo was a gentle soul, but many were fearful of his height.

And the men . . . well, Camlo's size and mental handicap made him a target. The men of the village mercilessly teased him or tried to get him to fight.

After finding her brother beaten and bloody a few years ago, Sabina had nearly packed their belongings and gone off to find their Romani family. The only thing that kept her from doing it was that she had no idea where they were.

When her mother took her from the Romani, it was the last Sabina had seen of them. If the family ever came close to Brasov, she didn't know it.

Sabina couldn't say she'd had a bad life. Within a year of moving to the area, her mother had met and fallen in love with Petre Negru. Nine months later, Camlo was born. Petre was good to Sabina and loved her mother dearly. Perhaps it was because of the happiness in the home that Sabina had been able to adjust so easily to remaining in one place after a childhood of wandering.

Most likely, it was because the house was situated in a valley next to the mountains that offered a willful child an overabundance of places to play.

Sabina looked over at her brother. Camlo lifted a rabbit from the pen and held it in his arms, stroking the fur as he began to sing to it. Sabina smiled while watching him, but in the back of her mind was always the nagging worry about the future.

What would become of her brother when she died? Part of all proceeds she made on her jewelry went into a fund set up specifically for just such an incident. She'd even found a home that took in those like Camlo.

She hoped she wouldn't have to worry about such things for many years, but it was on her mind more often than not of late. It was a sign. One that she couldn't ignore. Whether it was her early years living as a Romani or the Sight she had snubbed for so long, she knew that something was about to happen.

Sabina shut the door and turned in time to see a bolt of lightning far in the distance. It was too far away to hear any thunder, but it still felt as if the storm harkened an arrival of some kind. And she really didn't want to know what it was.

Her life was good. She didn't want anything to complicate things or upend what she had with Camlo. Both of them were happy, and that's how she wanted to keep it.

Sabina reached her computer and pulled up the online will she'd begun months ago. It was time to complete it. An hour later, she sent it off to the attorney in Bucharest, along with the payment.

One more thing off her to-do list. She closed the laptop and turned on music from her phone as she crossed her legs in the chair and focused her attention on the earring.

All of her designs were on the whimsical side. Ranging from earrings, necklaces, bracelets, anklets, and even rings, Sabina was always looking to expand her business.

Anything that caught her eye, she drew in her notebook as consideration for future jewelry. She often got requests for items, and she rarely turned down a job.

The sky grew so dark that she had to turn on the lights. So much for the beautiful day. The storm was bigger than she realized. None of the weather forecasts that morning had mentioned anything about a storm. It was supposed to be clear.

She lowered her hands and thought of her grandmother. No doubt Gran would have said that magic was at work. And no doubt she'd be right.

There wasn't a day that went by where Sabina didn't think about the story her grandmother told her the last night they'd been together. For years after that, Sabina searched the face of every man to see if he was a Dragon King.

Sabina never told her mom what her grandmother had shared with her. When Tereza left the Romani, she left that entire way of life behind. It's what her mom had needed.

But for Sabina, she didn't want to let go of that part of her life. Or the things she'd learned in the six years she'd grown up as part of the Romani.

If only she knew how to get ahold of them. Camlo might not be full-blooded Romani, but he was half, and that counted. They would take him in if anything were to happen to her. No one would ever hurt him again with the Romani there.

Unable to keep her mind focused on the earrings she was working on, she picked up her sketchpad and a pencil to take to the sofa. She curled up with a mug of tea and started to draw. She rarely knew what would take shape when her pencil first touched the paper, but it was always whatever her soul was trying to tell her.

She became absorbed in the drawing, pausing only long enough to take sips of the tea. Sometime later, she lifted her head and gasped when she saw the head of a dragon staring at her.

Her head swung to the windows and the rain that fell in thick sheets outside. But even as she watched, the clouds moved away. Within ten minutes, the storm had passed, and the sun was out once again.

"Magic," she whispered.

She looked down at her pad. She couldn't think of a dragon without wondering about the Dragon Kings. Her grandmother had said they were still here, walking among them. They could transform themselves from dragon to man and back again, which meant they could be anyone among the billions out there.

Sabina reached for her phone and did a search on dragons. Most of the links were about dragon facts, the top mythological dragons, and such.

Then she found a message board that caught her interest when she spotted a double dragon logo. She recognized it from somewhere. A few messages down, someone said *Dreagan*.

"The scotch," she said as it dawned on her how she knew the logo.

She kept reading about "the video on Dreagan," but no matter how she searched for a dragon video, she found nothing. A few messages later, she read that the video could no longer be found.

What had been on it that caused such an uproar? It made her wish that she had been able to see it.

A ding from her email about another order made her put aside the computer and get back to work on the earrings. She finished one before she needed to start dinner.

With a yawn, she rose and got everything out to cook. She glanced out the back window and saw Camlo coaxing a starving dog to him. There was no use telling her brother they couldn't take in any more animals because he refused to accept that.

His argument was always the same.

"If they didn't need us, they wouldn't find their way here, Bina."

And she didn't have the heart to do anything but smile.

She stayed at the window until the dog finally leaned out far enough to snatch the food from Camlo's fingers. Her brother's triumphant smile made her heart feel light.

When she finished cooking, she didn't even bother trying to get him to come inside to eat. Instead, she took a plate to him. As soon as the dog saw her, it scurried off, but the starving animal didn't go far.

"Here," she said, handing Camlo the plate. She then gave him a few pieces of stale bread. "Something for our new guest."

"She's pretty, isn't she?" Camlo asked.

Sabina glanced at the brown, matted fur of the dog. The animal didn't look away. Instead, she found herself gazing into the dog's sad, dark eyes. "She's very pretty. And wait until you're able to clean her up."

"She likes you," Camlo stated.

Sabina never questioned her brother. Half Romani or not, he had the Sight, just as others in her family did. "Tell her not to chase the chickens. Did you ask her name?"

"She won't give it yet." Camlo never took his eyes from the dog as he sat on the ground and began eating.

Sabina leaned down and kissed him on the forehead. "You know my rule. She's not allowed in the house until she's had a bath. I want her clean."

"She doesn't want to come in," Camlo said around a mouthful of food. "But she will soon."

Sabina found her gaze on the dog once more. Her brother's connection to the animals fascinated her. In many ways, she wished she could communicate with them as he did.

So many times, she had seen him work miracles. Like the time they'd found a wolf in a trap. The animal was trying to chew through its own leg to get free. He was frantic and terrified, but Camlo's mere presence had calmed the animal without a single word being spoken.

The wolf remained still while Camlo freed him and then tended to the wound. Before the animal left, he licked Camlo's hand and then trotted off.

That was only one of dozens of occasions. And just one of the reasons she kept Camlo secluded from the rest of the world. She didn't want anyone exploiting him or his abilities. Because there would be those who tried.

"I love you, little brother."

At this, his head lifted to her. "I love you, too."

She put a hand on his shoulder before she returned to the house. Sabina ate alone, as she normally did, her thoughts on the Dragon Kings. After she'd finished and cleaned up, she made herself get back to work on the other earring.

Not long after, she set it aside and went back to the message board to read more about the dragons since she couldn't stop thinking about them. She saw posts where people claimed to actually see dragons.

Some were obvious lies, but there were a couple that made her pause. She read one account from someone on Fair Isle, Scotland, that claimed to have seen a white dragon flying around the cliffs.

They described the dragon with such detail that it was hard to imagine the person was lying. Then again, there were some really good writers out there who could make someone believe whatever he or she wanted.

Sabina closed the laptop and leaned her head back on the sofa, her thoughts not just on dragons.

But Dragon Kings.

CHAPTER THREE

Roman circled the large property the Dragon Kings had snatched up several hundred years ago. Caretakers lived there to keep everything running smoothly, but Ryder had sent them away for the next week.

Roman wanted to make sure everyone was gone before he and V landed. The lights were on in the house, awaiting their arrival.

Roman glanced at V before they dove from the sky into the rain. They both shifted back into their human forms on the way down. Roman tucked his head, rolling his body so that he landed on a bent knee, his fingers on the ground.

He turned his head to the side to find V standing as he took in the residence. Roman hadn't seen the house since he'd brought some sculptures here years ago. He straightened and took in the contemporary look of the dwelling.

"Con has had some updates done," Roman said.

V made a sound at the back of his throat. "Of course he has."

"Come on," Roman said as they walked up from the back garden to the stone porch.

He entered the security code before using his magic to

lift the shield protecting the house from magical beings. Once inside, they padded barefoot and naked up the stairs to the bedrooms.

"How many bloody rooms does this place have?" V asked irritably.

Roman chuckled. "There are twelve bedrooms."

V shook his head as he stood in the hallway and looked at each of the doors.

"I doona think you were ever awake long enough for us to explain how the houses work. You'll be able to find them by the feel of our magic. You doona need the code to get in as your magic will suffice."

"You entered a code."

Roman shrugged. "Habit. Some houses are bigger than others. The villa in Venice is huge. But most were no' meant to hold all of us at once. Whenever you go to one of the houses, Con set up the rooms and closets alphabetically. Of course, if you're the only one at one of them, use the master bedroom."

"I doona think I'll learn everything."

Roman frowned at him, but before he could ask what V meant, his friend strode down the hall to the last bedroom and softly closed the door behind him.

After a moment, Roman went to his room and straight to one of the two closets. One of them was devoted entirely to his type of clothes. He missed wearing kilts every day. He still wore them more often than not.

He chose a pair of jeans, a gray shirt, and boots. When he returned downstairs, it was to find V standing near the indoor pool, his gaze out the windows to the mountains.

"You can go for a swim," Roman offered.

V calmly said, "Are we close?"

Roman didn't need to ask for clarification. All V cared about was his sword. He was the only Dragon King to have lost his, and V took it as a personal affront. But it was more than that. So much more.

"Did you recognize anything as we flew here?"

V's icy gaze swung to him. "If I did, do you no' think I would've stopped? I know I once ruled this land. There's no doubt about that, but I couldna tell you which of the mountains I used as mine."

Roman looked out the many windows to the back acres that stretched before him. "It's been named Romania."

"That means nothing to me."

"There is a legend here, V. One that involves you."

His dark brows drew together. "What legend?"

"Dracula."

V was silent for a moment, his frown deepening as he searched his mind. "Is that the movie Cassie and Elena made me watch? The one where the guy sucks other people's blood?"

"It's an adaptation of the legend, aye."

"Roman, just spit out whatever you're trying to say," V stated in frustration.

During the entire flight to Romania, Roman had thought of different ways to tell V, but he hadn't settled on an option. And now he was making a muck of things.

"Aye, V, you're the basis for the legend."

"I never drank anyone's blood," he said, clearly affronted. "That's . . . gross."

Roman ran a hand down his face. "You have the power to mask yourself in dragon form. Do you have any idea what you look like to others when you do that?"

"Nay."

"Bats."

V faced him then. "Bats?"

"Hundreds of them. Your body comes apart and turns into bats."

"Oh," V said after a moment as he let that sink in. "What is the rest of the legend?"

Roman blew out a breath. "Mainly that you're a vampire. Immortal and unstoppable."

"They got everything right but the vampire part." V swallowed. "It still doesna answer why my sword was stolen."

"We're going to get to the bottom of that as soon as we find it."

"My magic hasna been able to locate it. It's on this realm. I can feel it. Just out of reach. Always fucking out of reach."

Roman caught a glimpse of the suffering V hid from everyone. A Dragon King's sword was a part of him, an extension, just like their tattoos. But for V, his connection went even deeper.

It was why each time he woke, he went slightly mad the longer he was without the weapon. It was also why Con returned V to his mountain and made him sleep each time.

V cut his eyes to him. "I'm fine. Stop looking at me as if I'm going to start drinking people's blood."

The fact that V could be sarcastic despite everything relieved Roman. A little. He would still keep an eye on his friend. Not because he feared what might happen to the humans, but because it was time for V to finally stop suffering.

They had lost precious months since V woke and left Dreagan without talking to anyone. It had taken a long time to find him, and, actually, it had been Ulrik who sent V back to Dreagan. But was it too late?

Would V fall into his usual madness before they found his sword? Every second counted.

"You're going to get your sword back this time," Roman stated.

"Doona make promises you may no' be able to keep."

"I never do."

V released a loud breath. "I know.

Roman walked to the nearest window and gazed at the mountains. "These are the Carpathians, V."

"I know them well. They extend for nearly a thousand miles."

He looked back at his friend. "We'll walk and fly every inch of them until something comes back to you."

If Roman wanted a sign that that pleased V, he would be waiting an eternity.

V gazed at the ragged peaks without interest. "Our magic is the greatest on this realm. Nothing should stop me from discovering where my sword is. More than that, nothing should have been able to wipe the memory of where I was." His gaze slid to Roman. "No' from me. And especially not from the Keeper of History."

Roman held his friend's gaze, unease once more filling him. "You know Kellan looked through the history. In his mind, he saw your sword being taken but not the location of where you were."

"I can still recall the faces of the men who came into my cave," V said as he walked slowly toward him. "I can still smell their stench of fear and righteousness. How can I bring forth such minute details but not recall my location?"

"Did you tell Con any of this?"

"Aye."

Roman frowned, an uneasy feeling coming over him. "What did Con say?"

"He said that, no matter what, the sword would be mine again. I've always known that, but I can no' return to dragon sleep without it. No' again. Because if I do, I willna wake."

Shock went through Roman. "You can no' do that. Too much rides on you."

V smiled sadly. "I tell you only what I told Constantine."

"Bloody hell," Roman murmured. Why hadn't Con shared any of this?

He inwardly shook his head. Why *would* Con tell him? It changed nothing. V's sword had to be located and returned to him. They had searched for thousands of years, always hoping that V would remember something that would help them the few times he woke. But they had come up empty-handed time and again.

"Something worries you that you're keeping from me," V stated.

Roman debated whether or not to share his concerns, but in the end, he decided it was best to be open in their partnership. He needed V to remain calm and sane, and V needed him to be honest.

"You were no' at Dreagan when Dmitri and Faith found the wooden dragon."

"Nay, but I know of it," V interrupted. "I know the story and all that happened."

"But you didna see its power over us. Even Shara was affected."

V rubbed his chin. "You think the same mix of Fae and Druid magic could've been used on my memories?"

Roman shrugged. "It's a thought. The magic surrounding that wooden dragon was immense, V."

"You know what that means if you're right?"

"That the Druids and Fae involved have a grudge."

V's eyes grew colder, if that were possible. "If that magic can mess with my head and change our feelings toward mortals, what else can it do?"

"I doona want to find out."

"We're going to, sooner or later. And if it was that intrepid group of Druids and Fae, then that means they're responsible for taking my sword and keeping it from me."

Roman took a step back as the implications hit him. "That means they know what the sword is used for."

"Aye," V said with a twist of his lips. "It also means that we've wasted enough time talking about it. We need to get searching."

The two of them walked out of the house. Roman paused long enough to use his magic to secure the building. Then they headed toward the mountains.

"Do you think these allied Druids and Fae knew what would happen to me if I lost my sword?" V asked.

Roman glanced at him. "I think it's safe to assume they had a suspicion."

"It's as if they want humanity hurt."

"Or they want us to be responsible for it."

V let out a string of curses beneath his breath. Roman looked at the mountains ahead of them. It would be so much simpler if they could fly. That way, V might find the cave he'd once used.

Walking the mountain as a human would take time they didn't have. V might be able to hide his dragon form, but Roman couldn't.

"We take to the skies at night," V said as if reading his mind.

Roman looked up at the peak before them. "This area has tourists because of Dracula."

"I'd love to know who started that stupid legend so I can beat them," V muttered angrily.

Roman said with a grin he didn't try to hide, "All legends begin somewhere. I just happen to be standing next to one. Vlad."

He halted and faced Roman. "I was good to the mortals on my land. I never harmed them."

Roman's smile died. "I know."

"I never gave them reason to want to do me such an injustice."

Roman began the ascent up the mountain. "Mortals need no provocation to do such things."

"Aye. That's what worries me."

CHAPTER FOUR

Wake up! Something is wrong! WAKE UP!

Sabina's eyes snapped open. She didn't move as she listened to the sounds of the house. Nothing seemed out of the ordinary. Why then had she woken?

She tried to move her legs, only to find that one of the cats had curled up next to her. Sabina got out from under the covers without disturbing the feline and walked from her room to peer into Camlo's.

Her brother's bed was empty. She had long stopped trying to get him to make it each morning. It was one battle she'd given up on, focusing instead on other things. So she couldn't tell based on the mess if he'd come to bed and already left. Or if he'd never come into the house at all.

Sabina returned to her room and pulled on a pair of sweats and grabbed a jacket before slipping her feet into a pair of old boots with worn soles. Her gaze landed on the unlocked deadbolt as she reached for the door.

Camlo knew her rule of locking everything when he came inside. With her heart thumping in worry, she opened the door and looked outside. She didn't see or hear anything. Hopefully, Camlo was asleep in the barn.

She stepped into the night and immediately fought the urge to jump back inside. There was no explanation for it. She wasn't afraid of the dark, but tonight, she didn't want to be out in it.

Sabina fought against the irrational fear and slowly closed the door behind her. With that soft click disconnecting her from the safety of the house, her blood turned to ice. Her gaze scanned the darkness, searching for some foe out to harm her.

The Romani had many folktales that were passed down to their children, and the Romanians were no different. Sabina was well aware that every story got its roots from some smidgen of truth. It's why she never totally discounted any of the myths.

For some reason, her mind conjured up the tale of the *zmeu*, a shape-shifting creature that fed on human flesh and often kidnapped young women to be his consort.

Once her imagination was triggered, it went to the *varcolaci*, or werewolves.

Sabina straightened her shoulders. Her ancestors once walked into the cave of a Dragon King and stole his sword. She could face anything that came out of the dark.

The longer she stood there, the more every sound was a threat. She hurried away from the door and made her way to the barn. Careful to close the gates behind her, she all but ran inside the structure.

But her fear skyrocketed when there was no sign of Camlo.

She turned one way, then the other. "Camlo? Camlo! Answer me, please!"

Sabina, no longer concerned with being quiet for fear of waking her brother, threw open the barn door to look outside. "Camlo!"

Slamming the door shut, she started rushing through

the various pens, shouting her brother's name. They lived far enough out that if a vehicle came down their road, it was to see them since no one else lived down the lane.

They were also close enough to the mountains that wolves and bears were common, which was why all the animals were safely locked up at night. Since the pens were secured, that meant Camlo had seen to them before. . . .

Before what? Her mind was filled with all kinds of possibilities.

Out of the corner of her eye, she spotted a shape in the front yard. She instantly recognized her brother's tall silhouette and breathed a sigh of relief.

"Camlo," she said sternly as she made her way to him. "Didn't you hear me call you?"

His head was tilted back as he gazed up at the sky with a smile on his face. "I answered."

"I didn't hear you. I was scared something happened to you."

He frowned and glanced at her. "Like what?"

"Like you left."

"I won't leave you or the animals, Bina. You're the one who's going to leave."

She took a step back at his words. They sounded like a prophecy of sorts, and it sent a chill through her. "I'm not leaving you, little brother."

"Not now."

"It's late. Let's get you into bed."

He shook his head and pulled his hand away, shooting her an angry look. "I'm not going to miss seeing them again."

She thought of the fear that had assaulted her when she walked outside. "What are you looking at?"

"Look up," he said with a grin and pointed to the sky.

Sabina raised her gaze but saw only stars and the occasional cloud that drifted slowly past. "I don't see any-thing."

"They'll be back."

"Who?"

"Just watch. You have to see them."

She was quickly losing patience. Now that her fear was gone, anger was rising. "I'm not in the mood for games."

"No game. Look," he urged again.

Unable to help herself, she looked up. For just a heart-beat, she thought she saw something flying, but it was gone before it even registered in her mind. "What is it?"

"You won't believe me."

"Camlo, please," she begged. "I want to go to bed."

He looked at her, his eyes clear and bright in the moon-light. "Go. I'm safe."

She leaned her head back to glance at the sky once more. No matter how hard she looked, she didn't see any-thing again. She had wanted to see something, that's why her mind played tricks on her. There was nothing up there but planes and satellites with their blinking lights.

"Don't stay too late," she said and tugged on his arm.

Without taking his eyes from the sky, he leaned to the side and let her place a kiss on his cheek. Sabina gave him a pat and turned to make her way to the door.

When she came out to look for Camlo, he hadn't been in the yard. Nothing had been there. She was sure of that. Just as she reached the door, she heard Camlo laughing and clapping his hands.

She whirled around to see what had excited him so, but there was nothing there. Her brother had never displayed such behavior before. His mind might be that of a child's, but he wasn't insane.

That could only mean that he did indeed see something. She shivered and hurried into the house. After removing the boots, jacket, and pants, she climbed into bed again and found herself staring at the ceiling, wondering what her brother had witnessed.

And what she had caught a glimpse of.

She tossed and turned for hours, listening to hear if some wild creature might be outside. It was the wee hours of the morning before Camlo finally came into the house. She heard him lock the door and noticed he was singing softly to himself as he walked into his bedroom.

He only sang when he was his happiest. Within minutes, he was snoring. Sabina closed her eyes and sighed.

The next sound she heard was the rooster at dawn. She groaned, rolled onto her back, and threw an arm over her eyes. Just a few more minutes of sleep. That's all she wanted.

Camlo's whistling as he rose and dressed had her angrily grabbing her pillow and placing it over her head as she screamed into it. It wasn't her brother's fault that she hadn't gotten any sleep, but it aggravated her that he could get up with so little rest. And to add insult to injury, he was chipper about it.

The cat began to walk back and forth on her bladder as a way of getting Sabina up. She set aside the pillow and sat up to glare daggers at the feline. "Fine. I'll get up. And next time you're sleeping, I'm waking your lazy butt up. Don't think I won't," she said when the cat turned its back to her and began grooming itself.

"Just wait," Sabina threatened as she threw off the covers and got to her feet.

She dressed, repeatedly yawning before stumbling into the kitchen. While the coffee brewed, she poured the cat food and stood with her eyes closed while waiting for the coffee to finish.

As soon as it did, she fixed herself a cup and sat at the

kitchen table. With one hand propped up to hold her head, she closed her eyes and drank every drop of the java.

Now able to open her eyes almost normally, she poured a second cup. Only then did she pop four frozen waffles into the toaster for Camlo.

She went to the table she used as her desk and checked her emails. Camlo came in to grab his breakfast as she answered messages and tended to business stuff. She watched him leave with a big smile on his face.

Sabina finished the second earring from the day before and wrapped it up to take into town. She grabbed it and two other boxes and put them into the rusty vehicle that passed for her car. She wasn't sure how it still ran, but she was thankful that it did. The mechanic in town was a friend of her stepdad, so he made sure to keep the car running—while giving her a discount on the costs.

"I've got to run to mail some packages," she told Camlo as he milked the cows. "I'm thinking of picking up food for lunch."

He grinned at her. "Really?"

"Anything in particular you want?"

He shrugged and gave the cow a pat. "Whatever. You know what I like."

"I'll be back soon," she told him and returned to the car.

She got into the vehicle and backed up, but before she drove off, she looked up. Her brother had been staring toward the mountains. Not the ones nearest them, but the ones in the distance.

It didn't take her long to drop the packages off, pick up a few necessities, and then grab lunch before she returned home. She dropped everything on the table and put away the groceries before she went looking for Camlo.

He was behind the barn, staring off in the direction of the mountains that he'd been looking at the previous night.

When he saw her, he pointed at the peaks. "You can't see them now, Bina, but they're coming."

"Who?"

Camlo's lips split into a grin. "It's a surprise."

"Another bear? Or wolf?"

He laughed and shook his head. "Something even better."

"Better?" she repeated, her worrying growing. "Lunch is inside."

He crossed his arms over his chest. "I hate that I can't see them until tonight."

"So they're nocturnal?"

He shrugged. "Maybe."

"Well, if you want to watch them tonight, you need to keep up your strength. That means you need to come inside and eat."

"Can't we eat out here? It's a nice day," he implored.

She could never deny him. "Okay. I'll get the food."

"Yay," he said and pumped his fist excitedly.

Sabina put her hand on his cheek. Her brother was so handsome. If his mind were right, he would already be married and starting a family of his own. But he was trapped in a child's mind.

"I'm happy," he told her, gazing at her with his big, dark eyes.

"I'm glad."

"You should be happy, too."

Her face went slack. "Oh, honey. I am."

Instead of replying, he returned his attention to the mountains. Sabina sighed and turned away. When she came back with the food and drinks, Camlo had spread a blanket on the ground and was sitting on it with the mangy dog from the day before about twenty feet away, watching them.

Camlo reached for the food. They were so lucky to have such a good life. She didn't know how long it would last, but she would revel in every second she had of it.

Because no matter how bright the sun shone, there was always a storm coming sooner or later.

CHAPTER FIVE

This was much worse than he thought. Roman rubbed his eyes with his thumb and forefinger. He and V spent the night starting from the southern-most part of the mountains and working their way over the peaks.

Neither of them expected to find anything that first night, but it was still a blow to V. Roman watched him standing at the edge of the cave they'd found.

V remembered nothing of it, but Roman found evidence that dragons had used it. That didn't necessarily mean it was V's, but it also didn't mean it wasn't.

Roman walked to stand beside his friend. The view from the top of the mountain was spectacular. "I visited you here once, but I doona remember such beauty."

"The only place that can rival the splendor of the Carpathian Mountains is Dreagan," V replied. "How could I forget all of this?"

His words were tinged with anger but also fear. Roman couldn't imagine what V was feeling. Before Roman had become a Dragon King, he knew there was nothing on this realm that could rival them in power.

For untold millennia, that truth had stood.

Until now.

If Dmitri and Faith hadn't found the dragon skeleton and then the small wooden dragon, there would be no doubt in Roman's mind that they were still the strongest.

But the combination of *drough*, *mie*, Dark Fae, and Light Fae magic was a potent mix.

"Doona," V said as his head swung to him.

Roman gave a shake of his head in confusion. "What?"

"Contact Con."

He lifted a shoulder in a half-shrug. "I'm no' sure we can do this alone."

"Con has enough worries."

"He at least needs to know about your memories."

V shook his head. "No' yet."

"All right." Roman wasn't sure that was a good idea, but he would do as his friend asked for the moment.

"We could have the entire mountain range searched in a few days if we didna have to hide in the darkness."

Roman grinned at him. "You could if people didna see bats when you shifted."

V rolled his eyes as he shook his head. "Doona tempt me."

Roman wanted to pat himself on the back when he spotted the ghost of a smile on V's face. V had been solemn from the moment they arrived in Romania, and it had only gotten worse once they were in the mountains.

It was almost as if the closer V got to the place he called home, the further his memories retreated. At this rate, V would tip into his madness sooner rather than later.

"Shall we remain here until nightfall?" Roman asked.

V snorted. "No' bloody likely."

"We might miss something."

"Then we backtrack when we're in the air." V's gaze was fierce as he stared at Roman. "Someone took this place from me. Stripped my mind of it. But I feel it here," he said and jabbed at his chest over his heart with a finger. "They couldna take that."

Roman kicked at a rock that went bouncing down the mountain. "Lead the way."

V jumped the twenty feet down from the cave, landing with ease. Roman followed, and then they were off. They walked among the tall spruce and over boulders pushing up through the ground.

Several times, V halted and looked at something, his brow furrowed as if a memory teased him with answers. One such time, they halted near a peak where a razor-sharp boulder reached toward the clouds.

It was a place Roman would land if he were in dragon form. And no doubt V had done exactly that. The fact that it had caught V's attention was a good sign. Maybe now that he was here, walking among the land that had been his, the magic that shrouded his memories could be broken.

Neither of them had questioned why V had been targeted. The answer was simple. Why had it taken them so long to realize it, though? As soon as V's sword was stolen, it should have been obvious. But all the Kings could think about was the fact that the mortals didn't know what V's sword could do.

Perhaps they hadn't. But someone certainly did.

"Dmitri," Roman called through their link.

Almost immediately, Dmitri replied, *"Aye. How is everything coming? Have you found the sword yet?"*

"I'm afraid no'."

"Is V all right?"

The worry in Dmitri's voice reflected how Roman felt. *"For now. We've stumbled across something. I could be reaching, but it seems to connect."*

"What connects?"

Roman watched as V leapt into the air and landed atop a boulder. V squatted and looked into the distance.

"V doesna remember anything about the Carpathians."

"Nothing?" Dmitri asked softly.

"I thought once he was here, he'd recall where he was when the sword was taken, but he can no'. It's like his memories were stolen."

"We know a Druid can manage that kind of magic," Dmitri said. *"Eilish did it to Kinsey and Esther, but on a Dragon King? I doona believe a Druid's magic can do it."*

"No' alone."

There was a slight pause. *"Fuck me. The bloody wooden dragon wasna enough, was it? There had to be more."*

"V doesna want Con to know with everything else that's going on."

"Usaeil," Dmitri said, distaste dripping from each syllable.

Roman didn't take his eyes off V. He worried that his friend might shift, but Roman wouldn't stop him. The torment plaguing V was too painful to watch.

"Tell me exactly what's going on," Dmitri stated.

"V can recall nothing of this place. He can, however, tell me in detail what the men who came into his cave and stole his sword looked like."

"Part of me had hoped that he would remember once there, that it was all the centuries of dragon sleep and his fury over losing his sword that made him forget." Dmitri snorted loudly. *"The more you tell me, the more I see why you think it might be magic. I'd have come to the same conclusion. And we know just what the magic from the wooden dragon can do to us."*

Apprehension slid over Roman. *"So, we're no' as invincible as we've always thought."*

"Apparently, no'. Do you need help with V?"

"We're good at the moment. Has Rhi found out anything about those responsible for the magic of the wooden dragon?"

Dmitri sighed. *"She returned to Skye. Everyone hopes that she might find something with the Druids there."*

"What of the MacLeod Druids? Has Isla gotten any answers from the Ancients?"

"Shite. If only. It seems the more anyone tries to learn anything, the less there is to find."

Roman blew out a breath. *"No' the news I was hoping for."*

"Yeah, well, yours wasna what I wanted to hear either."

"I thought with Mikkel gone and Ulrik back at Dreagan, that everything would return to normal."

"You expect there to be normal with the Usaeil problem? And did you forget the Dark Fae?"

Roman rolled his eyes. *"How could I? With Balladyn now leading the Dark, things could get ugly thanks to the tiff between him and Rhi. But we've fought the Dark before. I'm no' worried about them."*

"Perhaps that's our problem. We've no' been concerned, thinking they can no' do any major damage."

"When, obviously, they can when they get Druids to help."

"Keep me posted on V."

"Of course," Roman said as he severed the link.

V suddenly stood and lifted his face skyward. Roman didn't call out, didn't remind him that they couldn't shift now. V knew all of it, and if he wanted to fly the mountains, then Roman wouldn't stop him.

To his surprise, V vaulted from the boulder to land beside him. He said not a word as he continued walking. Up and down the mountainsides they hiked.

Whenever they found a cave, they made their way to it and looked inside. Each time, V's expression tightened.

Roman halted when he spotted a brown bear. The large animal eyed them, understanding immediately who the dominant ones were. V strode past Roman and walked right up to the bear, stopping only a few feet from the animal.

The beast lifted its head and let out a roar before it turned and sauntered away. V didn't follow. He stood on the slope of the mountain and looked toward the valley.

Roman made his way to V. "We could have Tristan look in your mind."

"Why?" V asked indifferently. "To tell me what we already know?" Ice blue eyes turned to Roman. "We're no' alone here."

Roman frowned before his head jerked down the mountain. He saw the large man meandering idly through the trees, the bear headed straight for him. Roman started to call out, but V put a hand on his arm.

"Wait," V said.

Roman gaped at him. "You want the mortal to be killed?"

"Use your magic, Roman. This human is different."

Roman turned back to the man to see that he'd halted and was looking at the bear with a smile on his face. To Roman's shock, the bear walked straight up to the man and rubbed his large head against him.

The mortal scratched the animal's ears before his gaze lifted and met Roman's. Remembering V's words, Roman used his magic to feel the area. All he encountered was peace and innocence—not something he often felt with mortals.

The man lifted his hand and waved at them. V walked

past Roman toward the human. Roman could have remained where he was, but he was intrigued. He had to know if the bear was a pet, or if the human had a gift. It wasn't uncommon, but there were many mortals who chose not to accept such talents.

Several steps behind V, Roman watched as the bear swung its head toward them before wandering off. The man smiled after the animal. As V neared him, the human's attention shifted.

"I knew you'd come," the man said in Romanian, his smile wide.

The mortal stood as tall as Roman and V, his shoulders wide and his arms thick with muscles. He had black hair that was too long on top and kept falling into his face.

"I saw both of you last night," he continued, nodding enthusiastically.

V smiled at the mortal and asked in Romanian, "Did you now?"

"I watched all night."

There was a childlike innocence about the man. Roman instantly liked him. Their magic allowed them to speak any language, but he was curious so he made sure to speak in English. "You saw both of us?"

The man's dark eyes swung to him. "Yes. Light blue," he replied in English and pointed at Roman. Then he motioned to V and said, "Copper."

Roman raised a brow at the ease in which the man answered in English.

"What's your name?" V asked.

The man straightened and grinned. "Camlo."

V then pointed to the retreating bear. "Is he your pet?"

Camlo gave him a look that said V's words were crazy. "He's a wild animal. Not a pet, but a friend."

"You talk to them," Roman said.

Camlo's smile widened. "I do. Some think I'm crazy, but Bina tells me I'm not."

"Bina?" V asked.

"My sister." Camlo turned and motioned down the mountain.

Roman spotted a house with a barn through the trees. "Did your sister see us?"

Camlo laughed as he shook his head. "Nope."

"Do the animals talk to you, too?" V asked.

Camlo's smile dropped, and he took a step back as wariness stole over him.

"You doona have to be frightened of us," Roman said calmly.

"I know," Camlo replied.

V said, "Then you can tell us if the animals talk to you."

It was several tense moments before Camlo said, "They do."

"Incredible," V murmured.

"Camlo, step away," said a rich, throaty, feminine voice that made Roman's balls tighten at the sound.

He looked past Camlo and into eyes as dark as the night and as deep as the heavens. And was instantly drawn in.

CHAPTER SIX

Sabina didn't know what drew her into the forest. Camlo often walked among the trees, but today she decided to join him. She was taken aback to find him speaking with two men.

"Camlo," she repeated and motioned for him to join her.

"Bina," he said when he looked at her. His eyes were full of excitement. "They're here."

She eyed the man closest to her. He had short, sandy blond hair and eyes a vivid, turbulent green that reminded her of the sea—vast, dramatic, and perilous.

He was so very tall and stood calmly, relaxed as if he walked the woods with dangerous bears all the time. There was a sense of serenity about him that she noticed immediately. Yet she felt that just beneath the surface was a passionate intensity that waited to bust through. The emotions should be at odds with each other, but they were like two sides of a coin.

"We mean him no harm," replied the second man.

Sabina looked into his ice blue eyes. He held her gaze, slightly bowing his head of long, dark hair. The men spoke fluent Romanian, but she had heard Camlo talking to them in English so she decided to use that. "No one comes here."

"They're searching for something important," Camlo said as he walked to her.

She gazed up at her brother's face, her heart breaking for the compassion inside him because she knew that, one day, someone would rip it out of him.

Sabina looked between the men. "You should leave, and if you know what's good for you, you won't return."

"Your English is verra good, lass," the man with the green eyes said.

She paused at his accent, not quite able to place it. Taking in his long-sleeved, beige tee and jeans slung low on his hips, she couldn't help but notice the way his shirt clung to his wide shoulders and thick chest. "Thank you."

When she tried to turn Camlo, he wouldn't budge. "I waited all night for them, Bina. I'm not leaving."

She glanced at the duo and said in a low voice, "Camlo."

"No," he stated loudly.

He was rarely obstinate, but when he got like this, she couldn't budge him. Sabina had no choice then because she wasn't going to leave her brother alone with strangers. She glared at them, daring them to do or say anything to upset her brother.

"I'm Roman," the first man said. He pointed to the second. "He's V."

"V?" she asked with a raised brow.

V shrugged. "That's right. *Bina.*"

She cringed. How did he know that she hated the nickname? The only one who called her that was Camlo, and she only tolerated it because when he was little, he hadn't been able to pronounce her name. "My name is Sabina."

Camlo nodded as he smiled. "Yes, yes. Bina." Then he

looked at the men, pointing to the sky. "Can you do it again?"

"Later," V replied.

Roman frowned at V but didn't say anything.

"You didn't say what you're doing here," she said.

It was Roman who answered. "We're hiking."

"With no gear, jackets, or food? Try again."

"It's no' a lie," he insisted.

She crossed her arms over her chest. There was something about the men that was off. She couldn't put her finger on it, but there was certainly something peculiar about them. "What did Camlo mean when he asked you to do it again?"

Roman issued a movement that constituted a shrug. "I doona know."

"I won't let you hurt him."

V lifted his head then, his brow furrowing. "Why would you think we would harm Camlo?"

"That's what people want to do when they see my brother," Sabina said, her gaze darting between the men. "His size scares them, and when he helps animals, they don't understand. It's their small minds."

Roman grinned. "Small minds, indeed. But we're no' like that."

"So you say. I don't know you," she stated. Oddly, she didn't get the sense that she should hurry them away. Everything about this meeting should make her feel anxious and afraid. But it didn't.

Camlo jerked his head to her. "I do."

"Honey, you just met them."

He shook his head and pulled away from her. "I've known they were coming for a long time. The others told me."

Out of the corner of her eye, she saw the men exchange

a look. She kept her gaze on Camlo. "You never said anything."

"I have secrets, too," he declared and crossed his arms over his chest.

She blinked. "You make it sound as if I have secrets."

"You do," Camlo replied with a sour look.

Sabina glanced at Roman to find him watching her carefully. She returned her attention to Camlo, but she couldn't come up with an argument.

Her brother dropped his arms and turned to V as if he'd forgotten she was even there. She watched as Camlo began talking so fast that V had difficulty understanding him, but the man never chided Camlo.

It was always just the two of them, so anytime she saw her brother with someone else, she became protective, watching and waiting for someone to hurt him.

"What happened to your brother?" Roman asked as he drew near.

She shrugged, never taking her eyes off Camlo. "He was born like that. He sees the world differently. To him, it's nothing but good and beautiful with animals for friends."

"And you keep him here to shield him from the bad bits."

"Something like that." She glanced down and sighed. "Kids used to make fun of him when he was young. My parents kept him home and schooled him as best they could."

Roman looked over her shoulder at the house. "Where are your parents?"

"They died some years back. I've been taking care of Camlo for nearly ten years now."

"That's a long time."

She looked into Roman's sea green eyes and shook her

head. "Not really. His mind might be stuck in a state like that of a child, but he's a good man. He has a love of animals that goes beyond anything I can explain."

"I saw," Roman replied softly.

Sabina smiled as she thought of the bear. "He's always said he can hear the animals speaking, and he talks to them. Not in words, but there is obviously something going on between them."

"And you think we're here to exploit that."

She faced him and squared her shoulders. "I don't know what you're doing here, and I don't care. Return to the city and tell others. I'll be ready if anyone comes and tries to take him away."

"I'll no' be telling anyone," Roman assured her. "And neither will V. We willna harm or bring harm to you or Camlo, lass."

She wanted to believe him, but she couldn't chance it. "Sure."

He blew out a breath and opened his mouth to speak when Camlo started running up the mountain. He tripped, and V was there to catch him before Sabina could grasp what was happening.

The moment V touched Camlo, he stilled, an odd look passing over V's face before his gaze slid to Roman. V jerked and fell backwards.

Camlo began screaming as she and Roman rushed to them. Sabina wrapped an arm around her brother while Roman knelt beside V, calling his name while looking for injuries.

"I didn't do it," Camlo said and covered his face with his hands.

Sabina rubbed her hand up and down her brother's back. "You didn't do anything, honey. It's going to be fine."

"He's in pain. I felt it," Camlo wailed, crying harder.

Roman looked over his shoulder at her, worry creasing his brow. His eyes moved to Camlo and then down to V's hand. Roman lifted V's arm that had touched her brother and looked closely at it for a long while.

Camlo shoved her away and took off running down the mountain toward the house. Sabina watched until he was safely inside the barn, the mangy dog running in after him.

"Is he going to be all right?" Roman asked.

She turned her head to him. "You're asking about Camlo when your friend is unconscious?"

"Aye."

She swallowed. "The animals are where Camlo seeks comfort. If he gets upset, he runs to the forest. If something happens here, he runs to the barn. What happened to V?"

"I'm no' sure," Roman admitted as he sat back on his haunches. He placed his hands on his thighs and stared at his friend.

She wanted to return to the house, but she couldn't just leave Roman and V out there. What if there was something really wrong with V and he died? How would she live with herself then?

Dammit. She was going to have to invite them in. When all she really wanted was for the men to leave. Didn't she? Because she wasn't too sure since the thought of Roman remaining made a small bubble of excitement rise inside her. It wasn't as if she got a lot of visitors. That must be the reason.

"You better bring him inside," she told Roman.

His head snapped up to meet her gaze. "You doona have to do that."

"I'll only make the offer once. You don't have to accept it." With that, she turned and started down the mountain.

She only got ten steps before she glanced over her

shoulder. A smile played on her lips when she saw Roman following her with V slung over his shoulder.

Against her better judgment, Sabina slowed her pace until Roman caught up with her. Everything she was doing went against all she'd done for her brother through the years. She couldn't remember the last time there had been a guest inside her home.

"I'm not much of a healer, but I know a few things," she said.

Roman glanced at her and adjusted V. "He passed out is all."

"I saw his face, and that didn't look like he just fainted. But who am I to argue." She shrugged, but all the while, her mind replayed the moments right before V collapsed.

He'd touched Camlo. Before that, everything had been fine. V had also looked at his hand. The same hand Roman had inspected. She shifted and cut in front of Roman before turning to face him.

She put her hands on her hips and glared at him. "What aren't you telling me?"

He merely returned her look and said, "Quite a lot, I'm sure. We did just meet."

"V fainted when he touched Camlo."

"I saw."

She flattened her lips when Roman didn't continue. "Why?"

"If I knew, I'd tell you."

She raised a brow, silently questioning him.

"I would, lass," Roman assured her.

She looked away, wondering if she were doing the right thing bringing strangers into her home. This could all be some trick to . . . to what? See if Camlo could talk to animals?

Oh, God. She'd all but admitted it, and Camlo had said

as much, as well. What if they tried to take Camlo away from her? What if they said she wasn't—

"You're safe with us," Roman interrupted her thoughts.

She looked at him. "What?"

"You wear your emotions on your sleeve. You're worried about what our arrival means. It's just happenstance, I promise. As soon as V wakes, we'll leave. You'll no' see us again after that."

For some reason, that made her sad. It wasn't every day that she met men, much less a gorgeous man with haunting sea-green eyes and sandy blond hair she longed to touch.

"Camlo is taken with you. He doesn't normally talk to people. As I said, he prefers animals," she explained.

One side of Roman's lips lifted in a grin. "He likes you well enough."

"He doesn't have a choice. I'm his sister," she stated. Then ruined it with a smile. "I'm cautious for a reason."

"No need to explain."

She drew in a sharp breath and turned back to the house. They walked the rest of the way in silence. She spotted Camlo peeking his head out of the barn when they approached the house. Sabina gave him a smile as she opened the door to let Roman enter.

Right before he stepped over the threshold, she felt some force pass through her, like a warning that everything was going to change as soon as he crossed the doorsill.

Then Roman was inside with V, and there was no way to stop whatever was coming next.

"The storm," Sabina whispered and looked up at the clear sky.

CHAPTER SEVEN

Dreagan

For the first time, he truly didn't know what to do. He was Constantine, King of the Golds and King of Dragon Kings. He always had answers, always knew what direction to take in a crisis.

But not this time.

This time, he was on the edge of a cliff and looking into an abyss of . . . nothing.

He sat at his desk and drew in a breath as he raised his gaze from the papers he'd been pretending to read to find Kellan and Ulrik seated before him.

". . . we have no other option," Ulrik said.

Con blinked, completely at a loss regarding what the conversation had been about. He should've been paying attention, but he couldn't even remember them walking into his office. That's how deep his preoccupation went. Hopefully, Kellan and Ulrik hadn't noticed.

Kellan raised a brow at Con's silence, his celadon gaze locked on his King. "You heard none of our ten-minute discussion, did you?"

Damn. Con looked away from the concern in their eyes. He fisted his hand and felt something in his palm. When he glanced down, he found the pocket watch Erith—also known as Death—had given him many years ago.

Of course, he hadn't known who she was then. She had also given him the dragon head cufflinks that he wore every day. And the Montblanc pen that was his favorite.

"Con?" Ulrik called.

He closed his fingers around the pocket watch, hoping that it would somehow give him answers. But it didn't. "To answer your question, no, I wasna listening."

Con turned his chair and rose to look out the windows. He tried to remember why he'd wanted to be King of Kings so desperately. If he didn't have the weight of responsibility on his shoulders, he could be out there flying around Dreagan, letting someone else make the decisions.

"This isna like you," Ulrik said as he came to stand beside him.

Con drew in a deep breath. "You've been gone from Dreagan a verra long time, old friend. You doona know me anymore."

Ulrik let out a loud snort. "You're still the same obstinate, tenacious, persuasive, formidable arse you always were. If anything, you've become more so."

"My decisions led us here."

"You can no' take all the credit," Kellan stated.

Con turned his head to glance at Kellan before he looked into Ulrik's gold eyes. "Mikkel's defeat should have been the end of things, but there is much more spiraling out of control."

Ulrik inhaled sharply and slowly released the breath as he shifted to face Con. "To be fair, the situation with the Dark Fae has been ongoing for some time. I'll let you take credit for the Usaeil debacle, though. I doona know what you were thinking taking her to your bed."

"I was thinking that I was lonely." He closed his eyes

as soon as the confession passed his lips. No one else would've been able to get him to admit such a thing.

Ulrik stared at him solemnly for a long moment. "You doona have to be."

Con returned his gaze out the window, refusing to reply to the comment. "Becoming involved with a mortal, even for a single night of passion, wasna something I wanted to attempt. Usaeil had let me know for some time that she was interested. Before we . . . sealed our union . . . she promised that it would just be a fling for both of us."

"Friends with benefits," Ulrik replied. "I can see that."

"It got out of hand quickly. I saw it, but didna get out when I should have."

"It wouldna have mattered. I think Usaeil told you whatever you needed to hear to get you into her bed."

Con shrugged. "Possibly. She used me, but I was using her, as well. I wanted the Light army in case things with you went tits up."

"I would've done the same thing. It was a smart move. You had no idea she was tipping into crazy town."

"Usaeil has done more than set her sights on being my mate." Con gave a shake of his head as he turned and walked to the sideboard where he poured three glasses of scotch. He turned to hand one to Kellan, only to find the seat vacant. Con quirked a brow in question to Ulrik.

"He left to give us some time to talk," Ulrik replied as he took a glass from him.

Con tossed back the whisky and let the smooth taste slide down his throat to settle in his belly. "Handling me with kid gloves, huh?"

"Actually, Kellan wasna interested in hearing you whine," Ulrik replied with a straight face.

Con chuckled and reached for the other tumbler. "Nice try."

"I thought it was a damn fine try." Ulrik grinned before he raised the glass to Con in a salute and took a drink.

"The Dark are a minor concern. Usaeil . . . well, I promised Rhi that we'd handle that situation in a timely manner," Con said.

"I'm no' sure how long our friend will wait. Usaeil banished Rhi from the Light. That blow, combined with learning that Usaeil wanted her killed, and the argument with Balladyn, has hit Rhi hard."

Con sneered at the mention of the new King of the Dark. Balladyn had given the Dark free rein to kill as many humans as they wanted.

And to think, Con had had a chance to let him die recently. He hadn't, though. Because Rhi had asked him to save Balladyn.

"There's also the Reapers," Ulrik added.

Con shot him a flat look. "We've heard rumors about the Reapers for some time now. Even Rhi told us about them. A couple even visited me."

"Aye, but that was before you knew that their leader, Death, had come to Dreagan to see you several times over the last few centuries, disguising herself each time."

"Her name is Erith."

Ulrik shrugged. "Death. Erith. It's all the same. And our two groups could verra well work together soon. But that's no' what's really bothering you, is it?"

The control Con kept at all times slipped as rage and fear erupted within him like a volcano. He spun and threw his glass against the wall.

"That's what I thought," Ulrik said softly. "The weapon."

"It's gone!" Con bellowed, still unable to believe that the one item he was to keep protected had managed to be stolen.

The weapon could kill the Dragon Kings. And if it fell into the hands of any of their enemies, then the Kings were doomed. It didn't matter how much magic they had, it would be over for them.

Con walked to the window and looked out at the mountains of Dreagan, searching for the peace that he usually found staring at the peaks.

"We will find it."

Con's lips twisted as he shook his head. "Nothing could move through my magic without me feeling it, and yet, something did. And they took the weapon that can kill us."

"You *think* it can kill us. We're no' sure."

Con raked a hand down his face, weary to his very soul. "When I defeated Tarel to become King of Dragon Kings, all of the information he had was passed on to me. That's how I first learned of the weapon. As soon as I realized what it could do, I understood why it had been kept from everyone, and why Tarel went to such lengths to have it safeguarded."

"I know the weapon is powerful, but why would we keep something that could kill us in the first place?" Ulrik asked.

Con let his shoulders slump as he braced one hand on the side of the window and looked at Ulrik. "It wasna my decision to keep the weapon, but it became my burden to bear."

"You could've destroyed it."

"There wasna a need."

"There certainly is now."

Now that it was too late. Con felt as if everything that he had worked tirelessly to build for his brethren was unraveling at a rate that he couldn't keep up with or even think of rectifying.

"We'll find the weapon," Ulrik declared.

Con sure hoped his friend was correct. Otherwise, it might very well be the end of the Dragon Kings.

"Have you heard from V?"

Con huffed and squeezed his eyes closed for a moment, thankful to have another direction to turn his thoughts. Maybe now he could get a handle on his emotions. "I'd forgotten that he and Roman left."

What kind of ruler was he that he could forget when his men departed Dreagan for an important mission? He really needed to get his head right and regain the composure that had gotten him through so much.

"Sending Roman with V was brilliant," Ulrik said.

Con pushed away from the window and squeezed the bridge of his nose. "Was it? I no longer know. Perhaps you should've challenged me. I'm no' sure I'm the one who should be in this position."

"You're the only one who can do it."

His head snapped to Ulrik. His friend's gold eyes were locked on his face.

"You know I'm right," Ulrik continued. "You were born to be King of Dragon Kings, Con. Every leader stumbles now and again. You do it so rarely that, when it happens, you doona know what to do. That's why I'm here. To keep you on your feet and remind you who you are."

Emotion choked Con. He looked away, unable to hold Ulrik's gaze. It was usually Con who bolstered others, not the other way around.

Ulrik put his hand on Con's shoulder. "What is it you tell us? We're no' alone. Well, old friend, now I'm the one telling you. All those years I was banished, did you no' talk with any of the others?"

Con lifted one shoulder in a shrug. "They look to me to have the answers and make decisions."

"And you always do. It doesna make you weak to need someone every now and again. Though, I know it isna really me you need."

Con pulled away from him to walk off the irritation and . . . other emotions he refused to name. "Doona go there, Ulrik. I'm no' in the mood."

"You gave me relationship advice recently. I told you I'd return the favor eventually."

He halted and pointed a finger at Ulrik, anger rising to dangerous levels. "It isna now."

Ulrik paused as he stared at him. "You're right. Now isna the time."

Relief surged through Con as his arm dropped to his side because he knew he couldn't handle that conversation. It would break him as nothing else could.

If he were honest, it was nice to be able to share things with Ulrik again. He'd missed his friend, who was more of a brother than anything. Before the betrayal perpetrated against Ulrik—instigated by his uncle Mikkel, which led to the war with the humans and then Ulrik's banishment—Con and Ulrik had no secrets between them.

If there were ever something on Con's mind, he'd gone to Ulrik. For the last several millennia, Con had gotten used to keeping his own counsel.

Ulrik released a loud sigh. "We're going to have to tell the others about the weapon being stolen."

"I'm going to have to tell them the rest."

A deep frown creased Ulrik's brow. "Is that wise? You said yourself that the other King of Kings kept the weapon secret for a reason."

"If I ever knew that reason, I've long forgotten it. Besides, I'm tired of secrets."

"*All* of them?"

Con swallowed and looked away. "Aye."

"They're your secrets. You get to decide when they're revealed."

His secrets. What a load of shite. Con's gaze caught on the shards of glass from the tumbler he'd thrown. It had felt good to show that little burst of anger. It was dangerous, though. So very, very dangerous.

If he let more out, he might not stop. That's exactly where Rhi would want him when they faced Usaeil, but Con knew if there was a chance for the Queen of the Light to come out of the confrontation alive and be the Fae she'd once been, he needed to get his emotions back under control.

"Bend a little, old friend," Ulrik cautioned. "Lest you break. Frankly, we're going to need you after the Dark, Usaeil, and the weapon issues are cleared up. No' to mention that Death and the Reapers may call on us."

Con snorted. Ulrik spoke as if those problems would be fixed in a matter of days. Never mind that V hadn't found his sword yet, and that they still knew next to nothing about the Druids and Fae who combined their magic to not only kill, but hide one of Dmitri's Whites along with a magical wooden dragon that was an exact replica of Con.

Bend.

Ulrik was right. He had to be flexible, or he would crack under the weight of everything. That wasn't acceptable. He'd promised to guide the Kings. Not that they needed it. Each was incredibly strong individually—or they wouldn't be Dragon Kings.

But as King of Kings, Con was the strongest, the most powerful of all the Dragon Kings. He'd fought to the death for that right. He wasn't about to let his brethren down now.

He met Ulrik's gaze.

After a moment, his friend smiled. "That's the Con we need."

CHAPTER EIGHT

Talented. That's the first thought that went through Roman's mind about Sabina when he laid V down on the sofa. That's when he saw the half-finished piece of jewelry. He couldn't quite determine what it was, but the craftsmanship was obvious to even his untrained eye.

There were dozens of colored drawings of various examples scattered about. The skill that went into the sketches and coloring of each piece only paled in comparison to the photos of the actual jewelry that were attached to the pages.

"It's a mess," Sabina said and tucked a curl of hair behind her ear.

It wasn't hard to imagine that she had gypsy blood somewhere in her past with her rich olive skin, fathomless deep brown eyes tilted up slightly at the corners giving her an exotic look, and brown locks so dark they were nearly black that just reached her shoulders.

He wanted to wind one of her large ringlets around his finger and give it a soft tug. But he couldn't look away from her eyes. With one sweep, she seemed to take in everything and digest it quickly, each emotion showing on her oval face.

Her dark pink lips were full and utterly sexy. Her face was unblemished except for a small scar that bisected her left eyebrow and left the spot exposed.

In an age where women went to extremes with their makeup, especially their eyebrows, he liked that she left what some might call a flaw—but something that made her unique—natural.

Her dark red shirt hung loosely over her body, showing him nothing of her curves. The only glimpse he got was from the jeans that clung to her shapely hips and legs.

"Doona clean up on my account," he told her. "This is your workspace, I take it?"

She gave a single nod, watching him.

He leaned closer to look at the piece in progress. "You draw and then make these?"

"I sell them online. It's how I earn a living."

"I take it you're good?" he asked with a grin.

She smiled as she shrugged, modesty making her gaze lower briefly to the ground. "Well, the orders keep coming in, and the reviews are good, so I suppose so." She shuffled some of the papers. "Each piece is unique."

"You keep record of them, I see," he said, pointing to the pictures.

"That's because I had people requesting that I make something their friend bought from me. It was difficult to keep track, so I began taking pictures and keeping it with my drawing as a way to have a record. I need to file these."

"Or put them in a portfolio of sorts so you can easily find what you need."

She raised a brow, surprise in her eyes. "That's actually a good idea."

"I have them every now and again."

She laughed, which made her eyes crinkle. She fairly glowed from within, and he wanted to make her laugh again to see more of it.

"We need to stay here for a wee bit," V suddenly said in his mind.

"Why?" Roman asked.

"I felt something . . . peculiar . . . when I touched Camlo. I caught a brief memory of my cave before my sword was taken."

The news shocked Roman. *"Then we stay as long as you need. Are you all right?"*

"I'm fine. Keep her talking," V urged.

That would be no great hardship. Roman liked talking to Sabina and watching the expressions cross her beautiful face.

Roman stepped away from the table while she fussed over a few things. He moved to the wall where there were drawings of Camlo through the years. In each one, he was with a different animal, proving just how much he loved creatures.

"You drew all of these?" Roman asked.

Sabina came up beside him and nodded. "And Camlo made the frames."

Roman touched the scalloped edge of one casing. The edges were so precise that he could barely see the seam. "Amazing."

"In many ways, my brother is like a child, but when it comes to animals and working with wood, he's an entirely different person. He replaced the door and added the shutters to the windows. Everything you see out back, he made. My stepfather began the barn before his accident, but as soon as he was able, Camlo finished it."

In just a few sentences, Sabina had given Roman a lot of information. "What kind of accident?"

"It was during a fierce snowstorm. Petre drove into town, and on the way back, he hit a patch of ice. His car went off the mountain."

"I'm verra sorry."

Sabina shrugged, her gaze going to a picture sitting atop an accent table near the sofa. It was of a couple—a girl of about ten, and a young boy. "My stepfather was a good man. We all felt Petre's loss."

"And your mother?"

Sabina's smile was sad as she looked at him. "She had been sick for a while. She'd have good days and bad days, but for the most part, she put on a brave face. I knew it was serious. I could hear her and Petre talking late at night when they thought I was asleep. After he died, I confronted her about it. She refused to go to the doctor, believing that her herbs could cure anything. The last year of her life was one filled with tremendous pain."

"You took care of her," he guessed.

Sabina nodded slowly. "Mom wouldn't let me take her to a hospital. When she got so bad that I didn't give her a choice, I had Camlo carry her to the car. The doctors could do nothing for her by that time, she was too far gone. They made her comfortable, at least."

"Did she have a fear of doctors?"

"Just a stubbornness that the old ways were better." Sabina smiled sadly.

Roman wanted to push for more, but he held back for the moment. Instead, he let his gaze move around the house. It was small but efficient. Everything had a place, and there was no unnecessary clutter.

"Coffee or tea?" Sabina asked.

He gave a nod. "Either."

Roman followed her into the kitchen. The table was old, the dings and nicks giving it character as if every person who sat at it had left their mark in some way. There were four mismatched chairs, one stained dark while the other three were painted blue, white, and yellow.

It shouldn't work, but it did. Perhaps because of the dried herbs hanging on the ceiling and the many plants along the windowsill near the sink.

Sabina saw him looking at the herbs and shrugged. "Habit. Mom wasn't wrong in using them. I just think there are times when they won't work. When no medicine will."

Roman pulled out a chair and sat as she fixed two cups of tea and set them on the table with milk and sugar. "Have you thought about selling Camlo's work?" he asked.

"I probably should. There are about thirty frames of various sizes in the barn. You've taken a lot of interest in us, but you've not told me anything about yourself."

"You've no' asked," he said with a grin over his mug.

She held his gaze, silently waiting.

Roman sat back after taking a drink. "Fair enough. I'm from Scotland."

"I couldn't place your accent. Now it makes sense," she said with a nod. "You're a long way from home. What brings you to Romania?"

He turned his head to V, who continued to pretend that he was asleep. "We're doing a bit of traveling."

"Now why don't I believe that?" she asked skeptically.

Roman slid his gaze back to Sabina to find her elbows propped on the table as she held her mug between her hands and watched him with her large eyes. "Why would you no'?"

"You mean you want me to believe that, just like you

wanted me to believe you two are hikers? Even the most inexperienced hikers have gear," she stated.

He drew in a deep breath and looked into her dark eyes. "Would you believe anything I said?"

"If I saw the truth in your eyes, yes."

That made him smile. "All right. We're looking for something."

"That I believe," Sabina stated and took a drink of her tea. "What do you look for?"

Before he could answer, V shouted *No!* in his mind. Roman didn't want to lie to her, but he also understood why V didn't wish her to know more. "We're no' sure yet."

Sabina studied him a long moment. "That's not the whole truth, but I accept it."

"You speak as if you're reading me."

She glanced at the table and set her mug down.

"Another family habit?" he pressed.

There was a pause before she said, "Yes."

"A natural gift, or one learned?"

It was her turn to sit back. Her dark eyes shrewd as she studied him. "A little of both."

"Which is how you know English so well."

"There are a great many tourists who come through the area. They believe anyone living here is Romani. My mother took advantage of that."

"It helped that she was Romani, aye?" It was a guess, but Roman had a hunch he was right.

Sabina brought her cup to her lips and drank before lowering it back to the table. Only then did she say, "Yes."

"You doona like anyone knowing your heritage?"

"You obviously know little of life here. Romani are looked down upon. We're the lowest of the low. Even though probably half the population or more has Romani blood flowing through them."

He regarded her. "I doona think your heritage is anything to be ashamed of. Who cares what others think?"

"Why give anyone more reasons to fear Camlo? It's better that no one knows."

"Where is your father?"

Her gaze lowered to her cup. "He died when I was little."

Roman's attention turned to the door as it opened and Camlo looked inside. He spotted V on the couch before he found Roman and Sabina in the kitchen.

"V will be fine," Roman assured Camlo. "He's resting."

"I brought something to help," Camlo said and lifted his hands to show the rabbit.

"What does he have?" V asked.

Roman smiled at Camlo while ignoring V. "He'll love it."

"Roman," V growled.

But V didn't move when Camlo neared or when he placed the rabbit on his chest.

"I better no' be shite on," V grumbled.

Roman covered his mouth with his hand to hide his smile. He licked his lips and met Camlo's gaze after he got ahold of himself. "Thank you."

"I didn't mean to hurt him," Camlo said dejectedly.

Sabina pushed back her chair and went to her brother. "You didn't."

Camlo's eyes moved to him. Roman nodded then. "Your sister's right. You did nothing."

"Then why won't V wake?" Camlo asked.

"He will," Roman assured him.

Camlo bent and gave Sabina a quick peck on her cheek before he left. She softly closed the door behind him before returning to the table.

"I can remove the rabbit," she offered.

"Aye!" V yelled telepathically. *"The damn animal willna stop sniffing my face. The whiskers are tickling me."*

Roman shook his head. "I think it's just the thing to wake V up."

"Payback is hell, Roman."

"Tell me something else about yourself," Sabina urged.

Roman scratched his jaw. "I'm an artist, of sorts."

"Of sorts?" she asked with a grin. "What does that mean?"

"It's more of a hobby than something I do for money. I doona have a choice. Once the idea is in my head, I have to create it, or I go insane."

"Exactly how I feel about my jewelry. So what do you create?"

"Sculptures from metal."

She leaned her forearms on the table. "I don't get to talk to many other artists. This is truly a treat."

It certainly was, but not in the way she thought. Roman hadn't wanted to stop when they did, but now that he'd met the lovely Sabina, he was thoroughly enjoying himself.

CHAPTER NINE

It had been a very long time since she'd used the Sight passed down in her family, but Sabina couldn't seem to help herself when it came to Roman.

She had expected him to ask her to read his palms once he learned she was Romani, but he hadn't. That surprised her, but it also disappointed her. She actually wanted to look into his future.

Her mother had used her Sight to make extra money for the family, but Sabina had never been interested. Ignoring her gifts hadn't been easy, but it had become a habit over the years. Still, there were times that her gift rose up when she least expected it.

Sabina glanced at the sofa to make sure V was still asleep. The longer he remained unconscious, the longer she had to talk to Roman. How odd that all these years she'd thought she preferred the solitude, but now she couldn't seem to stop sharing things with Roman.

Perhaps it wasn't that she was starved for attention. Maybe it was Roman who was doing this to her.

Yes, she liked that explanation the best. Otherwise, she

would have to reevaluate her life, and she wasn't up for anything like that.

"What kind of sculptures do you make?" she asked.

Roman's beautiful green eyes held hers as he shrugged, the corners of his lips dipping down slightly. "Anything that strikes my fancy. How about you?"

"Essentially the same. I grew up listening to the myths involving Romania, which have always fascinated me. As a child, I used to go looking for *Pasărea Măiastră* in the woods."

"The Majestic Bird," Roman translated.

Sabina could barely contain her excitement that he knew the translation. "She is considered the queen of the Birds and a messenger of the fairies. It is said that the privileged few who get to see the unique beauty are graced by its celestial light."

"Her song can lengthen the life of any who hear it. And she is a righteous bird with splendid, multicolored plumage and inexhaustible power."

"You know the myth?"

He shot her a lopsided grin that made her stomach flutter in response. "Aye."

Sabina looked at the table as she was transported back to her childhood before leaving the camp. "My gran would tell me of The Other Realm where the Majestic Bird lived, and I just knew it was waiting for me to be alone to grace me with its presence."

"Did you ever see it?"

She shook her head as she raised her gaze to him. "But those stories stuck with me. Mom and I took turns telling them to Camlo, which kept my love of such things going. I know they're just stories, but they are part of my culture, and therefore, a part of me. I think that's why all the jewelry I create is based on creatures from those stories."

Roman's head turned to her worktable as his smile grew. "That's what you're designing now. *Pasărea Măiastră*."

"Yes."

He rose and walked to the table before picking up her drawing and returning to the kitchen. "This is verra good, lass."

Lass. Damn the man for making her want to smile each time he called her that. "I've drawn so many variations, trying to get the colors just right."

"I doona think you could go wrong with any color combination."

"The necklace will be one of my most expensive pieces. I'm not sure if it'll sell for the price I'm going to ask."

Roman placed the drawing on the table. "You could do more than one necklace using different colors."

"I've thought of that. I think it depends on how well it sells."

"Have you thought of an arm cuff?"

She jumped up and rushed to her table, where she found a notebook she jotted ideas in and hastily wrote Roman's suggestion.

"I take that to mean you like the idea?"

She looked up, embarrassed. "In my head, I replied to you," she said with a laugh and returned to her chair.

"I do things like that all the time."

Silence stretched between them. Sabina cleared her throat as she returned to the kitchen and her chair. "You've not asked me to tell your fortune."

"Does everyone ask that of you?"

"Those who know I'm Romani."

"Have you always lived here?"

She tucked a leg under her and pushed aside the cold remnants of her tea. "Would you be surprised to learn that for the first six years of my life, I traveled the mountains with my family?"

"A true Romani, then," he said with a grin.

Sabina chuckled as she nodded. "Very. I can't remember much from that time, but I do recall the caravans traveling from town to town. I remember late at night there being a huge fire where the adults would gather. Some would talk while others played instruments. That's how I fell asleep each night."

"Good memories."

"They certainly are." She moved a crumb from breakfast around with her fingernail. "It was nice to have all the family around. Both of my parents came from large families, so we were a huge group. There were always cousins to play with, aunts and uncles to talk to, and Gran, who shared the myths with me."

When she looked up, Roman was silently watching her. There was no contempt or scorn for her family on his face. Just . . . curiosity. If everyone treated her like this, she wouldn't hide the fact that she was Romani.

But she still recalled how the kids had called her hateful names when she and her mother moved to Brasov. It left a lasting impression.

"Why did you leave the camp?" Roman asked.

Sabina inhaled sharply. She hadn't thought about it in a long time, but she would never forget either. "We came upon this village that we had been to before. There were times when Mom would take me into town as a treat. She hadn't wanted to go that day, but I reminded her that she'd promised. Our walk there was uneventful, despite the fact that most didn't enjoy seeing Travelers pull into their towns. We went into a shop, and Mom bought me a red ribbon that I fell in love with. We were on our way back to the group when a man stopped Mom. I didn't hear what he whispered, but she was outraged. He grabbed her, and she tried to get away, ripping her shirt in the process."

Sabina paused and rose to walk to the back window to check on Camlo. "Mom gave me a push and told me to run for the camp. I didn't want to leave her, but I did as she told me. I ran as fast as I could. I was only five at the time so my legs couldn't go very fast, but it felt like I was flying. I tripped and fell, twisting my ankle and scraping my face. Still, I got up and continued running. Dad was the one who found me. Through my tears and ramblings, he and two of Mom's brothers got the gist of what had happened. They left me in the care of the camp and went to find her."

Sabina watched a bright yellow butterfly leisurely glide past the window. Once she saw Camlo feeding the chickens, she turned to face Roman. "I don't know what happened to Mom. When they returned, my uncles were smiling, their knuckles bloodied. My dad had his arm around Mom, and they disappeared into our caravan. Gran kept me with her, telling me that the two needed some time alone. I thought it was over. That everything would go back to normal."

"The townsfolk had other ideas, I'm guessing," Roman said.

The memories of that night rose swiftly from the past, swallowing her in the heartache and horror of it all. "It was our last night there. We always had people guarding the caravans, and after what happened with Mom, they doubled that. We kids used to go running around at night, but not that night.

"We were irritated to be kept within the camp and were making a lot of noise. So were the horses. My father scolded me for trying to sneak off with the others, then he went to check on the animals. I went back to playing with the other kids. I don't know how long it was before my uncle came running into camp. He'd found my dad with a knife in his chest.

"The blood on my uncle's hands was so bright in the firelight. My mother tried to run to Da, but her brothers stopped her. She was frantic, tears coursing down her face. Then she saw me. She'd never held me so tightly before. It hurt, but I didn't want her to let go.

"We didn't wait around for anyone else to die. Nor did anyone go into the village. The horses were loaded into the trailers along with the other animals, and we all packed up in the middle of the night. In less than forty minutes, we were on the road. I sat beside my father's dead body in the caravan as Mom cried, and my uncle drove."

She shrugged and picked up their mugs to rinse them in the sink. "Romani don't like to touch their dead, but we had no choice. We traveled deep into the mountains before we stopped. There's usually so much noise, but it was so silent that day. No one spoke. There wasn't even a song from a bird." She paused and looked out the window. "My father was taken and prepared for burial by my mother, Gran, and aunts. The men built his coffin. We laid him to rest in the mountains he loved. Mom was never the same after that. She wouldn't let me out of her sight whenever we stopped at a village, and I wasn't allowed to go anywhere near outsiders. She'd always been so vibrant, but she was sullen and withdrawn after. I'm not sure what brought her to the decision to leave the group. We were one of the largest sets of Travelers, made up mostly of our families, but she decided it would be better to give me a proper home."

Roman looked around. "This home?"

"The very one. We lived here almost a year before she met Petre. He'd come to do some work around the house. You could tell there was something between them immediately. They were married a year later, and nine months after, Camlo was born." She leaned a hand against the edge of the sink and looked at Roman. "Camlo and I have been here ever since."

"You didna ever think of returning to your family?" he asked.

"Of course. I've long believed it would be the best place for Camlo, but I'm not sure he'd leave this place. This is his home. And I have no idea where my family could be. My mother chose this place because the group had never stopped anywhere near here."

Roman pushed back his chair and stood. He briefly turned his head to check on V before he focused his sea green eyes on her again. The way he looked at her made Sabina's breath lodge in her chest.

It was as if his eyes stripped away all her defenses and left her utterly exposed for him to see each worry, every fear—and all her dreams.

Did he have the Sight, too? Because she didn't think there was a piece of her life—past, present, or future—that he didn't see with those amazing eyes of his.

"You look scared of me, lass," he murmured. "Why?"

"It's the way you look at me." She didn't bother lying. It seemed fruitless.

His brow furrowed slightly. "How's that?"

"As if you see all of me."

"And you doona like that?"

She shook her head.

A sandy blond brow rose. "Why is that, lass?"

"There are things I don't want you to see. And things I don't want to think about."

He made a sound in the back of his throat that reminded her of a purr. "Whatever secrets I uncover will remain with me."

For some odd reason, she believed him. It wasn't in Sabina's nature to trust so easily, and yet she did just that with Roman. And she wasn't sure why. "Since it appears that V might be out for a while yet, would you two like to stay for supper? I mean, that is if you don't have other plans."

Roman's lips turned up in a sexy grin. "We doona have anywhere to be at the moment."

"Good." She started to turn to the stove when she paused and said, "I should probably mention that I'm only passable as a cook."

"I'm no' concerned."

What was it about the Scot that kept her saying such things? There was the fact that Roman was mind-numbingly gorgeous, not to mention sexy as hell, but his mere presence made her want to tell him her entire life story—which she pretty much had already.

And she'd invited them to eat. Now, she would be stressed trying to come up with a dish that she was comfortable making that would turn out edible. Camlo never complained. He would probably eat pinecones if she let him, but Roman and V were much different.

She wanted them to enjoy their meal, not do their best to stomach the food because it was so bad. The fact was, she had only ever cooked for Camlo and her mom. She didn't know if she was good or bad.

All she had to go on was her own taste buds. And right now, that worried her.

CHAPTER TEN

"For the love of all that's holy, just kiss her already," V growled.

Roman ignored his friend, despite the fact that he very much wanted to do just that to Sabina. She was, in turn, confident then nervous. Open, then closed off.

She was like a coin spinning, unable to decide what she wanted to do or say. He was more than surprised by her invitation for dinner, considering she hadn't wanted Camlo near them to begin with.

The small frown upon her brow stated that she was just as confused as he was about the matter. But she didn't retract the offer.

Camlo shouted for Sabina. When she walked from the house, Roman followed her. He probably should've remained behind with V, but he was curious about Camlo's excitement.

It wasn't until they reached one of the pens holding the rabbits that he saw the reason. The babies had been born just moments before.

"I told you more were coming," Camlo told Sabina with a proud smile.

She put her hand on his arm and grinned up at him. "You certainly did. Though, we might need to separate them. We have enough rabbits."

His smile faded, his brown eyes sliding to Roman. "Would you want to be separated from your mate?"

It was never a question posed to Roman before, and that same feeling he had in Scotland filled him once more. "Nay, I wouldna."

Camlo looked at his sister. "I won't keep them apart. They're mates."

"Fine," she said and held up her hands in defeat. "We're going to be overrun with rabbits soon if they keep having a dozen at a time, but okay."

Camlo's frown deepened. After a moment, he looked at the rabbits and sighed. "I'll talk to them and see what I can do."

Sabina patted his back as she shook her head. Then she looked at Roman and shrugged as if to say *"this is my life."* After a few minutes watching Camlo coo at the kits, Sabina walked away and motioned for Roman to follow.

They meandered their way through the various enclosures. Roman noted that each of the animals was healthy, happy, and better cared for than many humans.

"I think, in a lot of ways, Camlo loves them more than me." Sabina shot him a grin.

"I doubt that," Roman said.

She shrugged. "It only takes a few minutes of watching him with the animals before you come to the conclusion that taking him away from all of this would kill him."

"He could bring the animals with him."

"Maybe," she murmured.

Roman cut his eyes to her as they stopped, and she patted a cow on the neck. "What's your plan? To remain here, just the two of you?"

"Yep."

"You doona wish to marry?"

She laughed and looked at him. "I never really thought about it. If anything happens to me, I've made arrangements for Camlo to be taken in by a place who will understand him."

"But he will be taken from here."

Sabina pressed her lips together and nodded, sadness filling her eyes. "What else can I do? I can't leave him here alone. He doesn't know how to pay bills or when to go to the store for necessities that we don't grow or have ourselves. And what happens when someone comes wanting to buy this place, because it will happen. They'll take advantage of him and send him to some horrid state program."

"Or you could find your family."

She blew out a breath. "I wouldn't even know where to begin."

Roman watched the sunlight dance over the strands of her dark locks, some angles allowing him to see shades of deep red. "You willna know until you try, lass."

Dark eyes met his. "You're right."

"Maybe I can help," he offered.

A brow arched up at his words. "In exchange for what?"

"Nothing," he said with a shake of his head. "I'm merely helping."

"Say I believe you, how would you help?"

He grinned, liking how she was wary and wanting to know every detail before she agreed to anything. "I've a friend who can do amazing things with a computer."

Sabina stared at him a long time before she started walking and said, "All right."

The hesitancy in her voice gave him pause. "Once you have the information, it'll be up to you what to do with it."

"Of course." She glanced at him and forced a smile. "I appreciate your offer. It's just. . . ."

"You like how things are," he finished for her.

This time, her smile was genuine. "It's easy to get into a routine."

"Verra."

She stopped as they reached the front of the house, but she faced the mountains. "I've spilled my life to you, and you've told me nothing of yours."

"That's no' entirely true. You know I'm from Scotland."

They shared a grin, but her gaze told him she wasn't going to relent. Roman blew out a breath and told a whopper of a lie. "There isna much to tell."

She stared unblinking at him for a long minute. "That's not what I see."

He looked away while concern grew that she might actually see the very thing he wanted to keep hidden. The Kings had long been lying to mortals about who they were.

The silence that stretched between them was uncomfortable. Roman tried to ignore it and focus on the beauty before him, but he could feel Sabina's gaze on him, watching and waiting. He should've known that her Romani blood would eventually detect something.

"You're trying very hard to hide something," she said.

He raised his eyes to the sky. "Doesna everyone? Camlo said you keep secrets."

"Hm. I can't dispute that."

He finally faced her. "Stop trying to use your Sight on me."

"Why? Because I won't like what I see?" she asked pointedly.

There was a part of him that wanted to find out how she'd react to the discovery that he was a dragon, but the more rational side of him quickly chucked that away. "Because I'm asking you to."

"People who don't want their lives peered into usually have a doozy of a secret. Or have done something criminal." She cocked her head to the side. "I don't think the latter applies to you."

He raised his brows. "Indeed? Why?"

"Camlo trusted both you and V immediately. And . . . even though I didn't want to trust you, I quickly found that I did. Camlo doesn't react to others like he did with you and V. That means something to me."

Roman briefly shifted his gaze to the house where V was still inside. Something had happened to his friend when he touched Camlo. It could be nothing. Or it could be something huge. Roman had promised V that he'd find his sword this time. He wasn't going to be the one to ruin V's chances.

"I'm no' a criminal," Roman said.

Her smile was soft. "I didn't think so."

"I didna lie when we first met. V and I are searching for something he lost."

"What did he lose?"

Roman hesitated. "Something he greatly values."

"Ah. Another secret, then." There was no anger in her voice or countenance. "I'm intrigued. So, how did V lose this item?"

"It was stolen."

A small frown flashed across her face, but it was quickly gone. "Stolen? Are you after those who took it?"

"Aye."

Her eyes widened in excitement. "Really? I love a good mystery."

He didn't want to talk about his secrets anymore. Roman had never had a problem with lying before, but for some reason, it left a bitter taste in his mouth this time.

The squeak of the front door caused both of them to turn their heads toward the house. V filled the doorway, his gaze locked on Sabina.

Roman frowned as he watched his friend make his way toward them. Sabina's welcoming smile faded with every step V took. There was an intensity about V that Roman hadn't seen in a very long time.

It was a sign that V might be reverting back to his former self, the Dragon King he'd been before his sword was taken. But it could also mean trouble if he were dipping into madness again.

"*V?*" Roman said via their link.

His friend didn't answer as he stopped before Sabina. V's blue eyes were brighter than normal. "How far back can you trace your family?"

"Why?" Sabina asked.

"Please," V replied softly. "Tell me what you know."

Sabina glanced at Roman and shrugged. "I'm not sure. My gran used to tell me stories of our ancestors, but she never said how far back they went."

"What kind of stories?" Roman asked.

Sabina crossed her arms over her chest like a shield. "Romani stories."

V's chest began rising and falling quickly, but his gaze had moved past Sabina to the mountains.

"I'm going to check on Camlo," Sabina said.

Roman gave her a nod and waited until she walked away before he turned to V. "What was that about?"

"I told you something happened when Camlo touched me. For a brief moment, I was transported back to when I still had possession of my sword. I was in dragon form deep within the cave. I'd just come from a flight over the mountains. It rained on me." V's gaze slid to him. "I felt the water on my scales as if I were still there."

Roman studied V and found his eyes clear. It wasn't madness that V was falling into—but the past. "Then what?"

"Movements from the men as they climbed up the mountain to my cave. I heard the beating of their hearts, thudding erratically from exertion and fear. And then . . . nothing."

In all the times they had asked V to tell them what happened leading up to his sword being stolen, V had never been able to. This was their first clue, and somehow, it involved Camlo.

"Do you doubt me?" V asked.

Roman quickly shook his head. "Nay. I'm shocked and excited that you've recalled something."

Rage filled V's blue eyes as he gave a loud snort. "The mixed Druid and Fae magic has kept my memories hidden all this time. Somehow, I managed to strip away a tiny part of it. I kept trying after I woke, but I couldna replicate what I'd done."

"Then that means that baffling mix of magic can be fought with dragon magic."

V's lips twisted. "Was it my magic? Or was it Camlo?"

"You're putting a lot of stock in a half-Romani man-child."

"What would you do in my place?"

Roman ran a hand down his face. "The same damn thing. So, what now?"

"I need Camlo to touch me again. Maybe then I'll learn more."

"V, you fainted the last time."

"Passed out," V stated flatly. "A Dragon King doesna faint."

Roman rolled his eyes. "Call it what you will, you were unconscious."

"But I got some memories back. That's worth however many times I pass out."

Still Roman hesitated. He wasn't sure what kind of connection Camlo had to V, and that troubled him. Because if Camlo, as only half-Romani, could do this to V, what would happen if Sabina touched him?

His gaze found the siblings with the animals. Sabina turned her head then, their eyes meeting.

"Somehow, they're key to this, Roman. You know that," V stated.

Roman pulled his gaze from Sabina to look at V. "I know."

"You also know that I'm no' going to leave until I have the answers I seek."

"Aye."

"Do you?" V pressed. "Because I saw the way you looked at Sabina as if you wanted to devour her."

There were so many things Roman wanted to do to Sabina, but that's not what they were there for. And he needed to remember that.

CHAPTER ELEVEN

Even from a distance, Sabina could see the storm that raged within Roman. It blazed in his eyes and hung about him like a dark cloud.

She didn't know what his conversation entailed with V, but whatever words passed between them, Roman was in full agreement. And she wasn't sure what that meant for her or Camlo.

Sabina turned to her brother. "I'm not certain about our guests."

Camlo shook his head at her, acting like the adult for the first time. "I am."

"How?" she asked, needing to know. "What is it about them that makes you trust so willingly?"

"You would, too, if you'd seen them."

She fought not to lose her patience. "Camlo, tell me what you saw last night."

He pointed to Roman and V, who were on their way toward them. Then he pointed at the sky. "Beautiful. Powerful."

"What does that mean?" she said with fists clenched in frustration that bordered on exasperation.

Her brother held out his arms and smiled. As if that were answer enough. She squeezed her eyes closed and bit back the harsh words that would hurt her brother. In his mind, he was telling her exactly what she wanted to know.

Normally, she could figure such things out, but this time, she couldn't connect the dots. She flexed her fingers as she opened her eyes to find her brother looking over her shoulder.

Camlo dropped his arms and said, "You're awake."

"I am," V said from behind her.

"I didn't mean to hurt you," Camlo said.

Sabina shifted as V moved to stand before him. "You didna. Actually, you helped me."

At this, she frowned and looked at Roman, who was watching Camlo and V closely. What the hell was going on? Because there was something, and she was on the outside looking in—a position she didn't enjoy.

"Really?" Camlo asked, his eyes bright with delight.

V smiled as he nodded. "Want to help me again?"

"Whoa," Sabina said the same time that Camlo eagerly said, "Yes."

V turned his penetrating blue eyes to her. "I'm no' harming him."

"Says you," she argued. "I saw what happened to you the first time, and you want to do it again?"

"Exactly. It happened to *me*." V inhaled deeply and released it. "Ask Camlo if he was hurt."

She didn't need to. If her brother had felt any pain, he would've let her know. That didn't make her feel any better about what was going on, though. Mostly because Roman and V seemed to know what had happened to V when Camlo touched him.

"Here." Camlo then held out his hand, waiting for V to take it.

Sabina stepped between them, facing V and Roman. "I've taken great steps to ensure that no one can exploit my brother. For some insane reason, he likes both of you, and, even stranger, I've opened my home to you. I'm about to rescind that offer if you don't tell me what's going on."

"Bina," Camlo said as he grabbed her shoulder and turned her to face him. "I told you."

"You've not told me anything other than you saw them last night."

He sighed dramatically. "They're friends."

How did she tell her brother that people lied? That while they might look and act like friends, they really weren't? Her mind made that argument, but her heart urged her to wait and hear Roman and V out.

A large hand softly touched her arm. She felt a sizzle of electricity rush through her, and she didn't have to look to know it was Roman. He had that kind of effect on her.

"We would never harm either of you," Roman said.

She looked over her shoulder at him. "Then tell me what's going on."

Camlo stamped his foot. "I have!"

Without warning, Camlo reached around her and grabbed V's arm. Sabina stood between them, and there was no denying that something passed from them and into her. It was . . . intense and yet gentle. Severe but smooth.

It enveloped her in a layer of . . . she had no word for it, but she knew that it was around her so profusely that she thought she might be able to touch it if she tried.

Suddenly, she was yanked from the bubble and pulled against a hard chest with strong arms wrapped around her. She tried to lift her head, but she had no control over her body. In fact, it felt as if she were floating.

"Breathe," Roman whispered in her ear.

She moved her eyes to the side and saw her brother and

V. They stood as still as statues. V's face was contorted in pain, while Camlo watched him. A moment later, V dropped to his knees. There was a smile on his face before he pitched forward. The only reason he didn't hit the ground with his face was because Camlo caught him.

"Bina?"

"She'll be fine in a moment," Roman answered.

Camlo grunted. "Too much magic for her."

Magic? Magic! What the hell? The fog in her head began to clear, though she was quite comfortable braced against Roman's firm body.

"Easy," Roman whispered against the top of her head. "I feel you stiffening. Everything is all right."

"No," she croaked.

Still, she didn't pull away from him. Her mind shouted for her to walk away, but her limbs refused to obey. Despite the confusion and worry, it felt too good to be in his safe, delightfully strong arms.

"Camlo, can you take V into the house?" Roman asked.

Her brother chuckled. "He needs more sleep."

"Aye, lad, that he does."

Sabina closed her eyes. Her perfectly ordered life was being dismantled by everyone, with very little effort.

Roman's hand splayed over her back, holding her tight against him. His other hand gently smoothed her hair away from her face. "Are you hurt?"

She shook her head.

"I'm guessing you wish to talk now."

The regret in his voice made her smile. She opened her eyes then. "Yes."

"This involves your Romani blood."

"Did you come to us because of that?"

Roman hastily replied, "Nay. We didna know anyone was here until we saw Camlo."

"But you were searching for something."

"We were exploring the entire range of the Carpathians, no' just this spot."

She could hear his heart beating beneath her ear. Strong and steady. Just as he was. Sabina drew in a breath before she stepped back. His hands lingered on her until he let them drop.

Sabina stared into his green eyes. "What just happened between V and Camlo? Why does my brother continue to say that he saw both of you last night in the sky? What does he know that I don't?"

"I'm no' sure you really want the answers to those questions."

Her mouth dropped open in astonishment. "I'm asking the questions because I want to know."

"You've denied your heritage and the Sight handed down to you from your ancestors."

She glared at him, hating that his words held more truth than she wanted to admit. "So?"

"Tell me, was it just the insults from others that made you reject who you really are?"

"I know who I am." How dare he? She was so mad she could spit.

A blond brow rose on his forehead. "Others may think you are less than because of your Romani blood, but you should be proud of it. It sets you apart."

"You speak of something you know nothing about."

Roman laughed, though there was no mirth in the sound. "Oh, lass, I know much more than you could possibly understand."

"Are you going to give me the answers I want?"

Eyes turbulent as a violent sea held hers as the seconds ticked by with no response. Then, he finally said, "Fine.

You want the truth? Here's the truth for you, my gypsy. V and I are dragons."

With that, he turned on his heel and strode toward the house. Sabina could only watch him go. Dragons. She started to laugh, but then her blood went cold.

"Oh, my God," she murmured as the story Gran had told her came back in vivid detail.

Sabina's knees went weak as she realized that V was none other than Vlad, the dragon who was the basis of Gran's story. He was the one who her ancestors had stolen the sword from—and Vlad and Roman were in her country looking for it.

She grabbed hold of a post next to her so she didn't fall. Her gaze moved over the various animals, and her face crumbled when it finally dawned on her what Camlo had been trying to tell her. He knew who Roman and V were because of his connection to animals. He'd *seen* them, had actually witnessed dragons flying in the sky the night before.

And she'd missed it.

With her hand on her throat, she dragged in a breath and tried to calm her rapid heartbeat. She was supposed to pass on the story of Vlad to her children, not be the one who came face-to-face with the Dragon King.

She didn't know what to do or say. Did she return to the house and act as if nothing had happened? Or did she tell them everything she knew? Her mind was whirling faster and faster.

Gran had said that Vlad was kind. Why then take his sword? Just because one of her ancestors saw something using her Sight? That was horseshit because their gifts weren't always right.

Something horrible had happened to V, simply because

of one vision. And now it was up to Sabina to sort it all out. Or was it? She could pretend that she knew nothing and let Roman and V go about their search.

But that was wrong, so very wrong.

There was a sound behind her. She whirled around to find Camlo. The look on his face was one of a man twice his age. She had sheltered him because his mind wasn't right, but she was beginning to wonder if he hadn't been the one protecting her.

"Do you see them now?" he asked.

Tears stung her eyes, but she didn't let them fall. "No."

"If you believed, you would." He closed the distance between them and took her hand. "It's your secret."

"Secret?"

He nodded. "The story you told Blackie."

There were no words. She hadn't stopped to consider that the story of Vlad and the sword was something her cat would repeat to Camlo. Or had she? She really didn't know.

"It's okay, Bina," her brother said. "You didn't think the story was for me."

She put a hand to his face. "No, sweetheart. That story is for everyone in our family."

"Then why didn't you tell me?"

"I don't know," she answered and lowered her arm. "I'm sorry."

He gave her a little shrug and looked away. "Roman and V need us."

"I'm not sure we can tell them who we are."

Camlo shot her a bewildered look. "They're going to figure it out as soon as V wakes up."

An idea suddenly struck her. "Do you know what happens to V when he touches you?"

"No, but I wish I did. I wonder if he'd let me ride upon his back."

Sabina looked at the house. "Once they know who we are, I'm not sure they're going to be so nice."

"That's because you don't know them. Vlad didn't kill our family back then, and he won't do it now."

She swung her head to her brother. "You do realize that Vlad is the same person the myth of Dracula is from, right?"

Camlo's smile was wide as he said, "Yeah."

CHAPTER TWELVE

Texas

There were so many options. Rhi loved options, and OPI never failed to give her that. She glanced at the bottles in her hand and actually found something to smile about. She couldn't wait to add the four bottles from the Iceland collection to the others.

It amused her to pay for things as if she were a human. Then again, as a Fae, her magic could get her anything she wanted. And she had everything.

Well . . . almost everything.

She carried the bag from the store and slid into the seat of her black Lamborghini. As she dropped the bag onto the passenger seat, she thought about the times that Daire had ridden with her, veiled and silent. But she hadn't been alone.

How she'd hated him following her at first. Now, she sorely missed him. But he was happy and in love. How could she be angry about that?

She hadn't spoken to him, but she'd found him and the pretty Halfling kissing in Ireland. Rhi had almost approached him, but she decided against it at the last minute. And she was glad she had.

The drive to Jesse's was short. But when she reached the salon, she didn't want to go in. She wasn't in the mood for conversation. While she adored Jesse, the mortal knew nothing of who Rhi really was—or the goings-on in her life.

Rhi turned the car around and drove through Austin to the storage unit where she kept the car. Once it was parked and locked with her magic, she gripped her package in her hand and teleported to the small isle she'd claimed as her own.

After the fight with Balladyn, she'd thought about finding another location, but it wouldn't do any good. Besides, she loved this beach. The sun, turquoise waters, and white sand were just what her soul needed when the darkness threatened.

She glanced at the waves rolling onto the beach. The water called to her, but first, she wanted to add her new polishes to the others.

Her collection was along the wall, in order of color, starting at white and ending in black. She pushed aside the oranges and made room for *I'll Have a Gin and Tectonic*. It took some doing to find the right spot for this complex shade that was somewhere between coral and tangerine.

Next was *That's What Friends Are Thor*. She quite liked the earthy brown shade and couldn't wait to match it with one of her gold colors. *Suzi & the Arctic Fox* made its way into the purples, while the dark ice blue, *Less Is Norse*, found its home.

Rhi stepped back and looked at the rainbow of colors. At one time, she'd had many more, but in a fit of rage, she'd destroyed them. She could've used her magic to replace them, but sometimes, magic was the easy way out of things.

At least that's what her mother used to say. Rhi hadn't understood it then, but she did now.

Just as she was about to change into a bikini to take a swim, she heard Phelan say her name. There were some that Rhi ignored, but never Phelan.

She still remembered when she'd found the Warrior. He hadn't known of his royal ancestry from both his human and his Fae sides. Phelan was like a brother, and she would do anything to keep his identity from Usaeil.

"Ubitch," Rhi said with a smirk.

Then she giggled. But it died a quick death. The sting of the queen banishing Rhi from the Light was still fresh. Actually, it was a gaping wound that festered.

And it did little to diminish the darkness growing inside her.

Rhi tried to set that aside as she teleported to Scotland where Phelan and his wife, Aisley, lived alongside an idyllic loch and forest.

"I wondered if you'd come," Phelan said.

She looked into his blue-gray eyes and smiled. "I told you, I will always come when you or Aisley call."

"That's what I told him," Aisley said as she walked up holding out a mug of tea for Rhi.

She accepted the cup with a smile and turned her attention back to Phelan. His long, dark hair was pulled back in a queue at the base of his neck, and there were lines of strain around his mouth.

Rhi sighed, realizing what the problem was. "Who told you?" she demanded.

Phelan's eyes widened as he looked at her as if she'd lost her mind. "You speak so calmly?"

"Who told you?" she demanded.

Aisley let out a loud sigh as she curled up on a chair

near Phelan. Her wavy, black hair was pulled up into a messy bun with tendrils falling around her face. "It was Fallon."

The leader of the Warriors. At one time, the Highlanders who had primeval gods inside them thought they were the only immortals on the realm. Until she made herself known and told them about the Fae.

And then, of course, the Dragon Kings introduced themselves to the Warriors and Druids of MacLeod Castle.

"I suppose Fallon heard from someone at Dreagan," Rhi stated.

Phelan gave a small shake of his head as he frowned at her. "I know you're angry. Why no' show it?"

"Because if I give in, I'll not be able to hold it back. And it isn't time for that. Yet," she added before taking a sip of tea.

Aisley cut her eyes to Phelan. "Told you."

Rhi gave a nod to the woman in thanks. She still wasn't quite sure what role Aisley would play in the future, but since she was one of the rare Phoenixes, it was bound to be important.

"Phelan, I'm livid," Rhi told him. "Just because I'm standing here instead of laying waste to Usaeil doesn't mean I don't intend to do just that."

Phelan held her gaze. "I'll be with you when that happens."

"No, you won't." Rhi set down her cup and straightened. "I've gone to a lot of trouble to make sure Usaeil doesn't know about you. The only other Fae who are aware of your existence are the Reapers, and they won't be telling Usaeil anything."

"How do you know?" Phelan asked.

"Because they told me."

At the sound of the deep voice behind her, Rhi froze. She turned her head to the doorway of the cottage and looked into eyes as black as pitch.

Constantine stood tall and stoic in his black suit and deep blue dress shirt. As usual, his gold dragon head cufflinks were in place. Everything was neat and orderly except for his short, wavy, blond hair that tended to do whatever it wanted no matter how much he ran his hands through it to put it in place.

"I wasna sure if you'd come," Phelan said into the silence. "So, I asked Con to drop by."

Rhi didn't like that Phelan turned to the Dragon Kings, but it wasn't as if she could stop him now. She tried not to fidget under the weight of everyone's gaze, but it was growing difficult.

It was Con who finally spoke. "I'll leave."

"Wait," Rhi stopped him. "What's this about the Reapers and Usaeil?"

If the King of Kings was pleased with her asking him to stay, he didn't show it. Then again, Con rarely showed much emotion.

But when he did . . . it was explosive.

Phelan motioned Con to a chair. "Aye. I'd like to know what's going on with the Reapers and Usaeil."

"It's no' pretty," Con said as he walked to the chair and unbuttoned his suit jacket. His gaze focused on Rhi when he lowered himself to the seat.

She'd known Con long enough to know that he was trying to figure out how to tell her something. "Just spit out whatever it is you're turning over in that head of yours."

"It's no' that easy," he said.

She barely managed not to roll her eyes. "Sure it is."

Phelan's brow furrowed as he looked between the two

of them. It was Aisley who put her hand atop his to stop whatever he'd apparently been about to say.

There was a time when Rhi had been a part of something special like that. When she'd known what her lover was thinking before any words were spoken. Everywhere she turned, there was a reminder of what she no longer had. Worse was the recollection of how wonderful it felt to be with him.

Her Dragon King.

She looked around at the people with her. She couldn't remember when she stopped seeing things as Fae and Warrior, Fae and Dragon King. The lines had blurred long, long ago. Just as she didn't see herself as Irish or the others Scottish.

Their friendship bound them beyond any other ties. Though that same friendship pushed the boundaries. Rhi knew that Phelan and Aisley would always be there for her, and she for them. It was the same for many of the Dragon Kings.

At one time, she'd considered Con an enemy that shifted to frenemy. Now, she wasn't sure what he was. And that bothered her immensely.

Especially now that he was handling her with kid gloves.

She met his black gaze and held it. It didn't take a whole lot to deduce that whatever he was holding back somehow involved her. It was becoming a pattern lately when Usaeil was mentioned.

"I'm a big girl, Con. I can take it," she told him.

He glanced down. "Do you remember the Reaper who disappeared when you fought with them a while back at the Light Palace?"

As if she would ever forget that battle. It was the first time she had actually come face-to-face with the Reapers.

That had been a doozy of a day that ended with an epic scuffle. "Eoghan, yes. Did they finally find him?"

"In a manner of speaking." Con rested his arm on the chair. "A Halfling with an affinity for music managed to reach him in whatever realm he'd been thrown into. Turns out, Thea was being tracked by a Fae who kidnapped her."

Now that got Rhi's attention. "I'm guessing you're about to tell me that Eoghan went after her."

Phelan snorted, shaking his head. "Of course he did. The woman brought him back from whatever realm he'd been sent to. He wouldna just let someone take off with her."

Rhi looked over to find Aisley smiling adoringly at her husband. Rhi turned back to Con, only to discover that he was staring at her peculiarly. "Go on," Rhi urged when he remained silent.

"It was Usaeil who sent the Fae to kidnap Thea," Con said.

Rhi reached for the chair nearest her and sank into it. "Bloody hell. Why? Usaeil has never given Halflings much consideration. To her, they are less than, not worthy to be considered a Fae because of their human blood."

"Obviously, something got her attention," Aisley said.

Rhi bit back a growl when Con didn't immediately pick up the story. "Con."

His head cocked to the side as he looked at her. "Did you know that Usaeil killed her bairns while they still grew inside her?"

She shook her head, feeling sick to her stomach.

"Did you know that she killed off her family to protect her throne?"

Rhi swallowed, her stomach rolling viciously. Her chest felt tight, her fingers numb as she clutched the arms of the chair. "She said her family went into hiding to protect themselves from the Dark Fae. Anytime I asked about them, she said they were enjoying living away from the life at court. I never . . . no one. . . ."

She trailed off, unable to finish the thought.

Con sat forward, resting his forearms on his knees as he clasped his hands together, his gaze never wavering from her. "Usaeil admitted to killing her family. She sent Trackers after them, wiping out all but one male. He's the one who kidnapped Thea. Neither he nor Usaeil knows of Phelan, and it's going to stay that way."

"No," Rhi said, shaking her head in disbelief. "We would've known if Usaeil did such a horrendous deed. Surely, someone would've discovered it."

"What's Usaeil's interest in Thea?" Phelan asked.

Thea. Rhi had forgotten about the Halfling with the other news. Her grip tightened on the arms of the chair, knowing that whatever Con was about to say would be big.

"She's Usaeil's daughter."

Coldness swept through Rhi. She felt detached from herself, as if she were looking down upon the entire scene. Her mind couldn't process Con's words at first. It took a minute for everything to sink in.

And with it came the realization of what had happened. "Usaeil killed her, didn't she?"

"She tried," Con replied. "But Thea was strong enough to fight back."

Rhi sat back slowly, a smile curving her lips because she knew what Con wasn't saying. Not only were Eoghan and Thea together, but Usaeil had failed. Oh, if only Rhi had been there to see it. But it was enough to have that information.

"Rhi," Con said, pulling her from her thoughts. "It's time we went after Usaeil."

"Yes, it certainly is."

CHAPTER THIRTEEN

Roman watched Sabina and Camlo through the window. His enhanced hearing picked up a few words, and it wasn't difficult to figure out what they were talking about—him and V.

He glanced at V, who was passed out—again—on the sofa. Roman turned away from the window and walked from the house. He went down on one knee and put his hand to the earth. Then he opened up his magic to feel for metal.

It ran all through the ground, but each ore sang a different tune. Gold, copper, lead, aluminum, mercury, silver, and platinum, to name just a few.

He felt each and every one. He knew when they gathered together or split off. But he couldn't get to them. That's when Kellan would usually come and call whatever metal Roman wanted to him. They often worked together in such circumstances, and it made Roman wonder if Kellan shouldn't be here with them.

Roman might sense which metals were which and work them however he wanted, but it was Kellan who could call them forth. And if V's sword were buried, Kellan would be the one to get it for V.

No matter how deep Roman sent his magic, he felt nothing that even came close to being V's sword. That metal had a sound all its own. Roman had listened for it last night but heard nothing. It was the same now. Romania was part of V's domain. It made sense that the sword would be here.

Roman felt Sabina as soon as she approached. She too had her own song, and it slid through him of its own accord, wrapping him in sensuality while an animalistic heat filled him.

He stood and faced her. The slight wariness around her made him frown. She shoved her hair away from her face and shifted her feet nervously.

"You're afraid of me. Why?"

Her shoulders lifted as she drew in a deep breath. "You're a Dragon King."

He could only stare at her in shock. "How do you know that?"

"Isn't that why you're here?" she asked, her brow furrowed in harsh lines. "You came looking for us."

"Lass, I think you'd better start at the beginning because you've lost me. We're looking for an object, no' a person."

"You're looking for a sword."

Roman gave a shake of his head in confused wonder. "Is this your Sight? Are you using your gifts?"

"I wish it were that simple," she murmured. She looked over her shoulder at Camlo, who was squatted down, holding his hand out to a mangy dog who leaned forward to sniff his fingers before inching closer. "Promise me you won't hurt my brother."

Roman grew more baffled by the moment. "We've no' hurt either of you, and we willna."

"You might think differently once I tell you that it was my ancestors who stole V's sword."

He couldn't believe what she'd said. This couldn't be true. Could it? His gaze shifted to the house. Is that why V had had such a reaction to Camlo?

V would be overjoyed when he heard this news. They'd found a connection to his past, which would lead to his sword. After all these millennia, V would finally have what was rightfully his.

Or . . . V's anger at the truth might get the best of him.

Roman slid his eyes back to Sabina. "Do you have any idea how much he's suffered? Can you possibly fathom what V has endured these past eons? Our swords are a part of us, like a limb. V's means even more to him—and to us. Tell me where it is. Have it ready to hand to V when he wakes."

"I would if I were able, but I don't know where it's at," she said.

Roman took a step toward her, but when Sabina retreated he halted. "Shall I tell you of his anguish? How about I list the distress, the agony he's borne since your people took it upon themselves to take something that wasn't theirs."

Sabina licked her lips and swallowed loudly. "I can't imagine. I'm sorry for what happened. I wasn't part of it, and if I could help, I would."

"You can help. Tell me what you know." Roman didn't mean his words to sound so harsh, but he was irritated that Sabina was involved, as well as relieved that they were closer than ever to getting answers.

She was cautious as she watched him, shifting so that she could bolt at a moment's notice. As if that would do any good. He was a Dragon King. He could have her in milliseconds. She might know what he was, but she knew very little of his kind.

"It's a story told to every generation," she said. "Gran worried that Mom wouldn't tell me when the time came, and she was right. So, the night before we left the camp, Gran came to my caravan and told me about how dragons are among us, and how a Dragon King used to rule over our land."

Roman clenched his teeth. "Did she say V was cruel to humans?"

"No," Sabina hastily replied. "She said that he was kind."

"Then why take his sword?"

Sabina took another step back. "One of my ancestors had a vision that if the sword wasn't hidden away, there would be death and destruction to all."

Roman wanted to laugh at the absurdity of this so-called vision. He wiped a hand down his face and turned his back to Sabina as he paced a few feet from her. One fucking vision had set things in motion. *One.*

There were times that the motives of the humans were as confounding as the beings themselves.

He faced her once more. "One woman says these things will happen, and everyone believes her?"

"Apparently," Sabina said with a confused shrug. "I don't exactly understand that either, but she must have done or said something to convince them."

Roman let out a bark of laughter. "Oh, there wasna much that needed to be done or said to push mortals to turn against us."

"What's that supposed to mean?"

"You doona know?"

She raised a brow. "Would I ask if I did?"

He leaned his head back and blew out a breath. "Tell me the rest, please."

"There isn't much to tell. Six of my ancestors climbed up the mountain and entered V's cave. They took the sword and left, each going in different directions."

Roman lowered his head to her. "Which one took it? Which direction did he go?"

She shrugged. "No one knows. The men never returned to the village. After they left, my family packed up and became Travelers, beginning the Romani tradition."

"There's nothing else you can tell me? Nothing more to lead us to V's sword?"

"I know only this."

"Then why pass down the story?"

She tucked her hair behind her ear. "Because my ancestors knew that, eventually, the Dragon Kings would find us."

"And do what? Did V retaliate and wipe out the village when the sword was stolen? Did he hunt your family?"

Sabina shook her head. "Not that I know of."

"I can tell you, he didna."

"You saw him after the sword was . . . ?"

Roman glanced at the house. "Aye."

"All these years, my family has believed that if V reclaimed his sword, the vision my ancestor had would come to pass."

"Did it ever occur to any of you that the vision might happen because V *didna* have his sword?"

"I suppose not," she replied in a soft voice.

Roman wanted to shout his frustration to the heavens. And if he felt this way, he could only imagine how V would feel. Shite. He couldn't tell his friend. If he did, V might fall into madness again and leave another catastrophe behind.

"I thought you figured out who we were and came to demand the sword," Sabina said.

Roman shook his head. "Nay, but I'm going to take V far from here."

"You think he'll retaliate?"

"I'm no' sure what he might do, and I'd prefer no' to find out."

Sabina lowered her head. "I understand."

Roman didn't move. Instead, he stared at the beautiful mortal before him. "Did the story mention anything about Fae or Druids?"

Her head jerked up. "Not at all."

"Could it have gotten lost in the retelling?"

"Possibly. Gran did say that there was a drawing of Vlad that was lost. She also made a point to tell me to memorize her words so that I wouldn't embellish or change anything. But I was only six at the time."

"And yet you remembered."

"It's not a story you forget."

"Nay, I guess no'," he admitted.

Sabina crossed her arms over her chest and rubbed her lips together. "What now?"

"We leave."

"If I were V, I'd want to hear everything for myself."

Roman started toward the house. "He probably will, but just in case V tips into madness again, I want him away from here."

"Madness?" Sabina repeated, her voice pitched high in shock and fear.

He halted and faced her. "Somehow, the people that took his sword also cast some sort of spell over V, making him forget where he was when he lost his sword and every-thing about that night."

"I always wondered why he didn't go after the men right

then," Sabina said. "If there was something stopping him, it would let the humans get far enough away."

"Exactly. That magic wound its way through V so that each time he woke from dragon sleep and went looking for the sword, he couldn't remember where he'd been when he lost it. And he'd go mad. The consequences were . . . devastating for mankind."

Sabina frowned at him. "Devastating how?"

"Does the Great Fire of Rome mean anything? How about the Black Plague?"

Her arms fell limply at her sides. "Oh, God."

"Exactly. It's why I'm here with V to help keep that from happening again. We've kept him sleeping for just this reason."

"Then why wake him now?"

"Because we had no choice. And it was time we helped him find what is rightfully his."

She blew out a loud breath. "Camlo wants to help V."

"But you doona," he guessed.

"It's not that I don't want to. I'm scared," she confessed. "Gran made it sound as if the Dragon Kings would come for us. Like a reckoning."

Roman twisted his lips ruefully. "We've hidden from humans for so long that no one knows of us anymore. It's how we like it after what happened in the war."

"War? What war?"

"The war between dragons and humans."

She blinked, surprise filling her features. "I think there's a lot I don't know."

"You could say that."

"Will you tell me? I'd like to know what I'm missing."

Her voice, the way her dark eyes held his without guile or resentment did something to him. "Aye. If you want to know."

"I owe it to V to give him some answers at least. It's not the same as his sword, but it'll be something."

"You understand that I can no' guarantee how he'll react?"

"Will you be there to stop him from hurting me?"

Roman shook his head sadly. "V has never intentionally hurt a mortal before, and he willna start now. But, aye, I'll be there to make sure of it."

"I want Camlo with us, as well," she said. "He already knows more than I do, and I won't keep him out of this."

"I'm no' sure that's smart."

"He won't tell anyone about you," she promised. "He didn't even tell me. He just kept pointing to the sky."

Roman nodded, realizing she spoke the truth. "Point taken. Go get your brother. We'll begin this evening."

She touched his arm. "I'm truly sorry for what happened to V. I'll help in any way I can, but I fear it won't be much."

He watched as she walked away, and Roman couldn't help but wonder if this were the beginning of something that none of them were prepared for.

CHAPTER FOURTEEN

She was well and truly into things now. If there had been a small thread of hope that Sabina might stop herself and Camlo from getting entangled with the Dragon Kings, she had snapped that in half by offering her help.

It was a crazy—probably stupid—thing to do. But the look on Roman's face as he described what V had been going through slammed into her like a punch. Her family was responsible for this, no matter their intentions.

Now, it fell on her to sort it out. Somehow. If she could. Most likely, she would muddy the waters even more. The only things she knew about the Dragon Kings were from the story Gran had told her. There hadn't been another chance to ask her grandmother for more information since Sabina and her mother left the next day.

The one time she had asked her mother about dragons, her mom had wanted to know which of the local stories Sabina wanted to hear. If Tereza knew anything, she hadn't passed it on.

Sabina was so wrapped up in thoughts of dragons and swords that she didn't worry about the food as she cooked. Camlo and Roman sat at the table, talking about the animals. V slept through the meal. Not that it mattered. Her stomach was so twisted in knots that she only managed a few bites of food as she wondered what would happen when he opened his eyes.

Camlo, however, didn't have any reservations about eating with two dragons in their house. He kept Roman occupied with stories. If Roman grew tired of Camlo, he never let it show.

By the time the meal was finished, Sabina wanted to wake V herself. She went about cleaning the table and was surprised when Roman helped. She met his gaze and found his lips curved slightly.

"You sure about this?" he asked.

She knew he was asking again about her desire to know of the Dragon Kings. How could she not? It seemed the only thing to do, because, otherwise, she would always wonder.

Sabina nodded and went back to washing, which gave her something to do other than pacing. All too soon, she was finished. She wiped her hands and slowly folded the towel to lay over the edge of the sink. Then she turned to the living area and found V sitting up, his blue eyes locked on her.

"Hurry, Bina," Camlo said as he patted the spot on the sofa between him and V.

While she'd begun to believe that V wouldn't hurt her, she didn't want to test the theory by sitting next to him. She swallowed, her blood rushing in her ears as she made her way to the chair she used at her worktable. She glanced at Roman, who stood leaning a shoulder against the wall.

Camlo held out his hand to V. "Do you need me again?"

V turned his head to her brother and smiled. "No' now, but thank you."

Sabina was nervous and anxious to get things started. She cleared her throat and met V's gaze. "I suppose you spoke with Roman."

"I want to hear it from you," V said in an even voice.

But there was no denying the anger that simmered just beneath the surface. Sabina pressed her hands together and shoved them between her legs in an effort to warm them since they were now ice-cold.

"Please, tell it," Camlo urged her.

Sabina gave him a nod and focused her attention on her brother. It was easier to look into his dark, eager gaze than think about what might happen when she finished.

She began the tale just as her grandmother had. Sabina retold the story, word for word. Camlo's eyes widened as he leaned forward, eager for more.

When she finished, Sabina glanced at V to find his gaze on the floor, his face lined with confusion and a wealth of hurt. Even by her grandmother's words, V had done nothing to warrant the humans turning on him, but that hadn't stopped them.

Warmth slid over the side of her face and down her neck. She turned her head to find Roman staring at her. His eyes moved over her like a caress. A shiver went through her that had nothing to do with the temperature in the room and everything to do with the fluttering of her stomach.

"That's all I know," she told V after pulling her gaze from Roman. "I wish I had more to tell you."

"It's more than I had before." V's chest expanded as he pulled air into his lungs. "Did your grandmother say anything about Druids or Fae?"

"Roman asked the same question. No, I'm afraid not."

Camlo made a sound in the back of his throat. The three of them looked at him, but his gaze was on the ceiling as he drummed his fingers on his legs as if waiting for someone to notice him.

Sabina frowned, unsure what her brother was up to. "Camlo?"

"Ask me," he urged excitedly, his body vibrating with whatever he was holding in.

She looked at V and then Roman before turning back to Camlo. "Ask you what?"

He sighed dramatically and looked at her. "What I know, silly."

Just as she was about to tell him that he couldn't possibly know more than she did, she recalled how he had learned of the story her gran told her in the first place—the animals. "What do you know, Camlo?"

"A lot," he replied. His smile was wide, and his eyes danced.

V shifted to face Camlo. "Will you tell us?"

Her brother's face suddenly creased into regret. "You're going to be mad."

"Nay, lad. I willna," V assured him.

"Please," Sabina implored her brother.

Camlo shifted to the edge of the seat. "The animals talk of the place all the time. It's dangerous and filled with magic."

"What kind of magic?" Roman asked as he pushed away from the wall.

Camlo shrugged. "The animals don't say."

"What does this place have to do with V?" Sabina asked.

Her brother gave her a flat look. "It's where his sword is."

It was a good thing Sabina was sitting down because she was sure her legs would've given out if she weren't. "Why didn't you tell me before?"

"You kept the story a secret," Camlo stated.

V caught Camlo's attention. "Where is this place?"

"Far from here. It's an isle of fire and ice."

Roman jerked and took a step back. Shock reverberated inside him as his gaze swung to V. A deep frown creased V's forehead.

Sabina looked at each of them, trying to figure out what had silently passed between the two men. "Do you know where this place is that Camlo speaks of?"

"Aye," Roman murmured. "Somewhere I've no' been to in many years."

V's blue eyes turned to her. "His home."

"Iceland," Roman said.

Sabina slowly sat back in the chair. Both Dragon Kings had left their homes and not returned. She really wanted to know why. That question would have to wait, though. "Camlo, are you sure you heard the animals correctly?"

"Of course. They talk among themselves like we do. There are places they know to steer clear of, and others that they want to visit." He smiled at V and Roman. "I've heard great things about Dreagan."

Sabina shook her head as she put a hand on her forehead. Dreagan. Like the whisky? She'd just seen that logo. And did that mean . . . ? Oh, God. It did. "I'm feeling a little left out. Is my brother saying that you're from Dreagan?"

"It's the home we made," Roman explained. "We've been there for thousands of years. We make our living by distilling—"

"Whisky," she said before he could.

There was so much about the Dragon Kings that she didn't know, and she was beginning to realize that the story her gran had shared was just the tip of a massive iceberg.

And Sabina was scared of just what discovering the truth might do.

"Iceland," V said to Roman. "Is it a coincidence that some of us are being brought back to the lands we once ruled? First, Dmitri on Fair Isle, and now you to Iceland."

"And you here," Roman added. He ran a hand down his face in a weary gesture. "I would never have looked for your sword in Iceland."

V's lips twisted ruefully. "I think that's the point."

"But I would've heard its song," Roman added.

Sabina was woefully unprepared to follow such a conversation, but she hung on every word. Gran told her that the Dragon Kings were immensely powerful and immortal, but it was obvious that they weren't all-powerful if someone could hide a sword from them.

Roman's eyes focused on her. "You said you would help us, but it seems that we're going to need Camlo."

Instead went unsaid, but she wasn't stupid. Sabina had feared the Dragon Kings at first, but now she was willing to go on this search to return to V what was rightfully his.

And pray that she didn't set off the vision her ancestor prophesied that began all of this.

"I'm ready. I'm ready," Camlo said, bouncing up and down on the cushion.

"You aren't taking my brother without me," she stated.

V grinned, but it was directed at Roman. It seemed as if a conversation passed between them that only the two of them could hear. Finally, Roman looked at her and gave her a single nod.

"You said you would tell me about the Dragon Kings," she said. "Help both me and Camlo understand."

Her brother shook his head. "I know everything already.

The animals told me. They've been talking about Ulrik's return."

V laughed softly and grinned at Camlo. "You have an amazing gift."

"Who's Ulrik?" Sabina asked, hating being the only one who didn't know.

Roman rubbed his eyes with his thumb and forefinger. "One of us."

"It was dragons who ruled this realm for eons," V explained. "Picture the skies filled with dragons, ranging from the size of your cat to that of a jumbo jet. Our numbers were staggering."

"Pretty colors," Camlo said.

Roman's lips shifted into a crooked grin. "Every shade of every color. And each had its own clan."

"And every clan had its own Dragon King," V explained.

Sabina was enthralled, her imagination filling with pictures from their words. "Go on."

Roman scratched the side of his cheek. "Dragon magic is the most powerful on this realm, and it's by magic that a King is chosen. It's no' a birthright, but the dragon with the greatest magic and the most power leads."

"Sometimes, we fight to the death to claim the position," V added and briefly looked at Roman. "Sometimes, the previous King is killed, which makes the way easier for the new King."

Sabina cocked her head to the side. "Gran said you were immortal."

"Only a Dragon King can kill another Dragon King," V said. "So, in many ways, we are."

She frowned. "Then how does a dragon wanting to be King manage it?"

Roman lifted his eyes to her. "His magic will be greater

than that of the present King. Essentially, it is a Dragon King fighting another Dragon King. But even we, as a whole, have a King."

"King of Dragon Kings," V said. "His name is Constantine."

"Ah. I see," Sabina murmured. "How do we—humans—fit into the picture?"

"You arrived one day," V said.

Sabina laughed because she thought he was joking. Then she spotted the seriousness on his face. Her head jerked to Roman. "We arrived? How? When?"

"How does any being move from realm to realm?" Roman asked with a shrug as if his words were answer enough. "There is magic involved. Which was why we were so shocked to discover that your kind was mortal and entirely without any magic."

V ran a hand through his long hair. "As soon as you arrived, each King shifted into a matching form so we could communicate with you. We made a vow then and there to protect your race, always."

"Each clan gave up land so humans could make this realm their home," Roman said.

Sabina inwardly cringed. "Then what?"

"Your kind wanted more. Always more," V stated harshly.

Roman's lips flatted as he nodded. "Some of the Kings took humans as lovers, and one, Ulrik, was set to marry one. Dragons mate for life."

"While we don't," Sabina murmured.

V snorted. "Nay, you doona."

"Nearly two hundred years had passed by that time, and tensions were running high between humans and dragons. But the magic here had found its way to your kind. Those mortals called themselves Druids," Roman said.

V nodded. "It was a Druid, along with Ulrik's uncle, who convinced the woman Ulrik was to marry to murder him. Con found out, and we stopped it by killing her."

"But Ulrik's anger was more than we bargained for," Roman continued. "He lashed out at the humans, which began the war."

Sabina couldn't believe what she was hearing. "It's obvious you should've annihilated us. Why are we still here?"

CHAPTER FIFTEEN

Why are we still here?

Sabina's question was a fair one. Roman wasn't the only Dragon King who had debated their decision throughout the years. "Our vow," he replied.

Her gaze shifted from him to V and back again. "You let us win?"

V let out a bark of laughter. "No' hardly. Ulrik's attack divided us. Some remained with Con, while others went with Ulrik. Thousands of mortals were killed. But so were dragons."

"Because those with Con asked their dragons to protect humans, and those same mortals killed them," Roman replied when he saw the question forming in Sabina's eyes.

She sat unmoving for a moment. "I see. Where are all the dragons? Please tell me they aren't dead."

"No," Camlo said and shook his head. "They left."

Roman looked at Camlo and smiled sadly. "We sent them to another realm to protect them. Then we hid on Dreagan until humans forgot about us."

"Can the dragons return?" Sabina asked.

V looked down at his hands. "No' without my sword."

"I don't understand," she said. "Can't any King use their sword?"

Roman moved to stand beside V and put his hand on his shoulder for a moment. "When we shifted that first time, each of us received two things. One is a distinct tattoo. The other, a sword. If two Kings fight in human form, they do so with their swords in order to get the kill. Otherwise, we battle in our true forms."

"As dragons," she murmured.

"Our swords are as different as our tattoos and are an extension of us. But for V, his is even more special because his blood is part of the metal."

Sabina's forehead creased as she digested his words. "Why only V's?"

"Because I can call the dragons home with my sword. No matter where they are, no matter how far away, they will hear its call and return."

She shifted in her chair, tucking one leg underneath her. "Did you use it to send them away?"

"That was done with our combined magic," Roman explained. "Each Dragon King gathered, and we opened a dragon bridge. We can open another and hope the dragons see it, but since we've no idea where they are, we need V's sword."

"And it's not exactly time for them to return, so you've not been in a hurry," Sabina concluded with a nod.

V clenched his fists. "Something like that."

"There's more." Roman waited until her head turned to him before he said, "Because of the war, Ulrik was banished. He's recently returned to Dreagan and is once more with us. Yet, we're not the only beings here."

Camlo whimpered. "Bad people with red eyes."

"The Dark Fae," V replied. "They also have silver in

their black hair. Steer clear of them since they feed off humans by sucking their souls while having sex."

"That's nice," Sabina stated sarcastically. She shuddered. "If there's dark, then there are usually light."

Roman bowed his head in acknowledgement. "There are Light Fae. One is a verra good friend of ours. Her name is Rhi. The Light are only permitted to have sex with a human once."

"How considerate." Sabina bit her lip and glanced at Camlo, who was listening intently. "You already told me of the Druids. Is there more?"

"One other," V said.

Roman glanced at his friend. "The Warriors. They came into being when Rome invaded Scotland, and the Druids gathered together and called up primeval gods from Hell that the strongest warriors in each family accepted into themselves in order to fight Rome. They won, but the gods refused to return to their prison."

Sabina blew out a breath. "Wow. Are they friends of yours?"

"They are," V replied.

Roman leaned back against the wall. "Just like the Fae, the Druids have their good and evil factions. We never paid much attention to the Druids because they were no' a threat. And while we were involved in the Fae Wars when they attempted to take over this realm, our magic is more powerful than theirs."

"So we do enough to keep the Fae in line." V shook his head, an irritated look on his face. "We should've kicked their arses out long ago."

Roman didn't want to get into a debate about the Fae because it always went back to Rhi. She couldn't be the only Fae allowed on the realm, and there was no way they would make her leave.

"A little while ago, Con sent Dmitri back to the islands off the coast of Scotland that were his domain when word reached us that a dragon skeleton had been found." Roman crossed his arms over his chest. "We knew that was no' possible because once we sent the dragons away, we destroyed the dead ones to leave no trace for the humans to find."

Sabina wrinkled her nose. "You might have, but you look at any culture around the world, and there is some type of dragon myth."

V shrugged as if to say, *"Of course there is."*

"The fact is, dragon bones were found by an archeologist named Faith Reynolds," Roman continued. "Dmitri helped to keep Faith safe because the Dark Fae have been trying to expose us to humans for years now. There was a video making the rounds a wee bit ago."

Sabina looked helplessly at him. "I don't follow the news, so I didn't see anything."

"You're one of the few, then. After Dmitri and Faith dug up the bones, Faith found a small wooden dragon carved to look exactly like Con."

Sabina's eyes widened. "How is that possible?"

V crossed his ankle on his knee. "Because magic was used. They incapacitated Dmitri's White dragon so that it couldna answer its King's call, and then they killed it. They used magic to hide the skeleton from us."

"But why?" she asked.

Roman glanced out the window at the growing darkness. "That was our question. We soon learned that wasna the extent of their magic. The wooden dragon is also a weapon. When a King touches it, they want to kill mortals. When a human touches it, they want to kill us."

Sabina's frown deepened. "I thought you said your magic was the strongest."

"It is," Roman answered. "But this power is different. This magic is from Light and Dark Fae as well as *drough* and *mie*."

"Bad and good Druids, respectively," V added.

Sabina's expression was one of shock. "They joined forces?"

Roman shrugged one shoulder. "Apparently, but we're no' sure how. There were no Fae on this realm during our war with the humans."

"Obviously, there were," she said.

V snorted cynically. "Precisely. I believe it's that same magic that's being used to block my memories of where I was when my sword was stolen—and it kept me from following the thieves."

"Not good," Camlo said with a shake of his head. He held Roman's gaze for a long moment. "Not good."

"We know," Roman told him. "But we have to find those that did this."

Sabina leaned an elbow on the arm of the chair. "Can you? I gather that the Druids aren't immortal. Are the Fae?"

"Druids doona live forever." V paused, then said, "Unless they have help from a Dragon King."

Roman thought about the rings Con had given the Druids at MacLeod Castle so they could live alongside their Warrior husbands. "The Fae are no' immortal either. They can be killed, but they do live an excessively long time."

"Now you know all about us," V said and slapped his hands on his legs.

Sabina's dark eyes were on Roman when she said, "I highly doubt that. But this is a start. This Druid-Fae mix of magic intrigues me."

"Intrigues?" V issued another snort as he got to his feet.

"Shite, lass. It scares the hell out of me. And for a Dragon King to say that . . . you should be worried."

Roman watched V walk from the house with Camlo quickly following. Once alone with Sabina, he dropped his arms and took a seat on the sofa. "We might be powerful, but we have enemies."

"Anyone in power has enemies," she replied.

"I suppose that's true."

She laughed softly. "You don't see it because you no longer think of yourselves in power because you hide who you are, but it's the strength of your magic that says other-wise."

He had to admit, she had a point. "In all the years we've known the Fae and fought against the Dark, no one has said anything about this mix of magic. The Dark hate us, but we've known that."

"How do you know the mixes of magic?"

"Rhi."

Sabina raised a dark brow. "You trust her?"

"Implicitly. There's no reason for Rhi to lie about some-thing like this. She's a friend."

"How is she your friend?"

"She was once a lover to . . . well, another Dragon King, but he ended it."

Sabina asked, "Does Rhi still love her King?"

"Aye."

"Then there's your motive for her lying."

Roman shook his head. "I can understand why you would say that, but you doona know who Rhi is. She is loyal to a fault."

"Ever hear the old adage of a woman scorned?"

"Aye," he replied with a smile.

"Is Rhi often at Dreagan?"

Roman nodded.

Sabina studied him closely. "There aren't many women who can love someone and still be around them or their friends without feeling resentment and lashing out."

"Aye." Roman thought back to a conversation he'd had with Rhi not that long ago. "I had that same thought once and asked Rhi how she was able to continue being around us and helping when we asked. She told me that in order for her to get on with her life, she compartmentalizes things."

Sabina thought about that for a moment. "I could see how that might work. She takes her lover and being jilted and puts them in a box, mentally closing the lid on it. I did something similar when Mom was sick. I had to be strong for Camlo. It wouldn't do him any good to see me falling apart, so I put all those feelings away and only took them out late at night when I was alone. Same when she died."

"That's Rhi. Every once in a while, she takes the lid off and delves into those feelings."

Sabina's lips turned downward. "That will only work for so long. What happens when she can't put the lid back on? What happens when she can no longer compartmentalize?"

He shrugged helplessly because he had no answer. It had never dawned on him that such a thing could happen. Rhi was strong. She'd endured thousands of years with her pain.

But things were shifting for her, and not in a good way thanks to Usaeil. Rhi was already on edge. It was something the Kings were concerned about, especially Rhys, who was one of those closest to her. He and Phelan spoke almost daily, but no one had any kind of answer for what to do.

V thought Rhi's cure would be for her to fight Usaeil,

but there was a good chance that if Rhi went up against the Light queen alone, Rhi would die.

"Can you fight this Druid-Fae mix of magic?" Sabina asked.

Roman was yanked from his thoughts. "It looks like I'm going to find out. That's what V has been doing. Each time he touches Camlo, he's given more of his memories, and his dragon magic is eroding whatever blocks were put in place. We had no idea magic had been used on him, or we would've been fighting against it this entire time."

"It looks like we need to go to Iceland to figure out the next step."

He looked down at his hands. It was the first time in eons that he saw blood on them. That's what the thought of his homeland did to him.

CHAPTER SIXTEEN

She was going on a trip. An actual expedition. Sabina wasn't sure how she felt about that. On the one hand, she was excited to see another country and have her brother along.

On the other, she was with Dragon Kings, beings that had been prophesied to cause death and destruction. Not to mention that she was leaving her home.

There was so much that could go wrong. She knew little about Roman and V, and it frightened her how easily she trusted them—because she normally distrusted everyone.

What made them different? Why did she want to be near them? Well, it was Roman she wanted to be next to. V was nice, but there was something about him that she sensed could explode—or implode—at any moment. It also didn't help that she knew he was Vlad.

The man all the vampire myths had originated from was befriending her brother. It boggled her mind. And Camlo was enamored with V. Not that she could blame him. Roman and V were *dragons,* after all.

She wouldn't believe any of it if her gran hadn't told her

the story so many years ago. It had never entered Sabina's mind that her gran had made it up or was jesting. Even at a young age, Sabina had known the impact of the story and how important it was.

Had her gran known Sabina's life would lead her straight into the path of a Dragon King—the very King whose sword had been taken nonetheless?

Sabina looked up to find Roman staring at his palms, his chest rising and falling rapidly as if he had run a great distance. Whatever he saw, he didn't like. She fought not to rise and go to him, to take his hand in hers and read it—and divine the parts of his past that he hadn't told her.

The longer she gazed at him, the more it was obvious that he didn't want to go to Iceland. Why wouldn't he wish to return to his homeland?

Suddenly, he lifted his head, his sea green eyes meeting hers. Whatever he felt, he kept locked away, showing very little. Was it because she was reading too much into his silence? Or because he truly wanted to keep something hidden?

"Are you all right?" she asked.

He fisted his hands before relaxing them. "I will be."

"Want to talk about it?"

There was such a long pause that she thought he might tell her, but ultimately, he shook his head. Disappointment filled her. She'd gotten a small taste of the Dragon Kings' life, and she found it fascinating, scary, and quite sad.

Which made her want to know more.

"When do you think we'll leave?" she asked.

"Soon. I'll no' keep V waiting any longer."

"Why do you call him V?"

Roman's brow furrowed as he glanced toward the door where Camlo had gone outside with V. "Habit. We have nicknames for some. We call Warrick War sometimes.

We'll tease Nikolai with Nikki just to irritate him. Sebastian is Bast. Halden is Hal."

"How many Kings are there?"

He sat back and made a face. "Much more than that."

"Are any of you . . . married?" She wanted to take back the words and rearrange them so they didn't make her sound so desperate. Then again, was there a way to ask such a question without sounding that way?

"Aye. At last count, sixteen Kings have taken mates, and there are another three planning to take their vows."

She was mildly shocked at the number. "Sixteen? So each of them is now mated for life?"

"That's right. There's no divorce for us."

"What if the woman wants out?"

He gave a shake of his sandy blond head. "No' possible. It's why the Kings make sure that they've made the right choice. We doona hurry into such things."

"Someone has to get it wrong, though. I mean, it happens."

"A King knows his mate, lass."

Warmth filled her at the endearment. At least she considered it an endearment. "What if the woman gets it wrong?"

"It's no' happened."

"Yet," she added. "Are you telling me that a King won't let the woman go if she doesn't want to be with him anymore?"

He rested his arm along the back of the sofa. "Of course, no'. If she wants to leave, then she leaves. But that doesna break or erase the vows that are taken."

"But none have left yet?"

"They've no'."

Then it suddenly hit her. She had assumed the mates were human. "Are there Dragon Queens?"

There was a sad smile as he shook his head once from side to side. "My sister wanted to be the first. She was strong, but no' strong enough."

"Oh. The magic thing."

"Aye," he replied with a soft chuckle. "There were many incredibly powerful females in each clan, and I think had we no' sent the dragons away, it was only a matter of time before we had a Queen. I'm no' sure how long she would've remained in power, though."

Sabina immediately took offense on behalf of this imaginary Queen. "Why? Because the males wouldn't be able to handle a woman in power?"

"Our culture didna look down upon females. They fought alongside us and held positions of power. The simple fact is that the male dragons are bigger and stronger, just like males in most animal species. The power I speak of is part magic, but also strength of body and mind. My sister was one of many who had the magic and the mind, but she lacked the physical power to back it up. Otherwise, Ragna would've been a magnificent Queen."

It was the first time that he'd given Sabina a glimpse into his past. And she was enthralled. "I would like to meet her."

"She would've liked you," he said with a grin.

Sabina wanted to kick herself for forgetting that his sister was with the others who were sent away. It must have shown on her face because his smile faded.

"We made a decision to save our clans," Roman stated.

She moved her leg from beneath her so her feet were on the floor. "But you had to say goodbye to your family."

"Aye. Every King did. There isna a day that goes by that I doona think of them."

"Were you close to your sister?"

"Extremely," he said. "We're twins."

Now that was an answer she hadn't expected. "Oh." Hoping to change the subject, she asked, "So, I'm guessing all the mates you speak of are human?"

"All but one. Shara is a Light Fae. Well, she was Dark but only because her family was Dark Fae."

Sabina glanced at her notebook, wondering if she should take notes so as not to forget anything. "They can change like that?"

"Every Dark Fae begins as a Light. They have to make the conscious decision to be evil in order to turn. It's the same with the Druids. They are born as *mies*, but choose to embrace the black magic to become *droughs*."

"Do many Dark revert back to being Light?" she asked.

He lifted one shoulder in a casual shrug. "I've no' cared to know, but Shara says it doesna happen often."

"What about the *droughs*?"

"There is no going back for a Druid who gives their heart to the Devil."

Well. That explained that. Sabina chuckled. "And to think, we Romani are just gypsies. Good, bad, and many in-betweens."

"No' for us."

"There are no evil Dragon Kings?"

He glanced at the ceiling and shook his head. "The magic that chooses us can sense evil within us and doesna give that dragon the extra boost to become a King."

"That's a tad lucky, isn't it? Everyone else has to figure things out as they go and deal with the highs as well as the lows."

Roman lifted the hand on the back of the sofa before he let it drop. "If you're wanting me to explain such a thing,

I can no'. Just as I can no' tell you where the magic on this realm comes from. I know it's slowly disappearing now that most of the dragons are gone."

"Shouldn't the Druids and Fae help to keep the magic here?"

"You'd think," he answered. "But it isna the case."

She picked at a chipped nail. "Do you think the magic is a living entity?"

"In some ways, I think it could be. For the Fae, Death is a being."

Sabina couldn't believe what she just heard. "Are you serious?"

"I am."

"Have you met Death?"

His lips curved into a secretive smile. "Actually, I have, though I didna know who she was at the time."

"She? *She*! What does she look like?"

"Stunningly beautiful."

Sabina tucked her hair behind her ear and looked down at her jeans, shirt, and old boots—a reminder of her simple life. "I guess any being of power would be."

"What do you think Death should look like?"

She hesitated as she searched her mind. "For humans, Death is usually thought of as a cloaked figure with a scythe. No one can see inside the hood of the cloak, so there is no face. But you see a skeletal hand."

"Perhaps Death for humans looks that way."

She wrinkled her nose in distaste. "I think I like the Fae way better. Is there a Death for your kind?"

"I doona believe so. Death for the Fae doesna just take souls. She is judge and jury for them. There is another group who are the executioners."

Sabina wondered why she was so surprised. Different beings would have different cultures. "I see."

"I'm no' sure any of this is helping you come to a decision about us."

"Us?" she asked, her voice cracking as her mind linked her and Roman.

He raised a brow in question. "The Dragon Kings."

She really should keep her mouth shut before she said something stupid. "Right. Um, it is helping. Some of it is scary, I admit, but it's not like I just found out there were dragons."

"You did just learn of the history of dragons and humans."

"True." And it was his side of the story. She wished she knew her ancestors' side, but if the story handed down by her gran were any indication, she wasn't sure she'd be able to come to a fair conclusion.

Roman's head cocked to the side. "You're no' sure what to make of me. Of us. The story you learned as a child has made you fear the Dragon Kings."

"Gran wouldn't lie to me, but I can't be sure that some ancestors weren't dishonest or made up a vision to steal V's sword. I don't know if you're lying to me about the dragons and humans. I just have your word to go on. How can I come to a conclusion about anything based on stories of events that I didn't witness and no one else is around to corroborate?"

"Or ask your gran to explain," he added.

She nodded in agreement. "Many would side with their family against a stranger. I'm sure some would side with you because you're here and sound very convincing."

"The Kings have had many chances to wipe out humanity. We've no' done it."

"There is that," she said with a smile. She enjoyed this conversation. He didn't seem perturbed at all that she didn't readily accept everything he said.

Roman scooted to the edge of the sofa. "V wants to leave in the morning."

"How do you know that?" she asked, looking around for V.

Roman tapped his temple. "Dragons communicate telepathically."

"Oh." Somehow, she felt as if she should've known that.

"You'll have plenty of time to get to know me and V on this journey. Maybe then you'll come to see that we're no' the villains of the story."

That took her aback. "I never said you were."

"You never said we were no' either."

Sabina was surprised to see the glimmer of hurt in his eyes. If even half of what he'd told her were true, then he and his kind had suffered unimaginably. It made her want to believe him, to tell him that he was the good guy.

But she needed the stories verified somehow. Until then, she'd withhold judgment.

Roman rose to his feet. "Goodnight, lass."

She watched him walk from the house and wondered if he were going to take to the skies. It was only then that she realized she hadn't asked him anything about his dragon—specifically for him to shift so she could see him.

Maybe tomorrow.

Sabina knew that she should go to bed, but she was too wound up. How in the world could she sleep now? She turned and looked at the necklace she'd been working on, but she didn't reach for it. Instead, she opened her laptop and stared at the open browser. She looked at the past sites she'd visited over the last week and smiled when she saw the *(Mis)Adventures of a Dating Failure*.

She clicked on the blog. It would be a nice opportunity to shut off her mind and keep it from the thousands of questions she couldn't get answers to—even if only for a few minutes.

Sabina scanned the rows of boxes that held the titles of the posts, the first few lines, and a picture. She was happy to see that a new post was up. She hovered her mouse over the picture of a black rose with dew upon its petals and clicked.

Take Two

Well. Where do I begin? All of you have read so many of my disasters that I don't know if I should continue to write them. Obviously, I will. It's what keeps bringing you back here to read.

And I'll tell you now, that the comments and emails I get telling me you suffer too help. A lot.

I'm not alone. You're not alone. We're not failures in dating.

At least that's what I tell myself.

Being single is hard. Being a single, successful woman is even harder. Come on, guys! It's the twenty-first century. You want women to ask you out and pay for dates, then you need to be fine with them making more money than you.

But . . . that's another post. This one is about . . . well, let's call him Jackass, Jack for short. I can tell you right now my first mistake. It was the bar. I'd learned my lesson long ago about finding blokes in a pub. I hadn't given guys the time of day in a bar in years. I was out of my mind with just getting over a cold.

That's the excuse I'm using for agreeing to go out with him. Except, I don't know if you can call meeting back at the pub the next night a date. He was nice enough, and very good-looking. He had David

Beckham hair and that same amazing jawline. In a word, he was H-A-W-T.

Unfortunately, he knew it.

So, we meet at the pub. I get there first and order a drink. When he arrives, he orders one as well and tells the bartender to put it on my tab. I let it go, thinking that I'd buy the first round.

We had barely said hello when three of his friends joined us. Jack tells them to put their orders on my tab. I'm so flabbergasted that I can't get the words out to stop it before it's happening. Next thing I know, food is ordered.

I get up to tell the bartender no more can go on my tab, and when I turn around, they've moved my chair away. Needless to say, I paid my bill and left.

I'm not even sure what the hell happened. And, as you know, I had to analyze it. I went back to my place and went through every conversation—not that there were more than a dozen lines or so—between me and Jack to look for something I might have missed or misunderstood.

If I'm making these mistakes, I want to know so I don't keep repeating my failures. But, honest to God, people, I couldn't figure this out.

I came to the conclusion that this guy was just an Ass of the First Order and left it at that. But, I also won't repeat my mistake of agreeing to a date of any sort with a guy at a bar.

There are my Words Of Wisdom for you today. I've got a carton of gelato and The Holiday *waiting for me to enjoy while I wonder why I can't meet a Jude Law.*

Until my next (mis)adventure. . . .

CHAPTER SEVENTEEN

Dark Palace
Southern Ireland

Things weren't going as he'd planned. Not that Balladyn expected they would. Nothing ever did. He'd come to realize this after he'd been left for dead on the battlefield and the Dark found him.

He'd always thought himself strong, but would he have given into the darkness so easily if he were? His memories of his life as a Light Fae were fading. But there was one person who stood out, one who would always shine brighter than any star.

Rhi.

He'd loved her for so long that he couldn't remember a time when he didn't. There were a few thousand years where that love had crossed a thin line and drifted to hate, but only because she hadn't looked for him.

It wasn't until Balladyn captured her, intending to turn her Dark, that he'd discovered that she believed he was dead. He wanted to think that's when he began to love her again. But that was a lie.

As soon as he'd sensed her in the palace that day, his heart had soared with excitement. But much to his chagrin, she'd been veiled.

He'd been flabbergasted to discover that she was still very much involved with the Dragon Kings. Her lover had ripped out her heart and stomped all over it. In fact, the damn dragon had destroyed her.

The vibrant, vivacious Rhi that he'd loved was forever altered. Her spark diminished.

And then she'd disappeared.

Balladyn had searched everywhere for her. He'd wanted to be the one to find her, the one who held her as she cried. The one who brought her back from the brink and gave her a reason to love again.

But it was the same bastard Dragon King who found her in the Realm of the Fae and carried her back. Rhi didn't know it was him, and Balladyn had no problem keeping that secret. He didn't want to give Rhi any more reasons to continue loving her King.

After all this time, she should forget the Dragon King and move on. But that wasn't Rhi. When she loved, it was forever.

Yet his capturing her hadn't been for naught. Their friendship was renewed, and Balladyn had finally told her of his feelings. The greatest day of his life was when she not only returned his kiss but also gave him her body.

Minus her heart.

He had denied the truth that was evident to everyone but him. No longer could he ignore the facts. Rhi didn't love him, not the way he loved her. She never would. But he didn't care. He still wanted her.

Needed her.

He rose from his bed and walked to the tall windows of his room at the top of the palace. Finally, he was King of the Dark. It was a position he'd been born for. All those years of leading the Light Army had helped him work his way up the ranks of the Dark to be Taraeth's right hand.

And from there, it was simply a matter of removing Tara-eth from the picture.

Everything had been planned down to the tiniest detail. Except Balladyn hadn't realized that Taraeth had drawn a weapon himself. So when Balladyn sank his blade into the former king, Taraeth also struck a killing blow.

The joy Balladyn felt at finally becoming King of the Dark was sucked away as he felt his life draining from him. All he'd wanted was Rhi by his side as he breathed his last. Rhi, however, had other ideas. She brought Constantine.

And what did that prick do? He saved Balladyn.

Perhaps Balladyn shouldn't have lashed out at Rhi for helping to save him. Maybe he shouldn't have unleashed the Dark upon the mortals. And he was fairly certain he should've thanked her.

He said her name over and over in his head, wishing that he could call for her. But he didn't. She wouldn't answer him, and he didn't want the rejection.

Balladyn blew out a breath and turned his head to the table of books that he'd been looking through. Before him was the largest collection of Fae books outside of the impressive library at the Light Castle.

He'd hoped to find something else on the Reapers to give him an excuse to seek Rhi out. It hadn't taken him long to find the book on the legendary assassin, Fintan. Balladyn was almost certain the white-haired Dark he'd spoken with a few months ago in Ireland was, in fact, none other than Fintan—though the assassin was supposedly dead by Usaeil's hand.

The Light Queen and Taraeth had traded favors killing each other's enemies. It was how Balladyn had ended up with the Dark. Though Taraeth hadn't killed him as he promised Usaeil. Instead, he'd turned Balladyn.

And that would end up being Usaeil's downfall.

Balladyn had loathed the queen for a long time, but that's what happened when someone learned that the person they'd given their lives to protect was not who they thought they were.

Usaeil had no business being queen. Not only because she'd had Balladyn removed since he loved Rhi, but because the queen had instigated the end of Rhi's affair with her Dragon King. Then there was the fact that Usaeil had tried to have Taraeth kill Rhi—which was why Balladyn finally took the King of the Dark out.

But the final straw was when Usaeil banished Rhi from the Light.

Rhi. The strongest, bravest of the Light. The one who thought of everyone else before herself. The one whose light beckoned all.

Balladyn was going to kill Usaeil for all that she'd done to Rhi and to him. The Light deserved a better queen.

They deserved Rhi.

His dream of him and Rhi ruling the Dark and Light together was most likely gone, but that didn't mean he didn't know who should rightly lead the Light.

Rhi.

Her name slid through his mind like a caress, his heart hurting at not being able to hold her. Unable to take it anymore, he teleported to Rhi's island, knowing that she had probably left to seek sanctuary somewhere he couldn't find her. But to his amazement, her things were still there.

He walked into the small hut and stopped to smile at the rows of nail polish. Her significant shoe collection was elsewhere, along with the rest of her things. The island was a place where she went to relax, somewhere she swam in the ocean and basked naked upon the sand.

They'd made love there numerous times. There wasn't

a part of the isle that he hadn't touched in some way. Had she remained because a small part of her wanted that connection to him? Did he dare believe that she might still care for him?

He knew her favorite places. And he knew the people she went to when she needed someone. It would be easy to find her. All he wanted was a glimpse of her.

Balladyn veiled himself and began teleporting to Rhi's favorite cities. He went to Rome first and the shops she often visited. Then it was on to Milan, London, and New York before he went to Austin, thinking she might be getting her nails done.

When he had no luck, Balladyn returned to Ireland and went to the Light Castle. For all he knew, Rhi could be there veiled, just like him, and he'd never see her.

Balladyn didn't go into the castle. Usaeil had things in place to make sure that no one could enter veiled. It was too bad that Balladyn didn't have the powers of a Reaper because then he could do as he pleased. Or so he'd read. He'd like to find out for himself.

There was one place that he hadn't looked—and wouldn't. Dreagan. There was nothing that could bring him back to that place. He hated all the Dragon Kings with a passion, and if he saw the bastard who broke Rhi's heart . . . Balladyn might attack him.

Not that he could kill the wanker. The damn Kings were impossible to get rid of. And that made Balladyn despise them all the more.

If only the Dragon Kings had never entered Rhi's life, then maybe she might have loved him as she was supposed to. Why wasn't he enough for her? Why did she cling to a dragon who didn't even acknowledge her? Who'd tossed her heart and her love away as if they meant nothing?

Balladyn didn't want to return to the Dark palace. He

was still too wrapped up in his love for Rhi, and being in the place they were supposed to share together only made things worse.

Though, to be fair, from the beginning, she'd told him they couldn't rule the Fae together because the Light and Dark could never coexist. He'd known she was right, but with her by his side, he could've done the impossible.

Because Rhi was that extraordinary.

Because Rhi brought that out in him.

Because he loved her more than he loved anything else in all the realms.

No matter how long it took, he would prove to her that his love was unfailing. He'd stand by and wait for her to return to him. He'd watch as she pined after the undeserving Dragon King. He'd keep giving her all the love within him. All because he knew something that she hadn't acknowledged yet—the darkness he'd called forth as he tortured her in the dungeons was growing.

During one of their kisses, he'd seen her eyes flash red. It had been just a moment, but he was well aware that once the darkness took hold, there was no running from it.

Rhi would realize all of that soon enough. There was no need for him to tell her because it would only delay the inevitable as she valiantly attempted to fight the darkness.

He hated himself for torturing her. It had been a means for him to lash out when he blamed her for him turning Dark. If he could turn back the hands of time, he would never have chained her, would never have hurt her. But it couldn't be undone.

And it might be the very thing that put her in his arms again where she belonged.

Her light will be gone. It's the thing you love the most.

That was true, but he could love the darkness, as well. He'd come to not only accept it in himself but embrace it, as well. Each time Usaeil hurt her, Rhi was giving into the anger, which in turn called to the darkness.

Yes, his beloved would become the very monster she fought against.

He'd tried to tell her once, but she'd disregarded him. Each time after that, she'd assured him that she would never become Dark. That's because she didn't understand the root of it. She understood the light with all its goodness.

But the darkness was another beast altogether. It was heady and seductive. Invigorating and reckless.

Exhilarating and carnal.

It was Rhi.

Balladyn remained veiled and teleported to the edge of Dreagan. He wouldn't get close to the invisible barrier of dragon magic that protected the sixty thousand acres. He hated Scotland, hated everything to do with the people and the country.

Because it held Rhi's heart, along with her King.

She denied it, and while Balladyn knew he was blind to a lot of things, he wasn't stupid.

Just being near the Dragon Kings made him want to lash out at them. Anger and resentment churned viciously inside him. His magic surged, while the darkness urged him to go after the King who had hurt Rhi.

Balladyn controlled his rage—barely. There would be a time when he went after the Dragon King, but it wasn't now. He returned to the Dark Palace and dropped the veil to walk the corridors. The Dark still celebrated his new reign because he'd let them have at the mortals.

Rhi's precious humans that she wanted to protect just like the Kings.

He knew he was hurting her with every mortal death caused by a Dark, but it's who he was. She'd known that when she kissed him. She'd acknowledged it when she held his hand. And she'd accepted it when she climbed into bed with him.

He'd never held anything back from her or pretended to be something he wasn't. In time, she'd come to see that.

A Fae stepped into his path. Balladyn drew up, not in the mood to deal with those who vied to be his lieutenant. As if that would happen. He'd had that position. He knew the power—and the betrayal—that usually came with the job.

Then he recognized the Light Fae he'd discovered using glamour pretending to be Dark recently. "Xaneth," he said, noting that the Fae was once more using glamour to fit in. "I didn't expect to see you so soon. Have you made contact with Bran?"

"Not yet."

Balladyn moved closer to the Fae and stared into his fake red eyes. "We had a deal."

"There's been a complication," the Fae hedged.

Balladyn raised a black brow. "What might that be?"

"People I don't want to mess with."

While Xaneth tried to put enough fear into his voice, Balladyn wasn't buying it. He knew full well that Xaneth meant the Reapers, but the Fae wasn't as terrified as he should be. Which could only mean one thing—he was now working with the Reapers.

One way or another, Balladyn was going to find his answers. "I suppose that means you want out of our deal?"

"I didn't say that."

Balladyn smiled. "I knew I liked you. Tell me what you know."

CHAPTER EIGHTEEN

Roman remained in the forest, looking up at the sky while Camlo and V talked. All the while, Roman went over his conversation with Sabina.

He hadn't spoken of his sister in ages. As his twin, they had known what the other was thinking and feeling. If anyone could truly understand what he'd gone through to become the King of Light Blues, it was she.

Ragna was there when it was over, comforting him while the rest of his family either despised him or ignored him. That was until he reminded them that he was their Dragon King.

How he missed Ragna. She would've been an amazing Dragon Queen if the magic had chosen her. Even though she had desperately wanted the role, she never complained that she had been passed over. She didn't have to. He'd felt her disappointment—and her support.

Roman lay back on the slope with his hands behind his head and looked at the stars. One of them could be the realm where his sister and the other dragons had found a new home, waiting to be called back. All of his family was dead by now. Whoever led the Light Blues would only know stories of him.

"I doona have to guess your thoughts."

Roman's head turned to find V leaning against a tree. "I didna hear you walk up."

"Because you were too deep in your memories. I hope you're thinking of the good ones and not the . . . others."

Roman sighed and returned his gaze to the sky. "A little of both."

V pushed away from the tree and lowered himself beside Roman before laying back. "It willna do any good to let those other memories back in."

"Unfortunately, learning that we must go to Iceland has busted open that door, my friend."

"Then return to Dreagan. I'll do this alone. You doona need that kind of misery."

Roman shook his head. "That's no' going to happen. It's time I go back, anyway. It's time to bury the past."

"I doona like any of this. It feels like a trap."

"How? I doona care who these Druids and Fae are that have mixed their magic, there is no way they could know that I'd be the one going to look for the sword with you, or that we'd meet Camlo."

V made a sound in the back of his throat. "We are made of magic, Roman. It guides us, chooses us, and defines us. How can you even contemplate that this was all mere coincidence?"

"Because to think otherwise means that whatever awaits us in Iceland is no' good."

V turned his head to him. "It willna be good. In fact, I expect everything to go verra, verra badly."

"That's comforting." Roman looked at V. "We should fill Con in."

"Nay," V stated firmly.

"I know your reasoning for keeping Con in the dark, but this is important."

V laughed wryly. "That it is. What do you think Con will do with the information? He can no' help us. It will add more worry to his already heavy burden."

"Someone should know in case . . ." Roman trailed off, unsure how to finish the sentence.

V's smile was a little sad as he once more looked to the stars. "In case the Druids and Fae have something waiting for me in your homeland."

"It's crossed my mind."

"And mine," V admitted. "It's why I've filled Ulrik in."

Roman crossed his ankles. "As long as someone knows. Con willna be happy about being kept out of the loop."

"Probably."

Roman was silent a moment, thinking of all the things that could go wrong. "If, as you say, this isna a coincidence, whatever awaits us can no' kill you."

"There are many worse things that can be done to us," V replied.

And no one knew that better than V. Roman should've thought about that before speaking. "How long do you want to give them to sleep?"

V sat up and looked down at the house. "Camlo just went inside. A few hours should be plenty."

"What did you see this time when you touched him?"

V pulled his legs up toward his chest and rested his arms atop his knees. "More clarity. I'm busting through the magic, but slowly. Too bloody slowly."

"Do you still need Camlo?"

"I'm no' sure. Possibly.

Roman glanced at him. "I told Sabina we were leaving tomorrow."

"You didna lie. You simply didna mention that it would be in the wee hours of the morning."

"Semantics."

V shrugged. "Truth."

Roman concentrated muscle by muscle to make his body relax. He needed to find some sort of peace before their journey began. Because if V were right, then what awaited them in Iceland could be worse than just his past.

Sabina was nudged from the deep recesses of sleep. She pushed away the hands, unwilling to wake. It had taken her forever to fall asleep, and if the person didn't stop shaking her, she was going to do bodily harm.

"Go away," she growled.

"Sabina."

The sexy brogue calling her name was all it took to wake her. Her eyes snapped open, and she rolled onto her back to find Roman bent over her.

Even in the moonlight, he was gorgeous. Without thinking, she smoothed a lock of hair from his forehead. Their gazes met, and she wondered what he dreamt about when he slept. Was it his sister, his family? Or was it whatever had happened on Iceland that he didn't wish to talk about.

Vaguely, she realized that it was still dark outside and that he had woken her. Her first thought was Camlo.

"Is something wrong?" she asked as she reached over and turned on the lamp.

Roman shook his head, his green eyes watching her carefully. "Get dressed."

"Why?"

"We're leaving."

She couldn't have heard him right. Sabina looked out her window before glancing at the clock on her bedside table. "It's barely one in the morning."

"I know. We should've left already, but you sleep like the dead." He straightened and walked to the door.

When he opened it, she saw the lights on and Camlo talking to V. This wasn't a joke. They really wanted to leave. Now. In the dead of night.

"Why now?" she asked before Roman could exit her room.

He paused and looked over his shoulder at her. "We doona want anyone seeing us."

"Oh."

She sat up as he walked out, but she didn't get out of bed. For the next few minutes, she wrapped her head around what was happening. She was leaving Romania for the first time. Ever. It wasn't that she didn't want to visit Iceland. In fact, she knew very little of the country. But that's not what bothered her.

It was all the things that could happen to them. The easy thing to do would be to remain. What would that give her, though? Even she had to admit that it was stagnant where she was. Safe. Comfortable.

But stagnant.

Her only option was to go forward and see whatever it was this new road she was on offered. Sabina threw off the covers and hurried to dress.

While she threw a couple of changes of clothes and essentials into a bag, she called out for Camlo to do the same. V warned them to dress warmly. Sabina layered her clothing and put on her winter boots. She then turned out her light and hurried to her laptop where she checked emails before closing it.

"We'll use our magic to make sure no one breaks in while we're gone," V said.

She glanced up at him and smiled. "That'd be great."

Sabina almost laughed out loud. Magic was being used

to protect her belongings. Her gran would be ecstatic. Well, perhaps she would. If Gran didn't hate the Dragon Kings. In fact, Sabina didn't know if Gran liked them or not.

Camlo made swishing sounds in his coat as he and V walked out of the house while Roman calmly stood at the door, waiting for her. Sabina ran her hands over the necklace she'd been making. It would have to wait. Carting it around with her while hoping she'd have time to work was ridiculous. She'd end up breaking everything.

"What of the animals?" Sabina asked as she tugged on her coat then swung her bag over her shoulder and walked to her purse. "I can't believe Camlo is willing to leave them."

"They'll be fine," Roman replied. "Camlo has already spoken to all of them, and V and I have made sure they'll have plenty of food and water while we're gone."

She eyed him as she walked to the door and stopped beside him. "Did you have to bribe my brother?"

"No' at all."

That made her frown. "How odd."

"Ready?" Roman asked.

She looked around her home. The road before her was scary, but she was ready. She hoped. "I suppose."

He opened the door and waited for her to walk out before he shut it behind him. Sabina only got two steps before she looked up and came to a halt when she spotted the very real, very large dragon in front of her.

"It's V," Roman said as he placed a hand on her shoulder.

Sabina could only stare numbly at the copper dragon that her brother was climbing onto. It was hard to see what V really looked like in the moonlight, but she got the gist of things. Especially the thick horns that came from V's temple and curled inward.

It wasn't until Camlo was seated at the base of V's neck and smiling at her that Sabina understood just how they would be traveling to Iceland. For some reason, she hadn't thought about how they'd get there. Probably because she'd assumed they'd fly or drive to the coast and then take a boat to the island.

"You doona need to be afraid," Roman said. "It's safe."

Safe? Was he serious? A bubble of laughter tinged with fear and sarcasm filled her. She stepped away from him and pointed at V, shaking her head in terror as the words refused to pass her lips they were so jumbled.

Roman held up his hands before him and moved to face her. "Easy, Sabina. V probably should've waited to shift so you could see him. I thought you understood what we are."

This time, she did laugh, and it sounded as crazed as she felt. "I know what you are."

"Then I doona understand the problem."

She shook her head as she looked at V and Camlo. "No."

"This is how we're getting to Iceland. It will only take a few hours," Roman said.

Sabina took another step back. "No." She couldn't do it.

She wouldn't do it.

"Bina, come on!" Camlo called.

The ground trembled when V shifted his feet and swished his long tail. His wings were tucked against him while his gaze was on the sky. Without warning, V jumped and spread his wings. She watched in amazement as he took her brother high into the clouds.

"He's safe," Roman said. "You will be, too. I promise I willna let you fall off."

She swallowed and backed up several paces. "I c-can't."

"We have to fly at night so the mortals doona see us, and we need to go now."

"No." What was it about the word that he didn't understand? She'd said it several times already. He should get that this wasn't happening.

Roman ran a hand down his face. "I'm going to shift now. Then, you'll need to climb up my legs to sit on my neck. After that, you simply hold on tight until we land."

"That's not happening."

"I have to tell you this now because, once I shift, I willna be able to talk to you until I return to this form."

"I can't do it!" she yelled.

He paused as he started to turn away. "Imagine it's like being on a plane."

"I've never been on a plane," she told him and looked away. There had been few times in her life where her fear had taken such a hold of her, but the grip it had right then was debilitating.

"Sabina," he said to get her attention. "Is it me you're afraid of?"

She shook her head as she looked into his face.

"Then what is it?"

"Heights. I'm terrified of heights."

He blinked. "I see."

"I thought if we were taking a plane, that I'd try to sleep or something and make sure not to look out the windows. But this," she said motioning to V flying above them. "I can't."

"Nay, I doona imagine you can." Roman sighed and then put his hands on his hips. "That leaves us only two options."

"Which are?" she asked, afraid she already knew what they were.

Roman nodded at the house. "You remain behind."

Sabina really didn't want to do that. For one, she didn't want to leave her brother alone, and two, because she wanted to see this through. She had to. She couldn't understand it, but she knew she had to get to Iceland.

"And the other?" she asked.

"I use magic to make you sleep, and I carry you to Iceland."

The world spun just thinking about being that high up. She reached out, and it was Roman who quickly grabbed her to steady her.

She didn't fight him when he wrapped his arms around her and held her against his chest. Just like earlier, she melted against him, soaking in his heat and his strength.

"I give you my word that I'll no' let any harm come to you," he said into her hair.

Sabina opened her eyes and looked at her house. She'd lived there—safe—for so many years that she didn't know what taking chances meant anymore.

"Okay," she agreed and looked up at him. She was placing all her trust in him.

His lips curved into a smile. When his head lowered, her eyelids closed. She felt his lips on her forehead and then . . . nothing.

CHAPTER NINETEEN

Every beat of his wings brought him closer to a place that he loved with all of his heart.

And hated just as deeply.

Roman ignored the many glances V gave him as they flew side by side toward Iceland. Fire and ice. He still recalled the first time his father had told him that's what the land was made of. And Roman could still remember the first time he'd told a human.

"There's still time for you to return to Dreagan," V said. *"We're passing over Scotland now."*

Roman knew exactly where they were. He beat his wings faster, showing V that he had no intention of turning away from their course. Someone wanted him on Iceland. He didn't know who or why, but one way or another, Roman intended to find out. Hopefully, it would also reveal V's sword.

"You could've just said nay," V grumbled.

For the first time in hours, Roman found himself grinning. He looked over at Camlo, who had yet to stop smiling as he rode atop V—and luckily, V hadn't passed out. Camlo's ability to make V faint must only happen when V was in human form.

Roman's gaze shifted down to his paw where he held Sabina. His magic kept her slumbering, and would until they reached Iceland. It had never occurred to him that she might be afraid of heights. Not only was it a considerable distance to the ground from atop a dragon, but then there was the flying itself.

Her fear had been palpable. If he hadn't realized that, it would've been impossible not to notice her pale face, her rapid breathing, or her dilated pupils. Something like that couldn't be faked, even by the best of actors.

When she'd listed to the side as if she were about to fall, he'd dragged her against him without thinking. She'd clung to him as if he were her lifeline as her entire body shook. All that just from talking about flying.

That's when he realized that she would never make the ride. But he wanted her with him. Roman didn't consider why, just accepted it as fact.

Her dark curls blew in the wind, the locks sliding against his talons like a caress. Her face was turned toward him while one of her hands lay against the inside of his palm.

"She's verra pretty."

Roman growled. "Shut up, V."

"Why? Because I state the obvious? Or is it because you doona want to admit that you like her? I've been asleep, Roman, not dead."

He blew out a breath, sparks flying upon the wind.

V laughed loudly in his head. "Do you know what I did when I woke and left Dreagan?"

"You went looking for your sword."

"Aye. But I also shagged my way across the land."

Roman jerked his head to him. *"Your point?"*

"When was the last time you had sex?"

"No' that long ago." V made some indistinct sound that had Roman frowning. *"What's that supposed to mean?"*

"It means that even if you'd had a woman last night, you'd still crave the one you're holding now."

"You've no idea what you're talking about."

V shot him a dark look. *"Why? Because I spent most of my time sleeping? I'm no' blind, you prat."*

"What the hell is that supposed to mean?"

"Are you really going to pretend you doona know?"

Roman blew out more sparks as his anger increased. It didn't help that he could see Iceland in the distance. *"Since I doona know, I guess I am."*

"You're attracted to her. And in case you didna know, she has the hots for you, as well."

"Stop," Roman begged him. *"It doesna sound right, you using modern terms."*

V laughed. *"Turn the conversation if you want, but I'll be around to see you give in to the temptation to taste the lovely Sabina's lips."*

Roman pulled his eyes from the horizon and the mountains of Iceland to V. It was only then that he realized his friend had been attempting to take his attention from their arrival.

"I'm going to be fine," Roman told V.

V cut his scarlet eyes to him. *"I never had any doubts."*

Roman considered taking them toward the Vestrahorn Mountains on the east side of Iceland, but he changed his mind and nudged V onward. They flew straight over the land until Roman spotted the area the humans dubbed Westfjords.

The Hornstrandir was the perfect place for them because it was isolated and uninhabited. He circled the area to make sure no one was about and then swooped in. Roman landed, careful not to disturb Sabina.

Within seconds, V had also touched down. Camlo slid off him and looked around in amazement at the vast, snow-covered mountains.

"Doona let him go far," Roman cautioned V.

V watched the mortal for a moment before swinging his head back to Roman. *"Tell me about this place."*

"It's been uninhabited since the 1950s. There are those who come during the day for tours as well as the occasional hiker, but no' during this time of year. The weather is too temperamental for humans."

V shifted to his mortal form and used magic to return his clothes. *"What are you going to do about Sabina?"*

"Wake her."

V nodded slowly. *"Let her see you."*

"Why?"

"Why no'?"

Why did V have to answer things with a question? It drove Roman mad. *"I doona want to frighten her."*

"Did she look scared when she saw me?"

Matter of fact, she hadn't. Roman had thought she was, but really it was her fear of heights.

"You're catching on." V sighed dramatically. Aloud he said, "I still have so much to teach you."

"Go away before I burn you," Roman threatened. But he was grinning.

V lifted his head and sniffed the air. "My sword is here, and we're going to find it."

Roman watched him walk after Camlo, who was headed to a cliff to look out at the churning sea. Only then did Roman lift the magic that kept Sabina asleep.

Her lashes fluttered before her eyes opened. She inhaled deeply and rolled her head forward. Their gazes met, and she stilled. Roman's heart dropped until she lifted a hand as she sat up and placed her palm along his scaly jaw. And just like it had when she swept his hair off his forehead, his heart skipped a beat.

Magnificent. Glorious. Resplendent.

Sabina could've gone on and on describing the creature before her. She gazed into the ivory eyes of the dragon and smiled when she recognized Roman.

His chest rumbled, and she assumed that meant he was pleased by her reaction. She stroked the pale blue scales beneath her hand, marveling at their warmth. But she wanted to see more.

As if understanding what she needed, Roman lowered his paw to the ground. Sabina climbed off and dropped her bag as she moved back to take all of Roman in.

"Wow," she murmured, trying to put every detail to memory.

His body was enormous yet elegant with its pale blue scales that turned a shade darker toward his hindquarters before they became thicker along his slender tail. She'd seen the single horn that projected above his snout, but now she got a look at the thick bone that protected the back of Roman's head and neck.

He gently folded his massive wings against him and watched her curiously. Much as she was doing with him. What else could she do? He was a freaking dragon.

And then just like that, the dragon disappeared, and Roman once more stood before her—completely naked. And seemingly unaffected by the weather.

Snow swirled around him as if the flurries wanted to touch the Dragon King as much as she did. Sabina only got a glimpse of his chest and what looked like a tattoo before he was clothed once more.

"You leave me speechless," she said, embarrassed by her lack of words because she was so in awe of him.

Both as a dragon and as a man.

He closed the distance between them, fire sparking in his sea green eyes. "How do you feel?"

Feel? How could he ask that after she'd just seen him as a dragon, and then only got a teasing glimpse of him nude—and what she'd seen had been fabulous?

"Good. I'm good," she hurried to say.

He watched her with amusement, those amazing lips of his curved slightly. "Welcome to Iceland."

Sabina couldn't believe that she'd forgotten about the trip. She jerked her head to the side and took in miles of snowy mountains and turbulent waters.

The flurries didn't hinder her view of the glaciers or the steam that rose in the distance. Part of her wanted to venture there and see the dried lava fields, and perhaps even the molten rock spewing from the ground.

She looked down at her insulated boots and jacket. Her attire worked well, but not that well. She wasn't chilled. At all. And she should be in this kind of weather.

"I doona want you getting cold," Roman said.

That was his way of telling her that his magic kept her warm. She shifted under the weight of her clothes. "If I'd known that, I could've just come in my underwear."

Was it her imagination, or had his eyes darkened?

Roman's gaze moved away as he bent and retrieved her bag. He slung it over his shoulder as he straightened. "The sun will be up soon, but the weather is unpredictable here. We shouldna keep you or your brother out in the elements."

"Why not?" she asked curiously. "Your magic is keeping us warm, right?"

He smiled and glanced at the mountain behind them.

"We use magic when we have to, but we doona rely on it as the Fae and Druids do."

"Understandable." She saw him glance around again. It wasn't a casual look, but one that spoke of uncertainty and unease. "Are you all right?"

Roman stilled and looked at her. "Aye."

"I saw your reaction at my house. I know you aren't keen on being here."

He glanced at the ground. "I'll be fine."

"By the way, thank you for getting me here."

His face split into a grin. "I promised I wouldna let anything harm you."

She returned his smile and fell into step with him as they started toward Camlo and V. Her brother's wide eyes took in everything as he turned this way and that to look around. But what truly held his attention was the ocean.

"Bina, look," he said gleefully, pointing at the water.

She smiled as she came up beside him. "It's beautiful, isn't it?"

He nodded enthusiastically. "And there are so many animals here. They're all talking at once. Can I go see them?"

"No' now," V cautioned. "The weather is about to turn."

Roman pointed to the mountain. "We need to find shelter before the blizzard arrives. I know a place."

Sabina walked a few paces behind Roman while Camlo and V brought up the rear. "Where on Iceland are we?"

"West side," Roman replied. "I brought us here because it is uninhabited. It's better for us, but it will also give Camlo some time to adjust."

"Thank you. Again," she said.

He flashed her a smile that made her feet forget how to walk. She tripped over herself and pitched forward. Her hands caught her before her face smashed into the snow, but she was mortified.

Roman was instantly there to help her to her feet. "There are lots of rocks. You probably stumbled on one."

She forced a smile and nodded in agreement, refusing to tell him that she was just an idiot.

Behind her, Camlo asked V, "What's wrong with her? She's acting weird."

Sabina stared straight ahead. She couldn't remember a time when she'd been so embarrassed.

"The cold does strange things to people," V told Camlo.

Sabina felt Roman's eyes on her, but she wouldn't look at him. She started in the direction they'd been heading and kept her mind firmly off the hot Dragon King next to her.

That is until his fingers brushed hers as they walked. Her head jerked to him to find his green eyes on her.

Hot.

And hungry.

CHAPTER TWENTY

The desire burned so hot and so bright that it could rival dragon fire. The embers had begun in Romania, but they burst to life when Sabina woke and touched him.

Roman could still feel her palm along his jaw. Scales or flesh, her touch scorched him, branding him as surely as his tattoo did.

V said it was attraction. But Roman had never felt anything so primal, so . . . undeniably carnal before. He was aware of every breath Sabina took, felt every heartbeat.

Each time her pulsed raced when she looked at him made him ache. It was a soul-deep longing, one that got into his bones and settled there, sending whispers of desire rushing through him. The need, the hunger grew tenfold with every breath. His hands itched to hold her, to feel her flesh against him.

He led them into the cave, forcing his gaze from her to look around. Both Sabina and Camlo halted near the entrance because their eyes couldn't penetrate the darkness.

"Wait here," he told them. Roman walked ahead since he could see in the dark as well as the light.

The cave was narrow, and the ceiling low enough that

Roman had to bend over to walk through. About a hundred yards later, the passage widened, and as Roman continued, the ceiling also gradually rose so that he was able to stand straight.

There were footsteps behind him. Roman didn't need to turn around to know it was V.

"You're on edge," V said as he came up beside him.

Roman looked into a crude opening in the wall and saw another passage that was too small for anyone to fit through. He glanced at V and walked onward. "I'm good."

"That's horse shite, and you know it." V shook his head after looking into another opening. "There's something about being back here that's affected you. The sexual tension between you and Sabina is off the charts."

Roman halted and braced a hand on the wall, the cool, damp stone beneath his palm a reminder of the volatile temperatures of the land. "I know."

"Is it Sabina?"

Roman shrugged. He had no answer for what he couldn't figure out himself.

"I could find another woman and bring her to see if she affects you as Sabina does," V offered.

He looked at V and glared. "No."

"Afraid that it's the lovely Sabina who has you wound up? Or are you worried that it could be your homeland that's doing this to you?"

Roman raked a hand through his hair. He'd felt the instant attraction to Sabina in Romania, but he couldn't readily accept that that's what had him so wound up. Because once he landed in Iceland, his emotions became charged, heightening everything.

"I doona fucking know, V. Okay? I doona have any answers."

"Good."

At V's response, Roman frowned. "You doona make any sense."

"It means that I'm glad you're no' trying to force answers that doona match the questions."

Roman briefly closed his eyes. "I could use a dram right about now."

"You and me both. Do you remember this cave?"

Roman looked down the tunnel. "The entrance was too small for dragons to use. I've no' been here before."

V shouldered past him and continued looking for a place they could sleep. After a second, Roman trailed after him. It wasn't long before V shouted his name. Roman hurried toward him and found V standing in an opening.

Roman came up behind him and gazed into the cavern. It wasn't overly large, but roomy enough for four people to fit comfortably.

"Do you want to get Sabina and Camlo?" V offered.

Roman shook his head. "I need a moment to myself."

"I thought you might. I doona see wood anywhere. Looks like we'll have to use magic to get a fire going."

"Aye," Roman replied.

A moment later, V walked away. Roman was used to living in caves. Each King had their own mountain on Dreagan where they hid from humans. It was a sanctuary for each King when they wished to have some time alone, or if they decided to sleep away a few centuries.

But the hard, cold rock was not something Sabina or her brother were used to. Since they were helping him and Roman, the least Roman could do was make them as comfortable as possible.

His dragon magic was always there, waiting to be used—though the Kings chose not to turn to magic so as not to become dependent on it. That was laughable since their very existence was because of magic.

Roman held out his hand to the middle of the cavern. He pictured a large fire, and almost immediately, flames leapt from the ground. The crystal chips within the rock acted as a conductor.

Next, his magic manifested two down-filled sleeping bags. He tried to think what else the mortals might need when he heard them approaching.

He stepped aside and faced the direction of the opening. There was a ball of light above them, illuminating the way for Sabina and her brother.

As she neared, Sabina's gaze lifted and locked with his. Roman instinctively reached out for her. To his delight, she immediately grasped his hand, her fingers curling around his. He pulled her close so Camlo and V could walk into the cavern, but the ball of light remained with Sabina.

Roman let himself drown in the dark pools of her eyes. "I doona think I thanked you for doing this."

"I've not done anything yet," she said.

"You're here."

She glanced down, smiling. "I wish I could take the credit, but without Camlo, I wouldn't know that this is where the sword is."

"Your grandmother told you the story for a reason. Your family is bound to it."

Her tongue peeked out as she licked her lips. "I know V wants his property returned, and I know why the sword is important to him and the rest of the Dragon Kings."

"But," Roman said when she paused.

"Are we doing the right thing? My ancestors felt the vision was enough to steal the sword and hide it. What if returning the weapon to V creates the very thing my family was trying to prevent?"

Roman glanced into the cavern to see V and Camlo deep in conversation near the fire. "I can no' answer that any more than you can. What I do know is that your ancestors didna act alone. Whether they were party to it or no', their actions allowed the Druid and Fae group to use their magic on V."

Her forehead furrowed. "You think the Druids and Fae used magic on my ancestor who had the vision?"

"It's a possibility that I can no' rule out."

Sabina sighed loudly. "And we can't ask her."

"She probably wouldna know if magic had been used."

"Good point." Sabina rubbed her lips together. "I hate not knowing."

Roman looked down at their joined hands. She hadn't pulled away, and that made him happy. "Neither do I."

"What's the next step?"

"I need to listen to the metals."

Her eyebrows shot up in her brow. "Listen?"

"Aye. I hear them, like a song. Each one has a distinct sound."

She moved closer to him. "Really? So you should be able to hear V's sword?"

"I hope. There's always the possibility that the Druids and Fae masked it."

"Can V not hear his sword?"

Roman grabbed her other hand. "Each King has their own power. V has the ability to mask himself while in his true form. He has no idea what others see, so until I told him, he didna know that when he shifts and veils himself, it appears as if his body is disintegrating into hundreds of bats."

Sabina laughed softly. "Dracula in all his glory."

"He's quite sickened that the legends turned him into such a monster."

"I admit, I feared him after the story Gran told me."

Roman turned them so that she had her back to the wall. "And now?"

"I see the way he treats my brother. And Camlo adores V. That's pretty much all I need."

Roman bit back a moan when she withdrew her hand from him and placed it on his chest. "And me? Do you fear me?"

"You know I'm not afraid of you."

"Aye, lass. I know." But he'd needed to hear it.

She smiled up at him, the curve of her lips sensual and welcoming. He was contemplating kissing her, learning the movement of her lips and the taste of her, when Camlo shouted for Sabina.

Roman stepped away from her, giving her room, but Sabina once more took hold of his hand. She held his gaze a long moment before she slowly loosened her grip and turned to walk into the cavern.

He scrubbed a hand down his face. How in the hell was he supposed to keep his hands off her? Maybe it was a good thing they weren't alone. With Camlo and V always near, it would force Roman to keep a safe distance from her.

But in his mind, he could envision all the wonderful, naughty things he wished to do.

Roman entered the cavern, and as soon as he did, V smiled at him. The bastard knew just how much Roman yearned for a taste of Sabina. No, that wasn't right. A taste wouldn't be enough. Roman wanted a feast.

V chuckled, causing both Camlo and Sabina to look his way. Roman ignored him. V was enjoying this entirely too much. While his friend had sexed his way across Europe, Roman hadn't met anyone that knocked him off his feet.

Whatever plans Roman had for putting V in such a position were cut short when he realized *why* V hadn't met anyone. How could he when V had spent more time sleeping than living? All because of the Druid and Fae pricks.

Roman squatted down near the back of the cavern, out of the light of the fire. He wanted to be in the shadows, needed them in order to let his thoughts delve into places they probably shouldn't tread.

Because if this unholy alliance between the Druids and Fae had managed to conceal not only what they'd done to V—and, he suspected, their involvement in pushing the mortals to take V's sword—but also their vicious killing of the White dragon and hiding the lookalike wooden figure of Con, then what else had they done? What else could they do?

It was a thought that left Roman cold to the very pit of his soul. How many times had Con said that they might be the most powerful beings on the realm, but it was only a matter of time before someone challenged them?

Roman hadn't given Con's words much credence since Roman truly believed that day would never come. But now he feared that he might have been wrong all along.

He dropped his chin to his chest as apprehension, thick and cloying, churned through him. The last time he'd felt anything even remotely like this was during the war with the humans when Roman realized the dragons would have to leave.

All the Dragon Kings had ever done was protect their home. As far as he knew, nothing had been done to the Druids and Fae that would warrant such an attack. Yet it was the idea that the two very different, usually warring sects of both beings had joined forces for one cause—to harm the Dragon Kings—that troubled him the most.

"Dragon Kings, hear me," Con's voice said as it filled Roman's head.

Roman stilled, not liking the hard tone of Con's voice.

There was a pause before Con continued. *"There are Kings away from Dreagan, which is why I've no' called everyone together. I didna want to wait to impart this information because of its importance.*

"It wasna long ago that I shared a secret with all of you, one that was to be kept by those in my position. It was the Darks—and Mikkel's—interest in gaining the weapon that led me to tell you about it. . . ."

When Con's voice trailed off, Roman lifted his head to look at V, who met his gaze. A frown was forming on V's face that Roman was sure matched his own.

"Unfortunately, that weapon is now gone," Con continued.

Shock went through Roman. How could this be?

But Con wasn't finished. *"The magic I had around the weapon wasna breached. I doona know who found my mountain or gained access, but all of you need to be aware that the weapon that can kill us is out there."*

CHAPTER TWENTY-ONE

The Light Castle
Ireland

There was a hum through the castle that used to soothe her. It was the magic of the Light Fae. But very little pacified Usaeil now.

In fact, it hadn't for quite some time.

She knew the cause. She'd outgrown the role of Queen of the Light. She needed a grander task, one that would eclipse all others. That of Queen of the Fae.

Her magic was powerful enough. And she was strong enough to do it. Though it would likely mean another war before the Light and Dark came to grips with things. Not that a war was bad. It weeded out the useless, the inferior, and the weak. What would be left would be a race of Fae like no other.

A commanding, effective race more powerful than ever before.

Why hadn't she thought of this sooner? Balladyn had already done her a favor by getting rid of Taraeth. As for Balladyn, Usaeil had no doubt that she could kill him easily enough. After all, she knew his strengths.

And his weakness.

For as formidable as Balladyn was, he had one failing that would be the death of him—Rhi.

Usaeil smiled as she sat in the tall-backed, white chair and rested one leg over the arm, swinging her foot. With one blow, she could wipe out two enemies at once. Then, after several decades of letting the Fae fight it out, she would step in and force them to realize that they were better joined instead of divided.

Any that opposed her would be struck down immediately. Much as she'd done to her family.

Her thoughts took an unexpected turn to Thea. She still didn't know why she hadn't killed her daughter as she had with all the others as soon as she discovered that her belly was swollen with child.

To this day, Usaeil had no idea why she'd given birth to Thea. She'd intended to kill the babe, but again, she hadn't been able to. Instead, she'd given the bairn to a children's home in Ireland and then promptly forgot all about Thea until a few months ago.

Usaeil didn't know what reminded her of the child she had given away or why she felt the need to find Thea again. Whatever reunion Usaeil thought to have with her daughter had been shattered when she realized that Thea was ungrateful and weak. In the end, Usaeil had to kill her.

Which she should've done years ago.

Usaeil drummed her nails on the arm of the chair she was leaning against. Thea's death should have been the end of things, but instead, she'd been dealt a blow she hadn't seen coming—Reapers.

And Death.

For months, she'd ignored the whispers about Reapers circulating around the castle. She'd even discounted the head of the Queen's Guard, Inen, when he cautioned her to find out more about them.

While she wanted to know how the Reapers knew Thea and why they would even come to find her, Usaeil was much more concerned with why Death had arrived.

Once, a very long time ago when she was just a child walking the many halls of the castle on the Fae Realm, Usaeil had overheard a Light talking about the Mistress of War and her lavender eyes.

As soon as the woman with lavender eyes confronted Usaeil, she'd known the being was the Mistress of War. Yet the woman wasn't dressed in chainmail and leather as the legends described. Somehow, the beautiful black gown made the woman even more terrifying.

But it was what Usaeil saw in the female's gaze that truly frightened her.

Death.

Usaeil had run away before she could form a thought. All her years of destroying anyone who got in her way, of ensuring that she was more powerful than any other, meant nothing when confronted by those lavender eyes.

But the Mistress of War and the Reapers hadn't come for her.

"Her first mistake," Usaeil said aloud.

What was one more enemy to add to her list? Usaeil made sure her opponents didn't remain on that list for long. As soon as they were inserted, she set about ridding herself of the problem.

Unfortunately, she'd had to add Balladyn back to the list since Taraeth had lied about killing him. She still couldn't believe that Taraeth turned Balladyn Dark and made him his lieutenant. Look what that had gotten Taraeth? Balladyn had executed him and taken over as King of the Dark.

He wouldn't stay there long, though. Just as Rhi would soon breathe her last. Not even Rhi's precious Dragon Kings would be able to help her this time. Usaeil was going to make sure of it.

As for Constantine, he would soon come to see that they were meant to be together. Usaeil knew men. She knew what to say, how to act, and certainly how to dress to gain their attention. Men were led by their cocks, after all.

Con, however, had proven more difficult than most to get into her bed. She had been patient, though. Gaining his trust by helping him with Kiril's problem with the Dark Fae, and then giving Shara the last little push to turn Light.

The King of Dragon Kings had been grateful for her help. And willing to meet with her whenever she asked. By their third meeting, she lounged naked on her bed when he entered.

Con hadn't hesitated as he strode to the bed, yanking off his clothes before his mouth was on hers, their bodies skin-to-skin.

Usaeil had assumed that Con was hers from then on. That had been a miscalculation on her part. She'd let him think he was setting the rules for their relationship, and for a while, it worked to her advantage. But then Rhi had to poke her nose into things as she always did.

It was the final straw for Usaeil. Con was hers. Only hers. She was the Queen of the Light, soon to be Queen of all Fae. And she shared with no one.

Once she found something she wanted, nothing got in her way. Not in the past, and certainly not now. Con would realize how perfectly they fit together. He would see that only she could match him in magic, power, beauty, and brains. They would rule the dragons and Fae together.

And the Fae would finally give the Kings the children they'd been longing for. Because it was the magic within the Fae that would bear the fruit the mortals hadn't been able to sustain.

Usaeil closed her eyes and smiled. Her plan was beautifully laid out before her. While she'd initially been scared of the Reapers and the Mistress of War, she was no longer. Because if they were able to take her, they would have already come for her.

No, Usaeil was untouchable. She'd known it for some time. It was about time others did, as well.

A knock sounded on her door. Usaeil looked at it with distaste. "Who is it?"

"Inen," the head of the Queen's Guard said through the barrier.

Usaeil blew out an exasperated breath. "Enter."

The door opened, and the Light Fae stepped forward. Inen was handsome, as all Fae were. He kept his black hair trimmed to his shoulders. His silver eyes didn't hold hers long as he looked just over her shoulder. Was it out of fear or respect? Or something that resembled . . . disgust?

Usaeil narrowed her gaze as she straightened in the chair. "Yes? What is it?"

"A hidden room was discovered in the library."

As if she cared about the library. It was a huge place with shelves that reached up to the sky filled with books she had little interest in. "So?"

"An old book was found."

Usaeil sighed loudly. "Inen, you say this as if I should care."

"It's very old, my queen. In fact, it looks to date back several million years to before we ever came to this realm."

She raised her brows and shot him a flat look. "So?"

"Perhaps if you looked at it . . ."

"There are Fae who do that sort of thing and report to me."

Inen shifted in his white and gold uniform. "I think you will want to see this first."

"And why is that? Because you want to bore me with this shite? Can't you see I've more important things to do?"

Inen's gaze briefly met hers, a spark of righteous anger flaring in his silver eyes for just a heartbeat. "Because it mentions the Dragon Kings."

Now that got her interest.

Usaeil pushed to her feet. "That can't be right. We didn't learn of the Dragon Kings until we came to this realm."

"There were a couple of Fae who knew."

"Bring me the book," she demanded.

Inen tilted his head briefly. "I can't do that, my queen."

"And why not?"

"Magic is holding it in place."

Just what the hell was going on? Usaeil strode to Inen and made him look at her. "Then take me to it. Now."

He turned on his heel without a word and walked away. She followed, ignoring the many Fae who stopped and curtsied or bowed as she passed.

It felt like an eternity walking through the huge castle before they finally reached the library. And the entire time, Inen didn't say a word. He nodded and greeted others, but he kept just a few steps ahead of her.

Normally, that would please Usaeil, but she knew he was angry that she'd banished Rhi. And Usaeil had a sneaking suspicion that Inen's refusal to look at or talk to her was his way of delivering the bit of revenge he could.

Oh, how Fae like him amused her. She didn't bother getting angry. No doubt Inen would be one of the first killed in the upcoming war with the Dark. She'd make sure of it.

She inwardly smiled at the thought as they entered the library through the gigantic double doors. The smell of the books made her stomach roil. Usaeil never came here. She hated anything to do with books, and she didn't understand why some revered them so. They were just pages with words on them.

Inen led her through rows and rows of manuscripts. She glanced up at the large, domed ceiling, unimpressed with the artwork.

Finally, they reached the back left corner of the library where two shelves had been cleared of books. They were now stacked on the floor.

"My queen," a Fae in his elder years said as he dropped to one knee, bowing his head.

Usaeil smiled graciously as the two other Fae, both young, one female and one male, quickly followed suit. "Please," she said. "Rise."

The elder got to his feet and grinned nervously. "I saw one of the shelves bending, which it shouldn't do. This entire area was built with magic."

"I know," she replied. She had been there with her grandfather.

"Right, right." The Fae cleared his throat. "Once I removed the books and took a closer look at the shelf, I realized it was actually part of a hinge. And well, see for yourself," he said and motioned her forward.

Usaeil followed him to the bookshelf as he tugged on the ledge in question. The entire section swung open to reveal a small room. She'd given her grandfather ideas when he built the castle, but she hadn't cared about this section. He'd wanted her with him, but Usaeil had ignored his call when it came to the library.

Just what had the old goat hidden away inside?

She pushed past Inen and the three others and walked into the room. With a snap of her fingers, she illuminated the room to find a pedestal with a single book.

Usaeil made her way to the book and looked down at the pages. She couldn't read the words since they were an old dialect, but she did make out Dragon Kings in the third paragraph. Curious as to what the rest of the book said, she tried to turn one of the pages.

Suddenly, the letters jumbled together and began to move about the pages in various speeds, never stopping.

"What the bloody hell?" she murmured.

CHAPTER TWENTY-TWO

How surreal was her life right now? Sabina smiled at the fire heating them without the benefit of wood. Nothing unusual when you had a Dragon King as a friend.

That caused her to frown. Was Roman a friend? Acquaintance, yes, but a friend? When did one cross from just knowing someone to being considered pals?

She licked her lips to stop from smiling. She never said *pals*. It was like being around Roman had opened up other channels she hadn't known were there.

Or was too complacent to look for.

But with him, she had no choice. Those invisible doors threw themselves wide open by his mere presence alone. My God. What could he accomplish if he actively set out to do something?

"Cold?" Camlo asked.

Sabina jerked her gaze to him, frowning. "No."

"You shivered."

She glanced toward the entrance, looking for Roman, but she didn't see him. Sabina then scanned the cavern until she found him half-hidden in the shadows down on his haunches with a deep frown on his face.

Her head swiveled to V, who wore a similar expression. She recalled that the two could communicate telepathically, so they must be talking. But whatever the conversation was about, it wasn't good.

"I need to pee."

Sabina bit back an embarrassed moan. Thankfully, it appeared that neither Roman nor V had heard her brother. She motioned for Camlo to follow her as she headed to the doorway.

"You can't do it in here," she whispered.

He grunted. "Why not?"

"We'd smell it. That's not nice."

"Where are you going to pee?"

It wasn't something she'd thought about until he mentioned it. And then, suddenly, she really had to go. She swallowed, intending to ignore the call of nature for as long as she could.

"Bina?" her brother pressed.

She threw up her hands as she peered out into the dark tunnel. The light V had conjured was gone, and it wasn't like she could grab a stick to light her way.

"I don't know," she answered.

Camlo blew out a loud breath and shoved past her. As he did, he pulled her mobile phone from the pocket of her coat and turned on the flashlight.

"Well. Don't I feel dumb," she murmured.

Camlo grinned at her. "You should."

She shoved at his shoulder as he turned to the left. The tunnel hadn't been an easy trek to the cavern as it wound this way and that, and she wasn't keen on her brother getting lost. So she started after him.

Camlo halted and turned, shining the light directly into her eyes so she had to raise her hand to block it.

"Camlo," she growled in irritation.

"I don't need you to watch me pee," he stated.

She spun around and threw up her hands. "Fine. Go."

When he stomped away, she used her hands to find somewhere she could relieve her bladder. As soon as she discovered a small room, she hurried inside and yanked down her pants.

There were times that her brother did act like a toddler, but those times didn't happen too often. But since V and Roman showed up, it was like he was attempting to act like a grown man.

It was sweet. And sad. She wished her brother had the mental capacity to be self-sufficient. He certainly wouldn't be at the house with her taking care of animals if he did. He'd find himself someone to love and be off living his life as he should.

Tears stung her eyes, knowing that Camlo would never have such things. She wiped away a stray tear and sniffed as she pulled herself together and stumbled her way back to the tunnel to wait for him. She didn't like to cry, and she certainly didn't do it in front of Camlo. It upset him, and it wasn't as if she could tell him that he was the reason she cried. It would destroy him.

Sabina dropped her arms and moved closer to the entry into the cavern. The red-orange glow coming from within made it easy to see. She looked around the corner to find Roman and V still engrossed in their mental conversations.

She looked over her shoulder to where Camlo had disappeared but only saw a wall of black. He should've returned by now. She faced the darkness and listened for him. In the next heartbeat, Camlo screamed her name, the sound full of terror.

"I'm coming!" she shouted and started forward, only to slam her leg against a rock.

She doubled over, pain shooting up the limb as she held her shin with one hand and put her other out in front of her so she wouldn't run into anything.

"Sabina," Roman said as his arm wrapped around her.

She sagged against him, fear surging through her. "Camlo."

"Take care of her," V said as he rushed past them. "I've got Camlo."

"Bina! Bina, help!" Camlo shouted.

She tried to follow V. "I'm coming!"

"Hold on," Roman told her. In the next instant, another ball of light zoomed above them.

Roman then took her hand and led the way. She limped after him, the pain barely registering as she tried to reach her brother. He kept screaming her name, and the longer it took to reach him, the more frightened she became.

They finally found Camlo in another cavern that was so large, a city could fit into it. The light above them rose higher, giving her a meager glimpse of the size of the place.

V was with Camlo, who had squatted down near the middle of the cavern. He had his hands over his ears as he rocked back and forth. No matter how hard V tried to talk to him, it seemed to make things worse.

"I'm here," Sabina said as she knelt next to her brother. "I'm right here."

He threw himself at her, knocking her over. She never loosened her hold on him, despite the fact that he was holding her so tightly that it was difficult to breathe.

"You're okay now. We're here," she said.

He buried his head in her neck and whimpered. She rubbed her hands up and down his back to soothe him. V stood next to them, but Roman walked away to investigate the area.

"What was he doing in here?" V asked her.

She kissed the side of her brother's head. "He needed to go to the bathroom."

"Oh," V mumbled and turned to see what Roman was doing.

Finally, Camlo eased his grip on her. Sabina took a deep breath. Then she asked, "Want to talk about what happened?"

He shook his head.

"Camlo, we need to know what scared you," she pushed.

Roman turned to look at her. "I think I might have figured it out."

"No," Camlo said as he jumped up and ran for the opening. "No. No. Nonononono."

Sabina sat up, but V was already after him.

"V will get Camlo safely back to the cavern," Roman said.

She hesitated, wondering if she should go after her brother. But he didn't call for her. Sabina decided to stay and see what Roman had found. Plus, it was good for Camlo to be around other people.

After climbing to her feet and brushing herself off, Sabina made her way to Roman. "What did you find?"

"This," he said.

She glanced from his perturbed face to the wall. At first, she didn't see anything. She shifted positions, hoping that would help, and it did because the ball of light hovered above her. But she couldn't make out what she was looking at.

"What is it?" she asked.

Roman put his hands on his hips and turned to look at another wall. "Fae."

"Fae?" Sabina moved closer to get another look at the design. It didn't appear to be writing, but since she had no idea what Fae writing looked like, it could very well be that.

Behind her, Roman let out a sigh. "And Druid."

She whirled around. "I can't see much."

"Sorry," he said with a shrug. "Dragons can see as well at night as in the daytime."

"Oh, lucky you," she teased, trying to lighten the mood.

He grinned, but it was gone in the next second. The ball of light above her grew brighter, and then he said, "Four walls. Each one has evidence of Light Fae, Dark Fae, *mie* and *drough*."

"You're saying that the group we've been talking about met here? In this cave?" She wrapped her arms around herself and looked at the walls, trying to determine which was which.

He lifted a brow and shrugged again.

She let out a snort. "That's rather hard to believe. What are the chances we'd come to this particular cave?"

"There's quite a lot that doesna make sense. This is just added to the pile."

Sabina looked at the walls, wishing she could read them. Then she paused. "If I couldn't see them, then Camlo couldn't have either. If that's the case, then what scared him?"

Roman bent and picked up her phone. As soon as he did, the light shone on the wall where there was a drawing of a dragon with a sword plunged through its heart.

"What the hell?" she asked and moved closer. "Is this Fae or Druid?"

"Neither," Roman answered. "This is simply a drawing. There are others between the writing."

She briefly closed her eyes and drew in a steadying breath before she faced him. "What do the writings say?"

He rubbed his chin, anger and agitation flashing in his

eyes. Roman pointed to the left. "That writing simply says Dark Fae." He then pointed behind him. "That says *mie*."

"That's the bad Druids?" she asked.

"Good ones."

She gave a nod. "Right. Go on."

He pointed to the right. "That one says Light Fae."

Sabina looked to the wall before Roman. "And that one says *drough*?"

"Aye," he said, his lips twisting.

"Why? Did they want to make sure you figured it out? It's almost like they're taunting you."

He glared at the walls. "That's exactly what they're doing."

"That's assuming they knew you would be here."

"Oh, I think they were counting on it. For all I know, they wanted us to find it thousands of years ago."

She shifted, the sound of her jacket rubbing together loud in the silence. "And the other pictures?"

As if on cue, the light moved to where Roman pointed. "This one is the wooden dragon found beneath the White on Fair Isle. That," he said shifting slightly, "is V's sword being stolen."

She looked in the direction where Roman had said was the drawing of a dragon with the sword through it. "The first two you know happened. What about this one?"

He released a long breath, his eyes sad. "That's V's sword."

"Who did he kill?"

"This one hasn't happened yet."

She glanced at him as she moved closer to the wall, needing to see the drawing better. "How do you know?"

When he didn't answer, she walked to him and took her mobile so she could shine the light on the drawing. She didn't need to see the dragon in color to recognize that it was Roman.

Her head whipped around to him. "This can't be right."

He swallowed, his shoulders drooping. "The other two happened."

"What of the last drawing?" she asked, walking to where it was. "Has this happened?"

Her words died when the flashlight on her phone shone on the gruesome drawing of dead dragons on the ground. She wanted to look away, but she couldn't. How did this group know all of this would happen?

And then the answer was easy. They instigated it.

She slowly turned to Roman. "They knew you would be here with V."

"They were counting on it, it seems. They put this here, on my land."

"That means they had to know that Con would send you."

He let out a dry laugh. "That means they know my power. That means this group knows all about the Dragon Kings."

CHAPTER TWENTY-THREE

The way Sabina's dark eyes filled with compassion nearly broke the tenuous hold Roman had on his anger. He turned away from the drawing, but the others were there, waiting for him.

Roman squeezed his eyes shut and ran a hand down his face. He knew in his gut that he had to inform not just Con but also all the Dragon Kings. They needed to know this new development. And he hated that it was coming right on the heels of Con's announcement about the weapon.

Who the fuck took the weapon? It had to be someone extremely powerful to not only get through Con's magic, but also leave it intact. There was something Roman was missing, but his mind was too filled with the drawings in the cave to focus as he should.

"Should I get V? He probably needs to see this," Sabina offered. "And I'm sure the two of you will want to talk."

Roman opened his eyes and looked at her. She was remarkably calm. Then again, she had no idea the kind of mess she'd been dragged into. Because she had been drawn, unwittingly.

The quicker he could get her safely back home, the better. For everyone.

"I'll show V later. We need to find the sword," he said.

She glanced at the drawing where V's weapon was embedded in Roman's heart. "Can you hear it?"

Roman rubbed his temple as he sighed. Damn. He needed to get his shit together. "I intended to try, but then I had to get you and Camlo out of the weather."

"Your magic was protecting us," she interjected.

He shrugged, not bothering to comment. "Before I could get everyone settled, we received a . . . message from Con."

Sabina's head tilted to the side, her deep brown waves moving with her. "I take it the message wasn't good?"

"No' in the least."

"Is there anything I can do?"

He grinned despite the situation. "I wish you could."

"Well, I'm not here simply for you to keep warm," she replied with a smile.

Suddenly, an image of them naked, their bodies pressed together as he kissed her passionately as the warm glow of the fire flickered over them filled his head. He grew instantly, achingly hard for her.

As if sensing his thoughts, her smile faded as she stared at him. Everything would've been fine had the longing and curiosity not filled her dark eyes. It was his undoing.

With one stride, Roman was before her. He lifted a lock of hair. The curl was cold and silky against his finger before he let it fall from his grasp.

Unable to stop himself, he ran the backs of his knuckles over her cheek before letting his arm fall to his side. They were in a dangerous situation and had no clue what awaited them. Yet Sabina stood with her back straight and chin lifted, almost daring him to touch her.

It was no wonder she and Camlo had survived so thoroughly. Sabina was a force to be reckoned with. But what made her even more special was that she had no idea. She simply knew what had to get done and did it without complaint.

"Does anything scare you?" he asked in a whisper.

Her lips flashed him a quick grin. "I seem to recall a certain panic attack when you wanted me to ride you here."

In his mind, her *ride* took on an entirely different meaning. His balls tightened, and his blood heated and rushed through him so quickly that he felt it scorching his body. "That's no' what I meant."

"I know what you meant," she replied, never taking her gaze from his. "Everything scares me. But why worry about something I have no control over?"

"Hm," he said and found himself leaning toward her. "That's a good attitude."

She lifted one shoulder in a nonchalant shrug, her body leaning toward his. "Some might claim that I'm burying my head in the sand. I don't do that. I face what comes my way."

"No one could ever accuse you of burying your head, lass."

At the endearment, he heard her pulse quicken. He wished he hadn't noticed because now he knew he would make sure to call her that every chance he got.

He stilled when her fingers touched his. It wasn't an accident, but an intentional movement. And it went through him like dragon fire.

She shifted closer. "You make me feel as if I can do anything."

"You can."

"I'm not sure," she whispered.

They were so close now that with just a small tilt of his

head, he could claim her lips. Her finger hooked around one of his, anchoring them together.

It was exactly what he needed. She rooted him not just to the land but also to her. The last thing he should do was muddy the waters by kissing her, but he couldn't think of doing anything else.

His free hand snaked around her and rested on her lower back, pulling her the last inch that separated them. Her eyes filled with desire as she lifted her face to him.

"Please kiss me before I melt into a puddle," she urged in a voice filled with yearning.

His mind cleared of everything but Sabina. He heard her heart beating rapidly as well as the quickening of her breath. He smelled the wind that clung to her hair and skin. He saw the softening of her lips as they parted, anticipating his mouth.

No longer could he wait to learn the taste of such an exquisite creature. She was an anomaly, a rare mortal that no one could come close to in matching beauty, talent, or heart.

"*Please*," she whispered.

"Och, lass. You ask for something I've wanted to give you since I first saw you."

She swallowed and rested her free hand upon his chest. "What stops you?"

"Knowing that once I claim those beautiful lips of yours, I'll never stop."

A shiver went through her, and she melted against him. Her palm flattened and shifted up his chest to his shoulder, then his neck, then his jaw, to finally come to rest against his cheek.

Desire crackled between them. Hunger, intense and demanding, had its claws buried deeply within both of them. But it felt so good.

His head lowered, and her eyes slid closed. He stopped just short of touching her lips. She held her breath, waiting for him, her fingers now gripping his shoulder.

Roman put that image to memory and closed his eyes as his mouth found hers. She let out a rush of breath and moaned softly. For Roman, a kiss was more intimate than sex itself. You could taste a person's soul, hear their thoughts. See their dreams, their wants.

Their desires.

He spread his hand on Sabina's back and held her against him, needing her close. His lips moved over hers softly, teasing and learning. Every sound, every movement, every touch let him discover more about her.

And just as he suspected, he needed more. So much more.

He took her top lip between his and ran his tongue along it. She jerked before sighing. Then she slid her tongue along his lower lip.

It was his turn to moan. His cock was so hard that it throbbed. He wrapped both arms around her and kissed her, slipping his tongue past her lips to dance with hers. She leaned into him, her hand clinging to him as she gave herself up to him. He deepened the kiss, letting the fiery craving envelop them both.

He couldn't wait to strip her and lick every inch of her body. It was too bad they weren't in a more comfortable place. As soon as that thought went through his mind, he remembered where they were.

And why they were there.

Roman ended the kiss and lifted his head to look at Sabina. Her lips were wet and swollen from his kisses, her eyes glazed with desire. If she looked this tempting after one kiss, she'd have him on his knees when he finally got to see her tousled and flushed from sex.

"You stopped," she said, confusion contorting her face.

He smiled and ran his fingers down her cheek. "We need to get back to Camlo and V."

At the mention of her brother, her eyes cleared. "Oh, no. I forgot them."

"So did I."

"Yeah, but you remembered. I wouldn't have. I was too wrapped up in you."

Roman actually fought not to remove her clothes, lift her in his arms, and thrust deep inside her. Her words and the aching hunger in her eyes made it hard to think of anything but claiming her.

She cleared her throat as she took a moment to get her bearings. Then she stepped back, pulling herself out of his arms. Roman didn't want to let her go, but he couldn't keep her there either.

If he didn't move, he would give in to the longing burning within him and pull her close again. He drew in a ragged breath and turned toward the opening. Sabina walked in front of him. He made the ball of light follow her despite the fact that she had the flashlight from her mobile still on.

Once the dark enveloped him, he ran his tongue over his lips to taste what remained of her. He bit back a moan and walked to the tunnel in time to see her returning to the cavern with her brother and V.

Within seconds, V strode out. Roman moved aside so V could enter. He waited as V found the first carving. His gaze was locked on his friend's face where a frown furrowed deeper and deeper. When V came to the drawing of his sword through Roman's heart, V's head snapped to him.

There was no need for words. What could either of them say? Roman had no intention of fighting V, and he was sure

V felt the same. But that didn't mean anything. This group of Fae and Druids seemed to have the upper hand.

After a moment, V returned his attention to the drawings. His face went slack when he came to the last one of the dragons lying dead.

"I'm no' sure I want to find my weapon now," he said.

Roman moved to stand beside him. "It's yours. It belongs to you. The mortals and whoever else was involved had no business stealing it."

V glared at him while pointing to the scene of Roman's death. "These individuals have a verra thought-out plan, Roman. Look! The other two have come to pass."

"And you believe this one will, as well?"

V threw up his hands and snorted as he took a step back. "Why would you think it wouldna?" He jabbed a finger against his temple. "They fucked with my head. They killed one of Dmitri's Whites. They stole my sword and introduced terrifying magic to a replica of Con in the form of a wooden dragon. Aye, I think they're capable of anything."

"But we're Dragon Kings. We're stronger."

"Are we?" V shook his head as he looked around the cavern. "They put these drawings here for us. On *your* land."

Roman raised his brows as he nodded. "That's true. Everything they've done has been to make us second-guess ourselves and our power. I did it just a few moments ago."

"No longer?" V asked, surprised.

"A wee bit. But I doona believe you would kill me."

V's brows drew together as his jaw worked back and forth. "Nay. But would you sacrifice yourself for the others?"

It was Roman's turn to frown. His head swiveled to look at the drawing.

"I'm no' there," V said. "It's just my sword. And you."

Roman quickly stopped the unease that began to grow within him. "The Druids and Fae have made a mistake showing us this. Now we know what to expect."

"I'm right," V said. "You'd willingly give up your life in order to save the other Kings. Or to return the dragons."

Roman let the silence be his answer. His eyes moved from V to the drawing of the dead dragons. "Are they killed here? Or is this on the other realm?"

"We willna know until I get my sword back."

And that's where the real crux of the problem lay. If they continued on this quest, Roman might very well end up dead. But how could they not? V needed his sword back for many reasons, one of which was learning the fate of the other dragons.

Roman squatted and placed his hands on the rocks at his feet. He opened his magic and listened for the songs of metal. Hundreds of melodies rose up, cascading over him in a wondrous, beautiful cornucopia of music.

But not one of them was from V's sword.

CHAPTER TWENTY-FOUR

Sabina was reeling from the swoon-worthy kiss she'd just shared with Roman. She'd never been swept away by anything so romantic or glorious or . . . erotic.

She was still unsteady on her feet, her lips tingling from the desire he fueled with merely a look. A look that had stolen her breath while making her feel as if she were floating as high as the moon.

It had been an oddly glorious feeling that she was eager to experience again. As her mind remembered the reason he'd stopped the kiss, Sabina looked at her brother. Camlo sat on a rock, staring into the flames with his hands flattened against each other and pointed at the ground as he held them between his knees.

He wore an expression of someone who had the weight of the world on his shoulders. Gone was his easy smile and laughing eyes. A man sat before her now. Whatever happened in that cavern had altered her brother significantly.

"Camlo?"

He didn't look up from the flames or do anything to let her know that he'd heard her.

Sabina made her way to him and sat on the ground beside him. She put her hand on his leg, looking up at him. "Hey, there. Want to tell me what happened in the cavern?"

"Bad things," he mumbled.

"Something was done to you?"

He gave a shake of his head. "We shouldn't have come here."

"I thought you wanted to help V and Roman."

"I do." Camlo's deep brown eyes slid to her.

She watched him for a moment. "I don't understand. What did you see?"

"Roman and V need to leave. No Dragon Kings should ever come here."

That gave Sabina pause. "They're powerful beings. You told me that yourself."

"Some want them gone. They want to do very bad things to the Kings."

She could tell he was beginning to get irritated again. Sabina moved to her knees and took his hands in hers. "Did you tell V what happened?"

"He didn't ask."

"Why didn't you tell him?" she pressed.

Camlo shrugged and looked back at the flames. "Because he knows bad things are here."

That wasn't much of an answer. For the second time in as many days, she couldn't figure out what her brother was attempting to say. He wasn't normally so cryptic, and it was starting to scare her.

She swallowed and gave his arm a shake until he looked at her. "I have to know what happened. Tell me everything."

"It won't change anything."

"You don't know that."

He looked away from her, refusing to speak.

But she wasn't going to give up that easily. "I saw what was on the walls. Did you? Is that what upset you?"

Camlo winced and pulled away as he turned his back to her.

Sabina was so surprised by his actions that she could only stare at him in shock. She climbed to her feet, suddenly feeling so cold that she couldn't stop shaking. "We came to help V find his sword. You gave him the information he needed to know it was here. Now you don't want to help him?"

"If I do, he'll die."

It was said in such a sure, adult voice that for a moment, she wasn't sure it came from her brother. Sabina walked around until she faced him once more. "Just because they find the sword doesn't mean any of those things on the wall will happen."

Camlo's eyes lifted to meet hers. "Bad things, Bina. Very bad things."

"You saw them?"

He shook his head.

She looked askance at him. "There are no animals here. They couldn't tell you."

"But there were," Roman said as he strode into the cavern. "My clan of dragons."

Her gaze snapped from Camlo to Roman. "But . . . how? There are no dragons now." She returned her gaze to her brother. "Camlo? How are you hearing them?"

"Not dragons," Camlo said and shifted to look at Roman. "All the other animals."

Sabina briefly squeezed her eyes closed as her head began to throb trying to figure out what her brother was saying. "Didn't you hear them when we first arrived?"

"No," Camlo said and looked up at her. "They were silent."

Was it coincidence that the animals began talking to him once he went into the other cavern? She looked at Roman and raised a brow in a silent question.

Roman drew in a breath and released it. "Another coincidence."

"I'm beginning to hate that word."

"Me, too," he said.

Sabina squatted in front of Camlo and took his hands. "What did the animals tell you?"

"That the Dragon Kings should leave." He looked at Roman. "Especially you."

Roman tilted his lips. "This is the land I once ruled. I'm no' leaving."

For someone who hadn't been all too keen on coming to Iceland, Roman didn't seem one to scare easily despite the drawing in the other chamber.

Camlo's grip on Sabina's hands brought her attention back to him. "What is it?"

"Bad things," he said again.

"What bad things?" Roman asked. "We need to be prepared so I can protect your sister."

Camlo shook his head in agitation. "We aren't in danger. You and V are."

That drew Sabina up short. She looked past Roman to V who stood at the entrance. "We're here for the both of you. We'll do whatever you want."

"I'm no' leaving," Roman stated.

V gave him a dark look. "We should. We can come back with more Kings."

"That wouldna be a good idea," Roman said. "If bad things are going to happen, we need to limit the number of Kings involved."

Sabina shifted her feet. The more Roman and V talked, the more she began to agree with Camlo. They needed to leave. All of them. She wasn't sure when the feeling began, but now that she acknowledged it, it felt like a pressure on her chest that continued to push harder and harder.

She released Camlo's hands, took a step back, and pushed away at the air in front of her, trying to stop whatever was happening. Her brother looked at her oddly. She kept trying to take a deep breath, but it was like someone had their hands clamped around her lungs so they couldn't expand.

Camlo jumped up and rushed to her as she reached for him, the words to request help lodged in her throat—along with her breath. He screamed her name. She wanted to tell him it would be okay, but she couldn't form the words. And she wasn't so sure everything *would* be fine.

In seconds, Roman and V were with her. The room began to spin, and she couldn't remain upright. Roman caught her when her legs gave out. She held him tightly, trying to let him know that she was scared . . . that she was dying. And all the while, she had her mouth open, desperately trying to drag in a breath.

She could see V and Roman talking, but she couldn't understand them or hear their words. Camlo was crying as he sat at her feet, his big eyes fastened on her as his lips moved. All Sabina could hear was the blood rushing in her ears. It was deafening.

And it was all too much. My God. She was really going to die. Her eyes closed. She was suffocating, and no one could do anything. The Dragon Kings were powerful, why wasn't Roman doing something? Anything? He could keep her warm, but he couldn't give her breath?

"Sabina."

The sound of her name from Roman's lips next to her ear broke through the cloud of fear. She opened her eyes. He looked down at her and smiled calmly.

"Listen to me," he said. "Can you hear me?"

She nodded. It was wonderful to hear again.

"Good. Focus on me. Can you do that?"

Why was he talking to her like she was an idiot? But she nodded again. She felt something against her hand and began to turn her head.

Roman's finger against her chin stopped her. "Look at me."

Out of the corner of her eye, she saw something glowing that grew brighter and larger. His sea green eyes refused to let her look anywhere but at him. That's when she realized that she was no longer gasping for breath. She still couldn't breathe, but there was no pain.

Roman's lips curved upward. "Just a wee bit longer, lass."

Black dots edged her vision. It grew harder to keep her eyes open. All she wanted to do was sleep.

"No' yet, Sabina," Roman said, giving her a shake. "I need you to stay with me."

Yes. She wanted to stay. And perhaps have another kiss. Roman kissed marvelously. It had been years since she'd felt someone's lips on hers, and she was ready for more.

All of a sudden, the weight on her chest was lifted, and she was able to drag in a big gulp of air. She was yanked against Roman as he held her, and to her surprise, she could feel a tremor go through him.

Sabina blinked against the tears and pulled in another deep breath. She shifted her head so she could see V. He was on the other side of her, down on his knees with his head hanging. Camlo was still crying as he petted her feet.

She leaned back to look at Roman and frowned when she saw the weariness on his face that he didn't hide quickly enough. "What happened?"

"Bad things," Camlo repeated.

But he'd said those things would happen to Roman and V, not her. Sabina returned her gaze to Roman. He lifted her in his arms and brought her to the fire, placing her on one of the sleeping bags.

When he started to leave, she grabbed his hand. She was too tired to sit up, but she would get her answers. "Roman."

"It was the Druid and Fae magic," V said as he sat on the other side of the fire. "Roman and I battled against it."

So they had saved her. "Thank you," she told them.

Camlo lowered himself near her head and stroked her hair. "This is not a good place."

"Nay, it isna," Roman said. "But we fought against them and won. That is something."

V gave a shake of his head. "It was too bloody close."

"The sooner we find the sword, the sooner we can all leave," Sabina said.

She turned her head and looked at V. He met her gaze and frowned. "You want to continue despite what has happened since we got here?"

Sabina nodded. "I do. I don't know what will happen once you regain your sword. For all I know, you'll slaughter millions of people or kill Roman, but there's this feeling inside me that says you should recover what was stolen from you. I felt it when you arrived, and now that we're here, I'm more convinced than ever."

"We're taking a chance," Roman said. "It's one V and I gladly take."

"Because you live forever," Camlo said.

Sabina reached over and took her brother's hand, threading her fingers with his.

Roman glanced at them before he nodded slowly. "Aye, Camlo. We are immortal. But the two of you are no'. I'd verra much like if you could tell us anything else you know before you return home."

"No," Sabina said and tried to sit up. After two tries, Camlo propped her up against him as she stared at Roman. "No."

Roman looked away, anger contorting his face as he shook his head in exasperation. "You almost died. How can you want to remain?"

"To help you. To right the wrong that was done to V," she explained. "Yes, I'll admit I'm terrified. But you'll be with me."

V placed his hand on the ground and leaned to the side. "We may no' be able to save you next time."

"I accept that."

Camlo placed his head against hers. "I do, too."

CHAPTER TWENTY-FIVE

Stubborn. That's what Sabina was. And determined.

Roman sighed. He appreciated what she and Camlo wanted to do, but there was a very real threat against them. One that worried Roman more than his concern for his own safety.

He stared at her, unsure of what to do. His hands clenched at his sides. He'd sensed her life draining from her, had felt her fear as she struggled to breathe.

Something sinister had held her in its grip. And it had taken his magic, combined with V's, to free her from it. But why had it attacked Sabina? She wasn't a Dragon King.

But she was helping them.

Roman's eyes swung to V. He lifted his shoulders in a barely discernable shrug. In other words, V was leaving it up to Roman.

"Don't do that," Sabina said.

Roman jerked his head toward her. "What?"

"Talk so I can't hear you." She closed her eyes as she pulled in a deep breath. Then her dark gaze locked on him. "This is my life. I get to make decisions about it, not you."

"And if something happens to you?" Roman pointed out, glancing at Camlo.

His question was obvious, and by the worry that filled her gaze, she had forgotten that problem.

"What?" Camlo asked as he watched them.

Sabina smiled sadly. "It's nothing."

"It is," her brother insisted.

Roman was surprised when Camlo's eyes came to rest on him, as if waiting for Roman to give him the answer. It was obvious that Sabina wouldn't, and if Camlo were going to continue helping them while risking his life, perhaps he needed to know.

"Your sister takes care of you," Roman said. "If something happens to her, someone will need to take her place."

Camlo was silent a moment before he looked down at his Sabina. "We must help them."

"Yes," she said. "We will help them."

Roman wasn't sure how he felt about the siblings continuing with them. On the one hand, he thought they might very well need Camlo. But it was worry about keeping them alive that settled like a stone in his gut.

It was easier to let Sabina and Camlo remain with them since it would take time to return them to Romania, but he didn't want their deaths on his hands. He carried too many ghosts from his past already.

"The decision is out of your hands," Sabina told him.

V gave a firm nod. "So be it."

"What's the next step?" she asked.

Roman ran a hand down his face. "Iceland is a significant territory. The sword could be anywhere, but I'm guessing the people who stole it put it deep within one of the mountains. I'd hoped once here I'd hear its song, but I can't."

V pulled up his knees and wrapped his arms loosely around them. "Camlo, did the animals happen to see where the sword was taken?"

"No," Camlo replied.

Sabina shifted her head to look at her brother. "Can you ask them?"

Camlo's lips twisted into a frown. "They don't like us here."

That got Roman's attention. "Here, as in Iceland? Or here, as in this mountain?"

Camlo shrugged, either unable to discern the answer or unwilling to say. Which didn't help at all.

Roman thought about the cavern with the drawings. He could've taken their group to any part of Iceland, but he'd brought everyone here simply because it was uninhabited and the chance of being seen was remote.

He didn't like the idea that the Druids and Fae had put things in motion so that he would come to this part of the island. Yet, there were other mountains around. How would they know he'd choose this one? How did they know he'd find the cavern? There had been no magic within the rocks. He'd searched for it before entering the mountain. So how had everything happened?

"Fuck," he ground out as it all came to him. He looked at V.

His friend's face was filled with remorse. "I figured it out a moment ago."

"What?" Sabina asked in confusion.

V turned his head to her. "Roman has been trying to piece together how everything has happened since we arrived. Dragon Kings can sense other magic, and neither of us felt anything when we entered the mountain. So it can no' be a spell waiting for someone to activate it. There is no magic here. I'm the trigger. It's what the Fae and Druids did to me that has set everything in motion since we arrived."

"I don't understand," she murmured.

Roman rested a hand on the wall and leaned against the rocks. "This group knew we'd never enter a mountain where we felt their magic without first destroying every spell they put in place. They put all the spells within V, and they initiated once we entered the cave."

"Bad things," Camlo said in a soft voice.

"Verra," V added.

Sabina looked from her brother to V to Roman. "Then what do we do? Turn back?"

"Nay," Roman said.

V's head snapped to him. "No one is going farther but me."

"This group doesna want you to find your sword," Roman said to V. "Let that sink in a moment. Then think about what has happened in the wee bit of time we've been here. They know our vow to the mortals. They know we wouldna allow them to go with us."

"And if you go alone, you fail," Sabina finished.

V got to his feet and stared aghast at Sabina. "If you or Camlo go with us, you will likely die."

"Why don't they want you to have your sword?" Sabina asked. "That question keeps going through my mind. The Fae and Druids had to know that you could return the dragons. They had to know that your sword would locate your brethren so you could see how they are."

Roman dug his fingers into the rock as a deep apprehension filled him. The Kings had no idea where the dragons were. They didn't know if any had survived or if they were all killed. What if . . . ?

No. He refused to even think that the Druids and Fae had anything to do with the fate of the dragons. Because if they did, that meant the group's hand in things had begun long before any of the Kings even realized it.

One way to get an answer was to find V's sword.

Roman dropped his arm and looked at each of the others. "We have to go forward."

"Aye," V said. "I'm going."

"We do this together," Roman stated as he moved in front of his friend.

"Then what's the next step?" Sabina asked loudly before V could argue.

V threw up his hands before letting them slap against his legs as he turned away in exasperation.

Roman knew his friend was upset, but he wasn't about to let V go on this quest alone. Nor would Roman let anything happen to Camlo or Sabina. He and V had saved Sabina once. They could do it again.

He thought about the metals running through the mountain. He heard their songs easily, and would follow them when searching for the particular metal they sought. But he had an idea. Roman returned his hand to the wall and let the songs fill him as he closed his eyes.

They were so numerous and loud that he had to shut them off when he wasn't actively searching, otherwise, they deafened him to everything else. As the melody of the metals filled him, he singled out each one and followed it, mapping it in his mind.

It didn't take him long to realize that there were tunnels that snaked all around them. Some passages had been created by humans, but most were lava tubes. The longer he tracked the metals, the more he realized that many had a large deposit several meters below them.

His eyes opened to find the others watching him. His gaze slid to V as he grinned. "I just mapped the mountain."

V's brows shot up in his forehead. "Have you done that before?"

"I've never had a need. The fact that there are so many metals within it allowed such a feat. The mountain is considerable in size with many tunnels formed from lava beneath. There are others, however, that were cut through the rock by something else."

V's lips flattened. "Mortals? Or Fae?"

"They all lead down," Roman finished with a shrug.

Sabina's dark eyes were troubled as she asked, "To what?"

"Metals run throughout the earth, zigzagging this way and that. But here, in this mountain, there is a place where many of them gather in large quantities before shooting off again." Roman lowered his arm. "The gathering area is a good size."

V asked, "Can you see what's in it?"

"I only see the lines drawn by the metals," Roman replied. "It's how I can tell when there are passageways or caverns, because of the places without the metals."

V rubbed an eye before glancing at Sabina and Camlo. "Then we just need to decide which way to go."

"Bad things," Camlo repeated.

Sabina pushed herself up on one elbow and smiled at him. "We know, but we're prepared this time."

"I need more of the Druid-Fae magic gone and my memories returned," V said suddenly.

Roman frowned as he slowly shook his head when it dawned on him what V was saying. "Do you really want to take the chance that you'll pass out for hours again?"

"We have to know where to go," V said. "I doona wish to wander the mountain for weeks or months. Or years."

"No. No," Camlo said, shaking his head.

Roman didn't like the idea of V being unconscious again for any period of time. The mountain itself had no trace of Druid or Fae magic, but the group had been there. And it left a bad taste in Roman's mouth.

No matter where V went, his mere presence could activate something that then triggered that violent, appalling combination of Druid and Fae magic. But there was something about the cavern that made Roman feel as if they were being watched. He'd felt that way ever since they returned from the other cave with the drawings.

He wanted away from it. As far as he could get. And he wanted the others with him. If Sabina, Camlo, and V remained, he had no doubt that bad things would indeed happen.

"Roman, it's my sword," V said. "It was taken from me by forces I didna remember until recently. There may be something else in my memories that could help us."

Sabina sat up, swaying slightly. "What about telling the other Kings what's going on? Shouldn't they know?"

"Probably," V answered before looking Roman's way.

Roman had been sure of things when he and V left Dreagan. He'd known it would take time, but he was prepared for any eventuality.

Or so he'd thought.

Since meeting Camlo and Sabina, everything was coming unraveled, as if he had no control over anything anymore. He was second-guessing every decision, and overthinking everything else.

Yet, Sabina was right. His brethren needed to know what they'd discovered in case . . . well, in case of the worst.

"Tell them while I'm passed out," V said.

Damn. They were back to that again. "I doona like this cavern."

"I feel it, too," V murmured.

Sabina frowned. "Feel what?"

"The eyes," Camlo said. "Watching us."

"Then why the hell are we still here?" she demanded, outraged.

Roman inhaled and released it as he stared at her.

She rolled her eyes. "Because Camlo and I are mortal and you're worried about us?"

"The tunnels are dangerous," V said.

Sabina slowly climbed to her feet. "Everything is."

"You need more time to rest," Roman said.

She shook her head while issuing a sarcastic laugh. "Nope. Let's go."

"Wait," Roman said as he hurried to her, reaching for her as she tipped to the side.

CHAPTER TWENTY-SIX

Why did being in Roman's arms make her feel so good? Sabina leaned her shoulder against him as the room finally stopped spinning. He held her tightly, securely. And she knew that she was safe.

Despite the attempt on her life earlier.

It was a crazy, weird sensation. To be both petrified from coming so close to death, yet also completely protected from the unseen horrors.

Roman rested his chin atop her head. "You shouldna have gotten up."

"We can't stay here. You said so."

"I was hasty."

Her gaze moved to V, who was watching them with his head cocked to the side as if the entire scene pleased him. How . . . odd. Then again, there was so much about the Dragon Kings that she couldn't quite wrap her head around.

Okay. That was a lie. But that's what made them so appealing.

Or, at least, why she couldn't seem to take her eyes off Roman.

"How are you feeling?" he asked.

She felt horrible. Her chest still hurt, and her head continued to buzz but, worst of all, was the weakness that she couldn't seem to shake off. "Better."

He chuckled softly. "Liar."

Sabina found herself smiling. And she noticed that V was staring at her intently. She cleared her throat and glanced at her brother. Everyone was on edge, though Roman and V hid it better than she did.

"She's right," V suddenly said. "We need to do something."

Camlo wrung his hands as he rose and began to pace. "Bad things. Bad things."

Sabina didn't know if her brother meant that bad things would happen if they remained in the cavern or if they continued onward. Or both.

"I know," Roman said tightly.

She kept her gaze on her brother. "Camlo? What do we do?"

He halted and looked at her, blinking as the shock of her question went through him. After a long pause, his eyes swung to V. "See more," he said and held out his hand.

V shot Camlo a grin. "Are you sure?"

"What do you see when my brother touches you?" Sabina asked V before Camlo could answer.

V's head turned to her. "Glimpses of the past. That's what allowed me to realize that the Druid and Fae magic was there, which then gave me what I needed to begin breaking through their spells. That's why I'm unconscious for so long afterward."

"Oh." That was the only thing she could think to say after such a statement. "And will removing the magic help us find your sword?"

The Dragon King slid his blue eyes to Roman before he shrugged. "It certainly can no' hurt."

"Do it," Roman told him.

Sabina gripped Roman's hand as V turned to Camlo. Her brother walked to V and grasped the Dragon King's arm. Except, this time, V didn't faint.

V winked at Camlo. "Thank you."

"Well?" Roman asked.

V gave a shake of his head, regret linking his face. "Nothing."

Sabina then held out her hand. "Try me. Camlo is only half Romani."

Without hesitation, V walked around the fire. He took her outstretched hand. The jolt that went through Sabina caused her to jerk, and Roman held her tighter. V yanked his hand away and looked down at his fingers with a frown.

"What happened?" Roman asked.

V's blue eyes glittered as he met her gaze. "Amazing."

"V," Roman said in a dangerous voice.

Sabina shrugged her shoulders. "I'm not sure what happened. I felt something go through me."

"But no' when I touch you?" Roman asked.

She glanced at him and shook her head. "Not like that, no."

Because she certainly did feel *something* with Roman. It was warm and tingly and felt so good.

"Again," V said as he held out his arm.

Roman shifted, turning her away from V. "No' until you tell me what happened. I doona want either of you hurt."

"I wasna hurt," V said. "The connection of her Romani blood to the spells put on me by the Druids and Fae is . . . substantial."

The more Sabina learned, the more she was sure her ancestors were involved with the Fae and Druids who were after the Dragon Kings. She might have learned about the Kings when she was a child and didn't hear their full story until a day ago, but the dragons hadn't hurt her.

The Kings hadn't hurt anyone in all the time they'd been on Earth. Why provoke them? Why would a group go after them?

She really wished she could hear her ancestors' side of things. She only had Roman's and V's word to go on. And for some unfathomable reason, she believed them. Mostly because they had been nothing but kind. And the simple fact that the Kings hadn't taken over the world and killed every human had a lot to do with her trust.

No matter how long she lived, she would never forget the sight of Roman in his true form. He was simply glorious, in a frightening and beautiful way.

"Take my hand," she told V.

Whatever was going to happen, someone had to take the first step. That now seemed up to her. She braced herself when V lifted his arm. Their fingers grazed, and once more, a jolt went through her.

Sabina gasped and closed her eyes as all sound was suddenly sucked away. When she opened her eyes, she was inside a cave, but it wasn't the one she had been standing in. There was no fire, but she could see despite the dimness. She turned and saw a form sprawled on the ground. She frowned when she realized it was V.

He lay naked on his stomach as if he'd just collapsed. His hair was long, the dark locks spread around him, partially covering the large dragon tattoo on his back. Her gaze was jerked from the tat when his finger twitched as if he were fighting whatever was happening to him. She could hear a man screaming, but it sounded distant.

She heard something behind her and spun, looking for Roman and Camlo, but they were nowhere in sight. When she spotted the entrance, she walked to it and looked out over the land.

There was no ice, no snow. The moon hung low and full in the sky, shining upon the land with such force that it looked almost like daylight. Her gaze moved lower down the mountain and past the thick forest to the houses in the distance.

She wished she could see more because it looked like a village of some sort. But a glance down showed that the only way for her to leave the cave was to fall several hundred feet.

That's when she heard a sound. She squatted and looked closer to find that it was six men climbing up the side of the mountain.

Sabina was so shocked that she jerked and fell back on her butt. She scrambled to her feet again and whirled around to V. Tripping, she righted herself and rushed to him, falling to her knees beside him.

"V. You need to wake up," she said and shoved his shoulder, unable to move him more than an inch or two. "V. V! Did you hear me? Wake up!"

His head shifted toward her, but he didn't open his eyes.

Sabina grabbed his hands and pulled them over his head as she attempted to drag him somewhere the men couldn't find him. Gritting her teeth, she pulled with all her might but only managed to move V a few inches.

"Shit," she grumbled. "You're heavy."

She did a double-take when she saw something out of the corner of her eye. As soon as she saw the sword, she froze. That's when she knew that, somehow, she'd gone back in time. She didn't know if she was there in reality, or if this were just a glimpse of the past.

Though the fact that she could touch V wasn't keeping her calm. Because if this were a vision, would she be able to touch him?

Her stomach roiled viciously as fear iced her blood. She didn't know what to do. Did she hide the sword? Would that do any good? Where were the Druids and Fae?

V's fingers suddenly wrapped painfully around her wrist. She looked down at him to find his blue eyes open and staring at her.

"V," she said

A frown furrowed his brow. He released her and rolled onto his side then pushed himself into a seated position while braced to the side with his hands.

The men were getting closer. She could hear them, and by the way V's head snapped up, he did, too.

"Get behind me," he ordered.

"They're here for your sword."

V gave a loud snort. "They willna be getting it."

It took a moment for Sabina to realize that they were speaking in Romanian. She swallowed and decided to do as V said. Sabina moved behind him. Then she turned her head toward the sword. If she prevented her ancestors from taking it, then perhaps the Druid and Fae magic wouldn't have V in its hold.

But it also meant that she'd never meet Roman.

She walked toward the weapon and gazed at it in wonder. It was huge. She honestly wondered if she could lift it, even with both hands. She knew next to nothing about swords, but she recognized the craftsmanship of it.

The blade itself was as wide as her palm. There was a Celtic-looking design near the top. The guard looked as if each side were a dragon claw, curved downward toward the blade. The grip was just as beautiful and intricate and appeared to be fashioned after dragon scales. The pommel was made up of double dragon heads, facing away from each other, their mouths open, showing their teeth.

Sabina glanced at V as the men finally reached the cave entrance.

A low sound rumbled from V's chest. "Leave," he ordered the intruders.

They continued toward him, though their steps faltered for just a moment.

"This is my domain," V told them. "You are no' welcome here."

"We're not here for you," one of the men said.

V's head jerked toward him. "Iacob? What are you doing here?"

"We've come for your sword."

V merely glared at them. "I may have sworn an oath to protect mankind, but if you attempt to take what's mine, I will burn you where you stand." His gaze moved over each of them. "*All* of you."

"We must. Ana has seen a prophecy where you kill all of us."

"If you take my weapon, then you'll ensure the prophecy happens," V told him.

But none of the men were dissuaded. There was a standoff, and then suddenly, one of V's knees buckled. He quickly righted himself, but he was too disoriented to remain on his feet.

He dropped down hard on his knees, his hands catching him as he pitched forward. V shook his head as if to clear it as his long, thick hair fell around his face.

"I've no' hurt any of you," he said to the men.

The one called Iacob came next to V and put a hand on his shoulder. "That's what makes this so difficult."

V fell to the side and rolled onto his back. He lifted his head to look at Sabina, his eyes blinking as if trying to clear his vision.

It took just a heartbeat for Sabina to realize that she

stood between her ancestors and V's sword. The fact that
the six men were looking at her made everything that much
more real. She was actually there, not just a visitor getting
a glimpse of the past.

"Give it to us," Iacob demanded.

She shook her head. "It's not yours."

"And it isn't the Others' either."

That made Sabina frown. "Others?"

"The ones with magic. They want the sword."

Her mouth dropped open. "I don't understand. I thought
you stole it for them."

"We're preventing something horrible from happening.
There isn't much time. They're close," he said and glanced
at V. "Too close. You need to give it to us."

"Me?" Now she was truly shocked.

Iacob smiled sadly. "Ana said you were from another
time. I look at your clothes and realize she is right, as usual.
We can't touch the sword first. Only you can, Sabina. You
have to give us the weapon."

Her stomach dropped to her feet. "I . . . I don't know."

"There isn't much time," Iacob stated. "The Others are
coming. Already, their magic affects Vlad. Ana discovered
their plans through a vision. We're putting our village and
families at risk, but we want to help the Dragon Kings."

Oh, God. What did she believe? Was this some trick
from the Druids and Fae? Or was it real?

Her head swung to V. His eyes were on her, staring
intently before his head dropped back.

"They're nearly here," Iacob murmured hurriedly.
"Make your decision."

Everything hinged on her. And she honestly didn't
know what to do.

CHAPTER TWENTY-SEVEN

"Sabina!" Roman shook her but she didn't wake.

He glanced over at an unconscious V, where Camlo was leaning over him. V had finally stopped yelling and thrashing. Roman didn't know what had happened, but whatever it was, he never wanted it to occur again. That was if he could get either Sabina or V to wake.

"Bad things," Camlo murmured.

Roman looked at the mortal. "What bad things, Camlo? I need you to be more specific."

His dark eyes shifted to Roman. "Sabina went to V."

What the fuck was that supposed to mean? Roman looked from V to Sabina. Went to V? V was right here. There was nowhere for Sabina to go.

"Far back," Camlo said and sat calmly beside V while crossing his legs. "She went to the beginning."

Roman couldn't believe what he'd just heard. He stared at Camlo for a long time. Surely, the mortal couldn't be saying what Roman thought he was.

"What beginning?" Roman asked, not masking the frustration or shock in his tone.

Camlo shrugged. "With V. But it can't be changed."

Changed? Roman wanted to know what the hell was going on.

"V can't go with you on the quest," Camlo continued.

Roman ran a hand down his face. "Why no'?"

"He will end up taking your life."

"He wouldna."

But Camlo's gaze said otherwise.

Roman glanced away, trying to sort through the jumbled mess that had started to pile upon them from the moment they arrived in Iceland. He'd known this was a bad idea. He'd known, and still, they came.

Because he owed it to V.

Hell, every King owed V.

"All right," Roman reluctantly said. "When V wakes, he'll get you and Sabina home."

"My sister goes with you."

The entire time, Camlo spoke with the tone of a man. That's what caught Roman's attention. "It's too dangerous."

Camlo nodded. "Bad things."

Roman would be happy to never hear those two words together again. If only he could grasp what Camlo was trying to tell him. If he had Tristan's power, he could get into Camlo's head and see for himself. But he didn't.

"Go," Camlo said. "Now."

"Why? What's the hurry?"

Camlo glanced at V. "He'll be angry at Bina."

Maybe it would be best to keep Sabina and V separated until Roman could sort things out. Right now, he felt as if he were chasing his own tail. For someone who kept tight control of all things, Roman hated this feeling.

"We'll be back," Roman said.

Camlo smiled as Roman gathered Sabina in his arms and got to his feet. He walked to the entrance of the cavern and paused to look back at Camlo and V one last time. They'd wanted answers. Roman could only hope that what they found wouldn't destroy V.

Roman walked deeper into the mountain, using the map he'd formed in his head from the metals. He was careful to keep from hitting Sabina's head against any rocks, but her feet weren't always so lucky.

He bypassed the cave with the drawings and kept going. The ground undulated, and the path twisted erratically. As he walked, his mind kept going over the moment that Sabina and V had touched. Thankfully, he was already holding onto her when she fainted.

V had stumbled backwards and started yelling, trying to hit anything and anyone near him, the rage within him evident in the agonizing sound of his screams. And then he'd collapsed, unconscious.

Roman walked for hours. He paused when the tunnel opened up to three times its size. He gently lay Sabina down and checked her. Then he straightened and blew out a breath.

"*Con*," he said through the mental link.

Immediately, the King of Dragon Kings replied. "*Aye?*"

"*We have an issue.*"

"*Ulrik and Dmitri already filled me in.*"

Roman closed his eyes and dropped his chin to his chest. "*V and I did that so as no' to add more to your already heavy burden.*"

"*It's my duty to carry such things, Roman.*"

"*Then you should know the rest.*"

There was a slight pause. "*Go on.*"

As quickly as he could, Roman laid out all the details since their arrival in Iceland. Con didn't interrupt once, letting Roman speak until he finished.

"*Bloody hell,*" Con murmured.

"Aye."

"Who's with V now?"

"Camlo."

Con said, *"I'll send Ulrik."*

"I doona think that's wise. There is something wrong here."

"Aye, and V being there makes it worse."

"But I think V needs to be here," Roman argued.

"Why is that?"

"How else will the spells work?"

"But he isna with you."

Roman opened his eyes to look at Sabina. *"Fuck, Con. I doona know. Nothing makes sense. I'm no' even sure Camlo knows what he's talking about. The idea of Sabina going back to the time when V's sword was taken is ludicrous."*

"Is it?" Con asked. *"Look at us, my friend. We're no' supposed to exist if you ask mortals."*

"I'm going to keep going. Camlo and V can catch up with us."

"And if Camlo is right? What happens if V blames Sabina for his sword being taken?"

Roman swallowed. *"The only one other than the thieves in the cave was V. Until he remembers, we can blame anyone we want."*

"The drawings concern me. Especially the one with V's sword piercing you."

Roman rubbed his chest over his heart. *"Aye. I'm no' exactly keen on that one either."*

"I knew it wouldna be easy tracking down V's sword, but I didna count on this."

"You couldna have. None of us could."

Con sighed. *"I should send more Kings, but I'm going to heed your words. For now. I know V's sword is important to him as well as us, but I'd rather have both of you safely back at Dreagan than a damn weapon."*

"We'll return."

"Doona make me come looking for you."

With that, the link was severed. Roman felt better relaying the information to Con. Now he could concentrate on locating the sword while the others pieced together this conundrum of Druid and Fae magic—and just how far back their involvement went.

Because Roman really didn't think he wanted to know the answer.

He went down on one knee beside Sabina. As he was bending to lift her, he caught a whiff of steam. He picked her up and spotted the small opening to the right. Curious, Roman made his way to the gap.

As soon as he reached it, he felt the heat from the hot spring and quickly ducked into the space. As he straightened, he smiled at the pool of water where steam rose up in twisting ribbons.

He found a place to lay Sabina before casting a small light so she'd be able to see if she woke. Hot springs did wonders for humans, and he quite enjoyed them, as well.

After everything Sabina had been through, he thought this might help relax her. Once she woke, that is. He was thinking about how long they had been in the mountains when he realized that she was probably starving.

Roman produced a bottle of water as well as food. Then he tried to contact V. There was no response, so he assumed that V was still unconscious. It took little effort for Roman to make sure Camlo had food and water, as well.

After several minutes of gazing at the heated pool, Roman stripped and stepped inside. The water would do wonders for Sabina. He couldn't help but smile as he thought of the other natural hot springs dotting Iceland's landscape.

The dragons had loved them. Although, there wasn't much about this land that his dragons hadn't adored. Snow and ice and fire and steam. They went hand in hand in Iceland.

He leaned back against the side of the pool and spread his arms along the rock. Thinking of the past dragged up memories he was ill-prepared for—but he'd been expecting them.

One particular icy day stuck out more than any other. It was the day he'd become a Dragon King. A day that had destroyed his family.

"I don't like whatever it is making you frown."

His head jerked to Sabina to find her on her side, watching him. Roman pushed off the wall and glided across the short span of water to the ledge nearest her. "You've been unconscious for some time. You had me worried."

"Obviously not too worried since you're swimming," she said with a grin.

He shrugged. "It's a hot spring. I couldna resist."

She sat up and looked around. "Where are we?"

"Deeper in the mountain. And before you ask, Camlo is with V back in the cavern."

He expected her to argue or be upset about them being separated, but she only nodded in response.

"You can stop using magic to heat me," she said as she scooted closer to the water.

It was his turn to smile. "I did as soon as we entered here."

"This place is as beautiful as it is eerie." She shrugged out of her jacket and then pulled off her boots.

"Aye."

"It feels different than the other cavern."

He nodded. Roman couldn't take his eyes from her as she stood and pulled off her sweater and the undershirt together. Then she removed her pants and socks. He took in her figure, letting his gaze run over her curves at his leisure, memorizing her sleek legs, hips, and her full breasts.

His cock jumped, eager to be inside her.

Sabina's gaze met his before she unhooked her bra and removed her panties. He held out his hand as she neared the pool. There were no steps, so he grabbed her by the waist and lowered her into the water.

"This is amazing," she whispered.

He smiled, liking the way her hands rested on his shoulders. She was so close that he was tempted to kiss her again, but there were things he needed to know first.

"What happened?" he asked.

Her gaze lowered to his chest as she inhaled deeply. "I don't know how, but I ended up in V's cave before his sword was stolen."

There was no use asking her to explain how she got there. She wouldn't have any more answers than he did. "Did you see anything?"

She nodded and met his gaze. "I found V unconscious. I tried to move him, and he eventually woke up, but he didn't seem totally with it."

"I'm guessing the Druids and Fae had already used their magic."

"That's my guess. He asked what I was doing there, and I told him someone was coming for his sword. Then the men were there, and V told me to get behind him. The one in charge, Iacob, told V they were there to help."

Roman frowned. "Help? How does taking his sword help?"

"He kept saying he was trying to stop the Others. I gather he didn't know who they were, only that they were powerful. It was Ana who had the vision, expect it was different than what my gran told me. Ana's vision told them to hide the sword so the Others couldn't find it."

When she paused, Roman urged, "And then?"

"V fell over. He didn't quite lose consciousness because he was watching me, but he couldn't move either. Iacob told me I had to give him the sword. Apparently, Ana told them that I'd be there, that I was from the future, and that I was the only one who could take the weapon from V."

How silly for Roman to think he'd figure things out once Sabina woke. "That's why Camlo said I had to get you away from V. Each time V has touched Camlo, he's seen more of that night. No doubt, after your connection, he saw exactly what you did."

"Then he also heard the men," Sabina stated.

Roman shrugged. "We can no' be sure of that. Did you give them the sword?"

She nodded slowly. "I've experienced what the Druids and Fae can do. If they're the Others my ancestors spoke of, I didn't want them to get their hands on the sword—no matter their reasons for wanting it."

"They couldna use it anyway."

"Are you sure?"

As a matter of fact, he wasn't.

CHAPTER TWENTY-EIGHT

Was it heat from the water or the desire pulsing through her that kept Sabina warm? She had a difficult time keeping her thoughts in order being so close to Roman.

His hands were on her bare waist. The water came to the tops of his shoulders, and the only reason she didn't have to tread water was because he held her.

The look in his eyes when she disrobed had made her stomach flutter in excitement while desire throbbed much lower. The warm water slid over her skin, but it was Roman's hands, Roman's body that she wanted touching her.

She knew he was intentionally keeping her from pressing against him. She was glad since it allowed her to actually form thoughts and put words into sentences.

It took her a moment to register that Roman hadn't answered her question. Because he was staring at her mouth. And dear Lord, the havoc that caused within her already heated body was catastrophic.

"Doona look at me like that, lass," Roman murmured in a deep, sexy voice.

Sabina swallowed. All she heard was *lass* in that heart-stoppingly sensual voice. Just that one word, said in his amazing brogue, could bring her to her knees.

The water rippled as his arms jerked. As if he'd almost brought her against him but thought better of it. Why was he torturing her so? She'd briefly felt his arousal when he brought her into the water. He wanted her.

And that made chills race over her skin.

They were both breathing heavily. The steam dampened her hair, making it stick to her face. Neither the ice nor the fire affected Roman. He stood immobile, resolute against it all.

"I'm not surprised this land is yours," she said.

His sea green eyes studied her a moment. "Why do you say that?"

"Passion burns within you as scorching as lava. But you're also as controlled and cool as the ice around us." She slowly caressed her hands over his shoulders. "Fire and ice."

Though no words passed his lips, he said everything through his beautiful, arresting eyes. His desire deepened. And he was pleased by her words.

Very pleased.

His gaze dropped to her mouth again. Breathing became impossible. She wanted his touch, needed his lips on hers again. Yearned to feel his arms holding her once more.

Sabina had always been on her own, and proud of it. She didn't turn to other people for help, not even when her mother and stepfather were alive.

But it was different with Roman. He didn't make her feel weak. In fact, he somehow gave her the sense of being stronger, as if his mere presence allowed her the courage to do things she'd never considered.

Like stripping and getting naked in a hot spring with a

Dragon King who was millennia old. She didn't question the attraction she felt or the undeniable longing that begged to be quenched. She only knew she would find what she needed with Roman.

His hands moved to her back. Slowly, his fingers spread. Then, he gradually pulled her against him.

The first contact of their bodies made her gasp. Her heart skipped a beat when his thick arousal pressed against her stomach. He didn't stop pulling her toward him until her breasts were crushed against him.

His eyes were like green embers, they burned so hotly. "I waited as long as I could before kissing you. With one taste, you shattered what little control I had."

Those words, whispered and laced with desire so thick she could feel it, brought a euphoria she'd never experienced before.

Their faces were breaths apart, their gazes locked together. This moment stopped time, cocooning them in fire while surrounding them in ice.

Her arms wound around his neck as she tilted her head to the side. Roman's head lowered, and his lips found hers. Sabina sighed as her eyes slipped shut.

His kiss was heavenly. The taste of him utterly and unreservedly carnal. His heat stole over her, wrapping around her as firmly as his arms. As the kiss deepened, her mind emptied of everything but the Dragon King in her embrace.

Unable to help herself, she rocked her hips against him. A low, strangled moan rose from his chest as he tore his mouth from hers.

He lifted his head and gazed down at her with ragged breaths. "I want you."

"I wouldn't have climbed in the water if I didn't feel the same. Don't you know that?"

He glanced at her lips and swallowed. "Returning here has been difficult. The sheer depth of the need I feel for you troubles me because I've no' felt it before."

"Stop," she said and put a finger to his lips. "You like to control everything. I get that. But, sometimes, being out of control is needed."

"You doona want me out of control."

She brushed her lips against hers. "Try me."

The words were barely out of her mouth before he swept in and ravaged her lips. It was scorching, blistering. And absolutely swoon-worthy.

He held her with one arm while slipping his other hand beneath her thigh and lifting her legs so he could grind his hard cock against her.

Then he was moving them. The water slicing over her only added to the bombardment of sensations that were swirling in, around—and through—her.

She sucked in a much-needed breath when he pulled his mouth from hers and turned her so that her back was against his chest. Sabina flattened her hands on his hips and shivered when Roman's hot breath brushed her ear.

"There's no going back after this," he whispered.

She tilted her head back against his shoulder. "I need to feel you. Please don't make me wait any longer."

"Och, lass," he said against her ear, his warm breath fanning her neck.

He pulled her up so that her nipples breached the water. Almost immediately, one of his large hands cupped her breast and massaged it. She bit her lip when his fingers hovered over a turgid peak.

She pushed her chest out, trying to make him come in contact with her. A whimper escaped her lips when he moved so as not to touch her.

"Trust me," he whispered.

Was he kidding? Trust wasn't the issue right now. Him touching her, giving some kind of relief was all that mattered. It was all she needed.

His lips met her neck and softly sucked. "I need you aching."

"I am."

"No' enough, lass. No' nearly enough."

His tongue traced a path along her neck in the same pattern that his finger caressed the area around her nipple. It was driving her insane. She couldn't rub against him to ease the ache in her sex, and he wouldn't squeeze her breasts.

Sabina dug her fingers into his legs. "Please, Roman. *Please*."

She was so intent on the teasing of her breasts that she didn't notice his other hand slowly moving down her body until his fingers caressed the swollen flesh of her womanhood.

Her body jerked at the contact. Even to her ears, her breathing sounded harsh and erratic. She needed . . . oh, God. She didn't know what all she wanted, but she knew the person who could give it to her—Roman.

"So beautiful," he murmured as he nipped at her earlobe and slowly ran his finger around her clit.

She tried to turn to face him so she could kiss him again. At least with his lips on hers, there would be some contact. What she had now wasn't enough. But he refused to let her budge.

"Trust me," he said again.

Sabina parted her lips to reply, but a moan came out instead when he slid a finger inside her. But the pleasure was short-lived because he wouldn't move his hand to give her the friction she so desperately needed.

Then, with the softest of touches, he ran the pad of his thumb back and forth over her nipple.

It was wonderful.

It was agony.

Each time he gave her a moment of pleasure, it was followed by the need for more, a desire that he blatantly ignored. She'd claimed that he was controlled, and this proved it. His cock pressed against her back, a constant reminder that he was aching just as much as he claimed, but you wouldn't know it by the way he touched her.

Yet, with every moment that passed, she'd never felt sexier. More desired. Words could never give her what she was experiencing now. Only actions.

"I'm aching, Roman," she said, turning her face toward him. "Can't you feel it?"

There was a beat of silence before he said in a tight voice, "Aye."

She shifted her hips and bit her lip when the action gave her the friction against his hand that she craved.

"I should punish you for that."

His words excited her, something she didn't expect. "H-how?"

He chuckled and gave her nipple a pinch. "Denying you a climax while keeping you right on the edge for hours."

She broke into a sweat just thinking about it.

"You quite like the idea," he said, surprise lacing his voice.

Sabina nodded. "Yes."

He made a sound that rumbled in his chest and vibrated through to his hand. She hissed when he pressed his palm against her clit and did it again.

She grabbed his hand with one of hers, but he stilled. No longer was he teasing her nipple or making that amazing sound. Sabina bit back a sob and returned her hand to his leg.

"There are so many things I want to do to you," Roman said. "So many ways I wish to claim your body. I want to know how long I can hold you on the edge of peaking. I want to know how much you can endure before you beg me for release."

She was begging him now. At this rate, she wouldn't last a minute, and he was talking hours? But she wanted to experience it—at Roman's hands.

He continued. "I want to hear you scream, cry, and plead for me to let you orgasm. I can feel you shaking. A combination of the need thrumming through you now and the thought of what I plan to do to you."

"Yes," she breathlessly replied.

"You're verra tight."

She swallowed and opened her eyes to look at the far wall and the shadows from the light playing upon it. "I need you inside me."

His chest rumbled again. She jerked when it ran through his hand in contact with her clit. One more like that, and she just might come.

Her nipples were stiff, her breasts swollen from his light caresses. And just when she didn't think he could arouse her any more, he leaned her forward until her nipples bobbed in and out of the water.

She had to touch more than his leg. When she felt his cock pulse at her back, she didn't think twice about reaching behind her and wrapping her fingers around his thickness.

"Sabina," he groaned.

Yes! Now, he would know how it felt to be teased so mercilessly.

But she was up against a master, and she lacked the skills to continue her assault.

Roman pressed the heel of his hand against her clit while sliding a second finger inside her. Then he thrust his fingers once, twice. She cried out, her hand pumping his arousal forgotten.

"You really want to be punished," he murmured against her neck.

"I just want you. On me. Around me. In me."

CHAPTER TWENTY-NINE

He wasn't going to last. Roman knew it even as he continued to tease Sabina. He couldn't seem to stop. Her delicious reactions were feeding his need—and it was breathtaking to behold.

Her breasts were more than a handful, her nipples ultra-responsive. He was using the lightest of touches combined with the water, and she was already close to climaxing by the way her body clamped around the fingers inside her.

He'd turned her away from him in a bid to hold off from sinking into her body. But the soft cries and moans falling from her lips were pushing him past the point of breaking.

Though it was her reaction to his desire to deny her that nearly had him spilling his seed on her back. By the stars, she was exquisite.

He was losing control fast. His cock twitched, desperate to be inside her, to feel the wet walls of her body sliding over him.

"Please."

Her final plea did him in. He turned her to face him. She smiled, reaching for him. But he had other ideas. He set her on the side of the pool and moved between her legs that dangled in the water. Her eyes widened as he leaned close to lick her.

"Roman," she whispered and dropped back on her elbows.

He watched her as he licked and sucked her swollen clit. Her hips began to move in time with his tongue. It wasn't long before her body tensed and she climaxed.

Roman hated that he couldn't see her face, but he would get to see the pleasure come over her because he wasn't finished with Sabina yet.

When her body stopped moving, he gently pulled her back into the water with him and held her between himself and the wall. She lifted her face to him and smiled. He couldn't help but grin, knowing that he'd given her that kind of pleasure.

"You aren't inside me," she said.

Roman raised a brow. "You're a wee bit demanding."

"When it comes to you, yes."

He didn't stop her when she wrapped her legs around his waist and then grasped his cock. Their gazes were locked as she brought him to her entrance.

Never before had he been so aware of another individual. Their breaths were in sync, their bodies intertwined. Her lips parted on a sigh as he pushed inside her.

Her arm wrapped around his neck, her fingers sliding into his hair while her other hand rested over his heart. Something passed between them. Something deep, something meaningful.

Something strong.

He didn't want to think about what it was. All he wanted to do was feel. To let go as she'd asked him to do. He was fooling himself because he couldn't completely give up his control. But he could allow more than he usually did.

Her lips curved slightly. Then she leaned forward, their eyes still locked until their lips met. The brief kiss wasn't enough for him.

He stopped her with a hand on the back of her head. His fingers gripped her hair to hold her steady. "You're no' getting away from me."

"Oh, Roman. I'm not going anywhere," she said.

Then she rotated her hips.

He moaned at the feel of her surrounding him. It was . . . amazing.

They began to move, their bodies sliding against each other. The water and steam only added to the event, heightening their arousal.

The rhythm increased as he drove deeper, faster inside her tight body. Her nails dug into him, her breathing ragged and harsh. Water rippled out, sloshing against them with their movements.

It was the most carnal, sexy, beautiful thing he'd ever been a party to in all his very long years. And it was all because of Sabina.

She whispered his name. The sound went straight through his heart, embedding in his bones, his soul, into his very psyche.

He wanted to make love to her for hours, to savor every inch of her beautiful body. But he was already edging around his own orgasm. It wouldn't take much to push him over, but he wanted to see her peak, to witness the pleasure pass over her face.

Her head dropped back, exposing her neck. He leaned forward and kissed down the column until he reached the base of her throat and flicked his tongue against her skin.

She raised her head and cried out as her body stiffened. Roman smiled as he watched the ecstasy fill her while her body clamped around his staff.

He was so intent on watching her that he lost control for a split second. No longer could he hold back his climax. Suddenly, it was there, and he was pumping hard and fast.

Her arms came around him as he buried himself deep and jerked from the force of the orgasm.

They held each other silently, their breaths filling the cavern as the water gently stilled. It was sublime, a moment that could never be taken from him.

Without a word, he pulled out of her but kept his hold on her and climbed out of the pool. He knelt and laid her on the rocks while resting on his forearm beside her.

She stroked a hand down his face. "Wow."

He didn't bother hiding his satisfied grin. "That's nothing compared to what I have in store for you."

"I can't wait."

He saw the slight frown. "But?" he pressed when she didn't continue.

"I don't have sex. I mean, obviously I have before. But not on a regular basis."

"And you're concerned about getting pregnant?"

She nodded, a worried look contorting her face.

He pressed his lips to hers and leaned back. "I forgot to mention that mortals are unable to carry bairns from a Dragon King. Few actually get with child, but the ones who do, doona carry the bairn to term."

"Dear God," she murmured. "Then I pray I'm not one of the few who get pregnant. I can't imagine losing a baby."

He grunted, not wanting to talk about that. "It probably willna happen."

"Probably isn't a certainty."

"Then we abstain."

She flattened her lips, not happy with his reply. "Can't you use magic or something?"

He laughed. "Nay, lass. I can no'. Using magic for something like that is risky, especially for the mortal."

"So you just chance it?"

Roman gave a nod. "Aye."

He then rolled onto his back. She immediately came up on her elbow, but it wasn't his face that interested her. He remained still as she ran her hand over the tattoo covering his chest.

"This is spectacular. You got this when you first shifted?"

He nodded, watching her. Her face was full of wonder and interest. He quite enjoyed the feeling of her fingers caressing his skin.

"Did it hurt?" she asked.

"The first time we shifted didna feel good. We were so shocked that none of us realized we had the tattoos. Everyone assumes we got them because we shifted."

"You sound as if you have another theory."

He smiled and put a hand behind his head. "Because I do."

"Well?" she urged.

"Who is to say we didna always have them? Maybe they just couldna be seen beneath our scales."

"But once in human form, they became visible." She twisted her lips and raised her brows. "I can see that."

He shrugged. "It's just a theory. We'll never know."

Her gaze dropped back to his chest. He knew his tattoo by heart. It was a dragon in flight, wings up and tail trailing behind as the dragon breathed fire.

"Mesmerizing," she said. "Just like you." Her gaze lifted to his face. "Both as a man. And a dragon."

He put his free hand on her back and smiled. She'd never know how much those words meant to him.

"And the ink?" she asked. "I gather it's exclusive to the Dragon Kings."

"Aye."

"Why black and red?"

He shook his head as he shrugged. "Why did each of us get the dragons we got? Why were we born into the clans we were?"

"Well," she said as she tapped his tat. "I know why you got this design."

"Do you?" Now he had to hear her thoughts. "Why?"

Her finger traced the outline of fire. "Because this is your land. Your dragon looks intense, controlled. Very much you. But I see the fire. Again, you."

He pulled her down on top of him. "I never thought about it like that."

"You just needed me to see it."

"I think I did."

They grew silent as their gazes held. It was Sabina who broke eye contact and rested her head on his chest. "As wonderful as this interlude has been, it doesn't change the fact that I'm the one who took V's sword. He'll never forgive me."

"I think Camlo knew somehow. He kept telling me to take you out of there."

Her breath fanned his chest as she sighed. "I can only hope that V was aware enough to hear the conversation I had with my ancestors. He has to know that I had no malice toward him. I was doing it to keep the sword away from the Others." She turned her face against him. "If I can believe what my ancestor told me that is."

Roman rolled her onto her back and waited until she looked at him. "You had moments to make a decision. You took what your gran told you, what you learned about the

Dragon Kings, and what we've discovered since we've been in Iceland. I would've done the same thing."

"What if the Others aren't the Druids and Fae?"

"I doona know. We'll cross that bridge when we come to it, and I suspect we'll learn verra soon just who was behind everything. My bet is still on the Druids and Fae. Your ancestors would probably have begun to know Druids, but they wouldna be aware of the Fae."

Sabina issued a half-hearted shrug. "I suppose."

He jumped to his feet and pulled her up with him. "Get dressed before I have my way with you again."

She laughed, but it was gone quickly as her thoughts turned back to their discussion.

He grabbed his clothes and yanked them over his damp skin. "What do we know for certain? Someone wanted V's sword."

"Right," Sabina said as she dressed.

"And we know that magic was used on him. Until we have Tristan delve into V's mind, we willna know what kind of magic, but my guess is that it was the same Druid and Fae mix as the wooden dragon."

Sabina fastened her bra and looked at him. "That's obvious by the drawings."

"Perhaps. I know the drawings are significant, as is what has happened to us while we've been in this cave. I've no doubt that things willna get easier as we get closer to the sword."

He finished dressing and waited until she put on her last boot and straightened. Then he said, "I believe that whatever you did about V's sword, you did it to help us and protect him."

"I was protecting you, as well. You didn't hear the fear in Iacob's voice, Roman. They were terrified of the Others."

"We assumed your ancestors left in fear of V's reprisal. No doubt they feared the Others, as well."

She crossed her arms over her chest. "But nothing happened to my family. They weren't harmed by V or the Others."

"Are you sure? If the Others are the Druids and Fae—and I believe they are—they've done horrific things to us. What do you think they'd do to the family who thwarted their plans?"

Her face paled. "But wouldn't someone have noticed?"

"Look how long it's taken the Others to get to us."

The breath left her in a whoosh. "Dear God."

CHAPTER THIRTY

Dreagan

Con stood inside the mountain connected to the manor, staring at the four sleeping silver dragons. He came to see them every day. Mostly to remember his past. Because it was becoming harder and harder to recall the time when the dragons ruled.

He didn't move when he heard someone approach. Con wasn't surprised to see Ulrik. The Silvers were of his clan, after all. Con kept his gaze on the dragons.

"Care to share what's on your mind?" Ulrik asked as he came to stand beside him.

Con gripped the pocket watch in his trouser pocket. "No' really."

"I know that look, old friend. Something troubles you, deeply."

"If you had the chance, would you wake your Silvers and release them?"

There was a beat of silence. Out of the corner of Con's eye, he saw Ulrik face him. He could well imagine the thoughts going through his friend's mind.

"After thousands of years of trying to stop me from

doing that verra thing, I want to know why you ask me this now?" Ulrik demanded.

Con looked at the floor and shook his head. "It's just a question."

"There's quite a lot of shite going on at the moment," Ulrik said. "Henry, along with Esther and Nikolai are on Eigg, digging deeper into Henry's and Esther's Druid roots. Dorian is in New York, tracking down the relic Ryder discovered. And then there's V and Roman, searching for V's sword."

Con stepped closer to the cage containing the dragons and put his hand on a bar. "That's only a drop in the bucket."

"I wasna going to bring up Usaeil, the Dark Fae, the missing weapon, or the wooden dragon again."

"We should've left with our dragons."

Those words had been rattling around in Con's head for over a year, and he finally spoke them. When silence met his statement, he turned his head and found Ulrik's gold eyes trained on him.

"This is our land, our home," Ulrik stated.

Con shrugged one shoulder as he dropped his hand. "Then we should've wiped out the humans."

"Where is this coming from?"

"Too many years of thinking and wondering."

Ulrik leaned a shoulder against the bars. "We're no' killers. It's why all the Kings agreed to protect the mortals."

"They destroyed us. We were vast in number and mighty in strength, and now it's all gone."

"It's no'."

Con raised a brow. "Really? What do you think will happen if V finds his sword? That we'll check on our dragons and that'll be it? What if they're dead? What if they're all gone?"

"What if they're no'?" Ulrik countered.

Con nodded, a rueful smile twisting his lips. "Aye. What if they're no'? Do we leave them there? We certainly can no' bring them home."

Ulrik looked away and sighed. "We can no' change the past."

"But we can stop making the same choices."

Ulrik's head snapped back to him. "Meaning?"

"If V reclaims his sword and the dragons are alive, I think we should go to them."

There were several beats of silence as Ulrik stared at him. Then he pushed away from the bars. "What of Eilish and the other mates? You want them to leave their people?"

"We sent our dragons away for the mortals. We've lived thousands upon thousands of years, hiding who we are while fighting to keep the mortals safe. And for what? They'll hunt us if they discover who we are."

"No' all of them," Ulrik argued.

"Some would. And you know it." Con walked around the cage until he stood opposite Ulrik. "I doona expect that all the Kings will agree with my decision. But think about this, Ulrik, if you had the chance to wake these last remaining dragons before you, those of *your* clan, and let them live free with the others, would you?"

Ulrik gave a single nod. "You know I would."

"I truly believed that one day we could resolve our issues with the mortals and return the dragons. It was a foolish dream, one that you knew would never happen from the start."

Ulrik strode around the cage to stop beside him. "This is more than what's going on. What have you found out?"

There was no use hiding it from Ulrik or the others. Con

twisted the dragon head cufflink at his wrist. "Roman contacted me."

"Good," Ulrik said. "I knew one of them would. Are they close?"

"I doona believe so. I let Roman know that you and Dmitri had filled me in on what had been going on. But it seems that both he and V were no' exactly forthcoming in what they shared with you."

Ulrik raised a black brow. "Meaning?"

"There is a verra real possibility that the Druids and Fae are also responsible for manipulating the humans to take V's sword."

"Bloody hell," Ulrik murmured.

Con glanced at the Silvers. "Both Roman and V are sure that the same group of Druids and Fae put a spell on V so he couldna remember where he was when his sword was taken."

"Why would it matter if he remembered where he was, though?"

"Because he would then link it to the mortal thieves."

"And then to Sabina's ancestors," Ulrik said, nodding.

Con dropped his hands to his sides. "Roman said that V touched the female. Both became unconscious, but Camlo was insistent that his sister and V be separated."

"Has either Sabina or V regained consciousness?"

"V willna respond to me," Con said. "Then again, it isna the first time he's done that."

Ulrik shrugged. "Then I will go to find him."

"Whatever spell was put on V, it was unlocked as soon as they entered the mountain. Sabina was nearly killed by an invisible force that tried to suffocate her. V's and Roman's magic stopped it, but it was close from what Roman said."

"And Roman?"

Con raked a hand through his hair. "He's no' checked back in with me yet. He intends to continue looking for the sword. He believes it's better if V isna with them."

"V willna like that."

Con looked at the ceiling over the cavern and blew out a breath as he put his hands in his pockets, his fingers grazing the pocket watch again. "Take all of this, coupled with the drawings they found in the mountain, and what does it tell you?"

"That the Fae and Druids have been working together for a long time."

"Aye. Why? When the mortals were first here, there were no Fae."

"Obviously, there were."

Con shook his head, not liking that statement. "Then why return much later and pretend as if they just discovered this realm?"

"Maybe only a few Fae visited," Ulrik offered.

"And they decided to team up with Druids? We're missing something."

Ulrik scratched his jaw. "Aye, but we willna find it standing here. Or by leaving this realm."

Con cut his eyes to Ulrik. "You think to change my mind?"

"You've never backed down from a challenge. Why start now?"

"Because we've lost everything."

Ulrik stared at him a long moment. "No' everything."

"You want to continue living like this? What about the mates going insane? Thanks to you, they all know that now."

"We'll cross that bridge when we come to it."

Con felt the anger he kept tightly leashed bubbling inside him. "As soon as Hal took Cassie as his mate, we came to that bridge. You saw Rhys when he thought Lily was dead. Magnify that a hundredfold when one of you have to decide whether to let your mate continue living in madness or take their lives."

"Neither Hal nor Ryder were the first to fall in love," Ulrik said, looking pointedly at Con. "Besides, the Druids at MacLeod Castle are handling it fine."

"Doona attempt to argue this with me. You know how true your words were when you told Darius that the mates would go insane."

Ulrik snorted as he shook his head in exasperation. "And you think taking the mates from their realm will help? Being away from their kind will only bring on the madness sooner."

"I know."

Ulrik's brows knotted as he took a step back. "We can no' wipe out the mortals and take back our realm either."

"I know." This was something Con had been aware of for eons.

"You still doona think we should've taken mortals as mates."

Con slowly shook his head. "You've found happiness, but how long will it last? The devastation of losing your mate will destroy you."

"I doona intend to lose Eilish."

Con didn't want to argue because only time would bring the answers each of them sought. He turned on his heel and started walking away.

But Ulrik's voice stopped him cold.

"You loved once, too."

Con looked over his shoulder at Ulrik. "And look how that turned out."

"That was your fault."

"Aye."

Surprise crossed Ulrik's face as he walked to Con. "You admit it?"

"I always have."

"But . . . why?"

"Leave it, old friend."

Ulrik glared, his gold eyes blazing. "I know you, remember? You wanted the same happiness I have, but you didna believe you could have it and be King of Kings."

Con held his gaze, not bothering to reply. There was no need to talk about any of this. What was done was done. And there was no going back to change any of it.

No matter how much Con might wish otherwise.

How different things would be if Con could. The Dragon Kings weren't killers, no. But had they refused the humans, things would be very different.

No doubt another Dragon King would have defeated him eventually. But he would've ruled the Kings. And maybe he would've found a dragon for a mate. Con wondered if he would've had children.

Life would have gone on as it had for millions of years. None of the Kings would've had the need to shift again, and none of the horrors they were facing now would've come to pass.

No doubt the Fae would still have come, but they wouldn't have stayed long. And Con never would have gotten mixed up with Usaeil, which had to be his biggest mistake.

V wouldn't have had to spend so much time sleeping because his sword would never have been taken because they wouldn't have had to use it to open the dragon bridge.

If only Con could go back and change that one important decision to open their home to the mortals.

"I'm right," Ulrik said.

Con lifted one shoulder in a shrug. "That had a lot to do with my resolve to remain alone."

"Are you sure it wasna because you were scared? Afraid of how it felt to be in love? To love so deeply that nothing else mattered—including us or Dreagan?"

"I've no' thought about that in eons," Con lied and walked away before Ulrik could ask any more questions.

CHAPTER THIRTY-ONE

"V?"

No matter how many times Roman called out to his friend, V didn't respond. Roman could only hope that V was still unconscious and not ignoring him as was his friend's habit.

"You want to go back, don't you?"

Roman turned his head to Sabina as she finished the last of the peanut butter and chocolate protein bar. After the realization that her family could still feel the retribution of the Others, Sabina had grown quiet as she shifted to internal thoughts.

He gave her the space because he had his own things to sort through. Namely, V and what to do.

"Aye," he replied.

"Then go. I'll wait."

He shot her a dark look. "No' going to happen."

"You've been trying to reach him through your mental thing, right?"

Roman grinned as he nodded. "Aye."

"And I take it he isn't responding."

"V can be stubborn that way. When we woke him from

his dragon sleep months ago, he left Dreagan without telling any of us to look for his sword. We couldna find him, and he wouldna answer us. No' even Con."

Sabina walked to him and put a hand on his arm. "I'll be fine."

"I doona want to test that theory. Nothing happened when we first arrived either."

She crossed her arms over her chest, her hip cocking out to the side as she gave him a stern look. "You can either go back to V, or we go forward, but sitting idle isn't doing anyone any good."

"You're quite bossy."

"You like it," she said with a wink.

In fact, he did. His arm snaked out and pulled her against him. He gave her a long kiss before he said, "V can always catch up with us."

"Yep."

"Are you worried about your brother?"

She glanced away, licking her lips. "Yeah."

"Want to go back?"

Sabina hesitated. "Yep."

"Then that's what we'll do."

She stopped him when he made to move. "Camlo wouldn't have made you take me away if it wasn't important. I don't understand how my brother knows these things, but he's never wrong. I have to trust that V will take care of him. And despite Camlo's mental challenges, he gets by pretty good."

Roman could tell she was struggling with leaving her brother. Roman couldn't imagine what she must be going through, and it was one of the reasons he was trying to get V to answer him. He was also concerned about Camlo.

"It'll be okay," Sabina said, turning her face away. "It has to."

He put a finger under her chin and moved her head so she looked at him. "It will be. Trust me?"

She smiled softly. "Yes."

"Good. Then onward we go. It's going to get colder outside of this chamber."

"Romania isn't exactly the tropics. I can handle it. If it gets too bad, I'll let you know." He made to argue, but she said, "Dragon Kings don't use magic like that, remember?"

He quirked a brow. "Aye, lass, but we do protect mortals."

The bright smile she gave him made him wish they had more time to spend at the hot spring.

Roman took her hand and led her from the chamber back into the tunnel. He might not be affected, but he felt the change in temperature as they entered the tunnel. He glanced back at Sabina to find her grinning at him.

"I'm fine," she assured him.

He continued onward, keeping the ball of light over her so she could see. The passageway was as black as pitch, and he didn't want her tripping.

As they walked, he opened the mental link and tried V again. When his friend didn't answer, Roman then called to Ulrik.

"Are you all right?" Ulrik asked.

"I take that to mean Con told you?"

"Aye." Ulrik sighed loudly. *"He's . . . no' himself."*

"I knew I shouldna have told him."

"No," Ulrik hastened to say. *"You did the right thing. He can handle it."*

That made Roman frown. He hid it while he jumped down a small drop and then reached for Sabina. *"You just said he wasna himself."*

"He's regretting everything. He's talking about leaving Earth when we find the dragons."

"Fuck me."

"He's shouldering the responsibility for everything."

Roman didn't like the concern he detected in Ulrik's voice. *"You're going to watch him, right?"*

"Con doesna need a babysitter. He willna accept what it is he really needs."

"You mean—"

"Aye," Ulrik interrupted him. *"That's exactly what I mean."*

"Do you think he'll do it?"

"No' in a million years."

Roman hesitated, hating having to bring up the reason he'd contacted Ulrik. *"You know we'll return as soon as we're able."*

"I know. I gather you didna call to check up on Con? What can I help with?"

"It's V."

"You have no' been able to reach him either?"

"No." Roman looked back at Sabina. She gave him a thumbs-up then pointed ahead, silently telling him to stop checking on her.

"You want me to go to him?"

"You still have the bracelet, right? I thought you could pop in and see if he's awake. Camlo, Sabina's brother is with him."

"She's worried about Camlo?"

"I am, too. I'm no' sure what V's going to do when he wakes."

Ulrik made a sound. *"Why do you think that? Shite, Roman. Have you found out something more since you spoke to Con?"*

"*Aye,*" he said, inwardly grimacing. "*When V and Sabina touched, I told Con that V began hollering before fainting as Sabina did. I didna know until Sabina woke that she was transported back in time. To V's cave the night his sword was stolen.*"

"*Shite. I doona even know how to respond to that.*"

"*It gets worse. She spoke with the men, her ancestors, who stole V's sword. They said they were there to make sure the Others didn't get it.*"

"*Others?*" Ulrik repeated.

"*I think they meant the Druids and Fae. Ana, who had the vision about the annihilation from the Dragon Kings, told the men that a woman from the future would be with V, and that she had to be the one to hand them the sword.*"

"*Please tell me V wasna aware of all this.*"

"*I believe he was. Or he is now.*"

"*Dammit,*" Ulrik muttered. "*Tell me exactly where on Iceland I need to go.*"

Roman gave the location, then said, "*I doona think V should leave the mountain.*"

"*We'll see how he is when I get there. I'll let you know.*"

Roman severed the link. The deeper he went into the mountain, the more nervous he became. It was relatively easy to navigate, other than the dark. But that would never hamper a Dragon King.

And the Others would know this.

They could be walking right into a trap. One no doubt set for V. Or any Dragon King.

Roman looked at Sabina, who was right behind him. She kept a tight hold of his hand as they walked. "Why do you think you had to be the one to give the sword to your ancestors?"

"I don't know," she answered. "I asked, but Iacob never

answered. There wasn't exactly a lot of time for conversation."

"I wonder if you touched V again if you could go back and get more answers."

She halted and waited until he looked at her again before saying, "I don't want to go back. Mainly because I feared I'd be stuck there. The entire episode was frightening. I couldn't shake the feeling that there was something ominous coming for me."

"Like the Others also knew you'd be there."

Sabina came even with him. "Yes. But if it'll help you and V, then I'll do it. I want answers as much as you. Well, maybe not as badly as V," she said with a grin.

He liked that she was trying to make him smile. He tightened his hand around hers and gave her what she wanted. "I doona want you to have to return to that time if there's another way."

"But there probably isn't one," she finished with a firm nod. "I understand."

"I keep expecting you to tell me that you've had enough and willna help me anymore. After all, we've taken you from your home, separated you from your brother, caused you to jump back in time, and nearly got you killed."

She faced him and put a hand on his chest. "First, you didn't make me leave my home. That was my decision. As for distancing me from Camlo, you did it because he told you to. And you had nothing to do with me time traveling or the decisions I made while there. And let me remind you that you saved me from suffocating.

"I'm not finished," she said when he opened his mouth to speak. "Secondly, I have this feeling I can't explain that keeps telling me I need to help you. It may go against the story my gran told me, but even she said stories change as they're passed down. She kept telling me to remember every word so I wouldn't change anything."

Roman took her hand from his chest and kissed her palm. "Aye, but something was obviously changed."

"On purpose, perhaps?" she asked, brows raised.

"There are a million guesses, and we're no' likely to learn the answers."

Her lips twisted as she rolled her eyes. "I don't like that."

He tugged her after him as he started walking again. "We're still searching for answers about the wooden dragon from a few months ago. We've learned a little more."

"Which only leads to more questions."

He grinned at her. "That's usually how it goes."

"It's beyond frustrating."

"Aye, lass, it is. I meant to ask, how did you get back to this time?"

She shrugged. "As soon as I handed over the sword, I was back here. I don't think I did anything."

They walked a little way in silence before she asked, "How far down do we go without finding the sword before we call it quits?"

"I'll stay down here until I find it. I have to."

She nodded, tucking her hair behind her ear. "You believe it's here."

"The animals told Camlo your ancestor brought it here. If it had been taken, they would've conveyed that to him. Why? What's wrong?"

She glanced nervously at him. "I can't put a finger on it, but the farther we walk, the more I want to turn around and run back the way we came."

"I can return you."

She shook her head violently. "No. I'm going forward.

I want to know how I'm involved. I *have* to know. My family began this, and now, here I am. None of it makes any sense."

"You'll probably never get answers."

"In other words, I'll never know if I'm helping the Dragon Kings or making things worse?"

He shot her a quick look. "What do you mean?"

"Ever since you told me that the Others could be biding their time to exact their revenge on my family, I've been wondering if my being here, helping you and V, might be the thing that prevents V from reclaiming his weapon."

A chill went through Roman. With what he'd learned of the Others, that sounded exactly like something they would do. Just to fuck with the Dragon Kings.

"Do you still want me with you?" Sabina asked.

He gazed into her dark eyes and smiled. "I'm a Dragon King, lass. The Others are going to find out just who they've picked a fight with. We protect our own, and those we call friends. And to answer your question, aye, I want you with me."

"Good," she replied and lifted her chin as she squared her shoulders. "Let's find the sword then."

CHAPTER THIRTY-TWO

Overconfidence. Sabina was pretty sure that wasn't exactly a virtue. Then again, it was hard to keep track when she was with an immortal Dragon King.

She covertly cut her eyes to him. And she'd made love to him. She still couldn't believe it. His hands, his mouth had been on her body.

And he'd given her pleasure, unlike anything she'd experienced before.

Granted, her so-called experience was on the almost non-existent side, but she did have a little. Honestly, she didn't think it would matter if she'd had hundreds of lovers. Nothing could have prepared her for Roman.

The fact that he continued to hold her hand made her absolutely giddy. Though that was paired down significantly because of where they were.

She was extremely grateful for the light he provided. Otherwise, she'd have had to hold her phone up and use that. There was no telling how long the battery would last, not to mention that her arm would surely get tired.

Sabina looked around the tunnel. The part they were in now made their progress slow significantly. The ground was littered with jagged rocks. The passageway was wide, but the ceiling was low enough that Roman had to walk hunched over.

It was weird to see the walls and ceiling nearly smooth and the ground so rocky. Several times already, she'd twisted her ankle. Had she not had hold of Roman, she would no doubt have fallen.

She picked her way through the rock, hoping they reached a smoother section soon. Her thighs burned, as did her arm that was holding onto Roman so tightly.

What seemed like an eternity later, the rocks finally began to lessen, making their walk easier. She inwardly snorted. There was no *their*. Roman made his way with no problem. It was almost as if the rocks themselves moved out of his way. She was another matter entirely.

As soon as she found a cleared section, she halted and bent over, bracing her hands on her knees as she drew in breaths to calm her racing heart. The muscles of her legs were fatigued to the point that she wanted to sit, but if she lowered herself to the ground, it was likely she wouldn't get back up for some time.

"Let's rest," Roman said.

Sabina shook her head. "I'm fine. I just need a second."

She didn't want to be the reason that they had to stop. They weren't on a timed schedule, but the sooner they found the sword, the better for everyone.

Her eyes snapped open when she heard something near her. As soon as she saw Roman sitting against the wall with his legs outstretched, watching her, she gave up her fight and sank to the ground.

"Needing to take a break doesna make you weak," he said.

She shot him a look. "You'd keep going if you were alone."

"Maybe." He held out his hand, and a water bottle appeared.

When he handed it to her, she couldn't get the cap off quickly enough to drink down the refreshing liquid. She'd been so focused on not falling on her face that she hadn't realized how thirsty she was.

"Hungry?" he asked.

She looked at him while finishing the last of the water. Sabina smacked her lips together and nodded. "A little."

"Doona wait to tell me you need food or water. I tend to forget such things."

Because he didn't need them. Sabina couldn't imagine a life where she didn't have to eat, sleep, or rest. Her productivity could triple. She could put out dozens more pieces of jewelry and increase her and Camlo's income drastically.

"Did you hear me?"

She turned her head to Roman. "I did. Sorry. I was just thinking how life would be if I didn't have to eat or sleep."

He chuckled, his lips curving into another of his sexy smiles. "Do you no' enjoy eating?"

"Not when I have to fix every meal."

"You willna be cooking now. What do you want?"

She leaned her head back and laughed. "Anything?"

"Anything."

"Really?" she asked as she looked at him.

He met her gaze. "Of course."

"I thought you didn't use your magic for things like this."

"Sabina," he said, his voice dropping an octave. "I'll no' allow you to starve. Now tell me what you want to eat."

So many things came to mind, but she focused on items that would give her energy to continue this harrowing journey. Maybe later, she'd ask for a slice of cake. "A ham, cheese, and tomato sandwich on a croissant. Also a banana and some cashews."

"That . . . isna what I was expecting."

In the next second, her order was in her lap. Sabina didn't hesitate to take a bite of the sandwich. As soon as it filled her mouth, her stomach grumbled, begging for more as if she hadn't eaten the protein bar at the hot spring.

Three bites later, she realized that Roman was staring at her. "What did you expect me to order?" she asked before taking another bite.

"Lobster, maybe?" he said with a grin.

"I've never had lobster. I might not like it."

He crossed his arms over his chest and made a sound in the back of his throat. He seemed content to watch as she finished the sandwich, another bottle of water, and was munching on the banana.

"I don't think I've ever had anyone stare at me while I ate. Want a bite?"

He grinned as he shook his head. "Do you want more?"

"I still have the bag of nuts," she said, holding them up. "I'm saving them to snack on later. They're very high in protein."

"Is that so?"

She nodded and finished the last bite of banana. After she'd swallowed it, she rested her hand on her stomach and sighed. "Thank you. I didn't know I was so hungry."

"It's been hours since you ate, and obviously, the protein bar didna do enough."

Sabina glanced around at the darkness that edged the soft light above her. "How long have we been down here?"

"About eighteen hours."

No wonder she was so tired. With her belly full, sleep called to her, but she refused to give in. "Shall we go?"

"No' now," Roman said. "Let your food digest."

To her surprise, he pulled her toward him so that her head rested on his legs. She sighed contentedly when he started playing with her hair.

"You really don't like being here, do you?" she asked softly.

"As in the mountain? I'm used to that."

"Iceland."

He was quiet for a heartbeat. "Ah." Another pause. "No, I doona."

"How long has it been since you've been here?"

"This is my first time back."

She rolled onto her back to look at him, shocked to her core. "Since the dragons left?"

He gave a nod as he looked down at her. The shadows hid his eyes, but she doubted she'd see anything in them anyway. Roman's control over his emotions when it came to his homeland was limitless.

"I see."

She rolled back onto her side, and he continued playing with her hair. But her mind couldn't help but try and figure out why he didn't like it here.

The land was harsh, yes, but dramatically beautiful, as well. She wished she could've seen it with him and his clan of dragons flying around. Their pale blue scales would look amazing against the bright white snow, the vivid green during the summers, the stunning waters from the outdoor hot springs and the glaciers.

"I told you I was a twin. But I didna tell you that I had an elder brother."

She remained still, barely breathing for fear that he wouldn't continue his story.

Roman drew in a deep breath and slowly released it. "Our family line had a history of Dragon Kings, so each time a new dragon was born, everyone expected them to be King. My grandfather, father, and four uncles didna claim the throne. So everyone had his or her hopes pinned on Freyr. To everyone's delight, he became our King."

Sabina put her hand on his leg, feeling the pain that he didn't allow to come through in his voice or words.

"My brother was a good dragon. He was very strong, his magic unbelievable. From an early age, my father and grandfather made sure he would be ready if the magic called upon him to be King. Freyr never wavered when he challenged the current King. My brother won, but it was close. Verra close. There were times I was sure Freyr would be defeated."

She rolled onto her back again to look at him, but Roman's gaze was directed across to the far wall. Sabina watched his face, her heart growing heavy when she saw the sadness etched on his features.

"Freyr would've led us a long time," Roman continued. "I'm sure of it. He was strong in all ways. Except when it came to my father and grandfather. They wouldna let him rule as he chose. They were there, constantly telling him what to do. And Freyr listened.

"A clan needs a King who knows his own mind. The fact that my brother ignored his own counsel and did as my father and grandfather wanted brought great dissension to the clan. It was Ragna who came to me and told me she felt something within her. Except it wasna her magic or power she felt. It was mine."

Sabina's heart missed a beat.

Roman's lips twisted ruefully. "I ignored it as long as I could, but when the magic chooses you to become a Dragon King, there's no running from it. I tried to talk to Freyr to get him to do the right thing, but he wouldna listen. I finally told Ragna I was going to challenge our brother. She stood beside me. The rest of my family disowned me as soon as I did it."

Sabina took his hand and enfolded it against her breasts. Slowly, his gaze lowered to her. With his other hand, he moved a strand of her hair. It broke her heart to see him hurting so. If only she had words to help heal the wound that festered to this day.

She didn't need to ask what had happened. Obviously, Roman won. But it had cost him dearly.

"I lost my family that day. It wouldna have mattered if I won or no'. I was dead to them," Roman said. "All but Ragna. She never wavered. I put her in charge when we sent the clans over the dragon bridge. She's fierce. I wouldna want to go up against her."

Sabina brought his hand to her lips and kissed his knuckles.

He flattened his palm against her cheek. "All I see when I'm here is blood and death. I had to kill my own brother. I was happy to leave, and I would've preferred to never return."

"You did what you had to do for your clan," she said.

He glanced away, shrugging. "It doesna make the pain any more bearable."

"How long were you King before the dragons were sent away?"

"Six thousand years."

She raised her brow. That was a significant period of time to her, but to a dragon? "Is that a long time?"

"The longest anyone in my clan has ever ruled. Freyr was King for only three years."

"Oh. But shouldn't your family have been happy that another one of their sons was King?"

Roman shook his head, a lock of sandy blond hair falling

over his forehead. "They knew they could control my brother. But no' me. They ruled through him, and that's no' how it's meant to happen. In my mind, they're the ones who put Freyr in that situation. But I blame my brother for no' having the courage to stand on his own."

CHAPTER THIRTY-THREE

Roman had believed he'd forgiven his brother and family for their actions, but returning to Iceland dragged all the nastiness back up again.

And forced him to confront the things he hadn't been able to before.

He wasn't sure why he'd told Sabina the story. Now, she would know how much blood was on his hands. There were some dragons who yearned to be King. But Roman hadn't been one of them. He'd been happy.

Yet the call from the magic was powerful.

"Hm," Sabina said. "I hear your words, and I think you believe them, but you don't blame your brother."

He frowned at her. "What?"

She took his hand and held it before her. "Do you know how many times I've seen you looking at your hands? You do it when there's talk of Iceland. I knew there was something in your past that bothered you. Now I know what it is."

Emotion clogged his throat when she kissed his palm and then did the same with his other hand.

"You see blood, don't you?" she asked. Her lips compressed. "You admitted you couldn't deny what the magic wanted of you. To be a Dragon King. But you don't blame your brother. How can you when you carry the weight of his death even now?"

Roman looked away because her words struck too close to home. "I'm the one who took his life."

"Did you murder him?"

He jerked his gaze back to her, offended that she would even suggest such a thing. "No."

"You fought, right?"

Roman gave a single nod.

"A fight to the death. You were either going to win or lose. Each of you gave it your all, but the dragon meant to be King is who won."

He put his hand beneath her shoulders and lifted her as he bent to kiss her. With just a few words, she helped to ease a lifetime of guilt.

With one last smile, Sabina's eyes grew heavy. Roman said no more as he found his fingers in her hair again. He couldn't stop touching the lustrous curls. Soon, her breaths evened into sleep.

He touched her cheek and felt the coolness of her skin. She didn't appear cold, but he hovered his hand over her, moving from her head to her feet, to cover her with magic to keep her warm.

His thoughts tried to take him into the past with his brother, but he stopped them. It would do neither of them any good if he stayed mired in the past. What was done, was done.

Freyr, Ragna, and the rest of his family had made their choices. They each had to live with them.

Con had once told Roman to let the past go, that it would

do no good to hold onto something that couldn't be changed. Roman thought he had. Until he returned to Iceland and learned that he'd merely buried everything.

Roman sighed and ceased the ball of light. Darkness fell over them softly, enveloping them in a heavy blanket. He opened his magic and listened to the songs of the metals.

The music was beautiful, the crescendos alternating between each metal in a symphony that only Roman could hear. It was sad that no one else could bask in such melodies, but he liked that they were for his ears only.

Calm in a chaotic, confused world.

He listened to the music for several minutes before he searched again for V's sword. Roman didn't expect to hear it. No doubt it was being blocked by the Others' magic.

Or was it?

If Sabina's ancestors took the sword to keep it from the Others, then how did the Others know it was in Iceland? Why did they choose this mountain?

There was no doubt in Roman's mind that they were headed toward something. Metals didn't gather for no reason. Something brought them together, something magical—like V's sword.

But if the Others were in the mountain, why hadn't they taken the weapon?

"Because they couldna," he said with a smile.

That grin slipped. Why couldn't they? A group with that kind of power should have been able to get nearly anything they wanted. They'd trapped a White, imbued a wooden dragon with dangerous magic, and messed with V's memories.

What could have possibly kept them away from the sword?

He lowered his gaze to look at Sabina. Iacob had said

that she needed to hand him the sword. Why Sabina? Why bring her back in time to take part in such an undertaking?

Roman drew back his magic so the music wasn't so loud. That's when he heard someone shouting his name in his mind.

"Dammit, Roman! When I find you, I'm going to—"

"Ulrik?" he said.

There was a loud sigh. *"Aye. It's me. I've been calling for you for over twenty minutes."*

"I was listening to the metals."

"Had them up rather loud, did you?" Ulrik asked sarcastically.

Roman grinned. *"Did you find V?"*

"I did."

But Ulrik didn't sound happy about it. *"Well? How is he? Is Camlo all right?"*

"Camlo is fine. He's with V, who is still unconscious. Camlo said that I can no' take V from the mountain, and he willna leave with me either."

"Camlo can be a little stubborn."

"Really? I hadna noticed."

Roman could hear the eye roll in Ulrik's voice. *"If Camlo says V has to stay, then there's a reason."*

"There're no animals around telling him any of this, Roman. So how can you be sure?"

"A gut feeling."

Ulrik grunted. *"I doona like this situation. Eilish thinks we—"*

"You brought your woman?"

There was a bark of laughter. *"You've met the love of my life, my friend. Tell me, does anyone tell her what to do?"*

"Nay."

"That's right," Ulrik continued. *"I told her where I was*

*going, and she came with me. I'm no' going to tell her to
go back. Are you?"*

"I'd rather no'."

"Exactly." Ulrik paused a moment. *"Camlo is quite
taken with her. I could barely get anything out of him, but
she managed to get more."*

"Probably because he's used to talking to Sabina."

*"I guessed the same. We'll be staying here a wee bit.
I'd like to talk to V when he wakes."*

"You and me both."

Ulrik chuckled. *"I'm aware of the situation. If anything looks like it could go wrong, I'll get them back to
Dreagan."*

"Good."

"How are you?"

Roman lowered his gaze to Sabina. *"Sabina is resting.
When she wakes, we'll continue."*

"How close are you?"

*"We doona have much farther to go, but what's left of
the journey willna be easy."*

"You mean it willna be easy for a mortal."

Roman twisted his lips. *"Aye."*

*"Since you are no' suggesting leaving her, I gather
Sabina needs to be there?"*

"There's a good possibility."

Ulrik made some indistinct sound. *"Be wary of everything, my friend. Even the rocks and your precious metals."*

The link was severed, but Roman barely paid it any
heed. He was stuck on Ulrik's warning. Why hadn't he
thought about the metals?

The Others knew enough about the Dragon Kings to
carve one in Con's image, to know that V's sword was
important to returning the dragons, and that Roman was

from Iceland. Why wouldn't they turn the metals against him?

Or one type of metal, in particular. Say, V's sword.

Rage rumbled through Roman. There was no way he could find the Druids who joined with the Fae since they were mortals and long dead. But the Fae . . . when he found them, because he would find them, he was going to happily bathe them in dragon fire until there was nothing left but ash.

Roman was going to make the responsible Fae suffer horribly. And he wouldn't be the only King.

He heard the change in Sabina's breathing and instantly returned the light for her. A few moments later, she opened her eyes.

She smiled sleepily up at him. "Hey."

"Hi," he replied.

She frowned as she sat up and looked at him. "You're angry. Did I sleep too long?"

"You didna sleep long enough."

"How long was I out?"

"A few hours."

She shrugged and reached for what was left of her water. "Then what's wrong?"

"I've been thinking."

She swallowed, worry clouding her face. "About?"

"You."

Sabina nodded slowly as her lips flattened. "And me handing the sword to my ancestors."

"Aye. I started wondering why the Others didna take the sword if they knew it was here."

"And?" she asked, brows raised.

"I think it could be because they were no' able to."

She stared at him a full minute before her mouth went slack. "You can't possibly think it's because of me."

"I do," he said with a grin.

Sabina rolled her eyes as she climbed to her feet and paced before him. "Admittedly, I have no idea why I was transported back in time—a very long way back, mind you—or why I had to hand the sword to my ancestors, but . . ." She stopped and faced him. "Oh, God."

"Exactly. Somehow, magic was used so that you had to be the one to take the sword, which is why the Others couldna get it. You said yourself that Iacob was adamant that you give the weapon to him."

She nodded before her face scrunched up. "How? I just don't understand."

"We'll figure it out when we get to the sword."

"If the Others couldn't take the sword, do you really believe they'll make it easy to get to?"

Roman used the wall behind him to get to his feet. "Of course no'."

He'd already thought about that. The Others would put things in place that would be simple for a King to get through, but not a mortal. And no doubt there would be some kind of surprise waiting for them.

"You're awfully calm about all of this," Sabina said.

Roman walked to her and took her hands. "I am. Because we're going to get through whatever awaits us."

"That's easy for you to say. You're immortal."

"I willna let harm come to you," he promised.

She put her hand on his chest, her eyes filled with regret. "I didn't mean that you would. I'm just scared."

"We'll be together through it all."

"Promise?"

He pulled her against him and gave her a long, slow kiss. "I give you my vow."

"Well, then," she said with a grin. "I can do anything now that I have that."

He laughed, loving how she could turn her fears into something else. Roman waited as she bent to retrieve her bag of nuts. He refilled her water bottle as she stood, which made her grin.

And then they were off.

He hid his worry because there was no need to share it with Sabina. But he knew that he would stay beside her no matter what. Because she was going to come out of this alive.

CHAPTER THIRTY-FOUR

At that moment, Sabina felt invincible. Hopefully, it lasted longer than a few seconds because she had a feeling she would need all the courage she could muster.

There had been no more attacks on her, but that didn't mean the Others were finished. In fact, she was sure there was more coming. It was not knowing when or how that made her nervous.

Their path suddenly dipped at such an angle that had Roman not pulled back on her arm, she would've gone tumbling down to . . . well, who knew what. She should've been paying attention instead of letting her mind wander.

"That was close," she said as she backed up a few steps to stand next to him.

Roman grunted, his gaze staring into the blackness that the ball of light above her didn't quite penetrate.

"What do you see?" she pressed when he remained silent. Because she wasn't going to look down. She didn't want another panic attack.

"Nothing good."

Oh, that made her feel *so* much better. A shiver went through her the longer she looked into the shadows.

"The fact we're still standing here isn't invoking confidence."

Sea green eyes slid to her. "It's going to be rough."

"Okay." That could mean any number of things. Should she ask exactly what? After all, knowing helped one to anticipate what was to come.

Unless you were encountering a great height, in which case, she wouldn't budge from her spot. Deciding which option to take was only making her anxiety grow.

She tried to give off the impression of confidence while with Roman. She didn't want him thinking that she was a silly human who couldn't handle a few bumps along the way. But now . . . now, she wanted to back up against the wall and curl into a fetal position.

Sabina might be many things, but she wasn't a coward. She drew in an uneasy breath. "How rough?"

"Verra."

That didn't give her much information, but she was going to take it to mean that she shouldn't know. "I trust you."

One side of Roman's lips tilted into a grin. "I'm glad to hear it."

Sabina shifted her feet nervously. "What now? Do we run, do we walk, do we slide?"

Suddenly, the ball of light extinguished. That barely registered before Roman released her hand and wrapped an arm around her, pulling her in so close and tight that it was hard to breathe.

"It's better if you doona see."

No sooner were the words out of his mouth than he jumped. There was no time for Sabina to ask him to wait, no time for her to get her bearings. She had no choice but to grab him and hold on for dear life.

And not look down.

Wind rushed past her face so quickly that it stung her cheeks. She spied the darkness, but quickly shut her eyes so she didn't see anything below her. Besides, it felt better to keep them closed against the wind.

But it was the falling that terrified her. She ended up turning her head into Roman's shoulder while stifling a scream as her greatest fear came to pass. Her heart hammered, blood rushed through her ears. She couldn't hang on tightly enough.

They were jarred slightly when Roman finally landed. He held her in such a way that she wasn't able to touch down. She ended up bending her knees so that her feet didn't become tangled in his legs.

Sabina might refuse the chance to look, but she could tell that Roman was now running. Downhill.

And he wasn't even breathing heavily.

"Drop your legs," he urged.

She didn't hesitate to do as ordered. Seconds later, he was maneuvering them from one side to the other. In her mind, they were on slaloming downhill.

The image brought a smile to her face, but that quickly vanished when Roman launched them into the air again.

Sabina wasn't sure why, but she opened her eyes and looked over his shoulder. There was only darkness, like before. But it was the faint glow below that caught her attention. Her eyes widened when she spotted the river of magma.

And they were jumping over it.

Then everything began to spin. Her eyes snapped shut, and she wished she'd never looked. But it was too late. She had. *OhGodOhGodOhGodOhGodOhGod*. She didn't want to die. She'd already come close in the cavern. But she'd known this adventure would be fraught with dangers.

Roman landed so hard that her head snapped to the side.

He didn't move for a long moment. Then he lowered her so that she stood on her own. "You can look now."

Sabina lifted her head and trained her eyes on him. Sweat ran down his face, but it had nothing to do with the excretion and everything to do with the heat from the magma. She was warm enough that she contemplated taking off her jacket.

Finally, she turned her head and looked behind them. Her mouth fell open when she saw the size of the chasm that Roman had jumped. No human would've been able to make that. Then again, he was a Dragon King.

She tried to see where they had come from, but the shadows kept the way hidden. And perhaps that was for the best.

Sabina shifted to follow the river of fire until it disappeared into a hole in the mountain. They were several hundred feet from it, yet she could feel the heat.

"Watch your step," Roman cautioned as he took her hand.

There was no need for his light. The glow of the magma was enough to illuminate everything. Sabina found her courage once more and took the first step. Roman was right beside her, his hand warm and secure around hers.

They walked up an incline until they reached a rounded peak. She winced when she saw that the river flowed in nearly a complete circle around the area of rock.

"How safe is this?" she asked, careful to keep her eyes anywhere but down.

Roman didn't look at her when he asked, "Do you really want the answer to that?"

"That's what I thought."

He winked at her before returning his gaze forward. Sabina had no idea what he was looking for. She was very thankful for his dragon vision. Otherwise, she'd be stuck there. Actually, she never would've made it down the slope alive. Most likely, she would've ended up in the river of lava.

She twisted her head from one side to the other and behind her. "We're on an island." She looked on the other side of the river to the wall of rock. "How do we know where to go?"

"By listening to the music," he said.

When she raised her gaze to him, Roman had his eyes closed, and his head tilted slightly to one side as if he were listening to something only he could hear. Sabina wished she could hear the metals as he did.

She couldn't take her eyes off him and the joy that spread across his face as he listened to his metals as they told him which way to go.

"There," he said as he opened his eyes and pointed.

Of course, it was across the largest expanse of river. But he didn't take her in that direction. In fact, they headed to the right, toward a narrower strip.

"Hold on tight," he said with a grin as he pulled her against him once more.

Sabina swallowed, fighting the wave of panic.

Roman smiled down at her. "Trust me. I'll get you across in seconds. You willna even know it's happening."

She wrapped her arms around him and kissed his jaw. "I think I'll keep you around. I'll never worry about having to cross rivers of lava again."

He chuckled, the sound rumbling through his chest. "So molten rock plays a large part in your life, does it?"

"Oh, definitely. It means you have to stay with me."

His face grew serious, his eyes intense as they held hers. "I need no reason to stay with you, lass, other than that I wish it."

She had no comeback for that because there wasn't one.

She could've said she was teasing, but in fact, she wasn't. Sabina very much wanted Roman around. The odds were against that happening, but she could dream. Right?

With fourteen simple words, he'd given her hope that she hadn't had before. Hope that she hadn't even known she yearned for.

"Do you ken?" he asked.

She nodded woodenly.

"Good," he said with a cocky grin.

Sabina was still staring at him when he took three running steps and launched them into the air. This time, she didn't close her eyes. This time, she didn't say a prayer.

Instead, she basked in the power of a Dragon King.

The fear that had begun to swallow her before was tamped down when Roman landed safely across the river. As soon as her feet touched the ground, she found herself pressed against a wall of rock with Roman's body trapping her.

"If you doona know how badly I crave you, then I didna do a good job of showing you before," he whispered in a voice deep with emotion—and desire.

He captured her lips, the kiss passionate and fervent as both succumbed to the hunger they each had for the other. It was a kiss fraught with longing and a yearning so deep that it could never be filled. It was a kiss of fire, an inferno of desire and need.

It was a kiss of unspoken promises.

And hope.

When he pulled away, she awkwardly opened her eyes, trying to regain the breath he'd stolen. Her knees were weak, her heart thudding in her chest. And a throbbing had taken up residence deep within her.

He rested his forehead against hers as they waited for their breathing to return to normal.

His fingers slid down her arm to intertwine with hers. Then he straightened, staring silently at her, waiting for her to tell him that she was ready.

Sabina smiled and squeezed his hand.

"The ledge is narrow, but I've got you," he said.

She didn't doubt it. "I know."

Together, they turned and began walking toward the opening Roman had pointed to. Sabina could just make out an entrance, and she was glad to have something to think about rather than the fact that she was walking on a narrow ridge against a wall of rock with nothing but magma below her.

If she didn't have Roman to hold onto, to give her courage, she'd never be able to do this. And if she thought about it too long, another panic attack would hit. She turned her head away, refusing to think about where she walked or where the heat came from.

Hopefully, the rest of the way would be easier than what they'd had to cross to get there. But they were across the river of fire. However, they were far from being safe.

Well, at least she was far from it. Roman had said nothing but a Dragon King could kill another King, and she didn't wish to put that to the test at the moment.

The ledge was littered with various rocks that slid out from beneath each step. Roman kept her steady—again. Even though she attempted to pick the best places to put her feet, she still slipped a few times. Roman, however, didn't so much as even have to catch his balance.

They were nearly to the entrance when there was a loud crack. Both of them halted. Roman's head swung to her. A scream tore from her throat as a part of the ledge crumbled beneath them.

She was going to die. Her hair was in her eyes, preventing her from seeing Roman and reaching for him. She wanted to be touching him when she fell into the river so she wouldn't be alone.

And oh, God. She was falling!

Suddenly, something gripped her hips. The wind whipped her hair from her face in time for her to look at Roman. She smiled, but it vanished when he chunked her upward.

Sabina had no time to think as she was flying again, this time up. She landed hard on her side, rolling several times before she stopped. She immediately scrambled onto her hands and knees to the side to look down, not even thinking about her fear.

She hastily searched for some sign of Roman while fighting the nausea that hit her at gazing down from such a height.

"Rooooomaaaan!"

A sob escaped when there was no answer. What the hell had just happened? How was she alive but he wasn't? How . . . oh, God. Her arms gave out as she fell onto her stomach, tears swimming in her eyes as she squeezed them shut. She couldn't even look for him.

"Roman," she whispered.

In the next moment, there was a loud noise. Her eyes flew open in time to see a form burst from the river and spread its wings as it soared upward. Sabina jerked up and fell onto her butt as she watched in shock as lava slid from Roman's pale blue scales without leaving a mark.

He dipped a wing and turned, his ivory eyes landing on her. He then flew straight toward her. Sabina scrambled to her feet and backed up against the wall of rock, giving him as much room as she could for him to land.

Her mouth parted in surprise when he dove toward her, tucking his wings and head. She blinked, and the dragon was gone, replaced by his human form as he landed elegantly on his feet, his legs bent and his hands on the ground.

She waited until his head lifted before she ran to him and threw herself at him.

CHAPTER THIRTY-FIVE

There was an instant where Roman wondered if he could save Sabina. Even when he fell into the magma, he hadn't been sure she'd made it back onto the ledge.

It wasn't until he emerged from the river and flew around that he caught sight of her. That's when the band of steel around his heart had loosened enough for him to breathe.

He closed his eyes as he held her against him. While his fall and reemergence had taken but seconds, that time had felt like eons. And during it all, he kept wondering if he'd be able to hold her again.

"I thought you were gone," she said, her hands shifting over his back as she clutched him tighter. "I thought you were dead."

"I told you, only another Dragon King can kill me." He didn't bother to tell her that he prayed he'd pushed her toward the wider section of ledge, or that his heart had stopped when he lost sight of her.

She shook her head against his neck. "You fell. Into a river of fire."

Roman pulled back to look at her. He grasped her face

between his hands and waited until her dark brown eyes were focused on him. "Lass, dragons are made of fire."

"So, even if you weren't a Dragon King, you would live?"

He hesitated.

"I knew it," she said, her face crumpling.

"But I am a Dragon King."

She swallowed loudly. "I know."

Roman yanked her against him once more. He couldn't stop touching her, holding her. There were few things in his very long life that brought him fear. Sabina dying was one of them. His heart still thumped erratically.

"Did it hurt?" she asked.

"What?"

"The magma?"

He rested his cheek atop her head. "I didna feel it."

That wasn't a lie. He'd been too concerned about her to think of anything but her.

They stood for several moments in silence, each lost in thought. He wasn't sure what he would've done had she not survived. But she wasn't dead. She was in his arms, safe.

For now.

"Was it the Others?" Sabina asked.

He knew she was referring to the rock's collapse. "I can no' be sure one way or the other." He paused, then said, "You doona have to continue."

She jerked back to look at him with a condemning glare. "You said I needed to be here."

"You probably do. I can have Ulrik bring you to Camlo, and then return you to me when I've found the sword."

Sabina stared at him for a long moment. Then she stepped back, out of his arms. "You don't think I can handle this. To be honest, I'm not sure I even want to. But I have to do this."

"It isna that I doona believe you can handle it. It's that when I thought you might be dead . . ." He couldn't finish the sentence. Emotion welled in his throat, choking him. He swallowed heavily. "That's twice now. I doona want to tempt the Fates a third time."

Her shoulders dropped as she pressed her lips together. "I want you to know something right now. If I do perish, whether it be because of my own stupidity, the Others, or simply Fate, it isn't your fault. I would never hold you responsible."

"But I hold myself responsible."

She smiled at him then. A curve of her lips that was full of defiance, acceptance, and gentleness. "You can't be held accountable for everyone."

"Just you, lass."

"Do you always say the right thing?" she asked.

He shook his head. "Rarely."

"I don't believe that for a second."

"It's true. I find peace when I'm alone in my workshop crafting designs from the metals."

Her brow furrowed deeply. "You can hear the metals, right?"

"Aye."

"And you can shape them?"

"Aye," he replied again.

The smile she gave him was slow and extremely sexy. "Have you ever controlled them within the ground?"

Now he frowned. "No. Kellan can call metal to him, so when I find it, he then brings it to the surface."

"Why haven't you tried to control it in the ground before?"

He shrugged, trying to figure out what she was getting at. "It's no' my gift. And there was no need."

"There may be now."

Roman glanced at the entrance that awaited them. "If I try to shift any of the metals here, it will crack the rock, and the mountain could crumble around us."

"I'm not talking about those metals. I'm talking about V's sword."

Roman blinked at her. "But I can no' hear it."

"Yet you know it's here somewhere. Right?"

"Aye."

"Maybe it's simply waiting for you."

He quirked one side of his lips. "Or the Others could prevent even that. I'm no' against trying to do as you're asking. I will. But only when we've found the sword. After this," he said, motioning to the river below. "I doona want to risk anything."

She smiled sadly. "Risking everything is exactly what we're doing."

"For me, maybe. But no' you."

"You can't make that decision for me. Besides, we both knew the risks."

He ran a hand over the bottom part of his face. "I did, but you didna. There is nothing wrong with stepping back."

"That's just it. I can't. You need to understand that. I'm part of this, remember? I gave V's sword away. And he may never forgive me for that."

"V is stubborn, but he isna stupid."

She huffed out a breath. "I'll admit I'm scared. Standing here surrounded by a river of fire and contemplating entering that," she said, pointing to the opening, "terrifies me. But I'm still going."

"You're verra stubborn."

Sabina shot him a sassy look. "Yep. I am."

"I suppose it willna do me any good to try and sway you to change your mind?"

"Nope." She shook her head as she removed her jacket and tied the arms in a knot around her waist. "Shall we go?"

He was well aware that she wasn't enthusiastic about going, but they had to keep moving. She held out her hand, waiting for him to take it. Then she faced the opening, took a deep breath, and began making her way forward.

Roman let her set the pace. He wanted to give her as much time as possible to change her mind. But, secretly, he was impressed and pleased with the courageous decision she'd made.

When they reached the opening, Roman had to turn sideways and bend his head to the side to enter. He went first because he wasn't sure if the Others had set any kind of traps or not.

As soon as Sabina crossed the threshold, he made sure the ball of light was with her. The passage was so tight that he had to wiggle through the protruding rocks. He couldn't look back at her, but the fact that she wasn't tugging on his hand to stop was a good sign.

"Are you sure this is the way?" she asked, breathing heavily from the exertion. "This doesn't look like it was used by people."

He paused and put their joined hands on the rock. "You can no' feel the metals, but they're there. Silver, gold, and iron, just to name a few. Some running in tiny veins that zigzag through the rock. Others in thick lines. And they're all headed this way."

"What do they sound like?"

Now he really wished he could see her face. "Imagine a piece of music that moves you so much that even, days later, you can hear it in your mind. That's what each of them sounds like to me."

"That sounds incredible. You're very lucky."

He smiled as he started walking again. "You're fortunate yourself. You have Romani blood and have the Sight."

"I've not used it in so long."

"It's still there, waiting for you to find it again."

He felt, rather than saw her smile. Roman was tired of scooting sideways through the passage. Not to mention that he'd really like to stand up straight. Sabina wasn't having the same issue with the ceiling, but even she had to turn to the side to move.

His hope that the tunnel would open up was dashed as it went on, and on, and *on*. Sabina winced as she banged her shoulder. He bit back a curse when he tried to move his head around a projection of rock from the ceiling, only to graze it with the back of his head.

Before he could warn Sabina, she yelped. "Damn. That hurt."

"Aye. It did," he grumbled.

Minutes turned into hours. They kept moving, no matter how slow their progress.

At one point, Sabina tugged on his hand. "I need to stop for a moment."

Roman went down on his haunches to straighten his neck. She pulled out the bag of nuts from her pocket, and he produced another bottle of water. She eyed him as she ate her snack.

"What?" he asked.

"Do you eat regularly? I know you ate at my house, but you haven't since then."

He nodded. "Aye."

"As a dragon? Like, swooping down from the sky and snatching a cow or two?"

Roman laughed and shook his head. "I've no' done that in ages. I get hungry, but I can skip meals if I have to."

"I'm guessing your stomach doesn't rumble?" she teased.

He grinned at her. "Oh, it does."

"How did the other animals view you before the humans came? I'm assuming there were other animals. You had to eat something."

"Do you think about how chickens, cows, or pigs feel about you?"

She shook her head.

"Neither did we."

"That makes sense," she said with a shrug. "I'm guessing V is still unconscious?"

Roman frowned. "Hang on." Then he looked away and opened the link with Ulrik. *"How's V?"*

"The wanker is still out," Ulrik grumbled. *"However, Eilish and I are learning quite a bit from Camlo."*

"Like what?"

"Like how he's always known of the Dragon Kings. Apparently, the animals told him."

Roman laughed, glancing at Sabina. *"I'd like to know what else the animals told him."*

"That's what Eilish is attempting to find out. So far, nothing. How are you two doing?"

"It could be better."

Ulrik harrumphed. *"How close did she come to dying this time?"*

"Too bloody close."

"And the sword?"

"We're closer, but we're having to go slow because of the tight passage."

"Well, keep me posted. I'm no' sure how much longer I'll let Sleeping Beauty rest before I slap him awake."

Roman was laughing when he severed the link and turned his head to Sabina. "V is still out."

"And that's funny?"

"Ulrik calling him Sleeping Beauty is."

Sabina's face split into a wide smile. "That is pretty humorous."

"I do believe it's going to be his new nickname, which will annoy the hell out of him."

"And why all of you will use it," she replied.

"Damn right."

She chuckled as she put the cap on her empty water bottle. "Another Dragon King here, huh?"

"And his mate, Eilish, who happens to be a powerful Druid."

"Let's hope they get V to wake. Any chance you can just punch your way through the rock?"

"I'm about ready to do just that."

CHAPTER THIRTY-SIX

Isle of Skye

"Ugh," Rhi said and shoved away the book she'd been reading.

She rose from the chair and paced the room, anxious and irritated. And the fact that she couldn't find what she looked for even among the Skye Druids made things even more annoying.

"Right about now, Talin would say he was vexed."

She halted mid-stride and jerked her head to the doorway at the sound of the Irish accent. As soon as she saw Daire leaning a shoulder against the entry, she smiled at the Reaper.

"By the way," Daire continued, "if you ever truly want to rile Kyran, tell him you're vexed. The word irritates him like nothing you've ever seen."

"That's good information to have."

She stared into the silver eyes of the Light Fae who now answered to Death. His long, black hair was pulled back in a queue, and he looked . . . ridiculously happy.

"How are you?" he asked.

She held out her arms and looked around the chamber.

"Yeah," he said with a laugh. He glanced at the floor

and took a deep breath before he pushed away from the door. "I wanted to tell you why I stopped following you. I wanted to do it the moment Death gave me new orders, but there wasn't time."

Rhi shrugged, shaking her head like she didn't care, but she did. Oh, did she ever. Daire had become a trusted friend. She missed him. Mostly because she didn't talk to many other Fae now, and the sound of his voice was sorely missed.

"I'm sorry, Rhi," he said.

She walked to the table stacked with books and turned to him. She put her hands on the wood and leaned back, bending one knee as she crossed her ankles. "You know I wasn't exactly thrilled with you knowing my every move, thought, and conversation."

"I never knew your thoughts."

She smiled tightly. "We both know you did. I let my guard down when I'm on my island."

"Everyone needs such a place."

"Why are you really here, Daire? I am happy to see you, and I appreciate your apology for bailing on me, but you haven't said where you went. And I don't think that's why you've come."

His chest rose as he pulled in a long breath. "I was sent to Killarney to find Bran's descendants—three sisters. Turns out, he wanted something on their land. Somehow, in all of it, I fell in love with the eldest, Ettie."

"I'm glad for you." She waited for him to continue. When he didn't, she said, "Now, how about the real reason you're here? And since they sent you, it must be bad."

He shook his head, grinning. "You always think the worst."

"Tell me I'm wrong," she said.

His smile faded. After a moment of staring, he walked

into the chamber and looked around at the shelves of books. "The Skye Druids keep meticulous records, don't they?"

"Daire," she warned.

He stopped and dropped his chin to his chest for a heartbeat. "We know about Balladyn's decree to the Dark regarding the humans."

We. In other words, the Reapers. And the decree was that Balladyn—her best friend and now ex-lover—gave the Dark he now commanded free rein to kill as many mortals as they wanted.

That went against everything the Dragon Kings believed. It— She halted her thoughts. She was a Fae. Even the Light had sex with humans. Granted, they didn't kill like the Dark did, but she shouldn't be so outraged by Balladyn's command.

And if she weren't still so wrapped up in the Dragon Kings, she wouldn't be.

When she raised her gaze, Daire was watching her. "So you know what Balladyn has done. You've had that information as soon as his decree went out. This is the last time I'm going to ask why you sought me out here."

"I thought you'd be less likely to get angry and start glowing if you were aware that this is the compound of the Skye Druids and that there are many humans around."

Rhi rolled her eyes. "Wow, dude. You really think what you've got to tell me will send me right off the rails?"

"You have been through a lot lately with your banishment and all."

As if she needed to be reminded of that. "Get on with it, smartass."

Daire looked at the bookshelf for a moment. Then his silver eyes slid to her. "You were at the Dark Palace recently. Veiled."

Well, shit. Rhi had gone in an attempt to see Balladyn and find out if he'd changed as much as she thought he had. "Only a Reaper can see another Fae who's veiled. What were you doing there?"

"I wasn't," he said.

Rhi lifted a hand and looked down at her newly trimmed nails painted with *That's What Friends Are Thor*. The brown was paired with the glittery *Gift of Gold That Never Gets Old*, each finger an alternating color. Her nails grew fast, and she'd let them get pretty long before having Jesse trim them, not that the length mattered at all in the designs.

"Rhi?" he pressed.

She raised a brow, reminded that she wasn't alone. "What? I'm the one who asked you a question."

"I asked first."

"What are we, five?"

He looked away, annoyance in the tightening of his face and body. "Fine," he bit out before swiveling his head back to her. "Reapers were there. As you've figured out. And it's Reaper business."

In other words, none of *her* damn business. "Funny how Death can get all up in my life, have me followed, learn my friends, enemies, decisions, lovers, how I like sex, and so on. But you can't answer a simple question. And here I thought we were friends."

"Rhi," he said in a low voice filled with frustration—and a bit of anger. "We *are* friends. Trust me when I tell you that, right now, it's better the information remains with the Reapers."

"And Death."

He gave a nod.

"I'm guessing another Halfling is involved, as well." She smiled when he didn't reply, but there was no humor in the motion. She almost mentioned Thea, but something held her back. It couldn't be about Usaeil's daughter because Con and the other Kings knew. "So, this doesn't just stay with the Reapers."

"What were you doing at the palace?" he asked.

She shrugged. "Having a look around. Remember, I was banished from the Light."

"Are you thinking of turning Dark?"

Rhi threw back her head and laughed as she pushed away from the table. "Oh, *puh-lease*, Daire. Of course not. And even if I was, do you really think I'd tell you? Or be there veiled? I wouldn't need to tell anyone," she stated, crossing her arms over her chest. "All I'd have to do is commit murder—of a Fae or a human or whoever. And the deed would be done."

The sorrow that filled Daire's face made her want to lash out at him.

"Don't you dare pity me," she told him, dropping her arms. "Don't you fekking dare."

He took a step toward her. "Look at what you've endured in the past. This is just something else to get over. You're strong, Rhi. You can do this."

"Maybe," she said as she retreated a step. "But do I want to? That's the real question."

"You should," he replied with a frown.

She arched a brow. "Really? That's easy for you to say, handsome. You say I've been through a lot. I have. More than most. And just when I think things might get better, the rug gets yanked out from beneath me again. Frankly, I'm tired of it."

"And the darkness is hard to resist."

Rhi stilled as she started to turn away. His words slammed into her with the force of a hurricane. She slowly turned her head to him. "What did you say?"

"Your light has always shone so brightly, Rhi, that

you've not felt the darkness like most. And when you did, it wasn't just the fringes of it but the entire, frightening mass. And it wants you. Badly."

She tried to look away, but she couldn't. Her eyes clouded with moisture, tears that she hadn't allowed herself to shed. "Yes."

"I might have been a Light, but every Reaper was betrayed and killed. Death chooses each of us, and once we accept the position as her executioners, we're no longer just Light or Dark. We're neither. And we're both. I understand fully what the darkness is, and how persuasive it can be."

"Stop," she told him, not wanting to hear any more.

Suddenly, he was before her, his hands on her arms as he bent his head to look into her eyes. "You're not alone. You've never been alone. In all my long life, I've never known another being to have so many friends who would do anything for them. The Warriors and Druids at MacLeod Castle, the Dragon Kings . . . me."

It was too much. Rhi tried to push him away, but he wouldn't budge. When the first ugly tear escaped, he gently wiped it away.

Rhi spun around, hating for anyone to see her cry. She buried her face in her hands. And behind her, the Reaper put his hand on her shoulder, silently giving her comfort and compassion.

"Turning Dark is easy," Daire continued. "Fighting the darkness is the hard part. It wants you so desperately because your light is so bright. Keep fighting it."

She sniffed and lifted her head, angrily swiping away the tears she hadn't wanted to shed. "I'm not thinking of any of that right now."

"But you were at the Dark Palace."

Rhi spun around to face him. "You know I was, since

a Reaper saw me. And if you must know, I went to find out if Balladyn is the monster I fear he's become. But I didn't see him. I didn't stay long."

"He can sense you when you're veiled. That's highly unusual, but that's because the two of you have a deep connection."

"Yes." But it didn't compare to the connection she'd had with her Dragon King. He was . . . well, everything. Even now.

"I can tell when you're thinking of your King."

She held up a finger. "You know the rule. Don't say his name."

"Why? You've said it before. I don't understand how you can continue to hold such love for him while suffering the loss of that love and still go to Dreagan again and again. Seeing him."

Rhi forced a smile. "It's easy, really. After he ended our affair, I knew I'd either have to leave this realm or learn to deal with it. There have been times I've kept my distance from the Kings. In order to get my life back, I created this little room in my mind. I put everything we had—every kiss, every word, every memory—there. And I locked it tightly away."

"It doesn't always stay there."

"No," she said with a shake of her head. "But more often than not, I can control it. So that's how I help my friends at Dreagan. That's how I talk to him. That's how I say his name. Because when it's about something else, I can do it. But when it's about . . . us . . . that's when everything I put away in my mind threatens to escape."

Daire's smile was sad. "I think I understand. Now, why don't you tell me what you're doing here? Is this about the wooden dragon?"

"It is." Rhi walked around the table to the book she'd been reading. "I'm hoping to find the Druids who joined with the Fae."

"Those Druids would be long dead."

She shrugged one shoulder. "Yes, but I could trace the family."

"That still won't find you the Fae."

Rhi blew out an exasperated breath. "No, it won't. And my fear is that those Fae are still around."

"If they are, they could cause serious issues for the Kings."

"I know."

Daire's lips flattened. "We have books from the original thirty Fae families. I'll see if River can find any mention of some pact with the Druids in them."

"That would be helpful. Thank you."

He grinned. "Remember what I told you. You're never alone."

When he teleported away, another tear slipped down Rhi's cheek.

CHAPTER THIRTY-SEVEN

The tunnel didn't get easier. In fact, the walls seemed as if they were closing in on them. Sabina never thought herself claustrophobic, but it was quickly becoming a phobia.

She had been joking with Roman about busting through the stone before, but now she wished he would do it. She was moving through the passageway sideways, shifting her torso forward or backwards to work around the walls.

And Roman . . . he was utterly silent. There were no sighs, no mumbled curses, no slamming his palm against the rock helplessly as she kept doing.

For the fifth time, Sabina banged her head into an outcropping of rock. She bit back a curse and rubbed the spot with her free hand. She didn't know how Roman wasn't smacking his head, but he must be, right?

"Stop," she said and drew to a halt while yanking on his hand.

Her head was facing him, so she was able to see how tightly he was held between the walls. There was no room for him to turn his head to her or even shift his body.

"What's wrong?" he asked.

"Well," she said. "First, I can't take the walls closing in on me any longer."

There was a beat of silence. "I suppose there's a second?"

She rubbed her nose with the back of her hand. "My bladder is about to burst."

"You did drink four bottles of water."

Were his shoulders shaking? As in . . . laughing? Her mouth fell open in dismay. "Find this funny, do you?"

"A wee bit," he mumbled.

"I'm smiling on the inside."

This time, she was sure she saw his shoulders shaking. Sabina rolled her eyes, but even she was grinning now. If her bladder didn't hurt so badly, she might even enjoy the moment.

"Can you tell how far the passage goes?" she asked.

"It looks to go on for some time."

Damn. "I don't suppose you can make the tunnel any wider."

He didn't answer. His silence left her uneasy. And it didn't take her long to realize that he didn't want her to know something.

"Roman? Please, just tell me whatever it is."

It took him a moment, but he bent his knees until he was down on his haunches. Then he was able to look at her. Instantly, she saw the worry he no longer masked from her.

"That bad, huh?" she said.

"The farther we go, the more magic I can feel. I can no' tell what spell is being used, but I recognize the mix of it."

Sabina briefly looked at their joined hands. "Others."

"I think they created this tunnel to be as uncomfortable as possible."

"In other words," she said. "They're counting on a King using his strength or magic to widen it."

He nodded his head. "Exactly. I suspect that if I do anything, the ramifications will be swift and severe."

"And you'll survive it, but I won't." Sabina snorted as she rolled her eyes. "I really, really don't like the Others."

"We'll get through this."

"I'm beginning to have my doubts. Tight spaces have never bothered me before, but it feels like they're reaching out for me."

"They are."

She gaped at him. "What?"

"It's the magic," he explained. "They want you to feel that way so I'll widen the tunnel.

Sabina closed her eyes. "I thought I could do this. I really believed that I could handle whatever was thrown at me." She looked at Roman. "But I can't."

There was no disappointment in his green eyes, no frustration. He accepted her words for what they were. "Ulrik can no' get to you here. We'll need to backtrack to the magma river."

"That's several hours."

"Aye."

She really wanted to stamp her foot right then. Or better yet, punch one of the Others—or *all* of them. "I don't like going backwards."

"It's your choice. I'll take you back."

"It's not as if I'd get lost."

Roman raised a brow and gave her a flat look.

How could she forget that she was surrounded by the magic of the Others? Being on her own would be worse than remaining in the tight passage.

She licked her lips. "Let's keep going."

"Let me know if you change your mind."

"As I said, I don't like going backwards. I'll deal with this."

"Doona go through it alone. Talk to me," he urged. "Tell me what you're feeling and experiencing. I'll do what I can."

He didn't move until she smiled and nodded. Only then did he slowly straighten, waiting to look away from her until the last minute. Once Roman's tall frame was squished between the walls again, he moved forward.

Sabina wasn't sure how long she walked until she realized she was no longer feeling as if the walls were going to cave in on her. And she knew the magic of the Others wasn't gone. Otherwise, Roman would widen the tunnel.

No, he must have used his magic on her once more. With the heavy feeling lifted, she was able to focus on what she was doing and think about what might be coming.

They shuffled another hundred feet or so before she grew too chilled to continue. "I need just a second to put on my coat," she told Roman.

The moment she released his hand, she felt his absence. Sabina hurried as fast as she could with her jacket, but maneuvering even a little bit was nearly impossible in the enclosed space.

She became a contortionist. She had to dip her shoulder and wiggle her arm just to get one side of the coat on. For her other arm, she had to squat and lean to the side while sliding her arm behind her in search of the sleeve. It took four tries and sweat now covered her—and made her rethink the coat. But after everything she'd gone through to get it on, she wasn't going to take it off now.

Sabina rotated her shoulder until the jacket was on correctly. Then she reached for Roman's hand. Except he wasn't there.

"Roman," she called.

The light was still above her, but it showed only darkness. Sabina walked forward a few steps because that was the only way Roman could've gone.

"Roman! This isn't funny."

She held her breath, trying to hear the tiniest of sounds. But there was only a deafening silence.

"ROMAN!"

Her heart was beating wildly, her blood turning to ice. Terror and worry knotted her stomach. He wouldn't leave her. Not willingly. Which meant this had to be the Others somehow.

If only she hadn't let go of his hand. She'd known as soon as she did it that it hadn't felt right. Why, oh why, did she have to put on her coat? Why couldn't she have just dealt with the cold? He'd told her to tell him what she was feeling so he could help.

"Roman," she whispered.

She'd thought he was dead when he fell into the river of lava. She knew that wasn't the case, but there was no denying that he was gone. She'd have to continue on her own. Something that he hadn't wanted her to do.

Sabina looked up at the light. Had it just flickered? With Roman away, would it remain? And what about the claustrophobia? Would that return?

"What if it does?" she asked herself. "You push through it, that's what."

Her little pep talk did little to inspire her. But she didn't like going backwards, and what would that give her anyway? She had no way of contacting her brother, V, or Ulrik. Or a way to get back over the river of lava. Which meant she had no choice but to keep going.

"Right," she said and took a step.

And promptly rammed her knee into the wall. She

grimaced, but she kept moving. Each step becoming a little easier. Her hand grew cold, missing Roman's strength and warmth. Something as simple as handholding changed everything.

"Roman, if you can hear me, I'm going to find you," she said. "I'll retrieve the sword, as well. I promised I would, and I won't let you down. Trust me."

Her throat clogged with emotion. How many times had he asked her if she trusted him? Now it was his turn to do the same with her.

"I shouldn't have let go of your hand."

She felt tears threaten and hastily blinked them back. There was no time for crying. For all she knew, the Others' magic would detect the weakness and use it against her somehow.

Sabina frowned, wondering if everything she said aloud could be used by the Others' magic in some way. She couldn't know for sure, but she'd rather be safe than sorry. So she stopped talking to herself, halted her attempts to reach Roman. If anyone could detect her in the darkness, it was he.

If he were able.

No. She refused to even go down that road. He'd said the Others' magic was powerful, but only because no one—including V—had realized it had been used on him. Even then, V was working his way to erasing all that had been done to him.

That led Sabina to conclude that even with the mix of Druid and Fae magic, the Others still didn't stand a chance against the Dragon Kings.

At least she prayed they didn't. Because she really needed Roman.

Sabina kept her eyes straight ahead. She focused on putting one foot in front of the other, ignoring her bladder and emptying her mind of everything else. If she allowed herself to think about her brother or what might have happened to Roman, she might just lose her mind.

She could hear Roman's voice in her head, telling her that she could do this, that she was strong enough. That made her smile. Her steps grew quicker as she ate up more space. As her confidence grew, her mind wandered.

Before she knew it, her thoughts had taken her back to when she gave V's sword to Iacob. V's blue eyes blazed with fury and anger, but it wasn't heat she felt from his gaze. It was coldness.

His mouth moved as if he were saying something. But that wasn't right. Sabina remembered looking at him before she'd given up his sword. V's head had dropped back, and his eyes were closed.

How then did she know that he spoke?

I will find you. No matter how far you go, no matter what you do. I will find you for stealing what's mine, Sabina.

She stumbled into the wall, slamming her chin into a protrusion of rock. Without checking, she knew her skin had broken when she felt a drop of something on the back of her hand. Blood.

Sabina was yanked from her thoughts. She blinked, unease coursing through her. She didn't remember how far she'd come. It was like she'd blanked out while walking.

For all she knew, she could've walked right past Roman and not known it. But that's what happened when she allowed herself to be taken by her memories.

Except, this one had been different. Her steps slowed until she halted. What she'd seen hadn't been a memory. She knew she hadn't heard or seen anything that V said after it appeared he'd fallen unconscious.

She refused to believe it was the Sight. The Romani saw

the future, not the past. And yet, that's exactly what she'd seen. It was the only explanation. Quite frankly, it scared the hell out of her.

When she started walking again, she realized that she was facing forward, not scooting with her shoulders turned to the side as she had been for hours. When had that changed? She really had to start paying attention. She was on her own now, without Roman there to save her.

As soon as she was able, she emptied her bladder to stop the pain that had her nearly doubled over. Her mind tried to pull her under again, but she resisted. More out of fear of what she might discover than anything else.

She wasn't sure if this were her Sight or the Others, and until she knew for sure, she wasn't going to let her mind wander.

CHAPTER THIRTY-EIGHT

It would be so easy to lose control, to give in to the unrestrained fury, resentment, and indignation. Those emotions were simple, powerful.

And obliterating.

Roman should know. He'd given in to them when battling Freyr, and again when his family—all except for Ragna—turned their backs on him.

It had gotten him nowhere. The joy he'd experienced in claiming the throne for the Light Blues was shadowed by the fact that he'd taken his brother's life.

No one had come close to making him lose control until Sabina. But with her, it was different. It wasn't anger or bitterness that assaulted him. It was a fervid desire, an uncontrollable need to claim her as his.

But all that had to be put aside. He had to focus on remaining calm, concentrate on finding serenity amid the turmoil of being imprisoned.

In his mind, Roman raged. He bellowed, he cursed.

He roared.

Outwardly, he kneeled on his haunches, serenely in the center of his prison with his eyes closed. There would come a time for him to give in to the anger, but it wasn't now.

The moment Sabina's fingers slipped from his, the sickening feeling of the Druid-Fae magic washed over him. He hollered for Sabina and tried to reach for her, but it was already too late as he was unceremoniously yanked from her side. Every time he tried to use his magic, the farther she moved away.

The pain using his magic caused him had been debilitating, but it was worth it to save her. And he would've continued had he not begun to yearn for the deaths of all mortals. The sensation reminded him so much of what the others who touched the wooden dragon had experienced that he instantly stopped using his magic. Thankfully, the need to kill humans diminished.

From the moment he appeared in the cage, he'd kept his eyes closed. It was also the way he remained composed. He used his other senses to give him the information he needed. On the right side, the unmistakable chill of ice brushed against him. His hearing picked up the drip of water into a larger pool, and by the smell of the steam, it was a hot spring.

But there was also the heavy smell of sulfur as well as the blistering feel of heat coming from his left side. Magma. The small gas explosions from the molten rock filled the silence.

Roman reached out with his mental link, but just as he expected, none of the Dragon Kings answered. That could only mean the Others' magic prevented it.

There was no way to see if V had woken, no way to let Ulrik know that Sabina needed help, and no way to alert Con of just how far the Others had gone.

Roman took a deep breath and slowly opened his eyes. The cavern was enormous. Several Kings could fly together and never bump into each other. It looked as if there were a glacier to his right with the water dripping from the slowly melting ice into a pool heated from the magma flowing beneath it.

And on Roman's left side, a large waterfall of magma poured from the mountain into a fast-moving river of fire. Flames shot up from the lava while anything that came near it was quickly devoured.

Dividing the two extremes was a teardrop-shaped mass that he was on. There was something below him, but with steam swirling around and clouding portions of the cavern, he couldn't make out what it was.

Fire and ice. It was a bit poetic for his tastes, but he supposed the Others had a plan. Just what that might be was the real question. Mainly because it would likely involve Sabina.

Roman's heart missed a beat when he thought about her being left alone. She was strong, with a backbone of steel. There wasn't much that could get her down, and he hoped this wasn't the thing that would change that.

She didn't like going backwards, which meant there was only one way for her to go—forward. He didn't bother shouting her name. She wouldn't hear him. No one would. Ever.

As soon as Roman realized that he was imprisoned, he'd tested the strength of the magic. Each time he encountered the Others' magic, it made him nauseous, but he knew he could break through it.

But what would be the cost?

Because there would be one. The Others hadn't gone to this much trouble for him to endure a queasy stomach. And that's what really worried him.

"V's sword, the death of the White, the wooden replica of Con, and now this. Why?" he murmured to himself.

There could be an argument that the White was killed to hide the wooden dragon, but that carving could have been put anywhere. Why the White? Why hide it?

The answer was because they knew Dmitri would be there with the skeleton. The Others wanted Dmitri to know that one of his dragons had suffered an excruciating death.

And they wanted Dmitri to find the carving. The Others knew he'd bring it to Dreagan. They'd put enough magic in that small object to affect Kings and mortals alike—with disastrous results.

That was assuming the Others suspected that the Kings would take mates.

Apprehension snaked down Roman's spine. If that were the case, then that meant the Others knew about Ulrik's betrayal since the reaction by the humans when they touched the carving was the same as what had nearly happened.

Fuck.

Roman fisted his hands atop his legs. He didn't want to go any further or think any more about the Others, but there was no choice. If not for Rhi, they'd never know about the mix of magic because each time a King touched the carving, the uncontrollable need to kill mortals assailed them. That meant none of them had time to digest what type of magic it was when they were fighting the urge to kill.

That brought him to V. Roman's earlier thoughts had sorted through that tangled mess, but that didn't mean he hadn't missed something. The longer Roman thought about it, the more he was sure that one of Sabina's ancestors had hidden the sword here.

But *why* here?

No matter how he looked at it, it wasn't a coincidence.

The Others might not have been able to get the sword from Sabina's ancestors in time, but they made sure the weapon went exactly where they wanted it—Iceland.

His domain.

Because they'd known he would be here to retrieve it. There were Druids who had visions, so it was conceivable that one of them saw him and Sabina together. Maybe that's how they linked them and made sure the sword came here. And that the Druid knew him and his domain. But that was hedging everything on a single vision.

Fae didn't have that sort of ability. And no Fae could travel through time, so that left him with the vision, once again.

The drawings they left, however, really bothered him. Why would the Others give him a heads-up on what was coming? Was it because they felt sure he wouldn't be able to change the outcome?

Roman tried once more to reach the Kings, to no avail. If he weren't expecting Sabina, he'd try to escape. But he wasn't sure what would happen, and he didn't want her somewhere he couldn't protect her. So he waited.

"Bad things. Bad things. Bad things."

Ulrik frowned as Camlo jumped to his feet and began to pace, wringing his hands as he repeated the words over and over. Ulrik looked at V, who had yet to stir. And he had tried his best to wake V himself.

"It's okay," Eilish said to Camlo as she rose to her feet.

Camlo rapidly shook his dark head. "It's happening."

"What is?" Ulrik asked as he stood.

Camlo ran out of the chamber. Ulrik and Eilish followed him into the cavern with the drawings. Camlo stopped before the one where Roman, in dragon form, was killed by V's sword.

Camlo then turned his head to Ulrik, his face filled with sadness. "It's happening."

"But V is still unconscious," Eilish said.

Ulrik pointed at Camlo as he told his mate, "Stay with him."

Ulrik rushed back to V. He stood over his friend, waiting for any sign of movement. The Dragon Kings were incredibly powerful, but they couldn't leave their own bodies like a ghost.

Yet, Camlo was insistent that bad things were happening, specifically Roman being killed by V's sword. But V was right here.

Unless . . .

"Shite," Ulrik muttered as he realized V didn't have to be there for the sword to be used.

Ulrik opened the link to Roman. *"Roman? I need you to answer me now. Roman!"*

When there was no response no matter how many times Ulrik shouted his name, he sent out a call to all Dragon Kings, *"Roman is in trouble. I can no' reach him, and . . . there's a verra real possibility that we could lose him."*

"I'm coming," Con answered.

There was something Roman had said in one of their conversations that made Ulrik immediately tell Con, *"You can no'. This is all a trap."*

"For Roman."

"Or for you. Roman didna want any of us here."

"I doona like this," Con grumbled.

"We're no' prepared for this, my friend. Any of it. These Others know everything we're going to do before we do it."

Con issued a harsh bark of laughter. *"No' all of us."*

Ulrik frowned as he tried to figure out who Con was talking to. Then it hit him. *"Oh, aye. You're right. I'll let you know how it goes."*

"If I doona hear from you in an hour, I'm coming there," Con threatened.

"Understood," Ulrik said before disconnecting the link.

When he turned, Eilish was there with Camlo. His mate studied him a moment. "You were talking to Con."

"Aye," he replied. "We're annoyed by the fact that the Others seem to know what we're going to do."

Eilish raised a black brow as she stared at him with her green-gold eyes. "I suppose by that stern look, you have a plan."

"I have you," he said as he walked to her and gave her a kiss.

Camlo moved to sit beside V, ignoring them.

"What is it?" Eilish whispered.

Ulrik cupped her face in his hands. "We need to think outside the box."

"How? You said yourself, the Others know every move."

"Ours."

She frowned. "And, apparently, Sabina's."

"But no' you." He glanced down at her finger rings that she used to teleport.

Eilish thought about his words a moment. "It might be a gamble that could backfire."

"We've no' lost a Dragon King in ages, my love. We can no' lose one now."

"Do you think the Others would know about one of their own?"

It took Ulrik a minute to realize she spoke about Rhi. "You want me to summon her?"

Eilish shrugged. "It certainly couldn't hurt."

"V remains unconscious, I can no' get ahold of Roman, and Camlo said that it's begun. Just think how bad things would be had we no' arrived."

"I think when it comes to the Others, you Kings need

to stop thinking you can do things on your own. Banding together makes you more powerful."

"Aye, unless there's a situation like this. Roman knew it was a trap, and I fear he's already in it. Any other King who tries to find him will end up the same way."

Eilish grinned. "Which is why you need a Druid and a Fae."

"If I'd set up something so elaborate, I'd wonder if one of my own might befriend my enemy along the way."

Eilish hesitated. "True, but even if that's the case, would you hurt one of your own?"

He shrugged.

She smiled.

Without missing a beat, he said, "Rhi."

Seconds later, the Light Fae appeared before him. She looked around the cavern, her brows furrowed deeply until her gaze landed on him. "I'm guessing someone is in some deep shite."

"Let's start at the beginning, but it'll be better if you're in the other cavern," Eilish said.

Rhi looked at Ulrik as she asked, "Other cavern?"

"Thanks for coming, Rhi," he said as Eilish led the Light Fae from the chamber. Ulrik looked at V lying on the ground. "All right, old friend. Time for you to wake. We're going to need you."

CHAPTER THIRTY-NINE

The slap went through V like a shot. He heard the movement of air as whoever it was swung their hand back to do it again. Right before they made contact with his cheek, he reached up and grasped their arm.

When he opened his eyes, he was staring into a gold gaze he knew well. "Ulrik?"

"It's about bloody time you woke."

V released him and sat up. He swallowed past the emptiness he felt in his chest. He had the answers now, but knowing the truth only made things worse.

"V?" Ulrik asked, concern deepening his voice. "Are you with me?"

"I'm here," V said. Though he wished he weren't.

V's gaze moved around the chamber, and he spotted Camlo off by himself. The mortal's dark eyes watched him carefully. Somehow, Camlo knew. He'd known all of it, and he hadn't said anything to either V or Roman—or even his sister.

"Do you have any idea how long you were out?" Ulrik asked irritably. "Not to mention, I've been slapping your face for a good fifteen minutes now."

That's why his cheek stung. V worked his jaw back and forth to stretch the skin. He knew Ulrik wanted him to say something, *do* something, but V couldn't. Mainly because he couldn't decide if he was angry or not.

"V, you've got to talk to me," Ulrik urged. "I'm beginning to get concerned. It's never a good sign when you're quiet."

He swung his head to Ulrik. "I was out so long because I was ridding myself of the Others' magic."

Ulrik slowly sat back on his butt. "I gather it was difficult."

"No' how you think. There were multiple layers of each of their magic. It overlapped, some parts threading into the others. That's what makes it so powerful. It's finding the part that's the weakest in order to break it all down that takes the longest."

"Do you remember it all now?"

"Every damn second of it."

Ulrik propped a foot on the floor and rested his arm on his knee. "And?"

"It was a normal day. I flew over the land as usual. I had to deal with some minor squabble between two of my dragons. It was after that when I began to notice something wasna quite right with me. I returned to my cave to determine what was going on. I struggled to stay awake, and it felt as if my mind was fuzzy."

"Magic of the Others?" Ulrik asked.

V nodded. "It was while I was fighting it that Sabina appeared. I didna know who she was. She was dressed oddly and talked strangely. But I could tell she was scared of the men climbing the mountain. None of the humans had ever been to my cave. I selected it so it would be risky for them to even try."

"Bina," Camlo murmured.

V glanced at the mortal before he turned his head back to Ulrik. "The magic was taking hold of me quicker than I could combat it. I told Sabina to get behind me while I took care of the humans, but I couldna do anything. I was rendered useless. I had no choice but to lie there on the ground and listen as Sabina spoke to her ancestors.

"I knew the moment they mentioned the Others that it was a new threat. I tried to hold onto the memory, but it slipped away like a leaf on the wind. I tried to shift, to holler, to do anything to stop Sabina from taking my sword. But she handed it to a man. As soon as he had it, he and the other five men left. And then Sabina was gone. I doona know how long I lay there fighting the sleep that tried to claim me before they arrived."

Ulrik's gaze narrowed. "Who?"

"The Others. I heard their voices. They stood over me, laughing at how easily they'd taken down a Dragon King. If I could've, I would've killed each of them in that moment." Reliving the memory sent a wave of fury over V because it felt as if it had just happened.

"Did you look at them?" Ulrik asked.

V shook his head. "I couldna open my eyes. A woman led them, though. By the way she spoke, she'd put the group together."

"Was she Fae or Druid?"

V shrugged his shoulders before scrubbing both hands down his face. "I couldna tell. There were three females and one male that I heard for sure, but I got the feeling there were others there, as well."

"Well, hello, handsome," Rhi said as she strode into the cavern.

V snapped his head to her. He frowned as he swung back to Ulrik. "What the hell is she doing here?"

"Just helping out. But I can leave," Rhi offered.

Ulrik climbed to his feet and went to Eilish. "He doesna want you to leave. He just isna happy that any of us are here."

"That's right," V said. "I'm no'. You all need to leave. Now. And take Camlo with you."

At the mention of his name, Camlo began vehemently shaking his head. "No. Nonononononono."

"Actually," Rhi said as she tossed her long, black hair over her shoulder. "It sounds like Roman and Sabina need our help."

V had been so wrapped up in his memories that he realized he hadn't asked about Roman. "What happened? Where are Roman and Sabina?"

"I'm no' sure," Ulrik replied. "I can no' reach Roman now."

V stood and ran a hand over his mouth. "He knew it was a trap. He said we needed to go regardless, that our magic was strong enough to break through the Others'. It is, but he doesna know how to do it."

"Then we tell him," Eilish said. "Rhi and I should be able to find them."

V was shaking his head before she finished. "None of you get it. The Others planned all of this. They *knew* what we would do. It's no' a coincidence that my sword is here or that Roman is with me. We didna find Sabina and Camlo by accident. This was planned."

"But how much of it?" Eilish asked.

Ulrik gave a nod of agreement. "That was a similar question between Con and I the last time I spoke with him. He's the one who suggested we do something we wouldna normally do."

"Like ask for help," Rhi said with a brow quirked.

V didn't like this. Any of it.

"We're a Druid and a Fae," Eilish said. "I doubt the

Others thought of us, much less imagined that we'd help you or work together. But even if they have, I'm willing to chance it."

Rhi shrugged. "Count me in."

V walked to Camlo and sat beside the human. "How long have you known that Sabina took my sword?"

Camlo nervously looked at V out of the corner of his eye. His shoulders lifted in a half-hearted shrug. "Always."

"You never told her?"

The mortal frowned. "No."

"Why?" Eilish asked.

Camlo brought his shoulders to his ears as he kept his gaze on the ground. "She wouldn't have believed me."

"But we do," Ulrik said.

V looked down at his hands for a moment. "What else do you know, Camlo?"

The man-child made an indistinct noise and appeared visibly unnerved by the question.

But V couldn't let it go. He had to have the answer. "Did you know that she went back in time?"

Camlo hesitated before nodding once.

"You sent Roman and Sabina away after V collapsed," Ulrik said. "Was that on purpose?"

Camlo made a high-pitched whining sound. His face was folded into lines of remorse. "They had to go."

"Why?" V pressed.

Camlo squeezed his eyes closed, refusing to reply.

Rhi went down on her haunches before Camlo and gently touched his hand. When he opened his eyes, she smiled at him as one would a child.

"Hi," Rhi said. "Do you know me?"

Camlo swallowed. "Fae."

Her smile widened. "That's right. I am Fae. But do you know *me*?"

"No," he mumbled.

"My name is Rhi. I'm friends with the Dragon Kings. We know you love your sister. It's obvious. I had a brother who used to protect me. That's what you're doing now."

Camlo's lips lifted in a quick smile. "Bina."

"That's right." Rhi held his gaze for a long minute. "She's in danger, isn't she?"

Camlo grabbed hold of Rhi's hand and held it tightly. V tensed, ready to act, but Rhi didn't seem upset by the move.

"Bad things," Camlo said.

V wasn't surprised by the words. "You've said that many times. But we don't know *what* bad things. Can you tell us something, anything? We don't want Sabina hurt."

Camlo kept his gaze on Rhi's hand. He stared at her painted nails. "They aren't together anymore."

Damn. V was hoping that Roman and Sabina had managed to remain with each other. Knowing they had been separated, either accidentally or intentionally, complicated things even more."

"I can find Sabina," Rhi said.

Finally, Camlo looked into her eyes. "She's not finished yet."

"What do you mean?" Ulrik asked.

Camlo's interest returned to Rhi's nails. "Bina didn't like our gifts. She ignored them, but I didn't."

V blinked as elation went through him. "Your Romani gifts? You have the Sight, Camlo?"

"Of course," the mortal replied, offended that the question was even asked.

Rhi put her other hand with the first. "You've used your Sight to see things."

"They were just there," Camlo said as if that explained everything.

"All of it?" Eilish asked.

He shook his head once. "I used it to see Bina's path."

V hated that they had to pull every answer from the mortal. "And?"

Silence filled the cavern for a long time before Camlo turned his head to V. "Bina took your sword. She'll give it back."

"Does that mean she'll survive whatever is happening to them?" Eilish asked the others.

Ulrik shrugged, Rhi refused to answer, and V wasn't sure he could.

"What about Roman?" V asked Camlo. "Have you used your gifts on him?"

"Can't," was Camlo's reply.

V wasn't sure if that meant that Camlo couldn't see Roman's future, or that his Sight didn't work on the Dragon Kings. Either way, V was left with nothing.

"Roman is here for me," V said as he rose. He had to move to get rid of some of the pent-up energy coursing through him. He began to pace. "I was targeted because the Others knew what my sword could do. They doona want the dragons to return. They knew there would be a war with the humans and that we'd send the dragons away."

Ulrik sighed loudly. "We know my uncle worked with a Druid to help him speak to mortals. Makes me wonder if Mikkel was in league with the Others."

"Or if they used him," Eilish said.

V watched as Rhi remained still while Camlo rubbed the pad of a finger over her nails. "I'm leaning toward the Others manipulating Mikkel to do what they wanted. I doubt it would've taken much. It would explain how your uncle suddenly found a Druid willing to help."

"For all we know, the Druid could have been one of the Others," Rhi said without looking away from Camlo.

Eilish walked to Ulrik and slid her hand into his, their fingers intertwining. "The Others seem to have orchestrated all of this, but surely that couldn't include the mates?"

"Why no'?" V asked.

Ulrik lifted their joined hands and kissed the back of Eilish's fingers as he met her green-gold gaze. "Right now, we have to consider that the Others had their fingers in everything."

Rhi gently pulled her hands from Camlo and stood, facing them. "But not the Fae. Why would they worry about their own?"

"The Fae were involved because they wanted this world," Eilish said. "And as Ulrik pointed out, if they knew so much, they'd know that one of their own might befriend a King."

Rhi shrugged, her gaze locked on V. "What do you think?"

V took a deep breath and blew it out. "I say it's a chance we have to take. I'm no' going to let Roman die, no matter what the Others drew in that chamber."

Rhi winked at him. "Then it's settled."

CHAPTER FORTY

The first thing Sabina saw was the mist. She paused in the tunnel because she wasn't sure what she would find once she stepped out.

The light stopped with her. She looked up at it. It wouldn't be much use within the fog. Somehow, having that orb of light made her feel like Roman was still by her side.

"I don't go backwards," she murmured.

With a deep inhale, she stepped from the tunnel into the mist. It swallowed her so that she couldn't see her hand waving in front of her face. And just as she thought, the light was useless.

The passage had been tight and uncomfortable, but this was scary. She didn't know what was in the fog. Or *who* was in the fog. That was the terrifying part. Someone could be there, watching her.

Sabina swallowed and took small steps. She waved through the mist, trying to move it around so she could see better. Off to her right, she heard a noise that sounded familiar—flowing magma.

But that didn't explain the fog. The last time there was

a river of lava, there hadn't been mist. Just sweltering heat that felt as if it were crushing her.

She decided to remain in one spot for a minute to see what else she could pick up with her other senses. As the heated mist brushed against her cheek, it reminded her of the hot spring where she and Roman had made love.

Would she ever see him again? Hold him? Kiss him? Or had the Others taken him from her forever? Sabina wished she had more information from her ancestors about the Others.

Then she remembered how her memories could pull her in and show her things. Perhaps it was a form of the Romani Sight, though she really wasn't sure. But right now, she could use all the help she could get.

Sabina lowered herself to the ground and sat cross-legged. The ground wasn't as warm as she expected it to be, but she didn't linger on that. She closed her eyes and thought of V's cave. There was so much going on around her, breaking her concentration, that it took several tries before she fell back into the memories.

This time, she found herself at the edge of V's cave staring out over the land. Once more, she spotted the village in the moonlight. As she turned her head, her eyes caught on something. She did a double-take and found a woman standing at the base of the mountain.

The men had already begun their climb by this time. But what shocked Sabina was that the woman was staring at her. Even with the distance separating them, Sabina could discern that.

"I've been waiting for you."

Sabina jerked at the sound of the woman's voice. It was like she was standing right next to her. Sabina's heart thudded, but then she realized that she didn't feel as if she were in danger. In fact, she felt . . . safe.

Much as she did when she was with Roman.

"Who are you?" Sabina asked.

The woman smiled, her dark eyes crinkling at the corners. "A *very* distant relative."

Sabina blinked, and the next thing she knew, she was standing before the woman among the trees on the slope of the mountain. The woman was strikingly beautiful. Her dark olive skin had a glow to it that only someone who spent hours in the sun would have.

Her eyes were almond-shaped, and her black hair hung over one shoulder in a long braid that fell past her breast. She wore simple clothing, just a long, dress-like garment in a sand color with a deep red strip of material wrapped several times around her waist before it was tied so the ends dangled down at her side.

"How is this happening?" Sabina asked.

"You are descended from a long line of powerful women who can see into the future."

"What about me? I'm seeing into the past."

The woman's smile widened. "Who are we to question what our gifts allow us to see? Or not see."

Sabina glanced behind her to the mountain. "Iacob said someone told him I was going to be here. Was that you?"

"Yes. My name is Ana, and I'm one of two women in our tribe who has the Sight. I began seeing your face when I was only a child. As I aged, I saw more and more until this entire moment was laid out before me."

Sabina frowned, unsure what to make of things. "This is my second time here."

"Is it?" Ana asked, her shrewd expression stating that she was well aware of more than Sabina realized.

"Why did I have to give V's sword to Iacob?"

"Our kind has always held respect for the Dragon Kings, but there has been a growing fear, as well. Vlad is good to us, as well as to his own clan. It was not my wish that he be chosen for any of this, but it is out of my hands."

Sabina moved closer. "You're saying the Others did this?"

"Yes. They know what his sword can do."

Sabina opened her mouth to speak when a roar split the air, followed by several more above her. She looked up, her knees going weak when she spied a group of dragons flying above her. She stared in awe at the moon reflecting off their copper scales.

Tears filled her eyes. She stood speechless as she watched them. With her eyes skyward, she realized that there were dragons everywhere, their shapes dotting the skies as far as she could see.

"They'll be gone soon," Ana stated sadly. "They're a magnificent sight to behold, and I'm truly going to miss them."

"They should never have been sent away," Sabina said, her heart heavy at seeing what none of the Kings had witnessed in eons.

Ana sighed. "Humans and dragons cannot co-exist."

"They can," Sabina said, returning her attention to Ana.

"The moment the Dragon Kings welcomed us, they sealed their fate."

Sabina's stomach crashed to her feet. "What? You make it sound as if someone set all of this in motion."

Ana smiled despondently. "Because they did."

"Who?" Sabina demanded to know. "Who did this? And where did we come from?"

"Your time is almost up," Ana said. "You aren't asking the right questions."

Sabina pushed her frustration down and fisted her hands at her sides. "What should I be asking?"

"How to get the sword."

"Okay," she said, nodding. "How do I get it?"

Ana glanced up at the mountain. "The Others have all sorts of spells in place. They're meant to stop you. Trust yourself. Trust your heart."

"What kind of spells?"

"The Others' goal is to stop you, no matter what. Our plan impeded them, but only for a little while. It gave one of our men time to get to the land of fire and ice and take the weapon deep within the mountain."

Sabina's stomach clenched at the mention of Iceland. "Why that land?"

"Because I've seen you and the King of Light Blues together. I told the men that the sword had to be in that mountain. He got it there in time, but the Others were waiting."

Sabina rubbed her temples. "Wait. Just wait. Now you're talking as if this already occurred. The men are just clim—" Her words trailed off as she looked up, and they were gone.

"Time moves differently for you and I in this place," Ana said. "The Others tortured the one who hid the sword, but he never revealed where it was located. The Others figured it out soon enough. Yet they learned they couldn't touch it. Only you or a Dragon King has that ability. So they made sure the blade would be impossible to reach if you ever went looking for it."

"They want to make sure the dragons can never return, don't they?"

Ana nodded her head sadly.

"I don't understand any of this. Who are the Others?"

"Fae and Druid."

Sabina snorted. "You mean humans."

Ana tilted her head to the side. "In a manner of speaking."

"What does that mean? Druids are merely humans who attained magic once they arrived here."

It was Ana's turn to frown. "That's wrong. The Druids have long held power and prominent ranks of position within our kind. There have always been Druids. Well before our race ever came to this realm."

Sabina's head hurt with the influx of information. "Is there anything else I need to know?"

"That you can do this. I've seen you succeed, but not without paying a very steep price."

"You can't leave it there," Sabina stated angrily. "Tell me the rest. What price?"

Ana shook her head. "I've long awaited a chance to speak with you. It's nice to know that our line lives on, and within someone like you."

"It's not likely to continue, though." Sabina wasn't sure why she added that part. It just sort of came out.

Ana chuckled softly. "It most certainly will."

"How?"

Ana ignored her question and put her hand on Sabina's arm. "Remember. Trust your heart. Always."

"You make it sound as if our time is up, but I need to find Roman," Sabina said.

"Trust your heart."

"Stop saying that," Sabina snapped. "I need answers."

Ana inhaled, a look of profound patience filling her face. "I've given them to you."

"No, I'm sorry, you haven't. You've kept repeating the same thing."

"Which is all the answer you need." Ana smiled. "Good luck."

And just like that, Sabina was hurdled back to the present. She drew in a shaky breath as her eyes opened to find herself back in the fog. She had spoken to one of her ancestors. The one who'd made sure that V's sword was taken far away.

Sabina looked at the mist. It parted just enough for her to get a glimpse of something beyond. There was a reddish-orange glow coming from off to her right. With the heat, she knew it was the magma.

But she wasn't sure about the left side. It could be just more of the mountain, but she had a sense it was something else. If only she could see.

For all she knew, she was on a ledge, and if she stepped the wrong way, she could tumble down to . . . whatever was below. Regardless, she wouldn't survive.

"Trust my heart, huh?" she murmured, thinking of Ana's words.

Well, her heart was telling her she had to keep going—cautiously. Something waited for her. She had helped to set things in motion that would stop the Others from succeeding. And it had nearly destroyed V in the process.

But she would rather one King deal with his missing weapon than see all the dragons destroyed. The memory of the drawing of the dead dragons haunted Sabina. Because she had a feeling the Others weren't drawing just any dragons, but the Kings.

She could hear her heart beating, and the rhythmic thumping helped center her. The Others had put spells in place to prevent her from getting the sword. Those Fae and Druids were like a group of toddlers. If they couldn't have what they wanted, then they would make sure that no one got it.

But it still brought her back to *why*?

Why did the Others want this planet?

Why were they doing everything in their power to remove the dragons?

And how in the hell did Druids and Fae come together and decide that the Dragon Kings were the enemy?

Sabina clenched her jaw in determination. Then she climbed to her feet. As she straightened, the mist moved just enough on the left that her eyes encountered the most magnificent blue. A glacier.

"Fire and ice," she said with a smile.

CHAPTER FORTY-ONE

As soon as he spotted the muted rays of light through the mist, Roman knew that Sabina was there. The movement of the fog prevented him from seeing more than the orb of light, but the light was meant to remain with Sabina even if he wasn't there. He hadn't wanted her to be stuck in the dark.

He looked at the bars of his prison. His first thought was to bust through and shift so he could get to Sabina. What held him back was that it was something a Dragon King would do. Which meant it was something the Others expected.

So he wouldn't do it.

But he couldn't remain in the prison either.

"Well, I have to say, I really don't like this place."

Roman stilled at the voice from behind him. He turned, shocked to see Rhi standing there with a smile and some seriously kickass black, stiletto boots with spikes on the heel. She was dressed in her favorite leather pants and a black corset over a long-sleeved black shirt.

"Is it really you?" he asked.

"You bet, handsome." She eyed the bars separating

them, her expression turning sour. "Same mix of magic as the wooden dragon."

Roman nodded. "The Others."

"Have you tried to break out?"

"Nay. I've a feeling that when I do, something worse will happen. Possibly to Sabina."

Rhi's silver eyes widened. "Ah. I see. Well, that makes things difficult. But then again, I live for difficult." She winked at him before walking around the cage he was in, looking it up and down.

"You shouldna be here, Rhi," Roman said.

She lifted a shoulder nonchalantly. "I shouldn't do a lot of things, but I do. When Ulrik couldn't get ahold of you, he called for me."

"These Others are no' to be messed with. Look what they did to V. Did Ulrik fill you in?"

Rhi halted before him and nodded. "I saw the drawings, and yes, I know about what's going on. The fact is, you need help. And I'm willing to deal with whatever comes from helping you."

"How's V? Is he awake? Is he angry at Sabina?"

Rhi held up a hand. "Slow down there, stud. First, V did wake after Ulrik slapped him around a few times. He's not exactly happy, but V is doing fine. The thing is, apparently, Camlo knew all of this would happen."

"What?" Roman shook his head. "That can no' be right. Surely, Camlo would've told his sister."

"I'm just relaying what I heard."

Roman glared at the prison. "I doona want to be here. I should be with Sabina."

"What happened?" Rhi asked as she squatted down to look at the ground where it met the bars. "How did you become separated?"

Roman sighed loudly. "We were holding hands. She let

go to put on her jacket. Next thing I knew, I was forcefully pulled from her. I countered it, and I was succeeding despite the pain it caused me."

"Then why did you stop?"

"Because there were flashes in my mind of dead humans and how good it would feel to kill them."

Rhi's lip curled in disgust. "In other words, the same type of response that Dmitri and Con felt when they touched the wooden figure."

Roman nodded. "Exactly. I didna want to chance returning to Sabina and then having to fight killing her."

"Which is also why you haven't busted out yet," she said as she straightened.

Roman shrugged helplessly. "Pretty much."

"I can tell you that V eradicated all the magic those jerkwads used on him. It took him time, though. He said there were layers upon layers of it, each one overlapping like a weave."

"So how did he do it?"

"He found the weakest spot," Rhi said. "It wasn't easy, but he said if you can find that, it will unravel everything."

Roman turned in a circle, looking at the prison, from the four sides to the ceiling, which was just more bars. "That was in V's mind. This will be different."

"But doable," Rhi added. "You're a fekking Dragon King."

He glanced at her, smiling. "Did you think I needed a pep talk?"

"Oh, honey," she said with a sigh. "All men—no matter the species—need a pep talk every now and again."

Roman chuckled. The ball of light drew his attention again. "As much as I appreciate you coming to find me and passing on the information, there is someone else who needs you."

"Sabina," Rhi said.

He nodded, looking at Rhi. "She's alone. She made it this far, but as you said, this place isna exactly friendly."

"I'm not here by myself, Roman."

He frowned, shock and anger mixing together. "This was a trap, Rhi. How do you know it isn't one for you, as well? Bloody hell," he said as he raked his hand through his hair. "Look where I'm at. Who knows what awaits Sabina, but I can guarantee you, it isna anything pretty."

Rhi arched a brow. "Are you finished?" she asked testily.

He flattened his lips. "For now."

"I'll tell you what I told Ulrik and V. I know all of you believe that these Others somehow know each of your decisions and movements—"

"Aye," Roman interjected.

"But why would they think another Fae or a Druid would help? That I—"

"Holy fuck. You brought Eilish," he murmured.

Rhi gave him a flat look. "I hate being interrupted. And, yes, she's here, but I didn't bring the Druid anywhere. Ulrik can't even tell her what to do. Now, as I was saying, that means that whatever spells these dirtbag Others put in place won't affect either me or Eilish."

"You're both taking a huge risk."

She moved closer to the bars. "It's a risk you'd take without thinking twice."

"That's right."

"Then why is it different for me and Eilish?"

Roman gawked at her. "You can no' be that dense. You are needed. No' just as a friend to us, but to your people. And then there's—"

"If you say his name, I'll leave your cute ass here," she threatened.

Roman glanced away. "There's you-know-who. And

what do you think will happen to Ulrik if Eilish is taken from him? We just got him back."

"I appreciate your thoughts, I really do," Rhi said. She smiled softly, but it faded. "But give me and Eilish some damn credit. We're smart and pretty damn powerful, if I do say so myself."

"You've no' encountered the Others, Rhi. Neither of you."

"Then it's time we do," she stated, hands on her hips.

It was like arguing with a rock. Roman looked down at the ground and briefly closed his eyes. "I doona care what happens to me, but Sabina is important. She's the only one who can get the sword."

"What? Why? What don't I know?" Rhi demanded. "Oh. It's because her ancestor made her give him the sword."

Roman lifted his head and twisted his lips. "Something like that. I think there's much more to it. This is a complicated story we're somehow just discovering."

"Now you know how the Warriors felt when they learned about the Dragon Kings."

Roman nodded, laughing softly. "Aye. The thing is, the Others want V's sword. They've made finding it difficult and no' something a human could do on their own and survive."

"I know they wanted you with her. But why?"

"To trap me."

She flattened her lips. "Again, why?"

"I'm no' sure. Yet. I hope I can figure it out before it's too late. Look, can you please find Sabina?"

Rhi rolled her eyes and reached back, winding her long, black hair up at the back of her head and securing it with what looked like a stick. "Did you miss the part where I told you Eilish was with me?"

"Right." Shite. He had forgotten that.

"Hey, handsome. You need to focus."

He threw out his arms. "On which part? The fact that I'm being held, the fact that the Others separated me from Sabina, the fact that the sword is close, or the fact that the Others planned all of this?"

"Fine," Rhi replied testily. "Point taken."

"I'm afraid of making the wrong decision," Roman admitted. "I know they've somehow figured out our moves, and I doona want to do something they expect."

Rhi met his gaze and nodded. "That I can understand. I've been on Skye searching through the Druids' records there since they've written down everything since . . . well, forever. I can't find any connection. I know there has to be one, and I was counting on finding the link with the Druids first."

"Because the Fae doona keep such records."

She gave a snort. "That's part of the reason, but also because as much as I hate to say it, it would be relatively easy for a Dark and Light to come together and join forces. Our two groups are in a constant state of war, but there are places, like Eilish's pub, Graves, that allow the Fae to mingle without fighting."

"We're never going to find the source, are we?" Roman fisted his hands. "We claim to have the greatest power on this realm, but we can no' even figure out who our enemies are."

"Because they remained dormant for so long. That's another thing that confuses me. Why would they do that?"

Roman pinched the bridge of his nose. "I doona have any answers. I only wanted to give V back what was stolen from him."

"Break free of this," Rhi told him, waving at the bars

in disgust. "Eilish and I can take you and Sabina out of here."

"So we have to do this all again?" Roman shook his head in refusal. "I promised V his sword, and I'm no' leaving without it. I doona care what spells the Others have waiting, but V has been without his blade for long enough. Whenever I think of what they did to him . . ." He trailed off, unable to finish.

Rhi nodded slowly. "I agree. We're going to find the Fae, and we're going to exact punishment. What I want to know is why the Reapers haven't stepped in." Her face furrowed in a deep frown. "Matter of fact, I want to know why Death hasn't judged the wankers."

"You have more of a history with the Reapers than we do. Hell, we're just finding out about them," Roman said. Then his face went slack. "You doona think they're part of the Others?"

"Oh, Lord, no," Rhi said with an exaggerated eye roll. "If you knew Death, you'd know that Erith is nothing if not about balance. She is meticulous in her judgment, and the Reapers are swift to carry out her punishment. I recently spoke with Daire. The Reapers have some ancient Fae books, so they're going to look through them and see if there's any mention of the Others or a pact with Druids."

Well, that was more than they had earlier. Roman swung his gaze to the ball of light. It hadn't moved since he first noticed it. "I care about her."

"That much is obvious," Rhi answered softly.

"I think . . . I think she might be my mate."

Rhi exhaled. "I've seen a number of Kings fall in love over the past few years, and I do believe you're going to be next, stud."

"I didna want this."

"It can be an amazing experience."

Roman looked at the Light Fae. "What if she doesna feel the same? What if she doesna want to be mine?"

"Then she isn't your mate."

Roman thought about that for a moment. "She is. I feel it," he said, placing a hand over his heart. "I want to show her everything about my life. No' just me in my true form, which she seemed to enjoy, but everything else. I want to show her my sculptures, take her around Dreagan, give her a tour of the manor."

"You're going to get to do all of that, Roman. Because you're going to break out of that damn cage," Rhi stated. Then she smiled mischievously.

CHAPTER FORTY-TWO

One step. Another. One more.

Sabina wasn't actually taking steps. They were more like shuffles, but at least she was moving. That was something.

She blew out a breath, watching as the mist moved away before curling in on itself as if trying to return to her. It was pretty, and she might actually enjoy it if she weren't trying to remain alive.

Her body stilled when she heard a cough to her left that sounded distinctly feminine. She concentrated, listening for another sound. It came again, louder, along with a low mumbling that was definitely English, and definitely cussing.

"Sabina? Are you here?" asked the woman with an Irish accent. "Look, I know you're leery of everything, but I'm a friend of Roman's. We're here looking for both of you." The woman paused, perhaps waiting for Sabina to speak.

Sabina wasn't sure what to do. Did she trust the voice? Or was it some trap set by the Others?

The woman sighed. "I suppose I should tell you my name. I'm Eilish. I'm Ulrik's."

There was a smile in Eilish's tone, her voice rising in excitement when she said the words. Still, Sabina remained silent.

Eilish chuckled softly. "Sorry. I haven't been saying that I'm his all that long, and if you knew what we went through to be together, you'd understand why I'm so . . . well, giddy about it. Oh, my God. I'm so glad no one else just heard me say *giddy*," Eilish said more to herself than Sabina.

Unable to help herself, Sabina smiled. She liked Eilish. If only she could trust her.

"Damn this mist," Eilish grumbled. She coughed again. "Sabina, please. We can't reach Roman. V woke, and he broke through the Others' spell. He remembers everything. Including the Others coming to his cave after the sword was taken."

Sabina turned to Eilish. She couldn't see her yet because the mist was so thick, but she really wanted to know what V said about the Others.

Eilish blew out a breath, her frustration evident. "I know you're here. That light above you is from a Dragon King, and it follows you. If you don't want to trust me, I understand. I'm a Druid. Rhi, a Fae and a friend of the Kings, is looking for Roman. We figured the Others wouldn't think their own kind would help the Kings. Find V's sword. I'll be right here if you need help. Just shout my name. I'll find you."

Sabina bit her lip, weighing her odds of talking to Eilish. She was tired of being alone, but Ana had cautioned her about the spells the Others could cast. And, frankly, Sabina couldn't take the chance.

She faced forward and continued shuffling along the path. It would be so much easier if she could see, but she supposed that was the point. Ana had said the Others would make it as hard as possible for Sabina to get to the sword. Because once she had it, she would return it to V.

And V could check on the dragons.

Maybe even call them home.

After watching them fly as she spoke to Ana, she wanted them back. Even as it broke her heart to know that the humans and dragons could never co-exist. Someone would have to give up their home.

She didn't want to think about that right now. Instead, she focused on moving forward. She didn't know how she picked the direction. But she had followed her heart, as Ana had told her to do. Repeatedly.

Shuffle. Shuffle. Shuffle. Shuffle.

She was about to take another step when the mist suddenly parted, and she was able to see the entire cavern. It was . . . colossal.

Her gaze moved from the domed ceiling above her that stretched for what seemed like miles, to the enormous glacier—and she suspected she was only seeing a portion of it.

The stunning variances of blues and white reminded her of the color of Roman in dragon form. The glacier was so beautiful. Her gaze followed it from the top down until she saw where the ice was melting, leaving a dripping runoff that fell into a pool about a hundred feet below her.

Her vision suddenly swam. She fought the rising panic and her churning stomach for a moment. Steam rose from the water, and she realized it must be a hot spring. Her head swung to the other side, and her knees nearly buckled when she saw the thick waterfall of magma that poured into the cavern below into its own pool.

Awed, Sabina slowly let her gaze roam over the impressive area. She spotted the protrusion of land that rose up between the ice and magma like an island. Her eyes were moving away when they snapped back.

Her heart skipped a beat when she saw the cage on top of the island—and Roman within it.

She covered her mouth with her hand, her eyes misting at the sight of him. She was excited, horrified, and scared all at the same time.

"Hi, lass," he called.

He was too far away for her to make out his expression, but she heard the crooked smile in his voice. Sabina spotted the woman with him, but she was too focused on Roman to care who she was. "Oh, Roman."

"It's going to be fine."

She wasn't so sure about that, but she decided to keep her thoughts to herself. Sabina looked around, trying to figure out how to get to him. Her gaze drifted down, which was the last thing she should've done. Her feet were inches away from the edge that dropped off into . . . nothing.

Sabina hastily took several steps back as the cavern began spinning. She heard someone shout her name, and she was dimly aware that it was Roman. Her legs gave out. She hit the ground hard on her knees, the pain reverberating through her. With her fingers clutching the rocky ground, she opened her mouth and took in deep breaths to staunch the nausea.

"I've got her," she heard someone say near her. "She's fine, Roman." A moment later, a hand touched Sabina's shoulder as Eilish knelt beside her. "You are fine, aren't you?"

Sabina continued to take in huge gulps of air. She was so far up. So. *Far.*

"Scared of heights, I'm guessing," Eilish said.

Sabina's vision swam. She hated the tears, but more

than that, she hated her fear. Because it stopped her from getting to Roman.

"I can get you to the bottom in seconds," Eilish continued. "I can teleport, you see. Because of these."

Something silver flashed in front of Sabina's eyes, but she didn't see what it was. She could only nod her head. The idea of getting off the ledge or mountain or whatever it was she was on and onto lower, solid ground again sounded too good to pass up.

"Hold on," Eilish said as she wrapped her fingers around Sabina's wrist.

She waited, but she didn't feel anything. And the ground looked the same.

"Damn," Eilish murmured. "Give me a second."

Sabina closed her eyes when Eilish removed her hand. She disappeared before returning a second later. Sabina knew without looking at Eilish that there was a problem.

"I'm sorry, but something is preventing me from taking you."

Of course, it was. Damn the Others.

"Let me try something. I'll be back shortly," Eilish said and then was gone again.

Sabina would have to do this on her own. The very idea made her throat close up as she started to hyperventilate. She was going to fail because of a stupid fear. The Others would win because she couldn't staunch the terror within her.

Did they know she had this phobia?

Had they given it to her?

"Sabina."

Her face crumpled when she heard Roman shout her name. Tears slipped from her eyes. She hated the weakness within her. She couldn't go onward, but she refused to go backwards. And she wouldn't remain where she was.

Which left her . . . what?

"Sabina," Roman said again.

She slowly lifted her head, careful to keep from looking down. Thankfully, the mist remained parted so she could look at Roman.

When their gazes met, he nodded his head of sandy blond hair. "It's okay, lass."

But it wasn't. It was as if the Others had put the fear of heights in her just to keep her from this very thing. Whether it was true or not—and she didn't put anything past the Others—it infuriated her.

There was a way to get to the bottom. And she was going to find it.

Sabina stood on shaky legs. She wanted to ask Eilish for help, but she was certain the Others would prevent it, just as they had the teleporting.

The longer she stared at Roman, the more courage filled her. Sabina wished she could see his eyes, his gorgeous sea green eyes.

With a deep breath, she turned to the right and walked as close to the edge as she could manage. She swallowed hard and slowly went down on her hands and knees to tentatively crawl to the edge. She didn't look over. She lay on her stomach and put her cheek against the rock to steady herself. Then she peered over the edge, looking for stairs or some way to get down.

Unfortunately, she saw it. But the slope took her dangerously close to the pool of lava, which she'd already come too close to for comfort.

Sabina scooted back when everything began to spin, then shifted to her hands and knees before getting to her feet. She made her way to the left, repeating the entire process. And just as she expected, there was another way down.

It wasn't exactly easy, and it would require some careful thought before she moved from one section to the other. When the ground started to spin again, she closed her eyes and pressed her cheek to the rock. When she thought she could, she took another look.

The first section was about three feet below her. She could climb that relatively easily. The second one looked about the same distance, but it was hard to determine from where she was. After that, she couldn't get an accurate determination.

If she started down, she'd have no choice but to continue. And there was a good chance that she would get stuck and have to climb back up.

Sabina slowly got to her feet and turned her head to Roman. He was standing utterly still, watching her. She would never have gotten this far without him. He'd given her the courage to face her biggest fears—and chance everything.

"This is not the end," she whispered.

His head cocked to the side, and she realized that his enhanced hearing had picked up her words.

"I'm pretty sure I've fallen for you, Roman. But you already know that, don't you?"

She didn't wait to see his reaction. Sabina turned and bent as she started her descent.

CHAPTER FORTY-THREE

No! The word roared in Roman's head as he took a step, instinctively wanting to rush to Sabina's side. He'd seen firsthand how badly she feared heights.

He was amazed that she had the wherewithal to attempt the climb, but he was afraid she'd get halfway down, and her fear would overtake her, causing her to lose her grip and . . . fall.

"She's ballsy," Rhi said. "I like her."

Eilish suddenly appeared beside Rhi. "I tried to teleport her, but something stopped me."

"We saw," Rhi said.

Roman didn't look their way. He was watching Sabina make her way down to the first section. Anyone with climbing skills, or those who weren't afraid of heights, could get down fairly easily.

"I'm pretty sure I've fallen for you, Roman."

Her words had been as beautiful as the music from the metals. He'd been so shocked that he hadn't had time to respond before she started climbing. And now he didn't want to break her concentration.

"She can no' fall," he said, more to himself than Rhi or Eilish. "She can no'."

Out of the corner of his eye, he saw Eilish and Rhi exchange a look, but he didn't pay much attention to them. There was something much more important—Sabina.

"Roman," Rhi said. "Look at what she has to climb."

"What?" he asked, perturbed that she was talking.

Rhi moved to stand in front of him, her silver eyes blazing. "Look!"

"You're in the way," he stated angrily.

She rolled her eyes and stepped to the side. Roman then let his gaze move down the mountain that the mist continued to swirl around. There was a drop of about twelve feet and another of at least twenty.

A good climber could find foot and handholds, but Sabina wasn't a climber in any sense. In that moment, that very instant, he knew the Others had set her up to fail. She was going to fall to her death, and there was nothing any of them could do about it.

"Obliterate this . . . jail that holds you," Eilish told him. "Go to her."

His eyes swung to the Druid. "If I do, I willna save her. I'll likely kill her."

"What?!" Eilish asked in a high-pitched voice filled with shock.

Rhi's shoulders slumped. "Remember, you learned what happened to Dmitri and Con when they touched the wooden dragon? The same magic is holding Roman."

"Well, hell," Eilish mumbled.

It didn't matter if Roman watched Sabina fall to her death or if he broke through the Others' magic and it made him kill her—either way, they didn't intend for her to live.

"I'm not giving up," Eilish said and teleported to Sabina.

Rhi rubbed her hands together. "It's time I give it a try, as well."

Roman knew it was useless to think that either of the women could help Sabina, but he held out hope anyway. It took less than three minutes for that same hope to wither and die a horrible death.

Roman dropped to his knees when Sabina's hand slipped, and she hurriedly regained her hold. His heart was in his throat, fear and panic holding him tightly in their grip.

As one of the most powerful beings on the planet, Roman was curtailed, limited.

Restrained.

He had more magic than any Druid or Fae, but he couldn't save the woman he loved.

His mind went blank before his heart filled with happiness. It was true. He loved Sabina. And he wasn't going to lose her. He couldn't.

She reached the second section and rested a few moments before she started on the third. He didn't know where Eilish or Rhi was. Since they couldn't help, it didn't matter. He remained with Sabina, watching every placement of her hands, every position of her feet.

He could feel her muscles shaking, hear the frantic beating of her heart. She was terrified, but she was battling through it. He'd never been more proud of her than in that moment.

Twice she had to pause because her arms grew weary, but somehow, she made it through the section without incident. This time, she rested for several minutes. Roman tried to use his magic to give her water, but nothing would penetrate his prison.

He never took his eyes from her. She didn't look his way, and he didn't call out. Sabina had found a groove, and he was loath to disrupt it in any way.

When she began climbing again, he wanted to tell her to rest more, but he didn't. It took her far longer because she was so exhausted. Between the strain and exertion of climbing, there was also the toll the fear was likely taking on her mentally and physically.

He frowned when he saw the grip she had. It wasn't a good one. In fact, if she didn't reposition, she would—

The moment her hand slipped and she fell, Roman bellowed her name. She was tumbling through the air, and he didn't even hesitate to thrust his hand through the bars—and the magic of the Others—to use his own magic to stop her.

Except it wasn't that easy. The feeling of the Others' magic swirled dizzyingly, repulsively through him until he couldn't concentrate. Sweat broke out on his brow as he pushed everything aside and yelled as he gave a burst of magic.

He saw Sabina stop inches from the ground. Roman tried to smile, but he couldn't. Already, he could feel the effects of the Others' magic.

The price for saving Sabina would be a hefty one.

The scream lodged in her throat, unable to break through. The fall was all too similar to when she and Roman had tumbled off the ledge at the magma river. It wouldn't be lava that killed her this time, but a slam against the earth.

The wind was loud in her ears, but even so, she heard Roman shout her name. She wanted one last look at him, but she couldn't figure out which way was up.

Then, suddenly, everything stopped as she jerked to a

halt. Her heart was pounding so hard, she thought it might burst from her chest. A moment later, she dropped a few inches to the ground onto her side.

She sat up and looked toward Roman. Without a doubt, he'd saved her. The smile she wore faded when she saw him clutching his head as if in great pain.

"Damn," a voice said from behind her.

Sabina jumped to her feet and whirled around to see two women standing there. Both gorgeous, both wearing black, and both with black hair, though one had silver eyes and the other's were a green-gold color.

"You made it down," said the one with the green-gold eyes.

Eilish. Sabina nodded as she recognized the voice and shifted her gaze to the other woman, whose hair was pulled back in some messy 'do that shouldn't look good but did. "Who are you?"

Silver eyes slid to her. "I wish there was time for a proper introduction, and for me to tell you how badass I think you are, but there isn't."

"Rhi," Eilish said with a frown.

Rhi! Of course. Sabina should've realized that's who was with Roman.

The Fae cut Eilish a dark look and pointed at Roman. "We don't have time."

"What's wrong with him?" Sabina asked as she turned to look at Roman again. The words were barely out of her mouth before she gasped.

Suddenly, he was in dragon form, the prison demolished. His ivory eyes scanned the cavern. But the kindness she was used to seeing in his gaze was not there. Instead, there was death.

"He saved you," Rhi said as she came up beside her.

"He had to push his arm through the magic of the Others in order to keep you from splattering on the ground."

Sabina winced. "And in doing so, the magic changed him. He said it made the Kings want to kill humans."

"That's right," Rhi said. Then she turned her head to Eilish. "You better get Ulrik or V. Oh, hell, get both."

Without a word, Eilish disappeared. Sabina froze when Roman let out an earsplitting roar before he spread his wings and dropped from the top of the isle. He soared toward the lava waterfall and then headed toward them.

"Get moving," Rhi told her with a hard push.

Sabina stumbled forward before she jerked around. "What are you talking about?"

"You need the sword," Rhi stated, and then she too was gone.

Sabina nodded to herself. "Right. The sword."

For the first time, she paid attention to her surroundings. Behind her was the mountain she'd just fallen from, the base wide as it narrowed to the top ledge where she'd first come into the cavern.

Fire to her right, ice to her left. But what was in front of her? Two huge chunks of rock rose up from the ground, soaring toward the domed ceiling. She couldn't see much from her position. She'd have to go between them. The closer she got, the more they looked like an entrance of some sort.

Once she was even with them, she realized that they were much wider than she realized. From the front, they looked to be about twenty feet across, but the width was easily fifty feet.

A roar sounded above her. She looked up and spotted Roman. He suddenly dipped his wing and swung back around, his ivory eyes locked on her.

"You know me," she said. "You know me, Roman."

She saw the red glow in his chest as he inhaled. But right before he breathed fire, a copper dragon slammed into him.

"V," Sabina said.

She looked ahead of her and started running. The sooner she found V's sword, the sooner they could leave. Once out of the cavern, maybe the magic of the Others would wear off. Roman hadn't let her die, and she wasn't going to let him.

There was another roar, a different one. She glanced up and saw a silver dragon join in the fight. No doubt that was Ulrik.

"Don't you hurt him," she yelled at V and Ulrik.

Sabina slid to a halt when the rock walls ended, and she saw what was ahead of her. What she hadn't been able to see before was that when the pools of lava and water overflowed, they fell into a river. Both rushed toward the center of the cavern.

The hiss of the water meeting the lava was loud, but she wasn't paying attention. Instead, she was looking at the magnificent sword that hung in midair, its blade pointing down directly over where the fire and ice met.

There was no way she could get into the lava. It'd kill her. She looked at the water. It rushed past her so quickly that no matter how well she could swim, the currents would suck her beneath the surface and batter her against the rocks.

But there had to be a way to get to the sword. All along, Roman had assumed she was meant to acquire it for V, but now she thought perhaps it was hanging the way it was so that only a dragon could get it.

"Here!" she yelled when V flew past.

His head turned to her, but he kept flying. She realized he must not have seen his sword.

"What now?" Sabina asked herself.

Eilish and Rhi were nowhere to be found. Sabina was on her own. Because that's how the Others wanted it to be. They wanted her to make a mistake, to choose the wrong option and die.

This was her final test. And it would be the worst one yet.

She heard Ana's voice telling her to follow her heart. But how could following her heart help her safely walk through magma or a rapidly moving river of water?

It couldn't.

Sabina sighed. No. There had to be a way. She just needed to find it. She walked to the left, looking for anything that she could use to either cross the ten-foot span of water or throw at the sword to dislodge it.

Since she had horrible aim and that could very well tumble the weapon into the river, she opted to look for ways to get to the sword. She wasn't discouraged when she found nothing. Retracing her steps, Sabina walked along the magma, searching for the same thing.

Finally, she ended up right where she started. At the convergence of fire and ice. Curious, she put her hand into the water. It was ice cold. Strange since there was steam coming from the pool, but then there was little that made sense in the mountain.

The whoosh of air near her had her head snapping up. She saw that Ulrik had stopped Roman from grabbing her with his long talons.

With a shudder, she resumed looking at the sword. She didn't take her eyes from it. It was just as beautiful as when she had first seen it in V's cave.

She hadn't hesitated to grab it then because it had been right there. Like it was waiting for her. Same as it was now. Waiting to be returned to its owner. She could be the one to do that.

The edges of her vision grew fuzzy. She heard roars and felt wind rush past her, but she didn't take her eyes from the weapon. She had no idea how much time passed. It could have been a millisecond or a million years.

But, suddenly, she was standing before the weapon, hovering over the churning gathering of the rivers. She wasn't afraid. Not even when she felt the sting of the icy water and the heat of the magma.

Because, somehow, the sword had brought her. She didn't know how she knew, only that she did. The weapon had been waiting on her, waiting for her to take it back to its owner.

She reached out and grasped the blade by the hilt, wrapping her fingers around it. As soon as she did, she was back on solid ground.

The hot breath of something large behind her fanned around her. She turned and saw Roman glaring at her with his ivory eyes. He inhaled, ready to engulf her in dragon fire.

Sabina couldn't control herself or the sword when it lifted. The blade swung toward Roman, and the next thing she knew, it plunged into his chest.

CHAPTER FORTY-FOUR

Everything hurt. His body screamed in agony, and every breath felt as if his lungs were being ripped out. Roman fell onto his back and blinked against the agony. He spotted the silver and copper scales as they stood on either side of him, the concern in his friends' eyes worrying.

Why did everything ache?

Then he saw it. The sword protruding from his chest. His head dropped back, and he looked up at the domed ceiling. Where was he? He'd been after something, the need to kill critical. Unrelenting. What was it? What had he been af—

A mortal.

It was as if a dense fog filled his mind, preventing him from seeing the entire picture. Because he knew it was important. The fact that both Ulrik and V were in dragon form and staring at him with uncertainty didn't help matters.

He shifted his shoulder and immediately knew that the pull he felt was the wounds from Ulrik's claws healing. Ulrik had jumped on his back, tearing at his scales because Roman had been about to kill a human.

But that didn't make sense. He'd vowed to protect them. He'd never hurt one. Not even when he wanted to.

"Easy," V said.

It was getting harder and harder for Roman to keep his eyes open. Bloody hell, it hurt. He managed to turn his head and look at V, who was now in human form. And, somehow, so was Roman. He didn't remember shifting. Shouldn't he have recalled that?

Damn. What was going on?"

"Oh, God," he heard a woman say, her voice pitched high with fear and regret.

He knew that voice.

"Remember her," V told him.

Roman saw V's blue gaze trained on him before Roman's eyes shut. It was just too difficult to keep them open. Too much effort was needed to breathe.

"What did I do? Oh, God. Roman!" the woman screamed.

He felt something touch his leg, but it was hastily yanked away. Roman heard Ulrik talking to her, trying to calm her down. No matter how much Roman tried, he couldn't place the voice, but he should. He knew her.

"Roman, you need to remember her," V urged as he squatted down beside him.

If only the pain would stop, he might be able to concentrate.

"He can't die," the woman said hysterically. "He can't. He promised me that only another Dragon King could kill him."

For some inexplicable reason, Roman wanted to go to her, comfort her. He wasn't sure why, only that he *needed* to. If he could move, he'd do just that.

"Take . . . it . . . out," he told V.

There was a hesitation, and then V said, "We've already tried."

What? That didn't make sense.

"Roman, I can no' tell you what happened. You need to remember," V said. "Trust me. I ken you're hurting, but forget that. Let your magic sort through the fog."

So V knew about that? That was odd. Wasn't it? Roman was sure he hadn't mentioned it. And if he hadn't said anything, then that could only mean that V had been through the same thing.

Out of nowhere, a memory barreled through his mind about V's memories being blocked from magic by . . . Why couldn't Roman remember what kind of magic? It was imperative, that much he knew for sure.

Every breath was excruciating. Even after his battle with Freyr, Roman didn't recall the pain being so debilitating. Then again, V's sword was inside him.

V's sword! They found it. After all this time. It should be a time for celebration. If only he could remember what had happened before.

"V," he croaked. "Your sword."

"You helped me find it, just as you said you would," V said.

A woman cried softly, pacing near his feet. The same woman who had been frantic earlier. Without seeing her, he could sense her trepidation, her worry.

For him?

"Roman? Can you hear me?" Ulrik asked from his other side.

He swallowed and tried to open his eyes, but he couldn't. "Aye," he murmured.

There was a growl from V, who then asked, "Why the fuck did he shift? He should've remained in his true form."

Roman had that same question, but he assumed V wasn't talking to him. Damn. The fog was getting thicker in his mind.

"You know why," Ulrik replied.

Roman clenched his fists and tried to roll over. He couldn't hold back the groan when the blade tore through more muscle and organs. "Tell. Me."

"You need to remember," V urged again.

"Let me touch him."

The woman again. He wanted to smile at her demanding tone. Good for her. If she didn't stand up for herself, then Ulrik and V would run all over her.

"I think you should let her," said another woman with a hint of an Irish accent.

He knew that voice, too. Her name was right on the tip of his tongue. He hadn't liked her at first, but now she was part of the family. Because . . . she was Ulrik's mate. He remembered!

"Eilish," he whispered.

Ulrik leaned close, a smile in his voice as he said, "That's right."

"Surely, you know me, too, stud."

The sassy tone, complete with a thick Irish accent was one he knew very well. She was his friend. Roman struggled to picture her face, but just as it was all coming together, it fell apart.

There were footsteps close to his head, and then a soft touch on his brow. "Don't worry about it, handsome. You'll recall everything soon enough."

Why weren't they bringing him to Dreagan? "Home," he said.

V blew out a frustrated breath. "We can no' take you. The spells prevent it."

"That's it. I'm done being nice," the first woman said.

Roman heard scuffling, and then another body knelt beside him. Soft hands gently took one of his into hers and held it against her chest. She hooked her thumb with his, their palms flattened together.

"I'm sorry, Roman. So very sorry," she said.

He wanted to look at her. He managed to turn his head, but no matter what he did, he couldn't open his eyes. Her words held such anguish that he longed to comfort her. Her touch, though, did wonders to ease him. "It's . . . okay . . . lass."

She sobbed, her tears falling onto his hand. He hated that she was crying, but somehow, the longer they touched, the more bearable the pain was.

Who was this woman whose mere voice affected him so? And her touch? He never wanted her to let him go. She was helping him. If only he could remember who she was.

"Take it . . . out," he bade her.

She sniffed and leaned close. Her hair fell against his cheek. "I don't want to hurt you more."

He sighed when her wet cheek pressed against his. His mouth craved her lips. He'd kissed her. He knew her taste, knew how intoxicating she was.

A face began to form in his mind. Eyes a deep, mysterious brown with just a hint of impishness and a wealth of courage stared at him. Then it faded into the fog.

"Have . . . to," Roman said.

"He's right," V said. "It has to come out for him to heal. We can no' do it."

Roman felt the woman's heart drum erratically against the back of his hand. She was terrified of hurting him, and it was obvious by the way she held his hand that she cared about him.

"I think I've fallen for you, Roman."

The words drifted through his mind like a caress. He latched on to the memory, grabbing on to it with all he had until he was able to dredge up the memory of a beautiful woman with deep olive skin, haunting eyes, and curls so deep a brown they were nearly black.

Then her name floated through his mind, wiping away the fog with one swipe.

"Sabina," he whispered.

"Yes," she said as more tears fell on his hand. "I'm here."

He'd made love to her in the hot springs. Even now, he could recall the softness of her skin beneath his palms. Hear her ragged breaths as he brought her ever closer to climax.

She was his mate, the one he loved.

And he really hoped that Ulrik and V had put on some clothes. The idea that they were naked around Sabina didn't sit well with him. At all.

Ulrik touched Roman's foot. "Figure out the rest, old friend."

He wanted to, he really did. It was the pain. He wished to get away from it. There was a place in his mind that offered him a way to escape. He drifted there without thinking. Just as he was about to surrender himself, Sabina squeezed his hand.

"Don't leave me," she said. "You promised you wouldn't leave."

No longer could he gather the energy for words. There was an explosion—imagined or real, he knew not. Something was there, with him, something he wasn't sure of. Then a smell assaulted him and reminded him of home. How he and his sister would fly deep into the mountains and play near the magma or slide down the glaciers.

Home.

"Don't leave me," Sabina whispered again.

Then she released his hand. He tried to reach for her, to find her again. She didn't want him to leave, but she had done just that with him. Roman tried to form her name, to get the word past his lips, but already, he was fading.

And he feared there would be no return.

The fog was gone, but whatever had him now was stronger, more insidious. And it wanted him.

Roman felt someone stand over him, their feet on either side of his hips. As soon as they touched the sword, sharp pain cut through him. He wanted to know what was going on, but that place in his mind, that dark, sinister place, kept pulling him.

"Roman, stay with me," Sabina said.

Her voice was over him. Was she the one holding the sword? No sooner had that thought gone through his mind than an image appeared in his head. He stood over Sabina in dragon form as she held V's sword.

But he hadn't recognized her. All he saw was a mortal. And in his mind, all mortals had to die.

Roman bellowed in pain and jerked upward as the sword was yanked free. The moment it was removed, whatever treacherous magic had ahold of him vanished.

He fell back, the pain gone and numbness taking over as his body threaded itself back together.

"He's healing," Ulrik said.

Roman opened his eyes and took a deep breath. His gaze locked on the defiant, exquisite gypsy standing over him, and his heart swelled. Sabina held V's sword as the blade dripped his blood onto the ground, her gaze locked on him.

"I didn't mean it," she said as another tear fell.

Roman smiled and held out his hand. She grabbed it but hesitated as she handed V his weapon. Then she was in

Roman's arms. He held her tightly, savoring the feel of her warm body on top of his.

"I may never let you go," he said into her hair.

She pressed her lips to his neck. "I don't want you to."

"I wasna expecting you, or the feelings between us, but I wouldna change anything."

Sabina stiffened in his arms. "I stabbed you."

He sat up, and she spread her legs, wrapping them around him. "You may have wielded V's sword, but you are no' a Dragon King."

"You couldna kill him," V said as he dipped the sword into the water to clean it.

Ulrik crossed his arms over his bare chest. "What do you remember?"

Roman smoothed hair back from Sabina's face. "Everything. How I saved my mate from dying, and by doing so, gave the Others access to me through their magic." He held Sabina's gaze. "I'm sorry for trying to kill you. I had no control."

"She knows," Ulrik said. "We told her."

Roman looked from Ulrik to V, glad they at least had pants on. That's when he realized that he was still very naked.

"Let's get out of here," he said.

Sabina sighed and nodded. "Yes, please."

She jumped up. Roman looked down at the wound that was already healed. He got to his feet and realized that Rhi and Eilish weren't there. Roman raised a brow at Ulrik in a silent question.

Ulrik shot him a dark look. "You were naked. I didna want my woman seeing that."

V shoved at Ulrik's shoulder and flattened his lips in annoyance before turning to Roman. "The girls are looking at some markings they found on the stone walls."

Roman decided to use his magic for more than just a pair of jeans. With a thought, his clothes were once more in place. Then he and Sabina joined hands.

As Ulrik and V went to find Eilish and Rhi, Roman hung back.

"What is it?" Sabina asked.

"I can no' help but feel that the Others are no' finished with us."

She rested her head against his shoulder. "I don't they think are. We unknowingly put their third drawing into effect."

"We need to find the Fae since the Druids who were part of this are dead."

Sabina frowned as she faced him. "I didn't get a chance to tell you, but I traveled to the past again. I spoke with Ana, the one who sent the men to steal V's sword."

"And?"

Sabina glanced away. "I can only assume what she told me is true."

"Tell me," he urged, wondering what it could possibly be.

"She said the Others instigated all of it. Including the arrival of the humans here. The minute you and the other Dragon Kings agreed to protect them, you sealed your Fate."

Roman shook his head. "No."

"You said yourself, you don't know where the mortals came from."

That was true, but still . . .

"Also," Sabina began.

There was more? Roman wasn't sure he could handle anything else.

"Ana said Druids didn't begin here. That the place humans come from always had Druids. That they rule there."

Roman blew out a breath. "That changes everything."

"I know it means more questions, but I just thought—"

Roman put a finger to her lips and pulled her close. "You thought right, lass."

Her dark eyes held his. "I was terrified when I fell, but nothing comes close to what I experienced when I thought you were dying."

"I know the feeling well. It's the same one I suffered when you were suffocating, and again when you fell. I didna care what happened to me, but I was going to save you."

He bent and gave her a long, slow kiss. When he lifted his head to look at her, he asked, "So you may love me, huh?"

"No," she said with a shake of her head. "I *do* love you. I love you with all my heart."

"And I love you, my gypsy."

CHAPTER FORTY-FIVE

"Where's my brother?"

Sabina couldn't believe she'd forgotten about Camlo. What kind of sister was she?

"He's fine," V said, stepping back between the stones to look at her. "Eilish took him home. He's no' alone, though. Keltan is watching over him."

Sabina looked at Roman. "Keltan?"

"Another Dragon King," he replied.

"Oh." That made her feel better.

They walked to Ulrik, Eilish, and V, everyone eager to leave the mountain. Sabina would be happy to never see the place again. It was terrifyingly beautiful, but the Others had ruined it. They dirtied it, destroyed it with their magic.

"This place," Eilish said as she and Ulrik came around the left-hand wall. She shook her head and frowned. "It's like I know it here," she stated, touching her chest. "That this has something to do with Druids, but I can't read it."

Sabina frowned. "Read it?"

"There are symbols," Ulrik said.

She and Roman walked around the wall to see for themselves. Sure enough, there was writing of some kind. It wasn't faded as she'd expected it to be, but clean and perfect. As if it had just been carved.

"These are no' natural," Roman said as he eyed the stone.

Sabina hadn't thought much about it when she first saw them. To her, they were nothing more than entrances to the sword. Now, she realized they were much more than that.

"How tall are they?" she asked.

Roman shrugged. "About sixty feet high."

"The writing goes all the way up," Eilish added.

Sabina craned her head back to look up. "I wonder what it says."

"Tell them what you told me," Roman urged her.

She lowered her head to find not just Eilish and Ulrik looking at her but also V. Sabina guessed that Rhi was looking at the other wall.

Sabina still wasn't certain how she felt about the information, but she relayed what Ana had told her about the mortals and Druids.

"I don't even know what to say," Eilish said.

Ulrik's nostrils flared, his chest rising and falling rapidly. His gold eyes sparked with anger. "These . . . Others," he said with disgust, "are responsible for *everything*."

"We need to get back to Dreagan," V said.

"Go," Roman urged them. "Sabina and I will make it out."

V let out a loud snort, his lips twisting. "Seriously? You think I'm going to leave you two? Give me some credit."

"V's right," Eilish said. "Besides, I can't let this feeling go that what's written here is important."

Ulrik glanced irritably at the wall. "It doesna matter if we can no' read it."

"It's too much to memorize," Eilish mumbled.

Sabina released Roman's hand and walked to the other wall. She was curious to see if Rhi was able to read hers. When she got there, the woman was staring wide-eyed at the stone, her face pale and her hands trembling.

"Rhi?" she called softly, not wanting to startle her.

The Light Fae stumbled back a step. She was breathing heavily, her gaze unfocused.

Suddenly, everyone else joined Sabina. It was Ulrik who calmly walked to Rhi and took her by the shoulders. He tried to make her look at him, but the Fae's attention was on the wall.

"Rhi?" Ulrik asked. "Can you hear me?"

Roman walked to the wall and looked at the place where Rhi was staring. "There's nothing here, so she's no' reading anything."

"Rhi," Ulrik repeated, giving her a little shake.

V made his way to her and grabbed Rhi's arm, spinning her away from the wall. Everyone held his or her breath, waiting to see what Rhi would do.

"Rhi?" V frowned as he looked down at Rhi.

She inhaled swiftly and issued a quick nod. "I'm here."

"I beg to differ," Ulrik said.

Rhi shifted to face everyone and smiled, but it was forced. "This place gives me the creeps, and I've been in a lot of creepy places. This one takes the cake."

Sabina didn't know Rhi, but she was as worried as the others. The Fae wasn't acting her normal, sassy, confident self.

Rhi was rattled. Deeply.

"Do you see writing?" Sabina asked, pointing at the wall.

Rhi swallowed, but she purposefully didn't look at the rock. "Yeah. Don't you?"

Everyone shook their heads.

Rhi shrugged. "It's Fae, but that's all I know. I can't read it. At times, I think it's Dark, and then it's Light. All very confusing. Let's go."

Roman stepped in front of Rhi when she made to walk away. "What are you no' telling us?"

"Nothing. I simply don't like this place," Rhi answered.

V made an indistinct sound. "None of us does."

"One wall Fae, one Druid," Eilish said. "It's significant. We could probably find out all we wanted from these walls. If we could read them."

Sabina noticed that Roman, V, and Ulrik all jerked their heads in the same direction in unison.

"Did you—?" Ulrik began.

V quickly replied, "Aye."

"Move!" Roman bellowed.

As one, the three Kings shifted. Before Sabina knew what was going on, she was clutched in Roman's paw. He flew straight up. She looked down, expecting to be overcome with fear. And she was, but it wasn't nearly as terrible as before.

Until she saw the magma roiling viciously, the molten pool and river gurgling and bubbling right before there was an explosion that caused magma to shoot up. After the first, others began in quick succession.

Then there was a loud crack coming from the glacier. A heartbeat later, a huge section slid off, slamming into the pool and busting apart the rock that held it.

It was a domino effect. One thing hit another, then that hit something else. By the time Roman had landed on the outcropping, she saw one of the stone walls topple. In the next instant, they were flying through the mountain. V was leading them, busting through the narrow tunnel with his magic and powerful dragon body.

The trip that had taken her and Roman hours to make,

took seconds to reach the surface. They burst out into the open to a sky drenched in darkness and snow.

Sabina was glad Camlo wasn't in the mountain because their escape came seconds before the mountain shot a cloud of ash heavenward into the night sky while lava flowed down the mountainside, melting the thick snow.

She clung to Roman's hand, burying her face near one of his long talons. The wind rushed over her, but she didn't feel the cold—and she knew who was responsible for that.

Just to be safe, she kept her eyes closed and thought of anything but the fact that she was thousands of miles in the air. Yet she couldn't pass up the chance to see dragons flying again, not after witnessing them in her vision of the past.

With a quick peek, she saw V on Roman's left, his sword clutched in his claw, while Ulrik, with Eilish on his back, flew on Roman's right. Sabina assumed that Rhi had left another way because the Kings wouldn't have abandoned her.

It wasn't long before Sabina was drifting off to sleep. She was mentally and physically—and spiritually—exhausted. She had to admit that it was a peaceful experience. There was nothing but the sound of wind and the beating of dragon wings.

She didn't know how long she slept before she felt a direction change, which woke her. The dragons dipped from a cloud in unison to pass over a striking piece of land with vast mountains. Her eyes remained on the horizon, so she was able to enjoy the ride.

And then, to her surprise, more dragons joined them. Yellow, emerald green, red, amber, bronze, deep blue, black, jade green, burnt orange, white, claret, turquoise, dark purple, ivory, gray, hunter green, steel, teal, orange, and many others that she couldn't make out in the night.

But there was no mistaking the gold dragon.

She couldn't get enough of the magnificent creatures. And to think that, at one time, there were hundreds of thousands of dragons. Millions of them.

All too soon, their flight came to an end as one by one, the other dragons peeled off and started flying to certain sections of the land. Roman, V, Ulrik, and a few other dragons made their way to a mountain.

Sabina spotted the opening in the stone. As they drew closer, a shape took form. It was Rhi standing outside as the gold dragon swooped in first. Sabina had thought he wouldn't make it, but the opening was much larger than she originally thought.

Ulrik went through next. She and Roman were after him. No sooner had they come to a halt within the mountain than V landed behind them. Sabina stopped trying to see the other dragons as she found herself in a section of mountain that had dragons carved and painted all over the walls in various sizes.

"It's a tribute to the ones we've lost," came a deep brogue behind her.

Sabina turned and found herself staring into pitch black eyes. The man was tall with wavy blond hair, a black suit with gold dragon head cufflinks, and an intense look about him. Along with a vibe that demanded that everyone near him recognize who was in charge.

"You're the gold dragon," she said.

He bowed his head. "Constantine. And you must be Sabina Gabor. I want to personally thank you and your brother for your help."

Holy crap. This was Con? The King of Dragon Kings. She leaned to the side against Roman, who had shifted into human form, Then, in a whisper, she asked, "Do I curtsy?"

Con's lips twitched.

Roman smiled at her and shook his head. "He's our King. No' yours, lass."

She looked into Roman's sea green eyes then glanced around at the others who stood bare-chested and shoeless in pants before she returned her gaze to Con. "I saw them," she said.

"Who?" Con asked with a frown.

Sabina searched for V. He had yet to let go of his sword, and he was watching her. "There were about a dozen of them. The copper scales were difficult to see in the moonlight, but they were truly a splendid sight. There were others, in the distance, but the group I saw was the closest. Their roars, loud—"

"And long," V said with a sad smile. "That was their call to me. You saw them?" he asked in shock.

She shrugged, suddenly uncomfortable now that everyone was watching her. "Ana, my ancestor, told me that I come from a long line of powerful women with the Sight. I'm the first who can see the past, not the future."

"And you spoke to her?" Con asked, stunned.

Roman nodded, smiling down at her as he wrapped an arm around her. "Sabina has learned some interesting things."

"Hell, we all have," Ulrik stated.

"Then it's the perfect time to hear it all," Con said. "Dorian has just returned from New York. Get your woman something to eat while we wait for the others to gather."

Sabina beamed. She was Roman's woman.

"Welcome to Dreagan, lass. It's your future, if you'll have it," Roman told her.

She faced him, shock going through her. "What?"

"A dragon knows his mate."

Her heart nearly burst from her chest she was so excited. "Me?"

Roman laughed and pulled her against him as others walked past. "Aye. That includes your brother, as well. There are many animals on Dreagan. No one will ever bother him here. I promise you that."

"He won't leave his animals at home."

Roman shrugged. "Then we bring them. We have sixty thousand acres. There's room."

Could this really be happening? She'd never felt . . . well, *any* of this. The love, the excitement, the danger, the adventure. It was a heady experience.

"Think on it."

She shook her head and rose up on her tiptoes to wrap her arms around his neck. "I don't need to. Just promise that we can have a hot spring."

Roman's eyes darkened. "Oh, aye. That we will have."

Sabina could barely comprehend everything. Her heart was so full that it was nearly bursting. She'd never imagined that she would find a love as pure and deep as what she felt for Roman. Or that she would want to embrace the Sight.

But she had a purpose now besides just taking care of Camlo. She was going to help the Dragon Kings fight against the Others.

And they were going to win!

Because love always won.

CHAPTER FORTY-SIX

Three days later . . .

Sabina ran her hands over the tops of the chairs in the kitchen as she listened to Camlo talk to the animals through the open window.

Eilish was using her finger rings to bring the animals to Dreagan, and Camlo proudly told everyone who would listen that the creatures were excited about it. Hell, even the mangy dog was coming with them.

Camlo didn't seem to care that they were leaving their home behind. He was too overjoyed about getting to have his animals and being around other Dragon Kings. Sabina hadn't realized how hard it would be to leave behind everything she'd known.

She came to her worktable and touched the half-finished necklace she'd been working on. Then, before her very eyes, wires rose up, twining around themselves in a beautiful dance. They moved fluidly, easily, as a shape began to form. Within moments, a pale blue dragon necklace that would drape beautifully around her neck lay before her.

"I was wondering when I'd get to see your gift," she said with a smile.

Roman came up behind her, wrapping his arms around

her waist. "No one said you had to stop making your jewelry. It's something you're verra good at."

She leaned her head back against his shoulder and covered his hands with hers. "That's true."

"And if you doona want to move to Dreagan now, you doona have to."

Sabina turned to face him, grinning. "Oh, I'm coming."

He didn't smile. "I've bought this place. You can return anytime you want. This is your home. I doona want you to think that you're leaving forever."

And this was one of the many reasons she loved him. Instead of trying to tell him through words, though, Sabina brought his head down for a kiss.

"Again?" Camlo exclaimed in horror as he entered the house. He let out a loud sigh and turned around and stomped off.

Sabina laughed as she buried her head against Roman's chest.

He held her for a long moment. "We have to get back soon."

"I know." She looked up at him, and seeing his frown, she rolled her eyes. "I'm perfectly fine with not being able to see the mating ceremony. I understand that it's only for the Kings and their mates."

It had been her decision to wait for their ceremony. Not that she had any doubts, but she wanted to give herself and Camlo some time to adjust to things. They were taking a big step. But nowhere in her heart did she doubt that she was supposed to be with anyone but Roman.

Knowing that she could return eased her tremendously. In two hours, their lives were packed and already waiting for them at Dreagan.

When she walked outside to join Eilish, Roman, and Camlo, her brother was excitedly jumping up and down, waiting to teleport to Dreagan. And a few seconds later, that's exactly where they were.

Ulrik was waiting for them, and together, he and Eilish took Camlo to see the animals. Roman put his arm around Sabina as they walked up the stairs to the room they would share. Camlo had chosen to stay in a small cottage on the property to be close to the animals—a dwelling that hadn't been there until he asked for it.

Sabina didn't know who'd crafted it, but she would be forever grateful. Already, she felt a part of the large family at Dreagan. And everyone had eagerly taken in Camlo and his array of pets.

"Tell me again why Eilish and Ulrik aren't doing the ceremony now?" she asked.

Roman closed the door to their room behind him as he went to change into the kilt—which, she had to admit, made him look even sexier. "With everything that happened to them, Ulrik and Eilish decided to hold off. But, I know that Ulrik has something special planned for her." Roman looked up. "Doona tell Eilish."

Sabina sat in the chair near the fireplace and smiled. "My lips are sealed. By the way, can I say that I love the kilt? Can you wear that all the time?"

Roman paused in buckling his sporran. He grinned when he saw her staring. "If it makes you look at me like that, then I certainly will, lass."

Never in her wildest dreams had she ever thought she'd marry a Highlander, much less a Dragon King. "Can I at least see the others as they come down?"

"Aye," he replied as he raked his hand through his hair then held out his hand to her. "Ready?"

Was she ever. She'd heard all about the ceremony from the other mates, including that Con gave each of them special gifts. It was a personal touch that she hadn't expected from the King of Dragon Kings, but somehow, it seemed to fit the enigmatic leader.

At the bottom of the stairs, she found Eilish and went to stand beside her. Roman gave Sabina a quick kiss before he caught up with Ulrik and they disappeared into the solarium where the hidden door into the mountain was.

"I'm glad I'm not here alone," Eilish said with a grin.

Sabina felt the same. "Do you wish you were with them?"

"We both will be soon."

That was so true. Sabina let the conversation drop as Gianna descended the stairs. Her magnificent, long, red hair was left free, and it swayed against the fitted, sleeveless gunmetal blue sequin gown she wore. The neck dipped into a V in the front and the back, but it was the large octagonal gem the exact color of her dress—and Sebastian's scales—at Gianna's throat that Sabina couldn't take her eyes off.

It had to be the gift Con gave her.

Gianna touched the necklace and gave them a wink before she went into the solarium.

Next was Esther, who had arrived just the day before from the Isle of Eigg where her brother, Henry, remained. Esther's brown locks were swept softly away from her face and held up with pearl pins. Sabina immediately noticed the earrings that hung delicately in the wispy strands of her hair. How Con found a mother of pearl shade that matched Nikolai, Sabina didn't even want to know.

Then she forgot about it as she took in the simple but elegant spaghetti-strapped gossamer gown Esther wore with its plunging V neckline. Sabina smiled when she saw that the dress was held up in back by thin straps, but it was the sweeping train that she really loved.

They waved at Esther as she made her way toward the solarium. Both Sabina's and Eilish's heads whipped back to the top of the stairs where Con escorted Alexandra down the stairs.

The coral gown was a stunner, but then again, it would be for an heiress like Alexandra. The sleeveless, high-neck gown was covered with pearls in various shades of coral accented heavily around the waist and thinning out as they worked up toward the neck. Those same pearls thinned out as they reached her hips.

The voluptuous folds of the gown hid the daring slit over her left leg until she walked. Then you got to see a peak of sheer coral lace with pearls sewn in.

"Check out the shoes," Eilish whispered.

Sabina had just seen the stilettos the exact shade of the dress. Her gaze lifted to Alexandra's face to see her blond curls pulled gracefully away from her face in a half updo that had several curls falling alongside her cheeks.

At first, Sabina didn't see the jewelry. Then she spotted the sunstone gem on Alexandra's right hand. It was a beautiful, large, round stone set in a narrow, beveled, rose gold band.

Con gave Sabina and Eilish a nod as he and Alexandra passed them. And then the procession was finished. Sabina sighed.

"Are you ready?" Eilish asked.

Sabina frowned. "For what?"

Eilish rolled her eyes. "We might not be able to go to the ceremony, but there is a party afterward we can attend."

"Oh, God." Why hadn't Sabina thought of that? Why hadn't Roman said anything?

"Calm down," Eilish said with a chuckle. "I told Roman I'd take care of you."

Sabina stared wide-eyed at her. "Are you insane? I don't have anything. And there's no time to shop."

"Really?" Eilish asked, propped her right hand on her hip and waved the fingers of her left hand. "I am a Druid."

"I'm going to need a lot of help."

Eilish laughed and hooked her arm through Sabina's. "Nope. All you need is a dress."

"Then let's get going."

"About time," the Druid said and touched her finger rings together.

Roman looked around the party to find Sabina. The ceremony had gone smoothly, but he'd been anxious for it to finish so he could find his woman. He'd been too long without a kiss. His gaze scanned the area quickly, then his eyes jerked back when he spotted the red gown.

His mouth fell open when he saw her standing alone, her gaze on him. One side of her hair was pulled back, secured with some glittering pin that sparkled in her dark curls.

The red material crisscrossed over her breasts to disappear around her shoulders. The fabric hugged her curves—especially her waist—before falling to the floor, making his mouth water and his balls tighten.

He strode to her, pulling her against him and claiming her mouth in a fiery kiss. When he lifted his head, dark eyes gazed up at him with so much love that his heart missed a beat. "You take my breath away."

"Then you know how I feel every time I look at you," she whispered.

The noise of the celebration faded as he looked down at his woman, his gypsy. "I'm ridiculously happy. And selfish, because I doona want to share you with anyone."

"Do we have to stay?" she asked.

He gave a shake of his head. "Nay."

"Then what are we waiting for?" she asked with a sly grin.

"Och. I do like the way you think, lass."

Roman took her hand as they made their way to the exit. Con gave him a nod and a smile. Tonight was for celebrating. Tomorrow would be time enough to focus on their new enemy. And as far as Roman was concerned, nothing and no one was coming between him and his woman.

He didn't slow, even when they made their way deeper into the mountain and Sabina kept asking him where they were going. He'd been working on the surprise all week.

As soon as he tugged her through the narrow opening and steam hit them, he turned to her. Sabina's eyes widened, and her lips formed a big smile.

"Oh, Roman," she whispered when she took in the hot spring. "How?"

"It wasna that difficult."

She glanced down at her gown. "I'll need help getting out of this."

"That I can do," he said and made the dress vanish—along with his clothes—with magic.

Then he scooped her up in his arms and stepped into the water.

EPILOGUE

A week later . . .

Everything was perfect. Blissfully so.

But Roman knew it wouldn't remain that way, no matter how much he wished it. Miraculously, he and Sabina—along with V and Camlo—had survived Iceland. It had been close. Too close, actually.

In fact, there were times over the past week that Roman had woken in a sweat because he'd dreamed of Sabina falling—or worse, killing her himself while in the Others' hold. But she was always in his arms. He held her a little tighter those nights.

He walked into his workshop, smiling as he thought of his woman. She had taken Dreagan by storm. For a woman who'd spent many years alone, she'd become close to the other mates, much to his delight.

And Sabina blossomed. His gypsy wasn't timid or shy. She found her place and moved about the estate as if she'd always been there. And in some ways, she had. She had been in his heart as he hoped to find someone. One day.

Roman had never expected that day to happen, and yet

it had. He couldn't believe it. And a thousand years from now, he would still wonder at his luck at finding Sabina.

He moved to stand before the table where a chunk of rhodium sat. The extremely rare metal was highly prized by mortals, but Roman liked the way the silvery-colored metal moved.

For many moments, he stood over it as several images went through his head until he finally settled on one. He positioned his hands on either side of the rhodium and began to move his arms as he shaped the metal.

He didn't know how long he worked until he glanced up and saw his love leaning against the doorway.

"I could watch you all day," Sabina said as she pushed away from the door and walked to him. "You're amazing. What are you making?"

He turned the sculpture around and watched her eyes widen as she looked at herself. There were so many of Sabina's facial expressions that he wanted to capture, but he settled on the one where she'd confessed her love.

Her fingers shook as she tentatively reached out to touch the sculpture. "I look beautiful."

"Because you are."

Her head swung to him, a smile lifting her lips. "This is how you see me?"

"Aye, lass."

She swallowed, returning her gaze to the figure.

He drank in her beauty. "That is the expression that was on your face when you told me you loved me the first time."

When her dark eyes slid back to him, they glittered with unshed tears. "You're a marvel, my Dragon King. And I'm so glad you're mine."

"Always, lass. Always," he murmured before his lips found hers.

Light Castle, Ireland

She was all-powerful, but Usaeil couldn't get the letters on the page to stop moving. She'd tried all kinds of magic, to no avail. Everything she did only seemed to make things worse.

But she had to know what was in the book.

The fact that she couldn't turn the page either way was infuriating. There was information there, and she wanted to know what it was. Especially since she had seen the Dragon Kings named in the jumble.

She won. She always won.

And she'd win against this infernal book, as well. No matter what it took.

"Shite," Darius exclaimed as he came to a stop.

Cináed frowned after running into Darius's back. "What the hell?"

"Is that . . . V . . . *dancing*?"

Cináed leaned around Darius and looked toward the clinic Sophie ran in the village. A smile tugged at his lips when he saw V's head bobbing and his shoulders moving to a steady beat. "I'm not sure I'd call it dancing. Where's my mobile? I need to video this."

"I hear the music." Darius chuckled, shaking his head as Cináed began recording. "Claire always turns it up after the patients are gone for the day. She does love her music."

A moment later, V spotted them and stilled. He pushed away from the wall and stalked to them. "Delete that video right now, Cináed," he stated.

He laughed and put his phone away. "No' a chance, Sleeping Beauty."

"I'm going to kill Ulrik for telling everyone about that," V grumbled.

Darius asked, "So, you like Claire's music, huh?"

V glared at them. "You asked me to meet you here. I'm here. What do you need?"

Cináed slapped him on the back. "Why don't we go inside the clinic so you can hear the music?"

"I hear it fine," V said with teeth clenched.

Darius licked his lips to hide his smile. "I need your help with the supplies Sophie got in."

V rolled his eyes. "Use your magic."

"People watch us," Darius said as he led them to the back doors of the clinic where his mate was the doctor in residence, and Claire, her best friend, was the nurse. "We need to act normal."

Though V didn't say more, Cináed could tell there was something still bothering him. Despite having his sword returned, V remained aloof from the others. At first, Cináed thought it might be because V had spent more time than any of them sleeping, but he was beginning to wonder if there was more.

Cináed waited until Darius was talking with Sophie before he turned to V and asked, "Is everything all right?"

"Look around. Does it look like everything is fine?" V snapped.

He stepped in front of him and looked into V's frigid blue eyes. "What are you hiding?"

For several long seconds, V merely stared at him. Then he said, "I can no' use my sword."

Cináed ran a hand down his face, shocked to his core. He'd expected there to be a gathering where Con would ask V to use his sword to find their dragons. In fact, Cináed was getting anxious, waiting for such a time.

He never thought that V had already tried it.

"The others doona know." V released a long sigh, his shoulders slumping. "I knew something wasna right with the weapon once I had it back, but I thought maybe I was wrong."

"What do we do?" Cináed asked.

V shrugged. "The only thing I can. Fix it. But this stays between us."

With a nod, he agreed. "Of course."

Their conversation ended when a pretty blond walked up. Claire shot them a smile and said hello before she reached for a box. V quickly took it from her and walked away.

"He's a talkative one," Claire said.

Cináed shrugged and looked at V's retreating back. "He's going through something right now."

"Aren't we all?" she replied with a twist of her lips. "I'm Claire, by the way."

"Cináed."

"Kinnay? That's unusual."

"It's spelled much differently."

Her eyes widened with interest. "Is it Celtic?"

"Something like that," he replied with a smile.

"Claire!" Sophie shouted. "Elena just texted to say that another post was up."

The nurse laughed and said, "I'll be right there."

"Post?" Cináed asked as he lifted a box with the word *HEAVY* written on the side.

Claire shrugged as she stacked three smaller boxes on top of each other and gathered them in hand. "From what Sophie tells me, everyone talks about the *(Mis)Adventures of a Dating Failure* at the manor."

"Oh, that blog," he said as he followed her into the storage room. "So you're a fan, too? Do you know who writes it?"

She set down the boxes and waited for him to do the same before she said, "I know as much as you do."

"Apparently, a few of the mates have asked Ryder to find out who it is?" Cináed then frowned. "I assume you know who Ryder is."

Claire flashed him a smile. "I met him once. Sophie says he's a whiz with computers. Perhaps he'll track her down."

"Maybe so. How about you turn the music back up?"

She laughed and pulled out her phone from her pocket, turning up the volume on the wireless speaker.

As Cináed turned away, he saw V nodding his head with the music.

Somewhere in the universe . . .

"It has begun."

The woman turned from the fire and smiled. Satisfaction unfurled within her. She wasn't the first empress to wait for such words.

But now, they had been spoken.

Moreann stared at her advisor as she walked toward him. "I knew Tega and Arlain wouldn't fail us."

"Many doubted them," Orun replied, his faded blue eyes still holding doubt. He had his hands hidden in the wide folds of his white robes. "It has been a very long time."

Moreann clasped her hands before her, her fingers brushing the gold thread of the embroidered flowers that adorned her green gown. "The Fae warned us to be patient."

"And where are the Fae?" he asked, tilting his bald head.

"We've no need of them."

"No," Orun said. "We do not, but we joined forces with them against the Dragon Kings. We've taken their word that it all went according to plan."

Moreann inhaled swiftly before slowly releasing it. "Well, all your fears can be cast aside. You brought your own answer to me."

"Now that the Dragon King has his sword—"

She laughed, interrupting Orun. "You think Tega and Arlain would make it that simple?"

"You're taking a lot on assumption," Orun said, his close-set, deeply hooded eyes showing his unease.

She shrugged. "Why wouldn't I? I've had complete faith in our people. As has every ruler before me."

"The Dragon Kings are strong."

"So?" she said, unfazed by his words. "We found a way to beat them."

Orun walked to the fire and gazed into the flames. "Should we reach out to the Fae? The Light one was very . . ."

She knew he was trying to search for the right word. "Smug? Arrogant? Conceited?"

"Aye," he answered, glancing at her. "But I trust the Light more than the Dark."

Moreann barked with laughter. "This coming from a *drough*?"

"Who serves a *mie* empress."

A smile pulled at her lips. "Sixty years, and my family is still giving me an earful about that. All will be well, Orun. You'll see."

Also by
DONNA GRANT